SITTING ON A
RAINBOW

A 21ST CENTURY
IRISH AMERICAN
MORALITY TALE

JAMES PATRICK ROONEY

MINDSTIR MEDIA

Published by Mindstir Media, LLC
45 Lafayette Rd | Suite 181| North Hampton, NH 03862 | USA
1.800.767.0531 | www.mindstirmedia.com

Printed in the United States of America

ISBN: 978-1-958729-62-5 (paperback)
ISBN: 978-1-958729-57-1 (hardcover)

ACKNOWLEDGEMENTS

I would like to thank all the people who've helped me along my path to reach this moment, but my publisher advised otherwise. Thus, following my superb editor's prudent guidance, here are my brief expressions of gratitude.

My wife of 30-some-odd years, Cindy, and our two children, Patrick and Megan, come first, naturally. I know where my bread is buttered. They've shown their support by leaving me to my writing, or maybe they just had other things to do? Either way, it's in my support column. They've also provided excellent and loving company when I'm not writing. I'm blessed in this regard.

My early interest in writing was fueled by my friends at the Old Marsh Golf Club Reading Group. There are too many to mention individually, but they know who they are. The Chandlers and Bensons deserve a special nod though. I am forever grateful for their friendship and consistent encouragement. At some point, their question, "Hey Jim, when are you going to finish your book" got so annoying, I was forced to finish my book. Rest in peace, my good friend, Larry Chandler, who recently moved on to an even greater library than his own.

The creative writing courses I took at FIU in Miami, the Kravis Center in West Palm Beach, and Murder Bookstore in Delray Beach helped me immensely. Meaning—my writing would have been even worse without them. Also, I've sullied the pages of Stephen King's great book, *On Writing*, and I've taken more notes than I can store while reading my favorite authors including John Steinbeck, Wallace Stegner, Mark Twain, Marilynne Robinson, Ann Patchett, Pat Conroy, Bill Bryson, Erik Larson, Pete Hamill, Colm Toibin, Joseph O'Connor, Nora Ephron, and so many others. A special salute to Les Standiford, another favorite author who appeared at an Old Marsh Reading Group event and encouraged me to sign up for FIU's creative writing classes (where he was a professor). It was after a few glasses of wine. Or was that a few bottles? No matter—I followed his sage advice to my everlasting benefit.

While I'm dropping names, I must mention Larry Kirwan of the iconic Celtic rock band Black 47, and his extraordinary SiriusXM weekly show called *Celtic Crush*. Over the last two decades, Larry has almost singlehandedly kept my Irish fire stoked with his unique and brilliant storytelling and music, inspiring the literary direction of this project. The few times I've contacted him for guidance, he showed exactly who he is—a kind and generous man willing to help a total stranger. Probably because I fibbed once and told him I'd been to Mary's Bar in Wexford. It was so close to the truth that I went with it. Thank you, Larry, sincerely. You have touched more lives than you can count, and for that alone, your legacy is well secured.

My sincere thanks to a few special friends: Chuck, my music buddy and the best estate planning attorney in the world, and Doug and Rich, my college suitemates at "The U." These three friends voluntarily read my entire manuscript, and then told me it was good. That's why I selected them as my victims—they were always willing to lie to me, if necessary. For your selective morality, my friends, I am forever grateful. My younger brother and good friend, John, and a handful of other lifelong friends deserve special mention too. They also know who they are.

Finally, to my excellent publishing company, J.J. Hebert's MindStir Media, my project manager, Jen McNabney, my editor Lauren, the talented book cover artists, and the entire team behind the scenes. You have each been patient, kind and helpful, you've taught me to be a better storyteller, and let's not even talk about punctuation. What more could I have asked for? Don't answer that, especially if it's something substantial.

SITTING ON A
RAINBOW PLAYLIST

The author, James Patrick Rooney, grew up in the '60s and '70s—an exceptionally musical time. He associates nearly every notable event in his life with a song or an album or an artist. Following is a playlist of the music that inspired and drove his story forward. As you sit on the rainbow with Patrick Connelly, take a little time to listen to his music. Or create your own personal playlist. It will help bring the story to life, just as it did for the author. Thank you and please enjoy.

Chapter 1:

[1] – "Freedom" by Richie Havens (*Woodstock 1*, 1969)

[2] – "59th Street Bridge Song (Feelin' Groovy)" by Simon & Garfunkel (*Parsley, Sage, Rosemary and Thyme*, 1969)

[3] – "Come Saturday Morning" by The Sandpipers from *The Sterile Cuckoo* (1969)

Chapter 2:

[4] – "Rocky Road to Dublin" - written by D.K. Gavan, 17th century Irish poet.

Chapter 3:

[5] – "Tonight" written by Elton John and Bernie Taupin as performed by George Michael on the 1991 tribute album *Two Rooms*.

Chapter 6:

[6] – Van Halen. "Hot for Teacher" (I highly recommend the 1984 music video)

Chapter 7:

[7] – "Both Sides Now" written and performed by Joni Mitchell (*Clouds* 1966) and made even more famous by Judi Collins.

Chapter 8:

[8] – "Dancing Days" by Led Zeppelin (*Houses of the Holy*, 1973)

[9] – "A Song for Ireland" by Mary Black (*Collected*, 1984)

Chapter 11:

[10] – "Celebrate Me Home" by Kenny Loggins (*Celebrate Me Home*, 1977)

[11] – "Over the Rainbow"—written by Harold Arlen and Yip Harburg; performed by Judy Garland in *The Wizard of Oz* (1939)

Chapter 13:

[12] – "Whiskey in a Jar"—written in the 17th century; made famous by Thin Lizzy and performed by several other artists including The Dubliners and Metallica.

Chapter 14:

[13] – "As If We Never Said Goodbye" from the Andrew Lloyd Webber musical *Sunset Boulevard*; performed brilliantly by Glenn Close.

Chapter 15:

[14] – "Comfortably Numb by Pink Floyd (*The Wall*, 1979)

Chapter 18:

[15] – Any pipes-driven lament by The Chieftains, Planxty or The Bothy Band; or better still—all three.

[16] – "For Emily (Kewpie), Wherever I May Find Her" by Simon & Garfunkel (*Parsley, Sage, Rosemary and Thyme*, 1966)

Chapter 19:

[17] – Anything "wall-thrashing" from the genius Wolfgang Amadeus Mozart.

[18] – "Into the Mystic" by Van Morrison (*Moondance*, 1970)

Chapter 20:

[19] – "Dreams Are More Precious" by Enya (*And Winter Came...* 2008)

Chapter 22:

[20] – Listen to a mix from The Chieftains voluminous catalog on your favorite streaming service.

Chapter 24:

[21] – "I've Got the World on a String" by Frank Sinatra (*This is Sinatra!*, 1956)

[22] – "Scenes from an Italian Restaurant" by Billy Joel (*The Stranger*, 1977)

Chapter 26:

[23] – Once again, a mix of The Chieftains from your favorite streaming service would be a good backdrop to the redecorating underway at the Connelly home in SoSo.

[24] – *The Celtic Harp* by The Chieftains (1993)

[25] – "Hard Times Come Again No More" written by Steven Foster (1854) and performed by many wonderful gospel singers over the years.

Chapter 27:

[26] – Listen to any mesmerizing harp music you prefer.

[27] – "L.A. Woman" by The Doors (*L.A. Woman*, 1971)

Chapter 28:

[28] – "Do You Believe in Magic?" by The Lovin' Spoonful (*Do You Believe in Magic*, 1965)

Chapter 30:

[29] – "But I Might Die Tonight" by Cat Stevens (*Tea for the Tillerman*, 1970)

Chapter 32:

[30] – Put on a mix of two of Patrick's favorite Irish pub bands, The Pogues and The Dubliners, while you're reading this chapter. Or any other time at all.

[31] – Listen to any traditional Celtic music of your choice, including The Chieftains, Planxty, The Dubliners, etc., while you celebrate a very special St. Patrick's Day weekend along with Finnie and Patrick.

[32] – "A Song for Ireland" by Mary Black (*Collected*, 1984); This time, listen to Luke Kelly of The Dubliners' version.

Chapter 33:

[33] – "Caoineadh Cu Chulainn's Lament" from *Riverdance* (1993)

[34] – Listen to cheerful Irish reels and pub music by The Chieftains and others on your preferred streaming service, and don't forget to visit the bar three times (if you're of age).

Chapter 34:

[35] – "The Gambler" by Kenny Rogers (*The Gambler*, 1978)

Chapter 35:

[36] – If you're not tired of The Chieftains by now, play some of their uplifting instrumental music (i.e., reels) in the background. Maybe a splash of whiskey will help matters (if you're of age).

Chapter 36:

[37] – "Turn! Turn! Turn!" written by Pete Seeger, performed by The Byrds (*Turn! Turn! Turn!* 1965)

While reading Chapters 36 and 37, listen to John Denver's entire Windsong album and reflect on the beauty and power of nature, and how blessed we were to have the beautiful songwriter and troubadour as a part of our lives.

Chapter 37:

[38] – "Looking for Space" by John Denver (*Windsong,* 1975)

Chapter 38:

[39] – "Woodstock" written by Joni Mitchell; performed by Crosby, Stills, Nash & Young (*Déjà Vu,* 1969)

Chapter 39:

[40] – "Me and Bobby McGee" by Janis Joplin (*Pearl,* 1971) Patrick has found that if you adjust the lyrics to "Me and my friggin' Marie," the song may resonate more in the context of this chapter.

Chapter 40:

[41] – Listen to any number of Irish pipe-driven laments while enjoying May Eve at Murphy's. Stream something from the catalog of the iconic piper Davy Spillane, for example.

Chapter 42:

[42] – "Purple Haze" by Jimi Hendrix as performed at Woodstock, 1969

[43] – "Skating Away on the Thin Ice of a New Day" by Jethro Tull (*War Child*, 1974)

[44] – "Bewitched, Bothered and Bewildered" written by Rodgers and Hart; performed by Ella Fitzgerald (*Ella Fitzgerald Sings the Rogers and Hart Book*, 1956)

Chapter 44:

[45] – "Brand New Day" by Van Morrison (*Moondance*, 1970)

Chapter 45:

[46] – *Astral Weeks* by Van Morrison (1968) Play the album lightly in the background as you read this chapter. Then play it again. It grows on you.

[47] – "Sweet Thing" by Van Morrison (*Astral Weeks*, 1968)

[48] – "Ball of Confusion" written by Norman Whitfield and Barrett Strong; performed by The Temptations (1970)

[49] – "Abraham, Martin and John" written by Dick Holler; performed by Dion (1968)

[50] – "The Way Young Lovers Do" by Van Morrison (*Astral Weeks*, 1968)

Chapter 46:

[51] – "We Are the Champions" by Queen (*News of the World*, 1977)

[52] – "Let's Live for Today" written by David "Shel" Shapiro and Mogol, with Michael Julien; performed by The Grass Roots (*Let's Live for Today*, 1967)

[53] – "Life's a Long Song" by Jethro Tull (*Aqualung*, 1971)

Chapter 47:

[54] – "On Raglan Road"—published in 1946 by Irish poet Patrick Kavanagh as "Dark Haired Miriam Ran Away." It was later turned into the great Irish folk song "On Raglan Road," performed by The Dubliners (*Hometown!*, 1972)

[55] – "Landslide" by Fleetwood Mac (*Life Becoming a Landslide*, 1975)

Chapter 48:

[56] – "Tomorrow is a Long Time" by Bob Dylan (1971)

Chapter 49:

[57] – Once again, listening to any of the pipes-driven laments from the great Irish pipers (Paddy Moloney, Davy Spillane, Liam O'Flynn, etc.) would be the perfect backdrop to this chapter.

[58] – "Into the Mystic" by Van Morrison (*Moondance*, 1970)

Chapter 50:

[59] – "Skating Away on the Thin Ice of the New Day" by Jethro Tull (*War Child*, 1974)

Chapter 51:

[60] – "War Child" by Jethro Tull (*War Child*, 1974)

[61] – "*Mo Ghile Mear*" from the poems of Sean Clárach Mac Domhnaill (1700s); lyrics by Dónal O' Liatháin, early 1970s; performed by The Chieftains and Sting; Mary Black, among others.

Chapter 52:

[62] – "The Town I Loved So Well" by Luke Kelly and The Dubliners (*Plain and Simple*, 1983)

[63] – "Sweet Thing" by Van Morrison (*Astral Weeks*, 1968)

One looks back at one's youth as to a cup that a madman dying of thirst left half tasted. I wonder if you feel like that.

W. B. Yeats
(From a letter to Olivia Shakespear, December 6, 1926)

1

A STOUT HEART

Tossing his black Tumi shoulder bag across to the passenger seat, Patrick braced himself, thrust his folded chair in the open back, and pressed up and into his beloved silver bullet. Beloved for its utility and dependability, certainly not its sex appeal. A decade-old minivan is anything but sexy. He was sick to death of this same old routine. But what choice did he have? What reasonable choice, that is? He used to do it joyfully, for his family, his clients, and his own self-interest, of course. But not now, not like this. The idea of it had become nearly unbearable.

Scooting down the brick-paved driveway, he glimpsed the early morning, sun-sparked chop of the Intracoastal Waterway before turning west past lush tropical foliage. Usually taking more interest in the architectural nuances of his historic neighborhood, he blew through it this day, his mood anything but leisured. He was late for a meeting. One he had no interest in attending. Dialing his Sirius radio to the Classic Rock channel, Richie Havens's "Freedom" coursed through the cabin like an urgent cry. [1] Turning right at Olive and heading north, he moved along briskly. The heavier commute hadn't finished showering yet.

Patrick Connelly—Pat or Paddy to longtime friends—was moving steadily through his fifth decade and feeling every bit of it. Two grueling years spent in the entanglements of divorce had seemed like ten. The textured plaster and beamed interior walls of his Mizner-inspired house were lined with boxes he hadn't yet labored to open. He retained the structure in the settlement only because Becky wasn't interested, but its soul was long gone, in addition to most of the furniture. The process hadn't been pain-free, that's for sure. Going their separate ways was little different than their twenty-five years of wedded bliss had been. A daily grind where nothing came easy. Two well-meaning but mismatched people, each deserving better, he'd ascertained.

In pursuit of that idealistic outcome, the brutal process of decoupling had left him wholly diminished, especially financially. That was the toughest part because finance was his business.

Born in an ascending Bronx still aglow with the second war's decisive triumph, Paddy resembled a brick outhouse—some said it more graphically. He was a picture of sturdiness and vigor in a never-ending pursuit of the distant rainbow of success. Not just a win or even several wins. He'd had those. It was an enduring state of well-being he craved. Firm evidence he'd crossed the finish line and been declared champion. There were times he felt close, like he was leaning in toward the tape. But just when it seemed within reach—poof—it would be violently wrested away. Time to start again. And he would. He always would.

In his youth, he'd extracted himself from a regrettable family ecosystem and learned how to win—and lose—with dignity. The magic formula was his immersion in team sports—the more physical, the better. And despite taking a couple of massive shots to the gut that may have kept any other baller or rink rat prone, he never failed to get back up and push ahead. After earning an economics degree at the infamous "Suntan U" in Coral Gables, he landed a challenging job in stocks and bonds. He soon married Becky, and they started a family called Liam and Erin. The job turned out to be more about sales, less about economics, and Patrick, a cerebral sort, found himself a misplaced introvert in a fast-paced and shrill world. But with years of hard work and training, he learned his craft well and built what many would call a lucrative life.

His base of operation was northern Palm Beach County. Not a particularly common homestead in those days, it had something to do with 1970s heartthrob Burt Reynolds raving to Johnny Carson and the world that he made his home in Jupiter, Florida.

"WhereinthehellisJupiterFlorida," read the skintight black t-shirt just below his beaming smile.

This caused Patrick's mother to pine for a visit to Burt's hometown, which caused his reluctant father to veer off I-95 and into the slough of Jupiter's cow pastures and orange juice stands. The next day, Eleanor and Seamus were plunking down a cashier's check and taking possession of the Connelly's first and only vacation home along the untamed Loxahatchee River. You know how those heartthrob things go.

The timing was impeccable, if not unplanned. After graduation, Patrick migrated the few hundred miles up the coast to West Palm Beach, where the urban action lay in this neck of the Everglades. If "action" was the appropriate word. He took up residence in this small, manageable city with its "redneck" tropical breeze pace, conveniently flat terrain, and curb cuts in the sidewalks—just his speed. Largely invisible on a national scale, West Palm had grown steadily through the good and the bad of the past few decades, thriving in boom times and surviving the brutal busts along the way. Today, a new boom is underway. The downtown abounds with upscale hotels, condos and office towers, prominent theaters and museums, a university, a library, a cozy bookstore, coffee shops, sidewalk cafes, restaurants, wine bars, and one especially notable Irish pub.

There is also a rather world-renowned playground just east of the city center—the tony island of Palm Beach. In sum, it was a good place to be a purveyor of securities—a money guy.

For a kid from the Bronx, Paddy was one hell of an ice hockey player. Fleet on his skates, he delivered thundering body checks and had a nose for the net. Against all odds, he thrived in junior hockey and earned his way into a nationally ranked college program after nearly losing his right eye at the age of three.

Are you sitting down?

Under the synthetic protection of his defective brother twice his age, he held a firm grip on the pair of sharp, opened scissors. He was playing an ill-advised game of poke the faux brass tack off the back of the speckled gray and white Naugahyde kitchen chair. One of his purposed swipes missed the tack—and the chair. A confusing, spinning, spidery kaleidoscope of rapidly flashing black and white, and mostly red, followed. Then the police car siren.

Upon its urgent arrival, his sobbing mother holding a towel to the right side of his face, he was given deputy control over the siren on the way to the hospital. The doctors saved his right eye but little of its former vision.

This minor setback didn't slow him down much, especially once the eye patch disappeared and he fully embraced life on the Connelly battlefield. His deranged older brother's daily dose of discord was as sure as the sunrise. To help quell the crazy, Paddy needed to jump into the fray; and he did jump in—head-first. A "deep dive," they call it now. It wasn't fun, but it taught him valuable lessons. For one: there are really shitty people in the world, maybe even in your own family, who need to be confronted. These people are bullies and generally cowardly, and in the face of passivity, their brutality becomes emboldened and more destructive. They can ruin everything, even maim people, if left to their own devices.

In his early teens, Paddy learned to play the equally contentious game of ice hockey with reckless abandon and no fear. He found the rink teeming with cowardly bullies who would shrink at the first sign of confrontation. What they were trying to hide was their lack of skill and their lack of courage. The potent combination of skill and courage always minimizes cowardly bullies. Amidst the fray, it never occurred to him that one errant stick or puck could take away his left eye, too, leaving nothing but the dark for a long, long time. Luckily, that never happened, not that he could be called particularly "lucky."

This whole "luck of the Irish" thing was a misnomer when he considered it. Haven't they been conquered, ostracized from their rightful land, starved, slaughtered, and regularly enslaved throughout their inglorious history? A few tomes about leprechauns and other such bastardized folklore didn't wash all that away, he didn't think.

When Paddy, now going by Patrick, was nineteen, just beginning to emerge, parting his shoulder-length red hair down the middle, zits clearing, young ladies calling, the "shot to the gut" that really floored him landed. An elbow injury from a check against the boards festered into an infection, probably due to rancid hockey equipment and diseased locker rooms. Mindless, unbreakable teenagers are fertile breeding grounds for such things. When the infection got worse, he did everything he could think of to make it better, including going to the college infirmary, the local hospital, taking medicine, taking a rest from the game, calling his parents, even attending class. It was working. The arm was less ballooning, less tender, less red hot. The blood-yellow pus had stopped oozing from the open wound on his elbow. Great news, he was back on the ice, even scoring three goals in a game and getting local headlines. Unfortunately, he missed the red line heading north into his armpit. The doctors did too.

A month later, on a perfectly crisp New England fall Saturday morning, he went on a first date with the prettiest girl in the world. And a junior, no less. She was the unattainable kind who usually dated the captain of the hockey team, which he was not. Adorably petite, soft-spoken, and sweet, her cropped blonde hair and radiant smile were known across campus to weaken knees. He had a fondness for petite, soft, sweet, knee-weakening girls. Still does. She was the kind you could wrap your arms around and make one with you, fully embedded, breathing in unison, immersed in a kind of primal hug.

He still recalls the day vividly. It was a delightful "59th Street Bridge Song," "Come Saturday Morning," kind of day. Maybe his best yet. So free he felt, so poised, so serene, so "coming-of-age." The soft, sweet sounds and lyrics of the moment still color his memory. [2, 3]

All was groovy. They drove up the long hill to Brown, where PC Friars rarely ventured, and walked amongst the perfectly quaint Ivy college town shops. They bought hippie shirts—soft beige cotton mesh with colorful beads trimming the open neck and splayed cuffs. He surprised her with a leather bracelet to match his. After lunch, hand in hand, they walked along the busy tree-lined streets. They walked and walked, with golden yellow, burnt auburn, and rich red leaves crushing under their feet. They walked until the fading sun had surrendered its power to warmly light their paths.

Making their way back to campus, lingering on the moonlit lawn just outside of her brown-bricked, pine-shadowed dormitory, they whispered their goodnights and embraced in a hug. You know—the primal kind. And they lightly kissed two times, no, three. Maybe four. Warm lips followed by rose-chilled cheeks, the polar tip of her nose, and then her tiny eyelids. They each said it was a special, memorable day. The start of something more. He was on the cusp of a whole new life and could feel it through every inch of his body—from head to heart to groin to the very tips of his toes.

It was the last time Patrick Connelly would remember feeling the tips of his toes, or his groin, or the lower half of his body ever again. It was the last time he would remember walking.

Oh, he walked up to his apartment on the third floor of the decrepit colonial house he leased at 140 Eaton Street. But his steps were oddly labored. His back started to hurt—really hurt. *This must be what sixty-five years old feels like,* he thought. His fever was back, the one he had a month earlier. Undressing as best he could, pausing at his bedside, he turned around slowly, unsteadily, and fell backward into the abyss.

Had he known it would be his last time standing under his own power, ever again, he would certainly have lingered a few more precious moments in its underappreciated glory.

He cried out to his best friend. "Bobby! Bobby, something's wrong. I need help. I can't feel my legs."

"Here, hold my hands, dude," he said. "I'll help you out of bed."

"No, Bobby. I can't fucking move, I swear; my back really hurts. Call my parents—please; tell them I'm in trouble. I need help."

"Okay, Pat, okay; please, try to calm down." Bobby sounded as petrified as his longtime friend. In their decade together of work and play, grinding and driving, winning and losing, he'd never seen his mate cry—never seen him so hopelessly out of control. "Calm down, Conns, okay? I'm calling them. I'm calling them right now."

"Take me to the infirmary, please, Christ—take me now." Bobby dialed 911. The ambulance's siren soon wailed louder than his friend's relentless scream. He held Patrick's hand tightly, and from their own unique positions of pain and fear, they each wept. Always in charge, always knowing what to do next, Bobby was at a loss. There was nothing to do but wait, and weep.

He couldn't move from the bed when they implored, so three large yellow gears lifted him onto the stretcher. The school infirmary wouldn't take him in, saying he was too sick, and they redirected the ambulance driver to the nearest hospital. He lay in the emergency room bed for what seemed like hours. "What did you take, son?" they asked repeatedly. "What drugs are you on?"

"No, no!" he yelled in protest. "I'm sick—my back hurts, it really hurts. I can't feel my legs."

"What did you take, son?"

"Nothing, goddamn it. I can't fucking move! Please help me." He was crying, screaming out for help. "My back is killing me— fuck, *fuck*—help me, please."

He was right—his back was killing him, abetted by these fucking doctors.

"Calm down, son," came the too-calm voice. "We need to know what's wrong before we can help you. Are you sure you didn't take anything?"

Bobby furiously paced the hallway as an hour passed, then another. "Listen to him, goddamn it!" he begged. "Help him, please."

"My back fucking hurts," Patrick pleaded. "I can't move; help me—please, please, help me."

"We're helping you, son—quiet down now."

"I need someone's help. Anybody—*anybody*—help me, please." His desperate cries caromed through the room, the halls, his head. "Did you call my parents? Are they here?"

"Yes, we called them—they're on the way," someone said while handing him a dixie cup with pills, then water. "This will help with the pain." A priest he recognized from campus was in the room. He stood over the inferno in his Sunday best, Bible in hand, making the sign of the cross. He was conducting the sacrament of Last Rites.

"Paddy, Paddy, we're here." He woke bleary to his parents standing over him—his mother holding his hand. He'd been moved to a different room.

"They found a blockage in your spine. You're going into surgery," his father said in an earnest tremor. "We're right here with you, Paddy. We love you very much—everything's going to be okay."

Everything wasn't going to be okay. Ever again.

Veering to the right now onto Flagler Drive, he took in the panoramic eastern views of the wind-driven, brackish water, the ever-shifting, multi-hued panoply of grays, greens, and blacks reflecting the morning's white light. The deep waterway harbored innumerable million-dollar yachts, providing an ideal foreground to the timeless, sunbaked Mediterranean splendor of the barrier island beyond.

"We're in the second Gilded Age," he would often tell his clients. "Look around—the evidence is everywhere." He wasn't engaging in hyperbole. Intracoastal and oceanfront mansions on the island were selling for ten million, thirty million, fifty million. Magnificent displays of boundless wealth were visible at every turn. *That's where Becky lives now,* he thought with remorse.

The same office building he'd driven to a thousand times loomed on the horizon. He clicked on his favorite classical station, a mindless impulse to quell a rising anxiety. Slowing his pace to match the baroque's antiquated resonance, he breathed deeply and thought, *No rush to get to that shithole.* Whenever one of his father's favorite Bronx vernaculars would surface, he'd smirk in reminiscence. As he crept closer, darker thoughts set in. If music is said to soothe the rising beast within, it was failing him at this moment. After flashing his ID card at the stainless sheen, the dusky parking garage's gate lifted, and a robotic voice greeted him with, "Welcome. Have a good day."

"Ha, that's a laugh," he chided aloud. "It should say, 'Turn around now while you still can.'"

Pulling into his usual space, sweat beading on his brow, a noticeable tremble overtook his hands as he gripped the wheel. Sitting still to catch his breath, pulling it down from his throat back into his belly, he whispered, "Today is my day for miracles. All the seeds I've carefully sown come to fruition this day." He didn't quite believe it, so he closed his eyes and repeated the affirmation.

So far, Patrick Connelly's story had been one of loss and recovery, loss and recovery. He lost half his sight at three and fought back. He lost the use of half his body at nineteen, forever to be paraplegic, and fought back even more valiantly. Now, approaching his mid-fifties, he was caught in the wretched grip of loss once more. His marriage was dead, his dream of financial freedom teetering, and now his business was at risk of disappearing too? All he worked for half his life—gone? Would this be the knockout blow finally leaving him mortally wounded?

Why does everything I have get cut in fucking half? he thought despairingly.

With neither the vitality of youth nor the enveloping support the child once had, he felt uncertain and utterly isolated. This time it would be up to him alone, or whatever was left of him. Sitting a moment longer, he wondered if he still possessed the stout heart he'd need for the approaching tempest?

2

SANCTUARY DUBLIN

Lifting the lively pint of Smithwick's, Patrick toasted his venerable server, "God bless you, Molly. Here's to your health."

Smiling, she returned the sentiment, "*Sláinte*, Patrick. And may I say you're looking mighty chipper today. Single life must be agreeing with you."

"That sounds like a compliment, my dear Molly, and I'll accept it as such."

"You heard right, good sir. I'll take my apron off this very minute and bring you home if you don't put away that smile."

"You'd better not offer twice, Molly, O Molly."

His grin broadened as she sauntered off to spread her sweet Irish cheer to the lucky inhabitants of the next booth. *My God*, he thought, *I love a hard-working woman with a sunny mood. Not to mention that delicious brogue.*

Settled at his usual table, Patrick was more at home amidst the stucco, brick, and thickly hewn, burnt oak beams of this ancient space than in his real home, or his office, or anywhere else for that matter. At old-world Murphy's in the heart of Clematis Street, his little slice of Dublin, he wasn't measured, judged, or criticized. Here in his literary and social nirvana, he read his books, wrote his thoughts, listened to his traditional music, drank his drink, and engaged in friendly conversation, frivolous or otherwise, with all types of passers-through.

Home was, in contrast, a chilly barrenness. The heated contentiousness he and Becky spewed in the later years had been replaced by a stark and echoing emptiness. When the kids went off to college and beyond, there wasn't enough reason left to keep up the battle. His Catholic upbringing chastised that divorce equated to failure and mortal sin. But it was only in surrender that their mortal distress might heal, came the rationalization of the modern-day wayward sinner.

The first notes of "Rocky Road to Dublin" raised the pub's spirit. [4] While merrily lifting his pint to begin the grief and tears smother, he dumped his Tumi's contents out on the carved testimonial of a table. Arranging his journals, books, and notepads just so, these would keep him company for the next few hours as he engaged in the part of the investment business he still cherished—the reading and the thinking. The research required to bring a good investment idea to his clients kept his motor running.

In sharp contrast, Patrick found distasteful the antiseptic, computer-driven processes of financial planning and asset allocation, and the hyper-focus on client acquisition in this more recent "wealth management" era. As important as each of these were, in theory and practice, he believed they created a robotic, impersonal office climate and a feeling of unnecessarily cutthroat competitiveness. Well, maybe the competition for client assets had always been "cutthroat." It's the money business, after all. But it never seemed to bother him like it did now. He reminisced fondly to an earlier time when he'd built his career in a "one-for-all, all-for-one" and "there's more than enough for everybody" collegiality. Could he be fooling himself, engaging in selective memory, recalling just the good times? A survival mechanism, perhaps.

In any case, the climate had undeniably changed, had heated up, since the two market crashes of the early 21st century. With barely a breather between the two—Boom, Boom—more than a few advisors were anxiously scrutinizing their own financial plans, particularly their balance sheets and income statements, while they hunted ever more fervently for lifestyle-saving business. Fervency wasn't Patrick's thing. He was more of a 'slow and easy' kind of guy.

Three decades before all this, with the ticker tape scrolling on the wall above, an old yellowing IBM computer on his desktop, along with a pen, legal pad, and tattered copy of the Wall Street Journal, and finally, an old-style dumb telephone held to his ear, he'd built one of the larger books in the Palm Beach region—more than $300 million of loyal client assets. A member of the "million-dollar club" since the late-'90s, he exuded pride at the accolades and the reward trips and the paycheck. It afforded him a prosperous and notable life. But "had been" is past tense, he'd often been reminded, not so different than "has-been."

Before the internet took hold, and before all the wine and cheese investment seminars and book clubs and other mass marketing schemes were commonplace, he'd send out glossy mailers provided by mutual fund companies to the richest neighborhoods in the area and then "pound the phones" to follow-up. It was effectively the only way to succeed. The grueling process entailed making a hundred calls a day (in theory) to pitch an investment idea, usually an "enhanced income" mutual fund (supposedly) yielding 15%, or a high-quality municipal bond (definitely) yielding 8%, 9%, or 10%, tax-free. It was a time of lifestyle destroying inflation and he needed an edge to compete with the local banks offering double digits on federally guaranteed certificates of deposit. Most prospective clients didn't trust the stock market after a decade-long period of treacherous up and down performance, so stocks weren't prominent on his menu.

His goal was to get five people a week to say "yes," another five to say "maybe," and then pray the "yeses" came in with a check to pay for the fund or bond as they'd promised. If he came close to those lofty ambitions, it was considered a big win. If they didn't show up with the check, he'd eat the 3% or 4% or 5% commission instead of a burger and fries at TGI Fridays that night. The "maybes" filled his pipeline of weekly call backs until they either said "yes," or screamed at him to stop calling before slamming the phone in his ear. That meant another ninety of the hundred daily calls (in theory) ended in some other type of rejection, not easy for the sensitive, introverted types like Patrick Connelly. He bought more than his share of psychological sales training tapes and spent a lot of Sunday nights staring at the bedroom ceiling. One way around the rejection, he found, was to hide from the phones as often as possible while still finding ways to survive another week.

Admittedly, the best way to grow the account base in the '80s and '90s was to simply not leave the firm, because almost everyone else eventually did. Otherwise known as resilience. The fortunate day when one of his colleagues announced their departure from the firm, or better still the business entirely, allowed for a rare breather from the daily grind of "dialing for dollars." Patrick couldn't even count the number of account distributions he'd participated in over the years. Usually, the news would break on a Friday at market close. The office manager would huddle with his staff behind closed doors for several hours organizing the departing broker's account pages, now free agents, while the remaining account executives (AE's) sat at their desks with sweat soaking their starched collars in anticipation. Sometime later that evening, depending on the size of the book, the manager's door would spring open, and the accounts would be doled out according to the size of the broker's production and length of service. The seemingly merit-based system had a serious flaw, though, the human characteristic called greed. Because the office manager was also a producer, meaning he had his own book of clients, the largest and most productive accounts would always end up in his pile. Always.

One of Patrick's early managers was infamous for his "one for you, three for me" policy. But he'll never forget the time when this guy met his match. The largest producer in the office, an extraordinarily obnoxious, selfish, but hilarious bowling ball of a guy from Boca, raged into the manager's office after he'd gotten his account pages, flailing his arms wildly and screaming that he'd been screwed. The manager's response was not to offer him a few more accounts from his own fertile stack. No— that would have been too close to honorable. Instead, he slinked around the office plucking a few accounts from each of the piles on the desks of vacationing or otherwise absent AE's, especially the females, until the screamer was satisfied. That manager drove a Jaguar, the screamer a Mercedes. Their clients probably drove Fords and Buicks.

One time, after waiting several hours into the Friday twilight, Patrick looked over his disappointingly short stack of account pages. The news got worse. The largest account he'd been given was a client who lived in Sweden, had a vacation home in Florida, and didn't have a phone number listed at either location. He never did reach the guy. It was hardly shocking that his scumbag manager didn't keep that one for himself. But Patrick didn't flail his arms and scream; he instead went to TGI Fridays for a burger and fries.

After one too many near office revolutions, the distribution policy was eventually cleaned up across the firm with the head of compliance stepping in for the producing managers.

Even with that, some of his best long-time clients came either from those distributions, or another relic from the day—the "walk-in" policy. Twice a month, he was the AE who would meet with any prospective client "walking in" and asking to see a broker. Once again, if the prospect was big enough, they'd never make it out of the manager's office. Except for the time when a wealthy prospect specifically requested a broker who didn't smoke, which narrowed the office field of fifteen down to Patrick. His Cub Scout training finally paid dividends.

But this was 2013 and times were different. Unrecognizably different. For one thing, they were no longer called "customer's men" or "stockbrokers" or "account executives," or even "financial consultants" or "advisors," and they no longer worked at "wirehouses" or "brokerage firms." They were "senior wealth managers" now working at "wealth management firms." And the days of distributions and walk-ins were long gone—no hand-outs or lay ups. The proliferation of the internet, with its discount brokers and shrinking fees and ubiquitous information in the hands (literally) of prospective clients was the root cause of the industry revolution. Those two stock market crashes—the Boom, Booms—flushed out the weaklings and accelerated the trend of advisors and support staff joining forces to form wealth management teams. Interest rates hovering near 0% for extended periods effectively killed the retail bond business and any retiree who had savings to protect. We were all stock investors now, for better or worse, and clients had more choices of where to put their money than they had time to decide.

One thing had remained essentially the same—Patrick's preferred style of doing business—the Mont Blanc pen, the heavy stock legal pad, and the grinding process of security-by-security selection, rather than farming it out to independent money managers and other platforms and spending all his time hunting for more assets. "Thinking a lot, doing a little," as famous billionaire investor Warren Buffett often said, was his mode of operation. He was considered ancient by his peers but that's what he enjoyed—stock-brokering the old-fashioned way. Add to this his penchant for rolling up his shirt sleeves, loosening his tie, leaving his suit jacket in the car, and making it to Happy Hour by 5 p.m., and it all combined to make him a lumbering turtle in a frenetic hare's business. And with his better producing days in the rear-view mirror, a prime target for planned obsolescence.

Just a short stroll from Murphy's, there was a markedly different vibe in his office—that of the frenetic hare. It was teeming with Jos. A. Bank value-priced, blue pinstripe suits sprinting here and there, accompanied by sharply pressed shirts, silk ties, and cuffs ornately adorned with initials. Equipped with fancy degrees and impressive accreditations up the yin-yang, "certified" this and "chartered" that, clutching their laptops like newborn babies, these were the brainiac know-it-alls—the new breed of wealth management advisors. As educated and talented as they undoubtedly were, they had a problem: the wealthy are generally as wary as they are wise. They do not trust their assets to the wet-behind-the-ears types no matter how many statistics they can spit out. Palm Beach's upper crust especially liked to see some well-earned gray in your hair and sunbaked lines framing your eyes before opening their vaults.

In short, it was increasingly difficult to build a financial advisory business from scratch. Nearly impossible, that is.

Regrettably, this new breed didn't have the luxury of time. They needed to build their books with affluent clients and they needed to do it rapid fire. Six to nine months of underperformance invites probation. One year without hitting their marks, eighteen months at the outside, and they'd be out the door. This volatile mix of extraordinary expectations and few assets to manage would destroy many an aspiring career. The virtue of patience—from both the firm and its eventual discards—was missing in action.

That made veteran advisors with established businesses their best targets, and the antiquity in the wheelchair nesting in the luxurious corner office was directly in the young gun's crosshairs. It was simple to grasp—they were ravenous, and he was food. He'd rebuffed a plethora of partnership offers over the years, becoming one of the few lone wolves remaining.

A few unsavory veterans were known to take full advantage by bringing younger advisors onto their teams with promises of future riches, only to chew up their asset-hunting enthusiasm before spitting out the remaining gristle. It was the way of the world on the money savannah, with predators and prey switching roles in their daily hunt for survival.

Patrick wasn't hungry for any of it. The business was competitive enough without doing battle on the home front. He just wanted to be left alone to enjoy his humble avocation, at his pace and in his time. But that was becoming more difficult by the day.

Given his teetering cash flow since the divorce settlement, this was a concerning development. Thus, he spent an unusual amount of his leisure time at his favorite table in his favorite drinking hole reinforcing his battlements.

Taking a long draw and emptying his pint glass, Patrick's eyes searched the pub room for Molly. They came upon something meaningfully less desirous. A group of a half-dozen young advisors from his office were flowing through the entrance and gathering at a large round table on the other side of the room. This was a first. He'd never seen even one of his officemates in Murphy's, never mind a brood. That's why he called it his "sanctuary," his "little Dublin hideaway." They were nice enough people, he guessed—smart, energetic, and impressive—but he shared nothing in common with them other than his chosen profession. Any small talk was just that, small, meaning irrelevant. If they had any interest in Patrick, it had nothing to do with his life or his personality or his hobbies or his Irishness—it was his book of business.

Thanks, but no thanks.

A member of the "gnat pack" recognized him, unfortunately, and hastened over to his table, saying, "Hey, Connelly, what's shaking, you old dog?"

"Me, now that I feel like I'm back at the office."

"Funny," replied Ian King, one of the firm's rising stars. He was toting his weaponry: two smart phones in a double holster. "One for business, one for pleasure," he'd proudly say while working them simultaneously. Tall and thick, the body builder type, with a copious head of wavy blond hair crowning his corporate blue pin-striped uniform, he certainly struck an imposing figure.

"What brings your posse into the dinosaur's den this evening, Ian?"

"Heading to a meeting at Capital Grille." In an instant he'd pulled out a chair and plopped himself down. "Thought we'd stop for a beer at your favorite hideout on the way."

"Lucky me."

King's eyes were nowhere in sight, focused down at one or the other of his screens. Glancing up, he asked, "You going?"

"Nope. I'm sitting right here working on my business."

"Oh yeah, that reminds me," he said while peering around the crowded table. "I saw the monthly production list; looks like your numbers are still slipping down, down, down. Man alive, Connelly—you're having your own bear market. Pretty soon, I'll have to lower my offer to take you onto my team."

"Flattery isn't your strong suit, Ian, that's for sure," he bristled. "What's 'my team' mean anyway? Would that be you and the assistant you share with three other guys?"

Molly floated to his table. "Shall I set a place for your friend, Patrick?"

"No thanks, Molly, he's not staying. But I'll take another Smithwick's. Want one to go, Ian?"

"No thanks. I'm a Bud Light guy." Ian King's eyes followed her as she walked away. "Holy shit, she's sure got game." Grimacing at the words, Patrick felt violated and protective, his sanctuary besmirched. "I'm growing fast," King continued. "You should jump on board while you still can."

"I'll stay right here in my life raft if you don't mind?"

"Suit yourself, but the days of pitching stocks to your book are gone—you're doomed."

"How so, Nostradamus?"

"Come on, Connelly. Really? Really?"

"Yes, really. How so?"

"I'm talking about your business model, cowboy. There's no money in it. You're working for sand and rocks while I'm coining gold. Last I looked, I'm at four times your velocity."

"Are you talking production or blood pressure?" he smirked. "I'm managing to scratch out a pretty good living."

"That's because your clients are loaded, and they're old, just like you. But they're all dying away. Speaking of blood, you need a transfusion."

"Nice sentiment, Ian."

Apologetically leaning in, Molly handed Patrick his pint. "Thanks, Molly."

"You're most welcome, Mr. Connelly."

Eyes trailing her vanishing rear end, King continued, "Are you profiling them—learning about their other assets, their children, grandchildren, education needs, charities, hobbies—their dreams?"

"Of course, I am," he replied. "All of that comes up in conversation, and a lot more. For instance, I've learned that one of their primary 'dreams' is having a financial guy who can pick a good stock and make them some money every now and then; one who's not trying to sell them a credit card or loan every time they speak."

"Anybody can make 'em money, Connelly. It's not about that anymore; it's about seventh on their list of priorities."

Looking bewildered, he asked, "They don't care about making money anymore?"

"Nope," King said definitively. "They just want me to care about them. I can do that with the best of them."

"So," Patrick asked, "you're more an actor than a money manager?"

"I don't have to act. I genuinely care about them, like they're members of my own family."

"I'm sure you do, Ian. It was a joke."

"And if we have a bad year or two in the market, who cares?"

"But you just said you 'care with the best of them.'"

"I can't control the market," King countered. "I farm all that extraneous stuff out. If it's not working, I fire the monkey pulling the trigger and move on. No harm, no foul."

"Suddenly, I feel like having a banana."

"No offense meant."

"Offense taken."

"Word is you're not even doing *that* well these days."

"Not doing what well, Ian?"

"You know, the monkey thing—managing their money."

"Who are you talking to?"

"The walls, Connelly, the walls." His eyes were roaming the room. "Here's another thing they're saying, banana boy. I can double and double again your book's revenue. All it takes is the caring. I take them out for dinner, help out their kids and grandkids, fix their hot water heaters, their pool pumps, meet their best friends at our wine events—"

"That sounds exhausting."

"You sound so old, Connelly. It's like I'm watching a Jimmy Stewart Christmas movie. Let me try one more time to modernize you."

"I can't wait."

***

After a lengthy swig of his Bud Light and a lengthier review of his phones, King plowed ahead. "The business today is about bringing on more and more assets and charging a reasonable annual fee for all those services I mentioned."

"Thanks, but I think I'll sit it out."

"Ha, ha. 'Sit it out,' that's a good one." King was nodding down at Patrick's wheelchair. When he noticed the glare, he said, "Oops, sorry about that. I thought you were making a joke." Hearing no response, he hit on his beer again and was back at it. "I heard you lost a big account last week."

"The walls again, Ian? The client died. The kids took the assets to Utah, where they live. End of story."

"I haven't lost an account in three years." He was flashing a triumphant smirk. "I know the kids better than their parents do. That's the business we're in, keeping and growing the assets, and getting paid a fair wage. If lawyers and doctors are worth $500 an hour and up, why not me?"

"Because they do more important work? Like, I don't know, protecting people's freedoms and saving their lives?"

"I like that, Connelly, I may use it on my website." Gesturing to the headline with his free hand, he said, "I protect financial freedoms and save financial lives."

"Knock yourself out."

"Don't mind if I do." Both phones now screaming some shrill rock refrain, King drained his glass and stood up to leave. "Saunders feels the same way, so you'd better face the facts—this isn't going away."

"Are you?" he asked, feeling as depleted as King's beer.

"It is what it is. See ya around the office, Connelly."

"Not too soon, I hope." Raising his glass of red ale high to the carved rafters, Patrick bid his colleague farewell. "*Slainte*, Ian."

3

ASS-WIPE RUMBLE

When they still thought there was something worth saving, they visited a marriage counselor friends had recommended. Once a week, they'd meet in the center of the ring the way two middleweights would. For clarification, one heavyweight and one lightweight, on average, equals two middleweights. Patrick was the lightweight.

"Okay," the referee instructed, "touch gloves and go back to your respective corners. When the bell rings, come out maligning, and let's have a clean denigration with no scratching, biting, nasty nicknames, or kicking in the balls. Best of luck to you both."

Round One: Becky comes charging in with tongue thrashing. "You never listen; all you talk about is money; you care about sports more than you do me; your dick isn't big enough, and it hardly ever works; and you're always wrong, wrong, wrong."

Patrick is backing up, on the defensive, warding off her blows the best he can. Dipping and dodging, he's looking for his chance to land the one knockout wallop. It's his only chance, and everyone in the arena knows it. He gives it his best shot. "Oh yeah? My dick seemed big enough when we were engaged—before you locked in my bigger house and bank account. And there was a time you thought my tongue did a pretty good job too." Then he snarls, "All I talk about is money? Are you friggin' kidding me? I'm a financial advisor, for Christ's sake. If you've forgotten, that's how we eat."

Glancing blows at best, if any even landed. Becky stands firm with jaw set. He added the part about the tongue more for the referee anyway. Round One goes to "Becky the Brawler."

Round Two: After coating his fragile ego with Vaseline, Patrick moves in first. "You don't love me now, and you never did. You married the West Palm home, the Loxahatchee River home, the Saab Turbo, the cash, the beach club, and my impossibly good looks. Let's face it, Becky, it was all superficial. You married the Palm Beach lifestyle—not me. You didn't realize I was a working stiff, always living above my means, or you'd have moved on long ago."

Valiant try, but his opponent is good. Real good. Besides her lightning sharp tongue, she wields the perfect defense—she couldn't care less what he thinks or says. Round Two is called a draw. He'll take it. The unfortunate "impossibly good looks" comment cost him two points and the round.

Round Three: Same script except with a kick in the balls this time. "You're just like your tyrant father and your loser brothers." She's sent back to her corner by the referee for brutality above and beyond while he gasps for breath. He couldn't reciprocate in kind because he actually respects her family, thinks they're nice people.

Becky's relentless barrage wins round-after-round, after which she leaves the ring just as she'd entered: Gloves in the air waving, calling for the adulation of the crowd. "See," she exalts, "I told you. I'm right, and you're wrong, as usual, ass-wipe."

Nasty nicknames are apparently okay once the match is over.

It feels good to be right. Becky's desire to be right exceeded desire, though. It was more a need—something warrior-like. Patrick liked to be right too. Who didn't? But he had an advantage. He didn't "need" it. He had learned to cope, make peace, with being wrong. The day-to-day realities of the money business taught him just how wrong even the most educated person could be. He'd tasted the sour tang of humility more times than he could count. A fellow advisor once aptly described the business this way: "I've failed my way to a pretty good living."

An educated and informed young woman, Becky was probably right a lot more than he was, although he never kept score. Their discussions gravitated over time to a competition—who knew more about this subject or that—a frustrating competition with no winner.

A synonym for it was arguing.

Whenever they'd get into it full bore, his blood pressure soared and he felt a dizzying futility which eventually turned to hopelessness. He'd retreat to his den and his Sonos and lament along to George Michael's heart wrenching version of Elton John's tragic "Tonight." It wasn't about being right or wrong—it was about being exhausted. [5]

He had a difficult time articulating it, but it was central to his belief about his failing marriage. He wasn't saying he was better than her in any way. Far from it. He'd lost that competition the day they met. But there was a difference between passive education—from professors and books and media input—with getting punched in the face every day by uncertainty at your place of business. The punch was the much more impactful lesson. Even worse was knowing that he sometimes didn't know the answer, that he needed to make it up on the fly, first for his own sake and then for his clients. Worst of all was knowing when he went to bed on Sunday night to sleep— if he slept—that he *must* bring a paycheck home this month to feed, clothe, shelter, and educate a young family. That their beautiful, innocent faces were depending on him, and him alone, in this respect.

That was the point he wanted to make. The difference between book learning and getting the emotional crap beaten out of you in the workplace was about as wide as the great Atlantic itself. And he craved hearing such acknowledgment on occasion, however rare it may be. Maybe the words he was searching for were empathy and gratitude?

Becky was a star athlete in multiple college sports and "cute as a button," as her mother liked to say—a little too often. Her multitude of impressive qualities—her mind, body, resume, steadiness—were what attracted him in the first place. Most of all, in retrospect, he was grateful—*there's that word*—for any woman who was unconcerned about the wheelchair. Only a remarkable individual, he believed, could take the giant leap of voluntarily sharing his burdens. And that she did.

But as time progressed and the honeymoon became parenthood, and the depth of his disabilities and idiosyncrasies and related anxieties were one-by-one revealed, their physical contact diminished, except as required for motherhood. Hugs and kisses were replaced by a growing vocabulary of unfriendliness, perhaps to fill the void, including her go-to "ass-wipe." He responded in kind, at times light-years wickeder to his deep shame.

Who could blame her? Who could blame him? The intimacy had faded—more like cratered. Reality had set in. It was too late to chase the rainbow together. They were two lonely souls making their way as best they could.

After a year of marriage counseling with no measurable progress, the "ass-wipe" was done with it, especially done with shelling out $150 an hour to absorb his weekly flogging. Towards the end, he accepted the hopelessness and dropped his gloves, refusing to fight back. Without a live punching bag, Becky dropped hers as well. The sessions did manage to keep them together for a few more years until the kids left for college. That was a very good thing, he knew. They were devoted parents—if nothing else. When the kids were home, they'd stay in their separate corners of the ring and keep the skirmishes to a minimum. But the moment they'd leave the arena, the bell would ring once again.

Round 1000: "Let's Get Ready to Rummbllle!"

It was the final round, they knew. The match was nearly over. "Let's ring the closing bell and get this over with," they both agreed heartily. In the end, it was all just a tragic passion play that needed to close its run earlier than they'd hoped.

4

SMOKING HOT THERAPY

Since the divorce, Patrick would schedule a therapy session on occasion. He enjoyed having someone to talk with, to try and sort it all out. Someone who'd listen with empathy, without judgment, and offer good, sound suggestions. Given he brought along his checkbook.

Kay Weinberg, MFT, LCSW, their former referee, was smart and good at her trade. Plus, she was smoking hot. In her executive suite waiting room, he'd notice the patients before and after him were almost always guys. Rarely a couple or a single woman. *Why?* he wondered. He figured the Connellys had followed the usual script. After taking an agonizing shot at marriage counseling, with the husband down for the count, the wife would declare victory, lose interest, or find a smoking hot male therapist. The soon-to-be ex-husband would remain a patient of Kay's. Unless, of course, the husband was gay, or the wife was gay or bi-curious. Then, the outcome might shift.

Thus, he figured, Kay's practice was 80 percent divorced guys who wanted her, and 20 percent divorced women who wanted her. Pity the tribulations of the smoking hot therapist. The tyrant Seamus would be proud of his son's considered analysis.

Arriving at six o'clock sharp, he was buzzed through the door. After Kay said goodbye to her previous patient, a guy, she beckoned him into her small, spare office. "How's everything, Patrick? You look healthy, and you're smiling from ear to ear."

"It's probably the Smithwick's talking, Kay; post-happy hour appointments are a bitch."

"Tell me about it," she parried. "Are you monitoring your consumption as we discussed?"

"Yes, of course. I watch every drop descend." Resting his eyes on her frowning lips, he said, "You're looking sharp and sexy, as usual."

"Thanks, Patrick. I do what I can."

"And you do it well."

Settling in across from her chair where she'd cleared a space, he glanced around the sparsely decorated and too brightly lit room. Kay was decoration enough, he decided. In fact, the room could be bare except perhaps an oriental rug and a rolling bar, and it would be better still. Kay was all of five-one and 110 pounds fully dressed, which today included a short black skirt revealing well-toned and tanned legs, and a white silk blouse billowing in the compressor and blower-driven breeze. But, billowing or not, a tent couldn't hide her femininity. With medium-length blonde hair adjoining a pretty face, highlighted by large, dark eyes, a delectable nose, and plump, succulent lips, she was one voluptuous Cameron Diaz-like package from top to bottom, front to rear. Her sides were worthy of an Oscar, too.

He wondered if such stunning looks interfered with her professional pursuits, even questioning his own motives. Did he continue coming back just to keep her image fresh—in case he needed it? Or did he believe one of those *Sopranos* scenes could possibly happen to him? Nah, he'd decided, that kind of luck wasn't typically in his script. Kay was smart and insightful, and spending time with her really did help him. She was the complete package, especially her intellect, humor, and kindness. The image refresh was just a bonus.

As she uncrossed her legs and shifted ever so slightly in her chair, his gut tightened. In a recent late-night production, this was the precise moment she parted her legs, shifted back more certainly, placed one leg over the chair's arm, and purred, "I forgot to put panties on today, Patrick. Does that make me a naughty girl?"

His answer, of course, was, "Yes, Kay, it makes you very naughty," before administering her well-earned spanking. This evening though, in the stark light and with eyes wide open, one bronzed thigh rested tightly on the other as she busily flipped her black pumps up and down, back and forth. Heel in shoe, heel exposed; in shoe, exposed. It was mesmerizing, like watching the sensual ticking of a fine calcaneus timepiece. He made a mental note of this foot action for his next screenplay.

"What's new, Patrick? Are you enjoying your home? It's more pleasant with Becky gone, I assume?"

"It's just so-so, Kay." This was one of his tiring quips. The historic city neighborhood where he lived had been dubbed "SoSo," for "South of Southern." He'd already begun writing letters to council people, pointing out the idiocy of this moniker, titling one "How to lower market values by 20 percent with one stupid, yuppie nickname." Noting a hint of professional impatience, he straightened up and said, "I'm enjoying life, working hard, having a good time, mostly. But you know what they say—when it's good, it's very good, and when it's bad, it's horrid."

"What's been 'very good'?"

"Well, let's see; my health is superb, all things considered. I live in a beautiful house; empty, but beautiful. And I have two healthy, happy kids, not kids anymore, really." He wore a warm, reflective smile. "I'll probably never miss a meal despite the divorce and my fucked up career, and I enjoy my pastimes like reading, writing, music, theater, history, antiques, a bit of the drink. So compared to the world condition, I'm a pretty lucky guy."

"Nice sentiment, Patrick, I like it," she said with a heartfelt smile.

"Look around," he continued in a softer voice, "People starving and suffering and dying everywhere. Their so-called leaders, the ones with all the power, robbing them blind, raping and pillaging, and leaving them for dead."

"It's true and so sad."

"And look in the mirror, Kay. Look who I get to complain to for only $150 an hour. All things considered, I've got it pretty good."

"That reminds me. My fee is going to $175 next month."

"Ouch, sorry I mentioned it. How much do you charge for forty-five minutes?"

"One-ninety—it screws up my schedule," she said with a smile. "Sorry about that, you know how it goes—the recovering economy, the rising cost of pumps, the drudgery of it all."

"Yes, Kay, I'm familiar," he said, returning the smile. "Other than the pumps, that is. And you're worth whatever you charge."

"Thanks, Patrick; I'll remember that. So, tell me, what's so horrid? Tell me about your fucked up career." He paused whenever Kay said the word "fuck." He loved watching her say it, or any derivative thereof, and didn't wish it to pass unacknowledged.

"It's how the business has changed; the constant pressure, the demands to open more accounts, generate more revenue. It never ceases." He was getting riled at the mere thought. "It's less about stocks and investing, and more about finding assets, selling services, getting referrals, team trainings, mandates, licensing, planning dinner seminars, luncheons, breakfast meetings. Next it will be midnight buffets. It's a non-stop treadmill. Nothing ever seems good enough."

"Maybe it's time for a career change?"

"That's what sucks so much, Kay."

"What sucks, specifically?"

He also loved when she said "sucks." He would be watching super slow-motion replays of her lips forming and releasing the word for the next several nights. His expertise in this area was due to endless meditation and visualization training tapes and *SportsCenter* replays. Trying to think of another word he could bait her with, nothing came to mind. With a noticeable shift in his body language, he said, "What *sucks* is that I *have* to do it; with the alimony check due every month now, I have no damn choice."

"Having 'no choice' seems to be a recurring theme of yours."

"It sure is. Nothing's really changed. I still feel trapped." He felt a rising sense of despair. "After all these years of hard work, what do I have to show for it?"

"A lot more than you're allowing for right now, I'm guessing," she responded.

"Okay, you're probably right. But I'm still a working stiff. I resent the freedom Becky has, and I don't—there's another theme for you. Her only worry is making sure the deposit hits her account. Then it's off to Worth Avenue."

"Worth Avenue? You don't pay her *that* much."

"Nice, Kay, thanks," he said with a smirk. "Truth is, I've built a damn good business over the years, and it's still a reasonable living if they'd just leave me the frig alone. All this client-centric talk is a bunch of crap. Every time they say relationship, they really mean revenue."

"Isn't that just business? Capitalism at work?"

"Sure, maybe, but there's still right and wrong. They're trying to influence how I do my business or outright take it away. There's not a chance on earth I'll let them do it."

Fuming, he paused to drink from the Zephyrhills bottle tucked in his chair and took a deep breath before continuing. "We're measured daily—my production is posted in the lunchroom, for Christ's sake. How's that for privacy? It's like posting my W-2. Isn't that illegal?" She shrugged her shoulders, encouraging him to go on. "There are never-ending strategy meetings about growing the business and increasing our penetration."

"What do you mean by penetration?"

"Just like it sounds—how deep you can 'enter' the client." He was flashing the air quotes.

"Oh my," she said, fanning herself and feigning a swoon.

"Tell me about it," he said in reaction. "Sorry for the reference."

"I've heard worse."

"Like what?"

"Well," she said, "I could check my notes from our last few meetings, but why not just forge ahead instead?"

Nice try, he thought, before following her apt advice. "They're incessantly telling us to deepen the penetration, broaden the relationship, offer more services and products. Like you said, growing revenue is an important part of any business, and they just want more of their client's assets to manage. Believe me, Kay, I understand. But Jeez, there's barely time to breath, never mind smell a rose. These are supposed to be my reward years where I can wind it down a few notches."

"Sounds pretty bad. Can't you switch firms? My broker's done it three times."

"Three times? That's crazy; He's only moving for the bonus money, regardless of what he tells you. It's not about you, the client, believe me." He was speaking with a grizzled authority. "Why do you stay with him?"

"He makes me money, and besides, he's kind of a stud muffin," she said with a giggle.

"Oh, for Christ's sake, is there no sanctity left in the world?"

"Who are you, the Pope?"

"Hardly. But how would you feel if your patients—other than me, of course— came to you only because you were a 'stud muffin'?"

"Duh. Hate to tell you, Patrick, it happens all the time. Some people have advantages; no one said life is fair."

"I think I'm getting depressed."

"I've got a scrip for that."

"Oh yeah, whaddya got?"

"It was a joke."

"Too bad."

"The question is," Kay continued, "what do we do with our power? Whatever reason my patients come through that door, even if it's to ogle me, what do I do with that? I can't help them if they're not sitting right where you are."

"I'm sorry, Kay, I wasn't listening." He was doing his best ogle.

"You're a riot, Patrick."

"Thanks. Seriously, I admire you for using your power thoughtfully. You want to help all people—even the sleaze balls."

"I appreciate that, I think." She was getting good eye roll practice. "Everyone on earth in any position of power has the same responsibility. Use it wisely, benevolently, or else."

"Well said; or else you'll burn in hell? That's what my Irish Catholic upbringing tells me."

"This Jewish girl agrees with you—other than the burning part; that seems a little much. Maybe that's where your anger issue started?"

"What's it to you?" he said with faux agitation.

They both chuckled before Kay continued, "You know what Freud said about the Irish, don't you?"

"I do not."

"He said the Irish are the only people who can't be helped by psychoanalysis."

"What did that loser know anyway?" he said with eyebrows raised. "I guess he meant we're stubborn?"

"I was thinking beyond hope."

"That's what Becky used to say," he shot back.

"What does that loser know anyway?"

"Good answer." Patrick leaned in for an amiable fist bump before continuing. "So, Freud would recommend I don't even bother coming to see you, is that correct?"

"Umm."

"Add to that your egregious bump in fees," he continued. "What do you think he'd say to that?"

"It depends if he got a good look at me, I suppose. He invented libido, after all."

"Nice recovery."

"Speaking of my fee," she said with a noticeable shift in her chair. "Our time is up today. This is your last chance at my old bargain rate."

Reaching into his Tumi for his checkbook, he said, "I love a bargain. Maybe I should stay another hour?"

"Sorry," she said with a glance at her dinging phone. "I have an appointment waiting in the lobby."

"A guy?"

"Yes, why?"

"No reason."

"Seriously, Kay," Patrick said, "you specialize in takeaways, something for me to put into action. What's my takeaway today?"

"Well, your main issue right now, I think, is how to protect your business and how to deal with your coworkers."

"Especially my manager, Jeff Saunders, who'd love to pilfer my assets and eventually get rid of me."

"Okay. So, how about if we commit to a mission?"

"Sounds good. Tell me."

"The mission is to acknowledge your power and do the right thing with it every day. Your power is your brilliant mind; your eloquence, wit, and good humor; your handsome face; your health; your solid business; your children; your ex-wife, who isn't a loser, and I'm certain still loves you; your home; your hobbies. The list goes on. All in all, you've built an extraordinary life."

"Thank you, Kay, that's very kind, if not tragically embellished."

"You know it's all true," she countered. "So, no matter what pressures you're facing, no matter who's trying to steal from you—

remember your power and fight them till the end. Trust yourself, and turn up the energy, work harder at growing your business."

"That sounds good, Kay, except for the 'work harder' part. I'm feeling kind of lost in that department right now, like my light bulb is fading."

"Then grow a pair of balls."

"Whoa," he said, scribbling notes furiously. "Balls" was a first; it earns a special place on his list for sure.

"Look in the mirror, Patrick," she said in a challenging, less patient voice. "Look at your life, all you've accomplished, all you've overcome; the three decades of hard labor it took to build that business. Think about all you still want to accomplish. You are resilient, a powerhouse. You've just forgotten it."

"I like it, Kay. I really like it."

"No one's going to take away your power, Patrick, without your permission. This is your life we're talking about—your business, your clients, your revenue—you built it, you own it, and you need it right now to live your life to the fullest."

"Goddamn right, I do."

"Then get your Irish up and tell them all to go fuck themselves. Nobody fucks with Patrick Connelly."

"I will, Kay, I will." He was flushed, blood boiling, feeling his power—like the times he went to the Tony Robbins seminars. "Thank you, Kay, really outstanding."

"You are very welcome."

"Do me a favor, though," he asked while handing her the check. "I'm taking notes as fast as I can. Will you repeat that last part one more time?"

"I said, tell them all to go fuck themselves. Nobody fucks with Patrick Connelly."

"Beautiful, Kay, beautiful. Once more please, and slow it down this time, will ya?"

5

THE BOSS

The eastern view from Patrick's top-floor corner office was one of the best in downtown West Palm Beach. "To die for," some have said. As one of the few leading producers in South Florida who hadn't jumped to a competitor in recent years, choosing instead to remain loyal to the firm, he had earned his premier location. Or so he thought. Since the two market crashes, office managers, advisory teams, and other staff members seemed to be on a conveyor belt, arriving and departing in rapid order. The latest guy in charge, from some fancy management school up north, reminded him often that "earned" was past tense. If that was a "best management practice" he was deploying, it wasn't working so well.

The wide Intracoastal was choppy this January morning, with a stiff northerly wind buffeting the tide's natural flow. Through the oversized window, he noticed a small caravan of determined seamen fighting the swells, driving their crafts toward the inlet in a sun-infused dance with the salt spray. These were the true working men and women of West Palm, hustling out to their favored fishing spots before the high noon sun beat down. The leisure vessels with their air-conditioned teak chambers and private crews were still tethered snugly to the pilings of their private docks. They might venture out later in the day, perhaps after a champagne brunch, a spa treatment, and a chat with their financial advisor.

Rapidly blinking red and green lights on large dual screens drew his attention back to the desktop as domestic markets began their trading day. Each flash was a trade reflecting the moment-to-moment assessment of the value of stocks, bonds, gold, silver, energy, coffee beans, livestock, food stocks, and currencies—green for a buy, red for a sell. Apple, the world's most ubiquitous brand and one of its richest companies, had just crossed $600 a share. Millions of dollars of wealth were being created and destroyed, transferring from losers to winners in the blink of an eye.

In all, Patrick felt privileged to have his unique window into the world of the global financial markets. To be a miniscule part of it gave him the sense of purpose that we all seek.

Patrick Connelly's investment style was old-school, developed over the years the hard way, through trial and error. But he had it down now to a simple, time-honored practice which could be summed up with the following morality fable: slow and steady wins the race.

"First, we buy shares of the world's greatest companies," he would tell his clients. "Some thoughtful mixture of established dividend-paying blue chips and faster-growing companies in emerging industries. Next, we keep plenty of cash on hand for the inevitable rough waters—it acts like a life jacket." For those still listening, he would wrap it up with: "Finally, and this is the hard one, during stormy weather, we must hold our ship steady and buy more shares at bargain prices when others are jumping overboard." He would finish off his sermon with, "We must remain optimistic when others are despondent, when there's blood staining the waters. It runs counter to human nature, and most investors cannot do it. That's our advantage."

He lifted the entirety of his investment credo from famous investors, including Sir John Templeton, Warren Buffett, and Peter Lynch, and he believed it like he believed in nature's cycles. The sun rose, the sun set. The tide rolled in, the tide rolled out. Winter was followed by spring, then summer, and then fall. It usually brought animated nods of approval from his audience and sometimes even light applause. His encore would be, "And that's why you have me, so you'll never forget."

Roar of the crowd and a standing ovation.

A longtime client once responded, "Great in theory, Pat. But I'm eighty-two years old—my heart can't take all the ups and downs, and I can't wait a few years to make money either. It's today or never. Get me in at the bottom and out at the top, or you'll be carrying my corpse out of here one of these days."

"Just perfect," he laughed. "I'm a dinosaur stockbroker with a book of irrational clients dropping dead at the first downturn."

Rich, irrational, eighty-two-year-olds aside, he knew how to win in the game of investing, most of the time, but human emotion would always get in the way. Superstar investors like Templeton, Buffett, and Lynch knew it, and Patrick knew it too. His never-ending struggle was to remind clients, and himself, to keep the emotions at bay. "Decisions of this nature should be made with a cold, rational mind, not a heated, illogical heart," he would say. It was like telling them to keep their emotions in check when they're arguing with their spouse. Fat chance.

"Screw you."

"Oh yeah, well, screw you too."

"I'm leaving, lame-brain."

"Good, let me help you pack, numb-nuts."

The preaching was infinitely less difficult than the practice.

"Good morning, Marie." His longtime assistant had popped into his office to drop the morning mail on his desk.

"Good morning, Pat. Everything good?"

"No complaints, except for—"

"Oh, spare me, please. Save it for another time, will ya?" Her Jersey-accented cackle interrupted him on a regular basis. Truth was, he welcomed it. "We have to get to work."

"Yes, ma'am," he said with a salute. "What's on the agenda?"

"You tell me. Last time I looked, you were still the boss."

"You know that's not true, Marie; you've been running the show since I can remember, and splendidly I might add."

Nearly three decades earlier, Marie and Patrick started with the same brokerage firm just a few weeks apart. The first day they'd met, she acted like a tenured veteran of at least a decade. So confident, so in charge, so Jersey-ish. He knew right away who he'd be working with—or for—someday if he made it and could afford her, which was a long shot. It took a few years, but one day he popped the question.

"Hey, Marie—do you have a minute?"

"Hopefully, I've got more than that."

"I'm rooting for you," he said with a laugh. "I'll be quick."

"That would be novel."

"May I proceed?"

"I thought you'd never ask."

"You know, Marie, I'm doing pretty well now, growing the business, and I'm making a good living."

"Are you proposing to me?"

"In a manner of speaking."

"How much?" she asked.

"How *much*?"

"What are you, a parrot? How much are you offering?"

"Is that all that matters to you?"

"Oh no, Pat. As long as you promise to treat me with respect, honor my opinion, maybe throw in a meaningless title, I'll work for free."

"Really? That's great. How about 'Wise-Ass in Charge of Operations'? You can adjust it if you want. I completely honor your opinion."

"How much?"

He sharpened his pencil and made the deal, and he and Marie McCarthy grew up together in the money business.

While still the same ball of energy, she was looking just like he felt these days—a little worn on the peripheries. With enough time, this business does that to the best of them.

"Well then, as your boss," she said, "I'm telling you to get to work. Make some calls, sell something. Your name is sliding down the list every month."

"I hate those damn lists. It's a breach of privacy."

"You can hate them all you want, but they're not going away; and you didn't hate them so much when you were on top every year."

"I was the big hitter around these parts, wasn't I?"

"Yes, you *were*," she said to his beaming face. "And nostalgia doesn't pay the bills, Pat. I'm getting worried. I still have mouths to feed, you know."

"Of course, I know that, Marie," he said more somberly. "Christ, things aren't that bad, and you have nothing to worry about."

"I'm not so sure; the last of the Darby assets transferred out yesterday. That's a big hit. He was our second biggest account."

"I can't help that he died," he pleaded, "and that his daughter is a totally entitled, know-it-all who's never worked a day in her life. She's from the new generation that thinks everything should be free—that we have no value. Besides, they live two thousand miles away, and Mrs. D never liked Florida anyway."

"I know it happens, Pat, but the timing couldn't be worse."

"Yeah, especially for Darby."

"Now you're joking about death?"

"What else is there to do? Jack would approve. What an incredible guy he was—I really miss him. We spent many a St. Paddy's Day lifting a few pints together."

"You sure did, and now you have to lift yourself up that damn list. How about that? Do it in Jack's memory. He didn't buy that mansion across the bridge by sitting around all day."

"You're right, Marie. Jack would never stand for failure. Look here, my horoscope says good fortune is coming my way."

"Oh, for criminy sakes, would you put that stinking newspaper away and get on the phone?"

"For you dear, I will. By the way, got any good stock ideas?"

"Isn't that your line of work?"

"Yes, that's a fact, but I'm having a rough time of it these days, kind of like writer's block. I haven't picked a good one in a while."

"Then sell a bond, a fund, an annuity. Make something up and sell that; just get the frig going."

"If you're finished, Marie, I have work to do."

6

REPORTING FOR DUTY

"Please report to the conference room immediately. The sales meeting is beginning!"

"Oh, my good God!" Patrick cried out. "Another friggin' meeting? When in Christ's name do they expect us to call our clients and talk about, I don't know, the stock market?"

"Oh, stop your complaining and get it over with. You have no choice anyway."

"Right, no choice," he bristled. "Thanks for the reminder."

"You're welcome. Always happy to help, boss."

He could almost taste her wise-gal grin oozing through the wall. After taking care of some unfinished business, he trudged through the deep pile along the avenue of sterility, past empty clusters of drab-beige cubicles and the gray linoleum kitchen before finally reaching the cherry-veneered rear door of the conference room. Pushing it open, he clumsily shuffled a few gray metal folding chairs out of the way and not-so-silently slipped into the back of the packed room.

In the corporate blue-gray square of a space, six rows by ten chairs each, sat an arched-back assortment of plebes leaning forward in rapt attention on the dancing balls of their feet—a sea of prematurely graying and balding heads atop dark blue pinstripes swaying to the rhetoric. The women were equally tailored and serious but without the premature balding. Yet. The whole damn room was tailored and serious and perspiring.

There must be a battle raging out there somewhere, he mused, and this strategy session would be critical to our very survival. Having watched a recent episode of *24*, he surreptitiously glanced about the room looking for Jack Bauer. Maybe the only guy alive, fictional or otherwise, who could match the intensity level of office manager Jeff Saunders.

"Connelly, thanks for gracing us with your presence." Saunders interrupted his oration to offer this not-so-veiled admonishment.

Patrick responded with a half-hearted smile and wave. "Good morning, Jeff. Everyone. Apologies for my tardiness."

Tall, lean, and sharp-jawed, Jeff Saunders certainly didn't overdo the rations and was perfectly uniformed in his ready-for-battle military cut. He spoke with an urgency that raised one's jitters as much as any double cappuccino. "So anyway, team, as I was saying, we're rolling out a new system today to enable deeper client penetration."

Here the fuck we go, thought Patrick.

"It's the most efficient set of resources and tools we've ever produced—end of story. Write this down, people."

The sound of urgently flapping notebooks enveloped the room.

"This comprehensive, dedicated, client-centric website and dashboard is being rolled out worldwide this very morning. You are in the advent of a brand new Wall Street." Light applause sprinkled the room. Pausing for the crescendo that never quite arrived, he continued. "You can access this world-class platform 24/7, including the training modules, team formation protocol, book segmentation, marketing materials, seminar scripts, lead generation tips, best practices videos, optimum fee schedules, and so on." The troops were furiously scribbling. "And you are the only folks on the street with this capability, easily two years ahead of the competition."

"Sir?" One of the plebes shot his hand up. "I'm so busy meeting with my clients, cold-calling, planning my seminar calendar, and studying for the CFP exam, I can't imagine having even a few minutes to look at the site. I'm feeling a bit overwhelmed, sir."

"Thanks for your input, Kyle." Saunders angled away from the podium and in towards the group. "But yours is a pathetic, weak-assed attitude. The answer is you simply have to work harder and longer." A groan of incredulity rose throughout the room. "If you're working fifty hours a week—up it to sixty; if you're doing sixty—make it seventy; if you're working less than fifty— you'll soon be adding to the deplorable unemployment numbers reported this morning." In choreographed unison, the room anxiously thumbed their screens to get the report.

Surprised there were no further questions, Patrick leaned over to the sweat-beaded, pimpled face to his left and whispered, "I put in about thirty-five hours last week and was exhausted. This is not good news." It elicited a cautious grin before quickly returning his attention to the front of the room.

"I'm in this office on Friday night until nine p.m.," continued Saunders. "You know who keeps me company? The cleaning crew, that's who. They work harder than all you sad sacks combined."

That was a clean takedown, Patrick thought.

"You can't escape the facts, team, the competition is getting fiercer by the day, and they're coming after your clients. Within a mile of where you're sitting are the ten most powerful wealth management firms in the world."

"The enemy lies within is more like it," Patrick muttered.

"Something to contribute, Connelly?"

"I'm just amazed at how competitive our market is."

"You of all advisors should know this," Saunders drilled, "if you even bother to pay attention." The room shifted noticeably. "All that island money should be producing fees right here inside these four walls, and every last person sitting here should aspire to live across that bridge as soon as possible. You never quite got there, Connelly, did you?"

"What's across the bridge, Jeff? I never quite got there."

"That explains a lot."

The rest of the room was craning back and forth nervously, waiting for the next volley, which never came. Patrick wasn't concerned about all the worthy competitors in the marketplace because he didn't consider them competitors. And they certainly weren't adversaries. He had former colleagues across the industry, many trained in this very office. There was enough wealth in Palm Beach, in Florida, in the country, he believed, to feed all the hungry mouths in the money business. Fresh food regularly adorned his family's table without resorting to rummaging through competitor's trash bins looking for their client lists—while working substantially less than sixty or seventy hours a week. What did concern him was having to attend meetings such as this one.

"Getting back to our topic," Saunders resumed. "The site can now be accessed from your smartphones, tablets and laptops—so you can complete a training module with your breakfast or dinner." A wave of indigestion moved around the room.

What about midnight buffet? Patrick thought nastily.

"No excuses anymore, ladies and gentlemen," he warned. "There'll be a weekly assessment on your mandates page to complete, so we're sure you master the information."

The meeting was thirty minutes in with nary a mention of a stock or bond, or an investment idea or strategy. That didn't seem to bother the troops, but the idea of working sunup to sundown struck a chord. They were human, after all.

"One more thing, team," he droned, "blah, blah, blah, blah, blah, blah . . ." Patrick took the "blah, blahs" as his signal to depart. Moving toward the door, he noticed Ian King and Mia Wolfe glancing his way from their front-row perch. Worse, Saunders said, "Leaving early, Connelly?"

"Appointments."

"Would you stop by my office in half an hour?"

"Sure Jeff, sure." He pushed through the same rear door and plunged down the corridor past the little prison cells whose inhabitants were out for their morning exercise. Through the dull heartbeat pulsing in his throat, he muttered, "God help me, but this place totally blows."

Entering a corner office three times the size of his own, Patrick settled in beside two plush black leather chairs facing the genuine cherry wood desk. It was more a massive alter filled with awards and plaques trumpeting "manager of the year" and "rising young executive." *If there were a "Heart Attack in Waiting" award*, Patrick thought, *he'd be a shoo-in.*

"You don't mind if Ian and Mia join us for a few minutes, do you Connelly?"

"What's the point of that, Jeff?"

"Just doing a little brainstorming. They're two of my rising stars and may be helpful."

"What's the theme of the storm?"

Hesitating, then making the connection, he said, "Same as always: how to grow your practice. I spend half my time trying to trick you dum-dum advisors into making more money."

"Nothing wrong with that, assuming it serves the client's interest. You know that old saw: the client always comes first."

"Always, Connelly, they keep the lights burning in here."

"So again, Jeff, what specifically is on your mind?"

"Well, speaking of clients, I think you could be doing a better job helping yours."

"How so?"

"We're not really a stock brokerage firm anymore. We do wealth management now; you're not showing them all we have to offer—not even close."

"Are you getting complaints from them?"

"I'm getting complaints from my boss. That's worse."

"So, no client complaints? Meaning they're happy."

"They don't know what they're missing, Connelly. And you don't either. Here, look at this report." He handed Patrick a thick document called a "Household Profitability Analysis." The total score in a bold black box at the top was 22.

"Twenty-two? Is that good?"

"It's on a scale of 100 being the best. So, you tell me. Is that good?"

"Well, if I can get it up to 30, I'd be in the Hall of Fame." Saunders didn't crack a smile, not even close.

"Your clients, excuse me, *our* clients, use credit cards, they borrow money for homes and businesses, they buy annuities and hedge funds, they need insurance, and a whole list of other services. They're borrowing and buying, just not from us."

"I've offered my clients some of those products when it makes sense. But I specialize in stocks, and a few entrepreneurial income ideas; that's my strength, it's why I love the business. I don't love cold calling for checking accounts and credit cards."

"There's no profit in your model, Connelly, unless you charge an annual management fee. You've been unwilling to do that either."

"I have some fee-based accounts, the more active ones," he corrected. "But why should someone pay more for the same service I give them for less?"

"Because you're not giving them the same service, for one thing; there's a long list of benefits your clients aren't getting. And we're worth the fees—95% of the surveys we receive back say so. You're shorting them by not using your toolkit."

"It's just as well, Jeff, I'd be a terrible handyman."

"You're a terrible comedian too." Saunders bristled. "Face it, Connelly, you're doing your employer, yourself, and *our* clients a disservice. You're not standing up for the firm. Get it, Connelly, 'standing up'?"

"Got it, Jeff. Brilliant play on words."

"Excuse me, can we come in?" Ian King was standing in the doorway with Mia Wolfe. He didn't hesitate. It wasn't a question.

"Yes, yes—come in, take a seat," said Saunders after the fact. "Good to see you both—thanks for taking the time."

He sounded like an okay guy when speaking with them, Patrick thought cynically.

"Anything we can do to help, Jeff, you know that."

These two looked like they'd stepped off the cover of *Wealth Management Advisor* magazine. King was Disney prince handsome and perfectly groomed, as usual, all buttoned up in his usual pinstriped blue. But the star of this show was clearly Wolfe. She appeared to be older than King, or maybe just more mature.

Dressed impeccably in a coordinated, black-trimmed white blouse and gray suit combination, none of it hid her portfolio. Her abundance of jet black hair was held at bay by trendy, oversized, multi-color frame glasses, giving her striking face a studious accountant look. Black heels elevated her to just above that of a pint-sized dynamo of scrumptiousness.

Patrick's mind jumped to Van Halen's "Hot for Teacher" video [6], thinking the advisory business had been bereft of such talent for years. It seemed to him that most young, attractive saleswomen flocked to the pharmaceutical industry, becoming its secret weapons. They'd call on the multitude of philandering, god-like doctors, buying them fancy steak dinners at Ruth's Chris, Morton's, or Capital Grille to their clogged hearts' content. In doing so, they eventually gained access to their lucrative pill dispensaries. Wolfe would get fat in the pill-selling trade, he decided, while her colleague King would starve. Except for the bi-monthly free steak dinners. The tyrant Seamus was once again beaming with pride right about now, he knew.

Turning to his rising stars, Saunders said, "We were just exploring how Connelly here might expand the products and services he offers to his clients." Referencing his .3 velocity, a measure of revenue the firm collects on the client's assets, he gushed, "Ian's team is at 1.2—do you know what that number would do to your take-home?"

"May I borrow a calculator?"

"Don't bother, Connelly. Suffice to say you could finally move across the bridge to the big island."

"I like my neighborhood just fine," Patrick retorted snidely.

Ignoring him, Saunders asked King to describe his business model, which was just more "blah, blah, blah." After detailing his portfolio development and client review process, King then said, "Your paper calendar, day planner, and yellow legal pad style is ancient, like out of the '80s, if you don't mind me saying."

"Do you mind if I mind?"

Saunders glared, saying, "And he means the 1880s, in case you're confused. Go on, please, Ian."

"Thanks, Jeff. So, I could automate your entire business, shift your priorities, get you all fixed up in no time. You'd be working half the time you're working now."

I'm not sure that's possible, Patrick thought with a smirk.

"Within a few months your revenue, I mean *our* revenue, would begin to increase and I promise, *our* clients would be thrilled with the new service model. Not to mention, every time I meet with a client, I'm owed at least one referral. I never let them forget it."

"I'm sure they're excited for every opportunity," Patrick replied, noticing Wolfe's giggle. "That sounds a little more King-centric than client-centric."

"Wrong again," Saunders chastised. "His survey scores are higher than yours. That's why you're here, Connelly. I'm trying to save you from yourself."

The "storming" wound down with Saunders saying, "I'd like you three to huddle, do a deeper dive into the idea of teaming up. It'll be in everyone's best interest, especially Connelly's clients."

"We're looking for assets, and it sounds like you could use help with providing more services," Mia Wolfe said. "It seems like a match made in heaven."

"I appreciate the offer, Mia, I really do—you too, Ian; but I'm not looking for new partners," he said. "I am, however, looking for the door."

Saunders's stern jaw tightened further as he said, "I don't like your attitude, Connelly."

Feeling under full assault now, Patrick returned the sharp look. With a slight tremble in his voice, he said, "Teaming up is another way of saying you're handing a piece of my business, the business I built the last thirty years, to these two. That's a big decision, Jeff." After a pause, he continued, "Shouldn't I at least know who the hell they are—or if we'd be compatible? A partnership is like a marriage—isn't it?"

"Another thing you don't do so well, I understand," Saunders said derisively.

"What do you want to know?" interrupted King. "My favorite color is blue pinstripe; I run five miles every day at four in the morning; I eat Grape Nuts with almond milk for breakfast and drink ten to twelve cups of coffee before noon; and I sleep in the nude if I sleep at all. Oh yeah, and my velocity is 1.2 percent. Any other questions?"

"No thanks, Ian. I think that more than covers it."

One of King's phones started pounding and zapping and pitching. "Jeff, I got a big one on the line here. Gotta go. See you soon, Connelly."

"Can't wait."

"Go reel 'em in, champ," Saunders said, before once again facing his prey. "This is strategic, Connelly. You'll be filling voids for each other."

"It could be a good thing for you, Patrick, and for us too," added Wolfe. "A blessing all around." With King out of the room, her face seemed more relaxed, her voice softened.

"Sorry, Mia. I don't usually put bullying in the 'blessing' category."

Wolfe's cell phone now exploded with a different rock and roll riff, "The Rising of the Moon," if Patrick heard it right. King was summoning her for "a very important call." She reached out her hand, saying, "I must go, gentlemen. I hope you'll consider Jeff's idea, Patrick. Thank you for your time." Patrick released her hand and watched her step away double-time.

"Thanks, Mia—you're the best," Saunders said, before turning his focus back to Patrick. "Why don't we put a bow on this. Your buy and hold stock strategy, or whatever you call it, is yesterday's news. It's not working for the firm, and it's not working for you either."

"That's your opinion."

"Sorry, but we've run the numbers. Your client performance wasn't anything special last year."

"You can't measure performance over one year, Jeff, you know that. Look at the five-year numbers, the ten-year."

"No can do. This is a 'what-have-you-done-for-me-lately' business."

"Have you ever considered that my clients may not want your style of business?" Patrick's ire was on the rise. "The relentless pitch for more services, the constant pressure to be referral machines. They may simply want what I've been giving them for decades."

"You really are from another time, Connelly. Medieval, maybe?"

"If you try to change them," he warned, "they may leave."

"Are you blind? Did you see that young lady who just walked out that door?" He was pointing to the hallway "Your clients won't be going anywhere."

"So, Jeff, this is your brainstorm? Hand my clients over to a higher velocity guy and his attractive sidekick?"

"Don't go there, Connelly; that's totally uncalled for."

"I haven't even begun."

"You'd better be very careful, my friend," warned Saunders. "We can play nice, or this can get ugly—your choice."

"I'm not in the mood for playing, 'friend.'"

"It's not a game. Ian and Mia do everything the firm asks. They have spotless records and their clients love them."

"What if my clients aren't interested in this marriage?"

"It's your job to sell them, and besides, technically, they're not your clients. They belong to the firm."

"Wow—that sounds like a threat, Jeff. Like this isn't my choice."

"It's my considered advice, Connelly, and you should take it seriously. Think about it, and we'll talk again next week. I'm sure you'll make the right decision."

Acid eyes staring down at the carpet, Patrick propelled his chair back from his boss's desk and turned abruptly toward the exit. Hesitating, ready to spew his vomit, he thought better of it. Seething, he pulled open the faux cherry door and drove his powerful shoulders forward. Bursting down the corridor, he bellowed, "It is what it is!"

7

FROM WITHIN

*And where does the power come from, to see the
race through to its end? From within.*
Chariots of Fire

"Ice hockey? Are you kidding me?" Patrick's eighth-grade
friend had invited him to check out the local pond hockey.
"I don't even own a pair of skates," he reasoned. Bobby Kelly wasn't
a "no" kind of guy. He loaned his friend an extra pair of skates, a
hockey stick, and a dream.

The next absurdly frigid Saturday dawn, Paddy was tossing his duf-
fle bag over the guardrail near the highway bridge and following

it over. Descending the winding path's filtering light through thick groves of dormant elm, hemlock, and pines, he finally cleared the muted woods and reached the banks of Three Ponds. The largest of three contiguous bodies of water unveiled a sheet of sparkling black ice bordered by clumps of wilting golden reeds against the sharp, blue-skied sunrise. Animated with skaters, some twirling, others flopping, others engaged in a fast-paced game of hockey. Bobby was at the far end of the pond in front of a homemade wooden hockey net, apparently playing goalie.

"Hey, Kelly," he called out derisively. "I thought you needed to know how to skate to play goalie?" Sitting on a log by the pond, Paddy laced up the beaten skates over two pairs of heavy, gray woolen socks. It was the first of thousands of times he would repeat this glorious ritual over the following seven years.

Grabbing the stick, he stepped out onto the ice. *Whoops.* Up he teetered. *Whoops* again. Slowly grinding his way out towards the others, his friend encouraged him. "Come on, dude, come on." As Bobby cheered him on, he was whipping around the ice just as he did in life. Ever the show-off.

"Shit," Paddy despaired. "You can skate after all, you bastard."

"Oh, come on, Conns!" he hollered. "You can do it too."

Not quite. Taking tumble after tumble, his frustration swelled to match his ever-bruising butt sheltered in soaked jeans. But the game was on, and no one even noticed. As Alfred E. Newman was famous for saying, "What, me worry?"

The answer came quickly. One of the older guys, a bullying asshole named Steve, bellowed out, "Hey Connelly—get the fuck off the ice before you kill someone." The whole world paused and turned their glare to "Connelly." And he did "get the fuck off the ice" that morning with his burning red face having little to do with the biting weather.

He never forgot that bullying asshole's stinging exclamation. In fact, it drove him, compelled his every exertion those next seven years.

Paddy caught some amalgam of fire and ice. An inextinguishable flame hissed in his gut. He went to Three Ponds every chance he had that winter. But never again in prime time. Instead, he'd go before school, after school, after his chores, with or without Bobby, until the moon would light his way back up the woodland path. Day after day, night after night. "I'll get the fuck off the ice, Steve, you fucking asshole" became the mantra he'd repeat over and over while relentlessly pounding his thickening legs into the brittle surface, pushing ahead stronger and steadier by the day.

Toward the end of that winter season, a girl from town he barely knew drowned at Three Ponds. She fell through the creaking, fracturing ice at the first spring thaw, forever fracturing a family. He read about it in the same local newspaper he delivered to fifty doorsteps every afternoon. "Bummer," they all said. "Didn't she know the ice was thinning out?" It was obvious, the paper said, by the surface's ever-blackening color, its groaning against the weight of a passing skater, and the water pressing up from the pond's shoreline the way a drink does over bobbing ice cubes.

It could have been Paddy, or Bobby, or someone else who fell through to their horrifying end. Maybe it just wasn't their time, like it was the girl's?

Another pond regular's fate soon beckoned. The bullying asshole Steve was the only guy Paddy ever knew, however faintly, who died in Vietnam, fracturing yet another family in an increasingly fractured nation. He read about Steve in the same paper. They called him a "hero," and in an odd, unintended way, he was. *Thank you, Steve, for your service to your country, and to me,* the paper delivery kid thought, understanding his life had been propelled upward by that bullying asshole "hero."

Soon after, Bobby suggested joining an organized league in White Plains. "Are you nuts, man? I'm not good enough."

"Sure you are, dude."

"Oh Jeez," he said with a knowing acquiescence. He wasn't assessing the plusses and minuses or thinking at all. He was instead following his heart. He was game.

In the inky silence sat the brightly lit oval—a picture of both desolate gloominess and pure beauty. At his very first dawn practice, a Canadian glacial front whipped across the outdoor rink, welcoming him to what would become his second home.

The white surface was adorned with blue and red lines and circles, and real hockey goals, just like on television. Bundled head to toe in wool, barely able to bend over, he stepped onto a real sheet of ice for the first time. His sharpened blades crackled the superficial layer of the glassy, smooth surface just laid by the funny-looking machine called "Zamboni." Feeling safe within the confines of the red-trimmed, black-pocked whiteboards and tall chain link fencing, Patrick was a lifetime away from whoever he'd been before.

He was not a good skater, which unfortunately is a prerequisite to being a good player. Not yet anyway. But hell, he'd only been at it a few months. And he loved it. He absolutely loved it. Power skating was first with no pucks in sight. His quad muscles were dense by now, bulging even. "Thighs good for fucking, not for trying on pants," a clothing store clerk in White Plains once said to his reddening cheeks. He didn't even know what "fucking" was other than a word his father used when he was angry, which was often. But he knew just enough for his cheeks to redden anyway.

He pumped his "good for fucking" thighs up and down, over and over, driving his blistering skates into the ice, pushing out to the side, and propelling his mummified body forward. Pump, drive, push. Pump, drive, push. Up and down the ice he went, trailing the group and using his stick for balance. Time for back-skating. This would expose the pretenders. Digging his blades into the ice and pushing forward, he drove backward. "Shit, this is much harder," he said to Bobby. Mired in place, falling on his butt, jumping back up, falling to his knees, jumping back up, he dug in, pushed forward, and drove backward. Not a lot of movement. But he didn't quit—he instead dug in, pushed forward, and drove his body backward. One hundred and sixty pounds swayed like an oversized gymnast trying to hold his balance on the beam as sweat soaked through three layers of clothing, cooling his over-heating engine.

"Hey, Connelly—get the fuck off the ice."

"Fuck you, Steve, you fucking bully. I'll get off the fucking ice when you come out here and get me, you fucking asshole hero." Dig, push, drive. Dig, push, drive.

The large aluminum bucket of frozen pucks with a hundred black dents finally made an appearance. "Oh, thank God," he said, racing to pick one up and stick-handle toward the far end of the rink. He was Vic Hadfield and Reggie Fleming rolled into one. His buddy Kelly guarded the net in his signature crouch, shifting franticly to the left, then the right, ready to spring. The neurotic little Eddie Giacomin clone was flicking his catching glove and waffled stick glove in every direction to deflect the little black missiles coming his way. "You won't stop me," Paddy decreed. Doing his best Marv Albert, he sang, "He breaks in on the net, he dekes, he shoots, and he—"

"Ha, ha," laughed Kelly. "Stopped you, dude."

"Next time, you fucker, next time," he called back over his shoulder while pumping a little less awkwardly up the rink.

For the remainder of his first life, Patrick Connelly immersed himself in all things hockey: pond hockey, street hockey, driveway hockey, hallway hockey, game board hockey, rink rat hockey, prep school hockey, summer league hockey, junior league hockey, all-star hockey, Madison Square Garden hockey, ECAC hockey.

From driveways to ponds to rinks, Connelly and Kelly, two inseparable grade school friends, grew into young men on a mission. Teammates and rivals, from bantam to prep school to junior, and finally to Division I college hockey. Ever so briefly. [7]

8

WALKING THE EMERALD ISLE

"**S**orry, Sean. I'd love to, but no way I'm giving up summer hockey. I'm the captain of the team, for Christ's sake."

"Oh, come on, Paddy buddy, come on; you'll live to regret it. This is Ireland I'm fucking talking about—our ancestral home."

"I'm friggin' eighteen, my man," he shot back. "Last time I looked, we were still in high school; you're acting like this is my last chance at visiting Ireland—I've got all the time in the world." That was Patrick's final answer. A few weeks later, a Bobby Hull-like slapshot broke a bone in his foot. Hockey was out. Ireland was in.

Walking from the airport terminal into the misty, chilly Shannon summer felt oddly like a homecoming of sorts. When Patrick was a kid, besides "Paddy," adults called him "Red" for his tomato red hair. It embarrassed him, of course. Most things did then. Another disease he had was countless freckles. One time he tried counting them, starting on his left hand and heading north. He got dizzy and bored just above his wrist after the first thousand or so. His father, Seamus the tyrant, didn't think he was diseased at all, often calling him a live version of a Norman Rockwell magazine cover. "Vintage Americana," he would say with pride.

So, into the lush green landscape strode "Red," the tomato-headed, freckled Irish boy from the Bronx—vintage Americana—clad in jeans, hiking boots, and a salmon-toned *Houses of the Holy* t-shirt. They'd gone to Madison Square Garden to see the hottest band in the world, Celtic rockers Led Zeppelin, before heading out to Kennedy Airport in the wee hours of the morning. That t-shirt became a central part of his image, marking him a Celtic soul on a coming-of-age journey of discovery. All he needed for the month-long trip was carried on his broad shoulders: tent, sleeping bag, camera, Bunsen burner, franks and beans, three changes of clothing, toothbrush, and a few other sundries. He left his razor at home. This wouldn't be pretty.

Standing on the side of a Limerick motorway drenched through in stiff, wind-driven rain, thumbs out, the two travelers began shuffling in the puddles and singing. [8] "Dancing days" were here again as that summer evening grew, and they laughed and frolicked and did their best Robert Plant swinging the mic imitation. Then they were high fiving, Jimmy Page air-guitaring, and feeling the thrilling edginess of an uncharted crossing.

They stood in the torrent for hours, lines cast with no bites, and began walking and walking (and walking) to Christ knows where. They said "Christ" a lot in Ireland. It's not a sin, he was told, unless you add in an expletive or have evil intent in your heart. Their non-evil intent was to travel south and make their first stop at the most famous of Irish pubs, Durty Nelly's in Bunratty. There they'd have their opening Guinness on Irish soil, visit their first castle, set up camp in a nearby field sheltered by ancient stone walls, and do it again the next day, and the next (and the next), until arriving in Dublin in a month's time.

They were instructed not to go north of Shannon or Dublin because "the Troubles," a bloody religious and political war, was raging in Ulster. So south they walked. That first Guinness at Durty Nelly's was also Paddy's last. Plucked off a warm and dusty shelf, he found it a putrid grind and instead hoisted frosty pints of Harp Lager from then on.

Intending to stay in a B&B once a week, sleeping in an actual bed and taking a bath on occasion seemed a prudent plan. At the first, in the vicinity of Killarney, the proprietor carried bucket after bucket of boiling water from the kitchen to pour into his tub, and Paddy scrubbed away a week's worth of Pigpen-ness. They sat the following morning for a hearty Irish breakfast which was a little too close to consuming various internal body parts of a recently-live pig for his taste. "Do they really have to call it 'blood pudding?'" he said to Sean. They swam in the renowned lakes, or "loughs," traversed magical Dingle and the Ring, and then headed southeast with one goal in mind—to kiss the world-famous stone imbedded at the top of Blarney Castle in County Cork.

Trekking the vast, rolling green meadows and forested hilltops leading to the medieval limestone castle, they came upon the magnificent partial ruin with its still intact tower and embattlements dating to the 1400s. Directed inside, they circled up steep, moldy slate steps worn slick from centuries of passage. At the top, they took in the breathtaking views of the countryside while walking the embattlements toward two leprechaun-looking gents. Setting down their packs, they stared down at the legendary stone and practiced their best pucker. One of the men held Paddy by his belt while he lay down, leaned over backward, and tightly gripped the black wrought iron rails. Then, inching his way down the deep well, he planted his most enduring kiss on the polished stone, thereby joining a centuries-old registry comprising millions of lips on their own unique pilgrimages. The second man captured the magical moment on his Polaroid. This was about the extent of Ireland's tourism economy at the time.

Patrick felt an immediate change, like when the scarecrow was given a brain by the wizard. This was the moment he became a true Irishman through and through. Eloquence and charm were his newfound fortune. As they tramped away from the castle, his poet's tongue was already in evidence.

"I'm fucking starving, Sean; let's go to that pub we passed in Blarney."

"Good motherfucking idea, buddy." Sean had obviously gotten the magic too.

From the Woolen Mills in the castle's yard, he shipped home all the promised sweaters, caps, and knick-knacks. His tight budget was rapidly depleting, with many a pub still on the itinerary. It was past time to fire up the Bunsen burner. They skipped the B&Bs, washing in lakes and rivers and rolling out their sleeping bags in castle and manor house ruins. One morning, in a heavy grove of oak trees in the corner of an open field harbored by a tall, black moss-embossed stone wall, he woke to a herd of cows with one nibbling at his toes in a good morning kiss kind of way. They rode to a rock and roll show with a busload of local teens who may have mistaken them for monsters of Irish fable. Paddy did bear a strong resemblance to Tull's *Aqualung* by this time. If there had been cell phones in the '70s, they'd all have been hiding under their seats, hitting 911.

Their thumbs were luckiest with German tourists, oddly enough. The Irish citizenry weren't as jovial and friendly as he'd imagined, seeming wary of their guests—and weary. These were tough economic times, especially for much of the hard-working Catholic laborers of modest means. They closed the pubs at five in the morning, he was told, so that the men would go to work the next day. Stereotypes are usually based in truths. He was proud to see they absolutely adored their adopted president, the late John Fitzgerald Kennedy. In nearly every pub they visited was an American flag draped near his photo and a candle-lit altar honoring the assassinated president and his younger brother, Robert, who was murdered five years later.

In Waterford, they watched the famous artisans carve their crystal glassware, and in seaside Wexford, clearly a working person's town, a German man bought them each a sandwich and a Smithwick's. Paddy had a new favorite beer. The pub sandwiches looked nothing like he remembered from home. A sliver each of ham and cheese on two thin slices of brown bread with a spread of butter, if they were lucky.

What did they expect for a buck?

The adventurers were nearly broke by the time they reached the outskirts of Dublin. Feeling hungry and desperate one day, they stole sandwiches and ran from the woman. She took off after them in hot pursuit, cursing something in Gaelic. It didn't bother him at the time, but in retrospect, Patrick had his first and only taste of what hunger can do to an otherwise rational and law-abiding man.

In Ireland's most populated city, they walked the streets aimlessly and slept in hidden corners of public parks like the homeless people they were. They took photos of each other in one of the dozens of church graveyards with double-arched headstones framing their exhausted, scruffy Irish faces. They walked the famous Ha'penny Bridge over the River Liffey and viewed the grounds of historic Trinity College through ominous black wrought iron fencing crowning its dense, gray stone-walled perimeter. And they walked along busy, cobbled Grafton Street, unable to conduct even the most modest commerce.

Dodging endless late August raindrops portending the coming fall, Paddy tossed his few remaining odd-looking coins into the cup of an urchin inhabiting a street corner. "Thank you for your generosity," he muttered while peering up from his sprawl. Offering no eye contact, he then said, "It will never be forgotten."

"Stay well, young man," Paddy replied in a glum tone. "I wish I could do more." He wished he could do a little more for himself, too, at that moment.

Finally, they put out their thumbs one last time and made their way to Dublin's airport, as thrilled to be leaving the homeland as they'd been to arrive. He was looking forward to having his wheels again, not having to depend solely on his legs for travel like some old-world gypsy. He'd never lived on such meager sustenance for so long a time and wouldn't miss that either. But he'd been to Ireland, and by walking half the country discovered who he was. He got to the heart of the matter. Patrick Seamus Connelly was no longer just "Red," the Norman Rockwell magazine cover from the Bronx.

It was all in the archives, where everything eventually passes. But for Paddy, it was a first, and certainly, there'd be many more such experiences ahead.

Of course, there weren't "many more ahead," making this unintended trip-of-a-lifetime maybe the most important decision he'd ever made. Visiting his adopted homeland and seeing it in its proper context—as a young, healthy, free man—was one of his last vivid memories of unbridled physical prowess. To any red-blooded Irishman, competing in the physical world with a furious independence is a prerequisite to a life well-lived. For evidence, just watch one of their rugby matches and the pub action that follows. Treacherously soon, Paddy would need to turn his fury away from the physical; his very survival would depend on his remaining assets north of T-10—particularly his mind and his heart.

Right. Tell that to any strapping nineteen-year-old and be sure to stand aside for the ferocious reaction.

The kissing of the Blarney Stone, and his meager life on the streets of Dublin, however brief, became a metaphor for all he'd need for his uninvited mission ahead: A strong Irish constitution, including a sharp wit, an eloquent tongue, and most importantly, a kind and stout heart that would never quit. No matter what. [9]

9

TRACE

"Insert it like this; now, press down firmly." She encouraged him while gently directing his hand. "Easy, easy; keep sliding it in—that's better." It went smoothly for the first six inches, plus or minus. Then he felt a resistance. His penis recoiled like the rounded head was bouncing off a trampoline.

"This feels like it should hurt like hell," he said. Although it didn't. It was more a discomfort deep inside—like an unnatural violation.

"Here, let me show you." She held his flaccid penis gently with three fingers of one hand. (Patrick thought she used four fingers; she remembers using two; so we settled on three). With her free hand, she deftly inched it out, applied more K-Y jelly on the tip, and then slipped it back in again. This time she exerted enough downward pressure to push through whatever had been putting up the fight. "The sphincter valve opens naturally when it's time to void," she explained. "But invading from the north is abnormal and triggers the resistance." His lower body was jerking and kicking and screaming in spasm.

"This whole damn thing is abnormal," he whined.

Patrick was learning to self-catheterize. Three times a day, his nurse would arrive, break open a sterile package and hand him a long, sickly yellow silicone tube with a foil of K-Y jelly. He'd hold the length of his penis, using all five fingers, he recalled, press open his pee-hole, apply the jelly, and begin snaking the narrow, rounded end down his pipe with his free hand. Once it was fully inserted in his bladder, she handed him the ubiquitous urinal while directing the wider end of the tube inside to catch the first golden dribbles. "We have to make sure your urine is clear," she reminded him. "Remember to drink lots of water."

"What about Heineken?"

"Heineken's okay, but water is better," she said with a faint smile. One of his exciting new objectives was clear urine. "You're prone to infection, so it's critical we get this right." Once he learned to "cath" himself, she encouraged, he'd be a step closer to independence.

"Independence?" he repeated. "How fucking great is that." Locked inside a body that couldn't move, dribbling not-so-clear urine from a tube. "This is what you call independence?" he growled. The pretty nurse spreading K-Y on the head of his penis should have made for a better story. But her professional tone and pitying look, and the rank smell of urine, shifted the narrative.

"All done," she said brightly while withdrawing the slippery coiling tube, placing it in a waste bag, and pouring the smelly brownish piss in the toilet. She tossed the tube, rinsed the urinal, applied wet wipes to his traumatized appendage, tossed those, and peeled off her gloves. It was like watching an experienced NASCAR crew changing a tire. "See you at noon. Remember, lots of water."

"Fan-fucking-tastic," he said with a brash new sense of independence.

Patrick was also practicing transferring on and off a toilet surrounded by grab bars so that he could generate a bowel movement without some nurse's hand stuck up his ass. Only two fingers, he was nearly certain. The pretty one didn't do that. She had her boundaries, after all. He imagined what went on in the nurses' dressing room at the start of the day. The divvying up of the day's duties—or should it be "doodies"?

"I'm on piss today," the pretty one would say while looking at the board.

"You gotta be shitting me; that's totally not fair," came the plainer one's lament. "I've been on shit three days in a row. Do they think I'm some kind of asshole?"

"Stop your pissing and moaning."

"Easy for you to say, piss breath; I'm up to my eyeballs in shit is all I'm saying."

"Hey, don't kill the messenger; I'm just reading what's on the board."

"Well, *the board* is delivering me a shit sandwich."

"Why don't you tell someone who gives a shit?"

"Oh yeah? Whose shit are you cleaning up? As if I have to ask."

"Hey, watch your mouth, bitch; that's a pile of shit, and you know it."

Circumstantial evidence? Sure. Completely made up in an aggrieved mind? Absolutely. But the pretty nurse never stuck her hand up Paddy's ass, was all he knew. Whatever the story, he was spending more time on these two most basic of life's functions than he had since his days in diapers. Everything old was new again. He'd gone from the cradle of his youth to a view of the graveyard nearly overnight.

The team from occupational therapy arrived to dress him in jeans, sneakers, and a sweatshirt. Just a few weeks before, he'd whipped on the same clothing in a flash before speed walking across campus. Now it took two attendants half an hour to drag and shift and pull them onto his frozen lower body. The clothes looked different now, much less cool, more helpless. They looked crippled. His formerly cool clothes looked crippled. He could see the outline of the leg bag contraption and tube snaking down his left leg.

"My dick and bladder are strapped to my goddamn left thigh," he raged. "That's a good look."

The crew lifted him onto a raised mat, and from a slumped-over sitting position, he tried to hold his balance. "Come on, Pat, hold it, hold it," they implored as he fell into their arms. They slid a slick wooden board under his ass, signaling the "lift and slide" routine. This effort was to move him into his new mode of transport—a wheelchair. The same way port workers move heavy cargo from the loading dock to the truck. He was heavy, dead, pathetic, crippled cargo.

Once in the wheelchair, his jeans would be twisted underneath, zipper off-center, sneakers crooked on the gunmetal, dinner-crusted foot pedals. He hated looking at his frozen, misaligned legs and crooked feet on the disgusting old person's pedals. Insisting his feet be straightened, angled out slightly, and his jeans aligned properly, zipper directly over crotch, he felt slightly less crippled when everything was in alignment. For a moment, he looked almost normal until he glanced in a mirror.

"I'm a circus freak!" he cried. "A fucking grotesque Elephant Man!"

Physical therapy, his only real hope, was next. The idea was to keep him flexible while the swelling in his spinal cord diminished and his nerves reconnected so he could get the hell out of there—get back to school and on the ice again. They'd bend his legs in every conceivable direction, meeting strong resistance all along the way.

It sometimes took several minutes for the spasticity in his knees to unlock.

"Hamstrings stretch," she breathlessly replied to his question while holding his straightened leg aloft. "These are called range-of-motion exercises; we need to keep you stretched out and limber, and then we'll measure your function."

"What does function mean?"

"Your levels of sensation and voluntary motor function, what you can and cannot feel and do," she answered. "Okay, Pat, now—try to lift your left leg." The moment of truth. Straining to lift his leg—he tensed and jerked his abdomen, hips, chest, shoulders, and neck—gripping the mat tightly. His face turned beet red as sweat soaked his upper body. "Try to relax your upper body; just focus on moving your left foot now." She was flexing his foot, rotating the ankle, bending his toes up and down. "Move your toes; come on, move them. Lift them up to me."

He focused on lifting his foot up and down, wiggling his toes. Sweat and tears mixed on his cheeks as he tried to push against her, to kick her. He tried to kick her right in the face, watch the blood dripping from her lip. Then he'd apologize and hear, "*That's okay, Pat, that's real progress.*" Instead, she was saying, "Don't forget to breathe. You're pushing with your abdomen; just relax and focus down here, only on your feet." Her colleague was furiously jotting on a clipboard. She stretched his toes up and said, "Hold them up, hold them, hold them."

"I'm holding them up, aren't I? There's something there, right?" His breathless voice revealed desperation. She glanced at her partner without answering.

Stretching his toes up again, she urged, "Hold them up! Hold them, hold, hold." Shaking from concentration, struggling to comply, he was determined to beat this disaster. He'd show them all. "Push with just your leg, Pat, not your hip or torso." She placed his foot on her sternum. "Keep the rest of your body relaxed; just push with your right leg." Glancing again at her partner, their silent communication screamed volumes.

They called his function "trace."

"Great news Paddy—the house is ready. You'll be leaving here next week; you're coming home."

"But I'm not ready, Mom."

"Dr. Ernst says you—"

"Fuck Dr. Ernst and the tank he rode in on."

"Calm down, Paddy. He says you're ready; the staff says you're ready. There's nothing else they can do here."

"Nothing else they can do? What the fuck have they done? I'm still a cripple—now I'm gonna live in my parents' basement? How pathetic is that?"

"Come on, Paddy. Things will get better."

"I don't want to go home, Mom." He was crying uncontrollably. "I don't want to go home. I just got the hell out of there."

"Try to relax, honey; you're just angry now."

"You're damn right I'm angry; really fucking angry."

Nineteen years old. A rock and rolling hockey jock just a few months ago—Patrick Connelly was a paraplegic, an invalid, a cripple, a fucking useless piece of garbage in his own eyes. He hated it. He hated looking like a cripple, he hated being seen with other cripples, and he really fucking hated being a cripple.

What did he have left to live for anyway? Everything he was, everything he cared about, was dead. It had been wrenched away, the way a barbarian would pry open the lacerated rib cage of his wounded prey and rip its beating heart from the chest cavity for his supper. Blood spurting, guts in arrest, writhing in death's grip. He was dying a violent death inside, which would be a relief compared to the obscene nightmare he was living on the outside.

10

IRONSIDE

Of all the names they called him, he hated *Ironside* the most. He couldn't watch the show—couldn't even look at Raymond Burr sitting in his dreadful wide-load Everest & Jennings wheelchair. Watching the heavy-set guy rolling himself around the courtroom, strangling in his tent-like blue suit, made him want to puke. It was like looking at some distorted future mirror he couldn't bear peering into. Who gives a shit if he won every case he tried? He was still a fat, ugly, talking torso on a dolly, some two-bit ventriloquist's pathetic dead-bodied puppet.

"Hey, there goes Ironside." That was all the asshole said, along with a point of his finger. Like seeing a tall black guy, pointing, and calling out, "Hey, there goes Magic Johnson." Kind of silly and innocuous, right? Not to Patrick. He was embarrassed, felt all the world looking at him, laughing at him, pitying him.

After a deeply troubled period living in his parent's basement, he moved south to warm weather and flat terrain to complete his education. While in Coral Gables, his father explored suing the hospitals and school infirmary for misdiagnosing the staph infection. Patrick hadn't thought much about the ungodly amount of money they'd been shelling out for the surgery, the rehab center, modifying the home, the medical equipment, the living expenses, the private college tuition. No wonder Seamus was a powder keg ready to blow expletives at any moment.

What was an injury like his worth in a 1980s small-town New England court of law? To be determined.

In the meantime, he spent an inordinate amount of time at the campus swimming pool—the heartbeat of Suntan U. One day, finished with his laps and grabbing some rays before class, a sunbather he'd never seen before took residence in the lounge chair contiguous with his. As she settled in, the light cotton wrap fell from her lithe shoulders and down the length of her petite, feminine torso, revealing one of the most sensual scenes he'd ever witnessed.

Her string bikini left little for his active imagination to conjure. She was tan and freckled all over, including the triangular indents at the tippy top of her inner thighs. As she rummaged through her canvas beach bag, he observed sun-bleached hair brushing her shoulder blades and the peach fuzz that lightened her lean belly and thighs. Stretching out on that very same belly and thighs, she rolled from side-to-side applying Coppertone to her naked, perfectly taut rear end. Seeming pleased to have him for an audience, she gave a rousing performance. While maybe not the right girl to bring home to meet the mom, she was a perfect fit for his dorm room, and his head was swimming in the possibility.

Four years removed from his last hockey game, with the same devotion to the pool he once had for the rink, his 5'10" frame had shrunk to a muscular 160 pounds tightly wound around a 32-inch waist. With shoulder-length, strawberry blond hair and bright white teeth offsetting bronzed, freckled skin, he could've been a Suntan U poster boy. No offense meant to Norman Rockwell. And while you wouldn't know it from his log, meaning his record of amorous activity, he was at his physical and sexual peak at this precise moment, never again to register a higher testosterone count.

Together they bathed in the warm, intoxicating coconut aroma of the tropics and talked about whatever came to their unencumbered minds. He was gaining the nerve to ask her back to his room, where he always kept a supply of chardonnay, Heineken, Jarlsberg cheese, and Triscuits. His wheelchair was sitting prominently next to his lounger, so he wasn't too worried about shocking her. One time in a popular haunt, he'd transferred onto a bar stool with a friend tucking the wheelchair out of sight. An attractive young lady happening by leaned against him and invited him outside, expressing in graphic terms her intentions. Ashamed, his words fumbled out nearly inaudibly. He was a fraud, he knew, nothing more than a billboard. When told the facts by his friend, she sheepishly drifted away to direct her ardent pursuits elsewhere. He was careful to avoid such mortification after that. But here at this pool, on this day, and with this delectable morsel, he felt totally at ease. It had been so long, he thought dizzily, he couldn't even recall.

He was about to pop the question when a blind guy with wiry brown hair and oversized dark sunglasses, cane busily tapping away, came directly toward them. It may sound like the beginning of a tawdry joke, but it was really happening. The blind guy plowed forward through the lounge chair obstacle course like a tank through a forest, nosily scraping one chair after another along the coral stone deck. He was a regular at the pool, and this was his neighborhood, but—"Christ almighty." Patrick bristled. "Now he has to show up?" He finally settled in on her other side with his chair so close, Patrick had suspicions he may not be so blind after all.

"Would you rather be crippled or blind?"

"Say again?" He was stunned by his little companion's question.

"Well, I was wondering which you thought was worse, being crippled or blind?"

"I didn't realize I had a choice," he quipped, trying to lighten the suddenly dour mood. Speaking hesitantly through a markedly redder face, he then said, "I've never really thought about it, to tell you the truth, but my preference would probably be neither." Maybe he should have said, "Hey baby, I *am* blind for everyone but you." (Ba-dum-tssh.)

Instead, he engaged her in a laborious philosophical discussion comparing the relative downsides of various disabilities.

They were in an environment of learning, after all. Truth was, he'd thought about the subject on several occasions. It must be what people who keep losing things do. What's next on the chopping block? Choose your poison.

Being half-blind already, which his diminutive prospective paramour was unaware of, he had come to understand the risk he'd taken every time he stepped onto the ice rink. There were no face shields or cages in the '70s to protect his good eye while engaging in his stick swinging, puck hurtling passion. It was reckless, of course. His parents tried their hardest to talk sense into him. But the young rarely look at the risks of their bold and sometimes idiotic actions. They live from moment to glorious moment unimpeded by good sense, until on occasion, a poor decision's downside bites them in the ass. But Patrick wasn't young anymore. He was a wretchedly old twenty-three.

The brush fire at the pool suddenly smoldered and then fizzled out. He packed up and went off to a class he had hoped not to attend, never again to encounter the sexy little pool toy. He'd lost his nerve, been neutered, by the sudden focus on all that was wrong with him. It shattered his dreaming. *Sadder still,* he thought, *she probably ended up banging the blind guy.*

He never got to tell her that if he were lucky enough to have such an appealing choice, he'd rather be crippled than blind. So fuck that blind guy with the cane he stumbled in on. At least Patrick could half-see what he could never have.

That was a long way of saying he wouldn't have exchanged his ability to walk and otherwise function normally for blindness, or a billion dollars, or a trillion, or all the money in the universe. But in 1980s small-town New England, his injury was worth $3.5 million. That was the number the attorneys arrived at for medical expenses, loss of wages, and pain and suffering. The pool toy he never got to play with, and the girl leaning against him on his barstool who never got to take him outside, were meaningful illustrations of his "pain and suffering." Anyway, the number sounded good to him.

The trial lasted nearly a month, just for jury selection and the prosecution's case. The day before Patrick was to testify, his mother took the stand. She was beautiful and honorable and cried genuine tears during her answers. She told the court what it meant to have a hockey star son one day and an angry, crippled old man of a son the next. And the jury cried right along with her. That night, while he was reviewing his notes for the next day's testimony, his attorneys, parents, and the presiding judge came into the room.

"Paddy," Seamus began, "they made an offer we think you should seriously consider."

"Yes, Patrick," said his lead attorney, "it's the first real offer they've made."

"How much?"

"$1.1 million cash, net to you after all fees."

"Don't you think we can win the whole 3.5?"

"Maybe—but this is like winning $1.5 million with no risk, no delay, no appeals process. If we sign the offer sheet tonight, they write the check tomorrow morning."

"It feels like we're doing well so far," he said. "I heard Mom was great today; that's why they made the offer, right?" Reaching out to hold his mother's hand, his voice had the shake of uncertainty. "Maybe we should just keep going?"

"That's up to you, of course," said his attorney. "But the defense hasn't presented their case yet. They're good attorneys; they'll try to poke holes in our case, destroy our credibility. We're ready for them, but however the jury feels today may be very different in a few weeks."

"What do you think, Judge?" The room turned their attention to the stately, grandfatherly-looking man.

"It is a lot of money," he said. "This is Providence. The jury members are working-class people; you never know what they'll do. They may award you half of that, or less, and think they're doing you a big favor. I can't tell you what to do, but your parents and counsel are making good sense."

"Okay," Patrick said, "let's take the offer and go home."

They did, and they did. He had some mad money in a checking account and a million-dollar certificate of deposit in the bank earning 21 percent annually. Thank you, Jimmy Carter. Most importantly, he was looking out the windshield for the first time rather than in the rear-view mirror.

11

BEYOND THE RAINBOW

With blood coursing and butterflies dancing, Patrick watched three sets of double-doors open in unison as the *2001: A Space Odyssey* theme burst out on an icy-cold tailwind. He timidly trailed his fellow trainees as they streamed into the large conference room while friends, family, and volunteers crowded around the doors applauding, high fiving, hugging, and telling them to "Go for it!" Taking his place in the back row where a folding chair had been removed, he counted at least fifty chairs perfectly aligned with masking tape applied on the industrial blue carpet. Each inhabitant looked as pale and uncertain as the next.

A sharply dressed young man soon bounded onto the platform with a big smile, moving to the music, looking intently throughout the room. Behind him, a sign on the wall read, "What Are You Pretending Not to Know?"

"Holy shit, I have no idea," he said to his neighbor with his patented wise-guy grin. "And I'm not pretending."

The doors closed, and the music ceased. The man in front, now wearing a microphone headset, introduced himself as the head trainer. As his story went, the former IBM executive had taken the same training and was so drawn to the "human potential movement" and the difference it could make in healing the planet, he immediately switched careers. He went "all in." He told the room, "It's now your opportunity to do the same. You need to make a full commitment, or the training simply won't work."

Then he took care of some business by outlining the rules, such as: being in your seat on time; no talking without raising your hand and being recognized; no bathroom breaks without gaining permission; no drugs or alcohol for the five days of the training; and the "absolute need to take full responsibility for your experience." Each participant needed to "fully buy in." He wasn't referring to the tuition, which had already been paid in full.

Patrick was in the breathtaking Pacific Northwest visiting his Ireland travel buddy Sean. It had been two relatively aimless years since he came home to West Palm Beach with his injury settlement. He had no compelling career aspirations and was frittering away enough of his hard-earned money to cause concern. On top of that, his girlfriend had recently flown the coop. He went for a swim at a nearby Olympic-sized pool one night, as he did most nights, returning ninety minutes later to find she had vanished with about half the furnishings. Given the efficiency and thoroughness of her exodus, he suspected it was a pre-planned operation with a team of her Harpoon Louie's colleagues. Duh. Although she forgot to leave a note, she *was* kind enough to leave her cat.

When the invitation was extended, he farmed out the cat and hopped the next jet to Seattle—the Emerald City. He was barely settled in, thoroughly enjoying the mid-summer fifty-degree nights, his morning Starbucks cappuccinos, the insanely delicious salmon with mason jars of crisp Chateau Ste. Michelle chardonnay and long-distance swims in frigid Lake Washington when he found himself sitting in a Lifespring training room. His buddy had recently graduated and said it was "totally cool," and he should "go for it." He also said, "there are a million hot ladies in the training." That was an effective close. He failed to mention the "sign up a new trainee" mandate each graduate must commit to before the training ends.

During the next several days, each session lasting well past midnight, the individuals in the room became one unified unit. Those independent enough to raise objections or question the leader, the dissenters, were taken apart one by one. Scathingly at times. Their concerns were summarily dissected and dismissed. "Are you willing to accept that you don't know?" The trainer's tone was gentle, like an older, wiser friend. "Are you willing to replace your fears and worries with trust?" As the skeptics continued their insurrection, he was losing patience, beginning to chastise. "Is this how you show up in life—always the skeptic, the critic? Have you always been the know-it-all?" He would resort then to confrontation and denigration. "How's that working for you, tough guy? The floor is yours—please tell us all about your extraordinary successes."

Each day, the sign on the wall enlarged:

What Are You Pretending Not to Know?

Hour-by-hour, Patrick dropped his own pretending. He wanted to be "fully authentic," just like the handsome, brilliant, dynamic, confident trainer. Who wouldn't? They were led through various exercises—group mingles they were called—where he fixed his eyes on someone and said, "I trust you," "I don't trust you," or, "I'm not sure I trust you," while they did the same. There were one-on-ones where they were instructed to recall something bad that happened in childhood and fix it now by screaming at the perpetrator: a teacher, a sibling, a parent, and pounding chairs with pillows. Afterward, they shared their experiences with the room.

Over vibrating, emotionally wrenching music, the trainer called out his challenges: "Tell your truths, people—what happened? Who did it? How did it make you feel?" The room was on fire as he threw on more fuel. "What are you going to do about it now?"

In another exercise, he turned the tables by howling out: "You know who did this to you? I'll tell you who—you did it, that's who.

You gave away your responsibility. You gave away your power." The room was now bawling, awash in tears of guilt. "You let it happen—it was all you." The intensity surged, and they were given pillows once again to pound out their anger and vengeance, their self-loathing.

One by one, the trainer was picking off the quiet, reserved ones. Although he did his very best, Patrick couldn't hide forever. He took the microphone one time and did some flimsy-assed share like, "I get it, I finally get it," to the applause of his peers, only to be excoriated by the trainer laying in wait.

"Tell me what's really going on for you, Patrick; not that weak, pathetic drivel." He hated being yanked into the spotlight, but it was far too late. "Dig deeper, Patrick. You're living on the surface. I'll bet that's exactly where you live your life. What are you afraid to look at?"

His emotions were on fire. He cried, he hated, he lamented his family, his injuries, the doctors who'd destroyed him, all his bad luck and missed opportunities. Other times he smiled broadly, laughed out loud, and loved every inch of himself. He became a helpless, totally trusting child again, alive with possibility. He hugged everyone: men, women, dogs, women, women.

Patrick indeed "got" the training, feeling a power emerging like he never had before. He now understood he was responsible for everything that happened in his life—the good and the bad. Ruining his right eye with scissors and paralyzing his body was on him. He'd even chosen his parents and siblings. "I chose my angry father and insane brother? And I chose to maim and cripple myself? Why would I choose such a shitty life?" It was befuddling. Maybe he liked a good challenge?

On day four, in utterly vulnerable and emotionally piqued states, the challenge was given to call the person who had most disappointed them or harmed them and tell the truth of what they'd done. Then they were to absolve the perpetrator of their sins; exercise their newfound power to forgive and ascend. They all lined up at the payphones in the hotel hallway, which was a great opportunity to hit the head without negotiating for permission, and one by one, they made the calls. Patrick called home—collect. He wasn't certain what he intended to say or what he said, only that the call became known in family lore as "the mushy brown peas" incident.

Apparently, he told his mother that she was a lousy cook, maybe the worst ever, and that he was forced to eat overcooked, mushy brown canned peas all his life. He'd been harboring a deep resentment of her—until now—because he finally understood that she was only doing the best she could. He forgave her and loved her unconditionally for her effort. He now saw her lousy cooking as the act of love that it was meant to be.

Later they all shared their experiences. Some had forgiven their drunken fathers for abandonment. Others forgave an uncle or brother or teacher for rape. Others forgave a former friend for stealing from them and leaving them bankrupt. Patrick forgave his mother for imposing mushy brown peas on him. Sure, there were tougher things he could have said to his perpetually angry father or his insanely bullying older brother. Maybe he was too afraid, or blessedly, neither was home. Be it cowardice, timing, or that he simply didn't see the upside, his saintly mother took his flogging for a relatively minor infraction. While the trainer may have been right about him living on the surface, it was a hell of a lot calmer up there than risking the turbulence of any deeper dive. He was probably being smart, not opening any other cans besides the peas. He also decided not to share his conversation with the group, which was probably smart too.

After the "peas" call, his family became convinced he'd been absconded by his west coast, nut-job friend and forced to join a cult. They weren't that far off. But what did it matter? It was all his responsibility now. He'd chosen it all, and it was his alone to handle. In a way, he was God, in full control of whatever came next.

Graduation night was an all-out group hug and celebration. They'd found their authentic selves—the innocent, wide-eyed children they'd been all along. Amidst teary-eyed joy, Kenny Loggins serenaded each one of them home. [10]

Patrick celebrated himself home as a "giving, loving, and accepting man," the label he'd been given on his second training's graduation night. It would become an enduring mantra.

The human potential movement of the 1970s and '80s was extremely controversial, including stories of participants going off the deep end and the resulting lawsuits. He saw it happening firsthand. Those with serious emotional voids made Lifespring the new center of their universe, choosing to work for the organization full-time in a volunteering capacity. Their new intention was to heal the planet, and this would be their platform.

Some even soared into manic highs and had to be hospitalized, including his lifelong hockey buddy, Bobby Kelly. In the frenetic afterglow of his graduation, Patrick convinced him to travel to Seattle, saying something about there being "a million hot ladies in the training." It was an effective close for Bobby, too.

It was one of those "good ideas at the time" that worked out poorly. Very poorly. Too much buried pain surfaced for Bobby during his training. He couldn't handle the emotional intensity and was forcefully removed to seek the medical attention he needed. Which he eventually did. Not voluntarily.

More than a few trainees bugged out during the height of the West Coast's counter-culture, humanistic psychology movement. But not Patrick. He kept his wits about him, other than the "mushy brown peas" incident, and the training was just the boost he needed. It changed his entire self-awareness, his life's perspective, from "Paddy, the poor victim," to "Patrick, the man in charge who can do anything, and have anything the hell he wanted." What he wanted the most, besides the perfectly healthy body he'd never again have, was a real career and a woman to love—a woman who loved him and was grateful for him despite his disabilities.

After a few false starts in business where he frittered away even more of his dwindling nest egg, and a broken heart or two along the way, he decided it wasn't going to happen for him in Seattle. Sean's girlfriend (of the month) was a talented folk singer who performed a gorgeous version of "Over the Rainbow" whenever

Patrick asked. She hadn't taken Lifespring, so she was the most level-headed voice in the bunch. In fact, she thought they were all kind of bananas with their deep eye contact and hugging and "I got its" and "Go for its."

One time, he was lamenting a setback he'd suffered in his never-ending quest to walk again when she gave him a birthday card with a *Wizard of Oz* photo on the front. Inside, she'd written this note: "Maybe there is no Oz, Patrick. Maybe everything you're looking for has been right there at home all along."

With deep eye contact, he gave her a teary hug and said, "I got it," and, "I'm going for it."

His few weeks' visit to Seattle to see his Irish buddy had become two years, and it was past time to leave the Emerald City. The rest of his life, whatever that would bring, had been waiting for him at home in South Florida all along. [11]

12

A DAY IN THE LIFE OF A MONEY MAN

"**B**ob Reinworth's on the phone."

"Oh Jeez, Marie, can you tell him I'm tied up and I'll get back to him?"

"What good will that do, Pat? The pain won't go away. It'll just get worse."

"Thanks for the good news."

"Man up, will ya, and get it over with." Marie knew Pat better than anyone, including Paddy and Patrick.

"Crap, you're right; just put him through then." Adjusting his headset, he steeled himself and unlocked the mute button.

"Bob, good morning. What's on your mind?"

"Good morning, Pat. Not much. Hey, do you remember about two years ago—in fact, it was June 12th—I asked you if we should buy Netflix at 66. You told me no. Do you see where it is today, Pat?"

"Mid-300s?"

"No, it's 412. You told me not to buy it."

"Well, Bob, I think what I said *was*, it's a highly speculative stock, and I don't understand how they'll stay ahead of the cable companies, not to mention Amazon, Google, Apple, and all the other competition."

"Looks like they're kicking butt and taking names."

"Looks that way, but we're still inundated with entertainment choices, and there'll be lots of money made and money lost."

"Right, and I'm the big loser."

"I'm looking at your account now, Bob. Plenty of other stocks we've selected are working too. I don't think you'll be missing a meal anytime soon."

"Actually, I could stand to miss a few; my belt's getting a little tight."

"I hear you," he agreed. "Kudos, you had a great idea; they're doing much better than I expected."

"Better than expected? That's an understatement, Pat. Bottom line is I feel like crap. I was a fool for listening to you."

"Bob, I've said this before, and it's a good takeaway now." His voice revealed a tinge of growing agitation. "Always ask for my opinion and guidance, but if you have a strong feeling about something, for God's sake, man, follow it. You should have bought Netflix at 66 regardless of my input. You're the boss, after all." After a brief period of silence and furious tapping on his keyboard, Patrick gathered his thoughts and continued. "Remember just before the call you referenced when the stock had fallen from 400 to 66 in a few months' time? They were changing their business model from sending movies through the mail to streaming to Blu-Ray machines, and the jury was still out. There was even talk they might go bankrupt."

"Sounds familiar," Bob said hesitatingly.

"I recall you asking what a Blu-Ray machine was," he reminded. "You didn't even know how to work your DVD player and felt lucky when your TV turned on in the morning. Do you recall that conversation?"

"Vaguely."

"I remember it like it was yesterday, Bob. It's all the coconut oil I drink." More likely, it was the notes he took that day that he was perusing now. "You've also told me often you can't afford to take any big losses. You certainly remember that?"

"It makes sense; who wants losses?"

"You've said over and over that steady income is all that matters."

"I need to pay my bills."

"Right, I agree. I was being prudent, Bob, looking out for you."

"Well, let's not cry over spilled milk, Pat. What's a couple hundred thousand between friends?"

"Pocket change."

"Right," he replied, "for very large pockets. What about Facebook now? Or LinkedIn? isn't that one going public soon?"

"If I may ask, how old are you?"

"Just celebrated my eighty-first."

"Congratulations again. You do remember I called you to wish you a healthy and happy?"

"Of course, I do, Pat. Much appreciated."

"It's my pleasure. We've probably spoken on your birthday or met for lunch more than twenty times now. How lucky am I?"

"Well, you could be luckier. You could have bought Netflix at 66."

"Touché. Speaking of Facebook, LinkedIn, or anything else you have an interest in—I'll send you our latest research. Give it the once over and give me a call whenever you want to speak again. Does that sound good?"

"Perfecto."

"By the way, do you use the social networking sites?"

"What's social networking?"

"Never mind, Bob, we'll talk again soon; sound good?"

"Okay, talk again. Ah shit, Netflix just hit 415. See you, Pat."

He hung his head for a few moments—eyes closed, breathing deeply, rubbing his temples. Tapping in the symbol NFLX, it was 417 and change. He strolled out to Marie's cubicle, where she was picking up yet another ringing line. "Patrick Connelly's office. Oh, good morning, Mrs. Grossman. How are you?"

A warm feeling welled as he watched Marie manage their business like a maestro would her instrument. He couldn't remember the last time he told her how important she was to him. Probably because every time he did, it resulted in a pay increase. Being from Jersey, Marie was a better negotiator.

An explosion of argument quickly chilled the atmosphere. Looking to a bullpen of cubicles down the way to his left, Jeff Saunders and Ian King were standing face-to-face. The conversation was heated, something about an error charge and who was responsible. It looked like a couple of gladiators about to do battle. "I'm not taking the hit, that's for sure," he distinctly heard Saunders say.

Marie was looking past him with an equally disgusted look on her face. "Mrs. Grossman just needs a few minutes to run an idea by you."

"Okay."

"Hang on another minute, will you, Mrs. Grossman? He's just finishing up another call. Thanks."

Patrick handed her some written notes, saying, "Can you send Facebook research and that new social media report to Bob? And print me up Netflix research when you can. I love reading about all the money I've missed making."

"You're human, Pat. I don't see a crystal ball in there. You shouldn't be so hard on yourself."

"Thanks, Marie. I appreciate your support."

"You're not considering teaming up with King or Saunders, or both, are you?"

"Where'd you hear that?"

"Everyone's business is public in this snake pit. You know that."

"You're right," he growled, glancing again down the corridor. The public chastisement had finally abated. "Team up with one of them, or both? Not in a million years, if I have a choice."

"Don't you?"

"Maybe not. Saunders is bringing down the hammer on me. King may be an okay guy, I really don't know, but we have nothing in common other than we're both trying to survive."

"That's the story of our careers, Pat,"

"It sure is," he agreed. "And at this point, we have different survival needs—King needs assets to manage, and I need my peace and independence. I'm perfectly happy with things as they are, just the two of us. Besides, I already have one boss and that's plenty."

"Hey, watch yourself," she responded with a giggle. "I'm your number one survival tool."

"Don't I know it, Marie."

"I like our set up too, Pat, but everything's changing so fast. We don't have much of a say around here anymore. Can Saunders just force a partnership like that?"

"Not in the day, Marie, but you're right, it's a whole new world—they call it 'teaming' now."

"Some team they are," she said with a note of revulsion. "All I hear these days is work more hours, sell more services. When is enough, enough?"

"Never enough in this business," he answered. "They need more and more revenue to pay for all the litigation from the two bear markets; kind of like the Catholic Church—'Please donate more so we can pay off all our past sins.'"

"You just compared our business to the sexual abuse of children?"

"The common theme is unwarranted penetration."

"Are you gonna pick up Mrs. Grossman?" She was stifling a giggle so as not to reward his crassness.

"Go ahead and put her through," he said, turning toward his office.

"While you're on with her, Pat, could you do a little penetrating yourself? We need the revenue too."

"For shame, Marie." He picked up the call. "Good morning, Doris, sorry to keep you waiting."

"Pat, how is everything? How's the family?"

"Everything's fantastic, Doris—thanks for asking. I trust all is well?

"Just peachy."

"Great to hear it. What can I do for you?"

"I think I need to own more stocks. I'm missing out on this big move."

Tapping again at his keyboard, he opened her account and said, "Doris, you have about 40 percent of the portfolio in stocks—blue chips that pay healthy dividends. You have a big slug of AAA laddered municipals that pay tax-free income, average yield of 6 percent, and you have almost no duration risk. You own commercial real estate on the island that pays juicy income and is priceless. And you have no debt."

"Irv told me never, ever borrow money."

"And he was one brilliant man, Doris. We all miss him terribly."

"Thank you, Pat." Her cracking voice softened. "You've really filled a void since Irv's passing—you've taken good care of me. It's been a blessing."

"Thank you, Doris. As I've often told you, it is I who am blessed. Now, to business. You have more money than you can spend in five lifetimes. Do you really need to own more stocks?"

"The ladies at lunch are telling me I'm a dolt for not owning Tiffany or Sotheby's or Michael Kors. My friend, Charlotte, made a killing in Google. She said her broker got it for her at $200 a few years ago. She just bought a new Jaguar with the profits."

"You can certainly afford to buy shares in any company you'd like. In fact, Doris, I encourage it. If you want to buy Tiffany or Kors or Google, go for it. As my Italian friend from the Bronx used to say, 'Knock yourself out.'"

"Now you tell me."

"Now I tell you? Doris, for goodness' sake. Do you remember the last serious downturn just about five years ago? You were panicked, in tears, and wanted to liquidate your entire portfolio. I told you to keep 50 percent in stocks, go play golf, and please relax. Do you remember I convinced you to hang in there?"

"Of course, I remember, Pat. Do you think I have Alzheimer's?"

"God forbid, no; you're as sharp as a tack, darling. Then you also remember as stock values recovered, we reduced your position a few percent a year to our 40 percent objective, so you'd never feel panic-stricken again."

"And I haven't missed a night's sleep since."

"That's because the market's gone up four years in a row now," he reminded.

"It has been fun."

"Remember the pick and shovel story I told you?"

"Is that the store in the mall?"

"Close. You're thinking of Crate & Barrel, I imagine."

"Oh, that's right."

"The story was about investing in more certain outcomes, rather than riskier companies in brutal competition for your attention, say in clothing, jewelry, or housewares. We bought shares in the company they all pay rent to, Simon Properties."

"What do they do again?"

"You like shopping at Town Center in Boca, right?"

"Love it. We're heading down there this afternoon."

"Good; you can tell Charlotte that you own a piece of it, and you've made enough for five Jaguars."

"I own Town Center?"

"Let's say you own a small fraction of it. Simon owns Grade-A shopping malls all over the world, including Town Center, and as a shareholder, you're collecting rent from every one of them."

"Oh goodie, I'll tell the girls. Any other grand ideas? What should I buy today?"

"I'll look everything over and call you in a few days," he said with a silent smirk, still thinking of Marie, the Catholic Church, and his adversaries. No rush for this ancient tortoise. "How does that sound?"

"Perfect, Pat. Toodles."

"Bye, dear." He just wasn't in the mood for penetration today. He needed a few dozen more clients just like Doris Grossman, he was thinking. Such a pleasure to work with the likes of her.

His radar was starting to register a warning, though. When elderly clients start blaming him for missing huge moves in trendy stocks or when friends at the club are bragging about all the money they're making, his market light changes from green to yellow. It was probably time to raise some cash for the next inevitable downturn. Never easy to do in a rising market. He jotted some notes to that effect. He'd also look at his own portfolio or what was left of it anyway. Becky's attorney, the king of penetration, had made off with quite a heist. But forget all that. Speaking with Doris had brightened his mood, and he wasn't going to let it dull.

The market was humming, and the hectic phone summoned him once again. This was the chaotic, surprise-per-minute life of a stockbroker, a money man, a financial advisor—the life Patrick had fallen in love with all those years ago. "It's Dale," Marie called out.

"Oh good, he must have gotten the research I sent on the pipelines; put him through." Dale was another one of the good guys who made the business a pleasure.

"Good morning, Dale."

"Pat, you're in early."

"Real funny." His watch was signaling the approaching noon hour. "I'm about to close up shop for the day to tell you the truth. How are you hitting 'em? Still beating your age?"

"Well, sure. Unfortunately, that's getting easier the older I get."

"You want to talk about the pipelines? Stable income, low risk, right up your alley."

"No, Pat; there's something else, and it isn't easy to say."

"What's that, Dale?" A sick feeling rose sharply in his stomach.

"I've decided to make a change."

"What do you mean, a change?"

"I've decided to move my account . . . to a team."

"For Christ's sake, Dale, we've been together more than twenty years; we're friends—and your account is in great shape."

"It sure is, and I have you to thank for that."

"This is an odd way to show it; what do you mean, a team?"

"I went to a fancy dinner at Morton's—met these impressive young people. They have a new way of looking at things, they said, a whole network of new services and support."

"May I ask what firm?"

"Oh, they're right in your office. You don't have to worry about me leaving your company."

"Who are they, Dale?"

"They call themselves the KW Group—a guy named Ian King and a gal named Mia. Let me see, I have her card here some-where . . . Here it is, that's right—Mia Wolfe. My God, she is quite a sight. Have you seen her?"

"Oh yeah, I've seen her. Can we meet for lunch and talk about this?"

"I've got a round today. Besides, I already gave them the go-ahead to take over the account."

"Dale. I've gotta talk to you about this."

"This has nothing to do with our friendship, Pat. I'll see you at the club and we'll have a few drinks soon. Take care."

About to collapse from acute disgust, Patrick threw off his headset and stormed from his office. When he got to Saunders's door, he blasted through without a knock. "Excuse me, Connelly, can't you see I'm busy right now?"

"Did you know about this, Jeff?"

"You'll have to give me a little more. I'm not a savant after all."

"Did you know King and Wolfe solicited my client Dale Wampler at one of their dog and pony shows? Did you know they're stealing my account?"

"Oh yeah, since you mention it—I was at that seminar and met Mr. Wampler. Fine chap, and very excited to hear about all the services we offer."

"You're on board with them soliciting within the office?" He was seething. "It's outrageous, against every protocol in the business since the beginning."

"This business has no past, Connelly; it's about today and tomorrow. Besides, it was his decision. See here? I have a signed letter asking me to make the switch."

"That's just a form letter. It's irrelevant."

"Have I mentioned King's velocity? I'm looking for home runs, not bunt singles."

"Dale is nearly eighty, for Christ's sake. He doesn't need home runs." He was fiery red and shouting now. "This is bullshit, Jeff; you're not getting away with it."

"Tsk, tsk, watch your potty mouth, Connelly, and put your accusations in a note to me. I'll be happy to pass it on to my superior."

Patrick was ready to explode, ready to expunge all the swirl of shit that had been building the past few years. But at this moment, in the presence of this tyrant who would exult in firing him, he kept his head and bit hard on his tongue. Gripping his wheels hard, he did a 180 and charged back through the door.

The first shots had clearly been launched, the smell of gunpowder sullied the air, and the full-on bombardment was nigh.

13

BUSHMILLS HOWL

Furiously gathering up his scattered desktop, he tossed the jumbled mess into his Tumi and spun rapidly out the door. Too embarrassed to tell Marie about Dale, he paused and gave her a tight hug, saying, "Thanks for being my steady rock and my good friend."

"What's wrong, Pat?"

"I gotta get the hell out of this shithole; I just need some time to think."

"What happened?"

"Just another day in paradise, Marie," he said while rocketing away. "But we'll be alright; we'll get through this one way or the other."

His words of assurance didn't alter much her worried look.

He settled into a booth in the shadowy backroom of Murphy's, the booth he inhabited when he didn't feel especially social or had serious thinking to do. At this very table, he came to terms with his divorce and its implicit failure. And here he was again. His breathing was shallow, and the dizziness he'd felt since Dale's call hadn't quieted. He was in trouble and had no illusions about it.

When a bear market hits in stocks, bonds, and real estate, the value of everything goes down except one entry on your balance sheet—the debt. You must pay back all the money you owe. Outstanding principal with stated interest. On time. No discount. The same was true here. While his business income was on the decline, his fixed expenses—education, property taxes, mortgage, utilities, maintenance, business costs, and especially the alimony check—all stayed the same, or worse. As the gap between his income and expenses narrowed, his worry expanded.

Staring down at his legal pad, he was feeling confused, barely knowing where to start. He wrote "Net Worth" on top and started listing everything he owned. Then he listed the associated debt. "Income Statement" was next. His shrinking business income and shrunken dividends. Then came his fixed expenses. He jotted down the bare minimum he had promised to pay Marie regardless of his income. His throat clutched. He'd done this exercise so often for clients from a position of authority: the master, the expert, the lecturer. But today, the rooting around in his own closet made him feel weak and ashamed.

"May I offer you something to drink, sir?" asked the small, unfamiliar server obscured in the dimness.

"Sure, thank you. I'll have a cranberry and club soda." He needed to keep a clear mind. "And a Bushmills Black on the rocks." *Just this one,* he thought.

He visited Bushmills on a family trip not long ago. Ireland's northern Antrim Coast was the most beautiful place he'd ever been. A palpable sense of peace embraced him at the memory. How simple a life it could be: a thatched roof cottage on a green grassy knoll overlooking the vastness of the foggy northern sea with only Scotland's rocky coast beyond. Watching the languorous sheep graze the mist gray days away. Maybe he'd own a little pub where he'd feature live traditional music. There he'd meet a sweet, unspoiled Irish lass, maybe a server in his pub; a hard worker with a sunny attitude whose only expectation was having a good man to share a life with.

Speaking of servers, his gently placed the drinks on the table and scurried away, leaving behind a menu. "Thank you," he uttered into her wake. As the first refrains of "Whiskey in a Jar" came wafting through the backroom, he sipped his Bushmills from a jar with a wry smile.

There's a synergy to the whole damn jumble, isn't there? he thought. [12]

How had things gotten so complicated, so fucked up? All the goal-setting, the affirmations, the visualizations, the workshops, Lifespring, Tony Robbins, Dale Carnegie, Wayne Dyer, the plans he'd written and updated annually for thirty years since college. He'd tried so hard—so fucking hard—but it didn't matter. None of it mattered. It was all falling apart anyway. Other than the kids, who he wouldn't trade for all the treasure in the world, what had he really accomplished? What did he have to show for all his labor?

He felt like a helpless child again, dependent on a volatile, unhappy home for his survival. He couldn't wait to escape it then, and now he was that same broken nineteen-year-old returning home once again in abject despair. Tears wet his cheeks until the flow flavored his whiskey.

"I can't do this, Dad," he moaned. "I can't do it."

"It'll be okay, Paddy, I promise; you can do anything you put your mind to."

"No, Dad, I can't. I really can't do anything. This is too fucked up. I'd rather be dead."

"Don't say that, please, Paddy. Thank God you're here."

"No, Mom, no," he sobbed. "I wish I were dead. I want to die." His mother was crying now. His father was half alive—still in shock, angry, dying to wake up from the sick nightmare they couldn't shake.

In the early morning, Patrick would lie in bed for a few moments until the haze cleared. Then he'd move to hop out of bed, stand up, and stretch, like he always had. That was when reality would smack him in the face, like a baseball bat landing at full force. Laying frozen on his back, a silicone tube snaking from his penis, he thought of his horror. *It's real. I'm really a cripple. My life is a nightmare.*

"Paddy, please listen to me," his father said. "Your life isn't ruined. It's changed, but it's not ruined."

"It's ruined," he whined. "Over."

"No, it's not; you have a new challenge, that's all. It's a tough break, but you'll beat this thing, just like you've beaten everything else. And you'll have a great life."

"No, Dad, no. It's not fair."

"You're right—it's not fair," he said intensely. "Life isn't fair, but you're a winner. Whatever shit comes your way, our way, we'll deal with it and fight back. You're not alone, Paddy. I won't give up, and I know you'll never give up. That's not who you are."

"I always believed that, I really did, but not this time, this is different. This is too fucking much." A stream of salty tears ran into the corners of his mouth. "I don't know how I'm gonna make it—I really don't."

"We'll all make it together," his mother whimpered while trying to take his hand. "You'll always be loved and protected."

"I don't want to be protected like I'm some baby," he groused while wrenching his hand away. "I want to skate; I want to get the hell out of bed; I want to feel my feet. I can't feel my fucking feet."

"Paddy, however bad it is right now, the pain you're feeling," his father said through his own crippling agony, "it's the worst it will ever be. From here on, it will only get better and better." The last two words he said before trudging up the stairs, head hung low, were "I promise."

It *had* gotten "better and better" in countless ways, just as his father promised. As his days of walking and ice hockey heroics faded, the pain lessened. Using his neck, shoulders, back, arms, and hands to transport his lower body on a four-wheeler eventually became the new normal. He'd adjusted to the loss of half his vision the same way. Squint one ruined eye to the glare, ignore the mocking, eventually, and see the left side of the world. Easy. But he was younger then, much younger, and surrounded by a horde of supporters to help push him forward. Today, he never felt so old and powerless and alone.

So fucking alone, he thought while glancing around the dank, barren, mid-afternoon pub room.

It wasn't true, of course. He had friends, a rich vein of them, really. But they weren't here in Murphy's, West Palm Beach, or Florida, for that matter. They were scattered around, mostly in the area surrounding New York; or dead.

His parents had recently passed; his mother succumbed to cancer far too early, and his father to despair soon after, maybe a year too late. He'd have been better off not suffering his lifelong partner's affliction. His siblings were up north, living largely colorless lives. They'd grown apart over the years, nothing much remaining in common, nothing good anyway. Volatile homes triggered by deranged older brothers and hyper-angry fathers can do that. If a parent's funeral and then another one didn't bring a clan together, there would be no coming together. They chose their middle son, Patrick, as the sole executor of the estate, the only one they trusted to do the job competently and with honor. It was like agreeing to several years of torture, which hadn't yet ended. After not a lot of thought, the best he could think to say to his siblings was, "Good riddance."

He perused the short list of his closest friends: Bobby, Sean, Larry, Cathy, Tommy, Robbie, Kenny, John, Rich, Doug, a handful of distant cousins and a few others. They were off living their own lives somewhere in the world, with families and jobs on Wall Street and other responsibilities. Florida just wasn't their thing, except for short visits in the dead of winter. Was it Patrick, or was it the 80-degree sunshine and the beaches and links? "Is it live, or is it Memorex?" The answer didn't really matter, so he never asked.

And then there was Albert, his Italian "goombah" from the Bronx. He was even further away. How do you just stop breathing one day at thirty-five? The answer, of course, was Marlboro. He was instrumental, heroic really, in Paddy's emotional recovery from his injury. They'd lost contact for about seven years, the hockey years, but when he needed his "Cuz" the most, he was there. He just showed up one day in the rehab center, saying he'd heard the news and would Paddy mind if he stayed awhile. He stayed more than a while. Loyal and strong, Albert remained with his frightened friend for the entirety of his post-trauma years until he'd adjusted well enough and until it was time for him to leave. In his last year, coughing uncontrollably, he'd quote Mickey Mantle in saying, "Cuz, if I knew I was gonna live this long, I'd have taken better care of myself." They'd both laugh out loud as Albert tapped out another smoke. Had it not been for his devoted friend from the Bronx, this story may never have been written.

Other than Marie, he had no close friends remaining in the business. They still referred to each other as friends but once they'd moved on to other firms, which they all eventually did, promises to stay in touch evaporated. He was no better. Life gets busy, complicated, much too serious. There's meaningful money to be made in wealth management, especially in moving one's practice to another firm. What are a few broken promises when you're in the money business?

Contemplating all that was on his plate, sipping from his jar of Black, he plucked a folded newspaper off a nearby table to distract from his roiling thoughts. Patrick was still an old-fashioned newspaper guy, a love he'd inherited from his father. As a regular reader of the Big Apple's big three, the *Times*, *Post*, and *News*, he was the most informed and conversant 'C' student you'd ever meet. He considered reading the paper properly an art form and an exercise in degrees of pleasure and pain. Being tragically human, he preferred pleasure and avoided pain as best he could. This wasn't news to anyone who knew him—especially Marie.

On the pain end of the pendulum was the front page, the geopolitical news of the day, usually like eating a can of mushy brown peas. Business news was next, more neutral on the scale, but often anxiety rendering, especially during bear markets. Being wrong, losing money, and questioning your value can do that to a person with a mind and a heart. His pleasure cruise always began with the sports section—except when his teams were consistent losers. His Canes, Dolphins, and Jets had made it a choppy sail of late. He referred to it as the "Curse of Tom Brady." The Yankees usually provided him some comfort. He was grateful Brady didn't play baseball.

Like capping dinner with a sweet bread pudding and Irish coffee, he'd then check the arts and leisure section for new restaurant openings, album releases, local concerts, and such. His pleasure now peaking, like pouring an after-dinner port and putting a favorite artist on Sonos, the comics were next. His longtime favorite was *Peanuts,* and just like Charlie Brown he wanted life to be fair, to work out well for everyone. He wanted justice. He also wanted the little red-haired girl to pay attention to him. He wanted to be loved. Who didn't?

A secret pleasure, like sneaking in one final pour before bedtime, were the horoscopes. He discussed his interest with no one, especially his clients. Knowing your stockbroker believed in universally derived messages delivered in the local newspaper was probably not good for business. Such a pastime seemed silly, he knew, but he needed to fill his forever curious mind with something, so why not something fun and cryptic and hopeful?

We make a lot of it up anyway, he thought, *so why not make up empowering stuff, or at least stuff that didn't crush the spirit?*

Sometimes he'd open a book to a random page and take the reading as a sign or a message. It amazed him how often they would have relevance. And if they didn't, so what? Toss them aside and move on. Same with the horoscopes. Many were generic nonsense, and he would indeed toss them aside dismissively. *"Be ready to meet the love of your life today." Christ,* he would think, *I'm ready for that every day.* But on rarer days, the messages applied so precisely that he couldn't ignore them. Like the one he'd clipped out and put on his desk: *"Today is your lucky day; a new source of income flows into your life. Be ready to answer the call and receive the good news."* That same morning a wealthy retiree called and said so-and-so at the club mentioned him, and he wanted to open an account. Just like that. There were enough such happenings to sit up and take notice. And he did.

Patrick was born in the shadow of Yankee Stadium on the Fourth of July, an Independence Day baby. That made him a Cancer, and he had all the resonant traits:

> *A homebody quick to retreat into your shell; you are moody and the first to laugh or cry; inherently kind and gentle of heart, you are nurturing and protective of family and friends; you can be tenacious and strong-willed, and you love to get your way; artistic, creative, highly-evolved, intuitive and spiritual, you pick up on others' energy and can almost read minds; music and writing are your perfect vehicles; you have a good memory and are a skilled storyteller; you don't ask for much: a comfortable home, someone to love and nurture, and a sense of peace is all; Cancer is ruled by the moon.*

Combined with his overt Celtic spirit, Patrick was a Cancerian on steroids. He was proud of his comfortable little life, and whenever he felt under assault, his world at risk, his ferocious Irish temper and need for independence would emerge. Today he felt the risk to his world as never before. "I'll have another whiskey, please, and a pint of Smithwick's," he said without raising his head from the paper.

"Absolutely, sir, right away," came her soft reply before making off.

Today's horoscope made no sense at all: *You've been on a roll this past week. Good fortune will continue to flow your way. Stay positive and excited about the future. The vastness of the ocean and the sky are yours for the asking.*

You've got to be kidding me, he thought. *This last week has been a friggin' disaster, never mind "good fortune flowing my way." This one's a throwaway.* The stars had been misaligned of late across the entirety of Patrick Connelly's universe.

Murphy's was filling up with a lively after-work crowd and both his vessels were nearly empty once again. With the afternoon largely frittered away, he signaled across the room for the check.

Spinning quickly through the paper's business section, he noticed the headline: "Disney Buys Cracker Barrel." *I must have been so distracted today,* he thought. *I completely missed the news.*

For years he'd tell anyone who'd listen that Disney should buy them. "A fairytale match," he would say. After all, Cracker Barrel was a successful, family-style restaurant and gift shop operation reminiscent of Disney's Fort Wilderness campgrounds and Hoop-De-Doo Revue. Its log cabin and country store theme appealed squarely to middle-class America, directly in the House of Mouse's wheelhouse. Their locations along major highways throughout the eastern half of the country, rocking chairs on front porches and all, made them highly visible and shouted everything Disney as much as any country song might. And Disney did family restaurants and gift shops better than anyone. Every time he passed by a Cracker Barrel store, it was jam-packed from the parking lot to the scores of people milling around and rocking on the front porch. The gift shops generated nearly 20 percent of their revenue, and now they would become purveyors of Disney kitsch.

"Well, look at that," he said, riffing aloud to himself. "They paid a 75 percent premium. Zip-A-Dee-Doo-Dah—my, oh my, what a wonderful windfall for the stockholders." He lamented not owning any shares. Restaurant stock values were generally erratic, rising and falling sharply with the economic cycles—not built for his typical client. Besides, most of his retirees weren't road warriors who hit all the country stores and motels on the way to the Tennessee mountains. Oh well, another brilliant unrequited idea comes off the board. Just the way his luck was going these days.

Tucking the paper into his overstuffed bag, he settled the check, finished the requisite departing pint of water, and bid Murphy's "*oiche mhaith*."

Motoring east on Clematis to the parking garage, he noticed the early evening moon peeking through the park's winter-bare oak tree branches. It was perfectly round and full. *That's odd*, he thought, *the paper said it would be a half-moon tonight*. Looking up, he let out an understated Bushmills howl, nonetheless.

14

EARLY MORNING MADNESS

When Patrick finished looking over the messages piled up neatly to the right side of his desk, he emptied his Tumi in the open space and started leafing through and prioritizing the new pile. This was his happiest and most productive time of the workday. He'd race to the office with the nascent sun ahead of the world and consciously sip the silence along with his first cup of Starbucks. Before the screaming phones, the constant interruptions, and the office chatter took hold, he was afforded the chance to think, to organize and plan his day.

Especially these days, he needed the sharp focus of the early morning to build his defenses against the mounting assault on his livelihood. He understood, clearly, he was not only in the fight of his life but the fight *for* his life. Everything he'd been until now, and hoped still to be, was on the line.

When prioritizing his return calls, he placed the most painful on top. He'd get them out of the way while he still had the spirit. These were the clients who always had a beef, a complaint, a criticism—the "Bobs" of his world. Luckily, or maybe by design, there were just a handful. He'd learned long ago to get the grimy work done early so he could breathe and cleanse the rest of the day. And when he forgot, when the perceived pain would cause him to deep-six a message, Marie was there to not so gently nudge him. "Oh, for God sakes, Pat, he's called twice; just get it over with, will ya?"

"Okay, Marie, okay. For criminy sakes, who are you, the warden?" He'd huff and puff but knew she was right.

Before he got it over with, though, he planned to call Larry Devlin, a former colleague and close friend at the firm until about a decade ago. He'd left for what he called "greener pastures," and they eventually lost touch—par for the course in the work-a-day money world. Seeking "greener pastures" himself was now a serious option, one he'd never really considered until the recent untenable circumstances. He had no choice.

"Oh yeah?" He was sneering at his absent foes. "No choice? Fuck you and your no choice." Old dogs like him were still in demand at rival firms, and he'd be handed a handsome check to come on board. But nothing in life, and particularly in this business, came without a price. The check would be exchanged for his signature on a contract, a seven- to nine-year commitment. The value of the deal would be enhanced or diminished based on his future performance. Meaning, they'd expect him to bring his best clients along and then generate noteworthy revenue from their accounts. He'd be working day and night, like a highly caffeinated rookie again—just what he was trying to avoid.

He'd seen such departures a million times. On the tumultuous day, nearly always a Friday afternoon to give the departing advisors an edge, the combat would begin. His book of clients was technically owned by the firm, as Saunders so caustically reminded him. A restraining order would be served, stopping him cold until the two firms worked out a settlement. On the down-low, he'd have already contacted his best clients, getting their buy in. Always subject to change, though, when the day arrived. One of the vagaries of human nature—people abhor change. They usually only do it when they have no other choice. "No choice." There it is again.

Meanwhile, soon after he handed in his resignation, his accounts would be doled out to the remaining producers in the office, including Saunders and King. It was rare that an advisor, or a team of advisors, would pull off the exodus without the firm being clued in. Saunders would be prepared. He'd call the largest clients requesting they come in for a meeting, showing them his love. Even the big boss, the regional director, would endure the two-hour limo ride up from Miami because losing firm assets to a competitor was a big no-no, on the list of "critical fews" never to let happen on his watch.

There are industry regulations as to what can and cannot be said to the clients—every one of them would be broken in those next few contentious weeks. The clients were considered orphaned, and Patrick the greedy, non-caring louse who'd abandoned them.

Advantage would go to the house because a pile of paperwork needed to be signed, and all other manner of inconveniences in moving the accounts were immense. He'd be burning the midnight oil and selling himself like a hooker in a late-night Okeechobee Boulevard strip club. Not that he'd ever been in one—or two. He would need to do everything but twerk on them. He'd even twerk, in a manner of speaking, if the accounts were important enough.

He recalled something a veteran told him in the early days of his career: "If you're willing to work like few others work for the next five years, you'll be able to live like few others live for the rest of your life."

That turned out to be a degree of the truth. But it left out the bear market setbacks, the unforeseen twists and turns, the divorce attorney, and the various adversaries who'd be coming after his business. Thirty years ago was then, and this was now. The mere thought of it all was exhausting.

Continuing to sift through Marie's pile, he noticed the Netflix research. The stock closed yesterday at $421 per share. *Just marvelous; that can certainly wait,* he thought, while placing it at the bottom. The sun peeked through the eastern window setting alight the pile emptied from his Tumi. The folded newspaper he'd absconded from Murphy's was on top. "Oh yeah," he muttered, "may as well check the action in Cracker Barrel shares." Tapping CBRL into his quote box, the stock sat quietly at $75.50, same as yesterday's close. Still two hours ahead of the opening, he expected to see high volume and the pre-market price in the vicinity of the $130 offer Disney had made.

A perusal of the company news revealed nothing about the takeover offer. The last story was about their eggs, bacon, cheese, and grits breakfast winning an award. *Couldn't be a low cholesterol award, that's for sure,* he thought snidely. Confused, he picked up the newspaper and looked again at the business section. There it was—Disney's $130 a share offer. He took in a few deep breaths and shook his head to disperse any remaining cobwebs. Scouring the morning's Journal headlines, flipping steadily from page to page, he saw that Disney was issuing $10 billion in ten-year notes but nothing about Cracker Barrel. Staring out the window befuddled, he noticed Marie setting up her desk and called out, "Hey, Marie, good morning."

"You're in early, Pat. Good to see you." Sitting down in the client chair across his desk, searching his face, she said, "I heard about Dale leaving. Bummer. You feeling okay?"

"Sure, sure, but Dale, of all people? It's hard to fathom and strictly against firm policy."

"They couldn't care less, I'm sure," she said. "They were down here sniffing around yesterday, looking at our office space. King actually had a tape measure."

"They both have a pair, don't they?"

"I don't really blame Mia," Marie said. "She seems more like his indentured servant."

"Hey, everyone makes their own bed. She has free will, doesn't she?"

"I guess. But we all have to pay the bills, so how free are we really?"

"Good point, Marie. By the way, what do you think about the Disney-Cracker Barrel news? Incredible, huh? How many times have I said Disney should buy them?"

"Like at every cocktail party for the past ten years."

"Thank you."

"So, it finally happened? I didn't hear a word about it. Guess I missed it."

"Look here," he said, handing her yesterday's paper. "Top billing—big premium too. Wish we owned some shares."

Looking at the paper, her face scrunched. "Funny, Pat," she said, tossing the paper back on the desk.

"What do you mean, 'funny'?"

"There's nothing there about Cracker Barrel or Disney."

"Come on, what are you talking about?" He opened the paper to where they could both see it. "Look, right . . ." He stopped in mid-sentence, blinking his eyes a few times. The Disney headline was gone, replaced by something about Europe sliding into recession. He madly flipped through the other pages. "What in God's name?"

"If this is some kind of game, please stop. I'm getting even more worried about you." A ringing phone startled them, and she hustled off to her desk.

"Sorry, Marie," he said, following her out the door. "You got it; it's just a dumb game I was playing, really dumb."

"Thank the Lord," she said, picking up the phone.

"Don't worry, I'm fine." He was frightened and needed a moment. "Just in a weird mood, I guess. I think I'll get some coffee."

Grabbing his favorite mug from the kitchen sink, he began scrubbing away the accumulated mold with the disgusting brown (formerly yellow) sponge before his turning stomach decided to abandon the rancid coffee excursion. Winding his way back the uncrowded way, meaning avoiding King and Wolfe's neighborhood, he closed his office door and pulled up to his desk. Taking a breath to quell his growing sense of dizziness, he glanced down at the still open newspaper. The headline screamed back at him: "Disney Buys Cracker Barrel."

Flush now, nearly faint, over-the-hill actress Norma Desmond's face flashed in his mind as Glenn Close belted out the Broadway showstopper "As If We Never Said Goodbye" from *Sunset Boulevard*. [14] Was this "early morning madness," or "magic in the making," or more likely some nasty trick being played on him?

He scanned the article. "After weeks of negotiation, Disney offered $130 a share," said the report. Pecking feebly on his keyboard, Cracker Barrel still came up at $75.50 with no unusual volume or breaking news. He typed in "Europe," and an article from yesterday reported the continent sliding into recession. Reaching for his bag, he fumbled with the cap on his anxiety medication before popping one and washing it down with the tepid remains of his Starbucks. His eyes darted out the window and fixed on the waterway beyond. Its undulating movement increased the wooziness, so he returned swiftly to the steadiness of his desktop. He looked down at the paper again, eyes settling on the date at the top of the page for the first time.

It said February 10th. The lower right corner of his screen displayed today's date: January 28th.

15

COMFORTABLY NUMB

When the bell rang, signaling the markets' close, Patrick quickly shut down his system and locked it for the first time he could remember. Gathering up his papers, he hustled past Marie, saying, "Gotta go, honey. I've got dinner reservations at Cracker Barrel."

"Ha, ha. Have the pancakes—they're to die for."

"Pancakes for dinner?"

"Until you've had pancakes for dinner," she answered, "you haven't lived."

"I'll do it. See you tomorrow."

He didn't stop racing until he rolled through Murphy's threshold. "Good day, lovely Molly," he said breathlessly.

"And to you, Patrick—where's the fire?" He sped past her pausing only for a drive-by hug. The booth he'd inhabited the day before was vacant along with the entire back room. He scoured high and low—booths, tables, chairs—all empty. No newspapers, no Samantha Stevens, no leprechauns, no nothing. He pulled up to a table and emptied his bag. "You're sitting all the way back here?" Molly asked. "In a private mood, are you, Mr. Connelly?"

"I can't stay long," he responded, still catching his breath. "I just want to read and think for a time. Say, Molly, would you do me a favor?"

"If you want to steal me away from this life, you'll have to give me five minutes to get ready."

"Wow, you're a tough sell. I wish it were that simple, but it's near the top of my to-do list."

"*Near* the top? My, you sure know how to flatter."

"*On* the top, Molly, I meant *on* the top," he said with a laugh. "And I promise, you'll live to regret being there." Meeting her eyes, he softly asked, "Will you help me now?"

"Tell me."

"Would you read this headline and tell me what it says?"

"Are you testing my eyesight or my reading skills?"

"Neither—I think I'm testing mine." He unfolded the paper and handed it to her. "Top right, what does it say?"

"It says 'Europe Sliding into Recession.' How did I do?"

"Perfect, that's exactly what I see. Now, at the top, what is the date of the paper?"

"That's not fair," she said with a smirk. "The questions are getting too hard."

139

"Just tell me the date, wise lassie."

"January 27th."

"Perfect again; I guess I'm not going blind or crazy after all," he said while giving her hand a gentle squeeze. "Thanks, sweetheart." He'd seen exactly what she'd read when he opened the paper in her presence. Folding it over, he said, "Next time through, would you bring me a pint and some soda bread, please?"

"I thought you'd never ask."

"In fact," he said with a smile, "in honor of the great Thornton Melon of *Back to School* fame: bring me a pint every seven minutes until I pass out, then bring one every ten minutes." She looked at him quizzically. "Not a Rodney Dangerfield fan, I'm guessing?"

"Rodney who?"

"True to your more intelligent gender, Molly. But you get the idea, right?"

"Absolutely, Patrick; if I see you passed out, I'll keep them coming anyway, but at a slower pace."

"Perfect. Thank you, dear."

After she left, he unfolded the paper and blinked to clear his sharp eye. Looking at the very same headline, it read, "Disney Buys Cracker Barrel," and the date at the top of the page read, "February 10th."

He sat in desperate silence contemplating his next move. For the first time since his injury all those years ago, he was afraid for himself. Even the divorce hadn't matched this. That was some mixture of anguish and perceived liberation where the costs could be weighed against the benefits. Here, there were no benefits to weigh. As his sweat-beaded gloominess swelled, he thought of calling Kay, or his internist, or just driving himself to the emergency room. But how could he explain this to anyone? They'd lock him up in a funny farm, or a not-so-funny farm; either way he'd surely lose his business. Of all the things he'd been worried about lately, the health of his mind, his very sanity, wasn't one of them. Were his days of lucidity over? Whatever the hell today was. Had he really traveled away with the faeries?

Nibbling on bread crumbles, drawing from his pint glass, brooding in the quiet, the first notes of Pink Floyd's classic "Comfortably Numb" floated from the speakers. "Perfect," he said aloud to a higher power. After taking a satiating swig, he sat reverently in concert. [14]

Slowly returning his focus to his surroundings, the rich wood in shades of red and black, the cracked green leather, the tarnished brass accents, he wondered if anyone was at home. Feeling comfortably numb, concerned that the dream was truly gone, he thought, *No one sings that chorus like Van the Man.*

Hanging on the walls throughout the room—amongst Guinness, Harp, and Smithwick's mirrors, Irish nationalist flags, and other references to the old country—were several blackboards scrawled with quotes. *It must be Samuel Beckett month*, he was thinking, as he moved about the room. Pausing in front of each board, reading them the way he might a horoscope or a random page in a book, he looked for the famed Irish playwright's resonant message.

The first board read: *You're on earth. There's no cure for that.*

Funny, he thought; dark, but funny. The next read: *We are all born mad. Some remain so.* He wore a knowing smile as he moved to another, which read: *Nothing is funnier than unhappiness. It's the most comical thing in the world.* His unhappy smile broadened. The large board on the back wall said: *Where I am, I don't know, I'll never know, you must go on, I can't go on, I'll go on.* Beckett was talking about human resiliency amidst all the absurdity, he was certain. The last board's message, authored by genius comedian Robin Williams, hit him like a whack on the head with a pewter mug. It read: *You're only given one little spark of madness. You mustn't lose it.*

Throwing cash on the table and packing up his Tumi, taking special care to tuck away his madness, he pulled out his phone and dialed up Marie. "Hey, honey. Do me a favor, will you?"

"Depends."

"Why do you care what I'm wearing?"

"What?"

"Nothing."

"That's what I thought," she said with an agitated tenor. "Where are you? Are you okay?"

"Sure, I'm perfectly fine—a little numb, but comfortable. I'm just heading home."

"Whaddya need?"

"Tomorrow morning, would you please submit a request for a hundred thousand shares of Cracker Barrel? The symbol's CBRL. I'll email you the bullet points later tonight."

"Sure, Pat. Wow, a hundred thousand shares? The pancakes were that good?"

"Nah," he said with a laugh. "I couldn't get near the place; the line wrapped around the building. That's why I want to build a position; it may be time to follow my intuition on this one. See you tomorrow."

He zipped his phone back into his Tumi's outer pocket and sat still for another long moment. It occurred to him that here, in the backroom of his beloved Murphy's, all by himself, he had officially gone mad.

16

PANCAKES FOR LUNCH

Finishing up his last morning appointment, Patrick slowly led his client toward the elevator. "Take care, Mrs. Mulligan," Marie called out. "It was so good to see you."

"You too, Marie; thanks for everything you do. You're a saint."

"See that, Pat? 'A saint,' she says. I told you."

"Be careful, Dolores," he said with a laugh. "Saints are in high demand these days. Marie might ask for a raise, and then I'll have to raise your commissions."

"She's worth a king's ransom."

"Believe me, I know. Watch that corner, Dolores—right there." He was pointing down. "The carpet's loose; your walker could get caught."

"Thank you, Mr. Connelly; I'm getting there, slowly but surely."

"Take your time; remember, the tortoise always wins the race. Will you be okay from here?"

"Absolutely, my driver's waiting in the lobby."

"Perfect, take care, Dolores."

When the elevator door closed, he turned back toward his office and saw Ian King standing at Wolfe's cubicle watching him. "I see your clients are getting younger all the time."

"Eighty's the new sixty, Ian, haven't you heard? She'll probably outlive us both. By the way, how's life out here in the cubicles?"

"You may be finding out soon enough." King's voice was harsher than usual. "Jeff just ordered moving boxes, enough for all three of us."

"Moving? Sorry to hear you're leaving so soon," Patrick said. "Oh well, please stay in touch."

"Don't worry, we won't be going far," King shot back. "And we'll definitely stay in touch."

With an exaggerated sneer, Patrick darted back to his office and grabbed his bag, saying, "I'm off to lunch with an old chum; probably be a few hours."

"I saw Larry Devlin on the calendar," Marie said, reminiscing. "Tell him I said hey and that we still miss him. What's the occasion?"

"Just catching up. I've missed him too. Guess I'm feeling nostalgic for the good old days."

"Tell me about it," she said wearily.

Arriving in front of Cracker Barrel's old country log cabin, he pulled into the only open parking space, a blue guy spot directly in front. *What a rare break—maybe the one benefit I get,* he thought wryly, while placing his blue-guy parking hanger on the mirror.

When the kids were young, the Connellys went out to dinner four or five nights a week, on a slow week. They'd come to terms with the fact that neither Rachel Ray nor any of her sous-chefs would be gracing their SoSo kitchen anytime soon. The outings became known as the "Connelly Supper Club," a comforting ritual after a good day on the battlefield and some of his fondest memories. When he pulled into any restaurant parking lot, then and now, the accessible spaces were invariably occupied. This was South Florida, after all. He bitched constantly about the throngs of able-bodied drivers with their fraudulently acquired permits taking the very limited spaces. The universal accessible image—the stick figure guy melding into the wheelchair on tall signs and painted on the asphalt—was prominently blue. His wise-guy kids started calling him "blue guy" and the wider parking spaces "blue guy spots."

Relative to "cripple" or "crip" or "disabled," or some other politically correct bullshit label like "physically challenged" or "otherly-abled," he preferred "blue guy." The moniker stuck, and a "blue guy" he'd be forevermore.

Ahead of the lunch rush, the backwoods porch rocking chairs were already oversubscribed. Passing through the entrance, he noticed most of the inhabitants could use fewer corn muffins and a few more sessions at the gym. Luckily, there were no available mirrors for his own assessment. The busy gift shop's lavender and cinnamon-sweet fragrances fetched him back to those supper club days with a note of melancholy. His spirit lifted immediately when he saw his old friend Larry waiting at the first dining table to the right. He pulled into the open spot where a chair had been thoughtfully removed. "Great to see you, Larry," he said while shaking hands robustly. "It's been too long."

"You too, Pat, way too long." He was standing to greet his old friend. "Interesting venue to meet."

"Well, it's about midway between our offices; besides, I have a hankering for some pancakes."

"For lunch?"

"Of course—you haven't lived without having pancakes for lunch," he said with a smile. "By the way, Marie misses you terribly and sends her love."

"Please tell her I said the same and that she's still the best. I tried to get both of you to join me in the 'burbs, you must recall. But your stubborn side won the day."

"More my lazy side. That's partly why I'm here, Larry. It may be time to revisit the offer you made way back when."

The two had been regular lunch buddies a decade earlier until Larry abruptly left the firm to set up his own shop. He opened an office in the burgeoning northern suburb of Palm Beach Gardens, bought a charming golf club home in an old marshland, and called his friend regularly in the first few months to convince him to join the independents.

"I'm finally free with no boss telling me what to do and how to think," he'd said. "And going the independent route means more take-home income on less revenue because we're not giving up 65 percent to the house."

Patrick considered moving, both his business and his home, but his risk-averse nature won the day. He resisted change, reticent to invite in all the conflict it would bring. Besides, he was happy living in the manageable city of West Palm Beach, and Becky had zero interest in moving any further away from the grand old island. Across the bridge was far enough. The domestic boss had spoken—end of story.

The old friends munched on syrup-slathered blueberry pancakes with sides of crispy bacon piled high while they reminisced and chatted away. "No wine list," Patrick said. "Too bad."

"Wine? with pancakes? with lunch?" Larry asked.

"You're right; it's a tough pairing," he responded. "I'm guessing a Sauvignon Blanc would work, maybe a Riesling, or certainly a sparkling wine, like a Brut."

"You picked the venue."

"Yes, I did," he said, feigning dejection. "We probably should have met a half hour early and tailgated in the parking lot."

"You haven't changed one scintilla, Pat," Larry said.

"Hey," he cracked back, "how does one change near perfection?"

After a good-natured laugh, Larry asked, "What took you so long, my friend?" Joining his firm was still the smartest thing to do, he said, but added, "I won't be there to help you along this time." He'd recently sold his business and took a consulting role on the way to retirement. He conveyed the news with a wide grin, like one of those "pancake-eating" grins.

"Congratulations, Larry," he said with a clumsily delivered fist bump. "Well done."

Larry went on to say he and Maggie, his wife of ten years, had been traveling to Ireland the past five summers and had fallen in love with the Emerald Isle. They'd recently bought a cottage on the Dingle Peninsula and planned to spend at least half the year there. "They were virtually giving them away, Pat," he said. "I'm even taking Irish mythology classes at a university in Galway."

Flummoxed at all the news, Patrick took a digestive moment and then asked, "What do you mean, mythology?"

"You know—faeries, shamrocks, leprechauns, kings, Merrows, giants, Banshees, Dullahans, the Blarney Stone, St. Patrick, the luck of the Irish—a whole litany of fascinating literature and history."

"Do you believe any of it?"

"Sure; we gotta believe in something, why not fun stuff like that?"

"Can't argue with that, my friend."

As Patrick reached to grab the modest bill, he said, "Jesus, ten years ago you left for 'greener pastures,' and now you're doing it again—this time literally."

"It's time, Pat," he said. "I couldn't be more ready."

"You're always three steps ahead of the crowd, and now you've found your pot of gold. You're like a much smarter version of me, which is why I've always hated you." They shared another hearty laugh, just like in days of yore.

"Really, Pat, I found my pot of gold when I met Maggie."

"That's heartwarming, Larry, if not a little sappy."

While sincere, especially about the "sappy," he felt a tinge of jealousy rising at all his friend's good fortune. Earlier in his career, he remembers a charismatic Wall Street strategist telling the audience the three most important steps to wealth accumulation: "Number one," he said, "under no circumstance should you get divorced. For numbers two and three, see number one." It brought a rabid round of applause, if not adherence. Patrick had broken this tenet, shattered it really, at a point in life when it may be too late to rebuild his dwindled pot. What he needed most was a wee bit of good luck, or maybe a changed definition of the meaning of wealth. After all, he thought, there's more to life than money.

"You should come over for a visit this summer. Dingle is truly the most magical place on earth. It's like stepping back into another time."

"Thanks, Larry, that's very kind of you. I'll take it under advisement." He reached up for a farewell hug. "It was incredible to connect with you again. I should have done it a long time ago."

"Me too, Pat, and I'm glad you did. Stay in touch."

They wound their way through the busy gift shop and out into the bright sunlight. Putting on his shades, Patrick noticed the porch and parking lot were even more rocking with eager, hungry patrons. "Hey, Larry," he called out. "I almost forgot; I'm buying shares of Cracker Barrel this week. Maybe you should too."

"What are the bullet points?"

"Simple—take a look around," he replied. "Oh yeah, plus, they've got great pancakes."

17

A CRAZY GOOD WEEK

The approval to solicit Cracker Barrel came on the first of February. Saunders grilled him on the whats and whys of his interest in positioning so many shares. Patrick gave him the basics: the stock's fundamentals, the crowds at the local store, the six hundred locations in forty-two states, the recession-proof nature of the business. Grudgingly giving the approval, he said, "I hope you're not trying to hit a home run at my expense, Connelly. I don't need dozens of unhappy clients demanding their money back if you whiff."

"I can't recall ever having a customer complaint, can you, Jeff?" he snapped back. "And it won't start now; it's been a solid hospitality business for fifty years. I'm not thinking home run or whiff. I don't take that kind of risk."

"Speaking of no risk, have you and the KW Group put your heads together yet?"

"We butt heads every time we see each other, if that's what you mean?"

"Are you still struggling with this simple concept, Connelly? I'm talking about saving your career by teaming with KW."

Bored with the redundant subject matter, he murmured, "I'm still thinking."

"Time is wasting. If you don't get the ball rolling, I'll have to do it for you. Oops, should I have said 'rolling'?"

"Thanks for the CBRL go-ahead, Jeff," he said, ignoring his awkward question. "Speaking of time's a-wasting, I'd better get rolling myself."

And "roll" he did, working harder in the next week than he had since he was a rookie. He'd convinced himself that if nothing happened on the 10th, his clients would own a good company at a reasonable price. No whiff there. But if this weird, fantastical dream turned into reality, he'd indeed hit a home run. Substantial upside, limited downside; just the kind of bet Patrick liked to make. Before dialing up the first client, he opened the paper again and again. The date on top was five trading days away, and Disney's offer was $130 a share. "I'm going to call this list, our top fifty clients," he told Marie. "I'd like you to call the rest."

"Every one of them?" Her voice was dubious. "That's over a hundred calls."

"Welcome back to the world of stock-brokering," he said, handing her the list of the company's virtues. "Here's the pitch. Keep it simple; just read off the attributes and say I recommend they own some shares."

"I hope you know what you're doing."

"So do I, Marie. So do I."

The next week flew by, and the hundred thousand shares flew off the shelf. With the passion they exhibited, it could have been twice as many. The other advisors took turns gliding past Marie's desk, glancing suspiciously into the coveted corner lair. They knew the effort underway was positioning Cracker Barrel's stock. In Saunders's little world, the walls spoke volumes. It may also be they'd never seen anyone work with such passion on an investment idea. Especially a stock idea. Most of them had never met one face-to-face. On Friday, just ahead of the closing bell, he handed the last order to Marie, saying, "It's all over but the shouting."

"Isn't that 'it's all over but the crying'?"

"God help us if it is," he said with a roll of his eyes. "Hey, Marie, nice job this week; yeoman's work, really." He extended his closed fist for a bump. He'd been practicing, so it connected this time. "Can I buy you a chardonnay at Murphy's?"

"That would be great, Pat. I'll meet you over there; I just need to finish up a few things here, like deciding where I'm moving if this doesn't work out."

"That's just what I'm doing. We can brainstorm over a few drinks."

"Maybe Vegas would be a good getaway," she said with a tired smile.

"Even hotter in the summer and dry as a bone—meaning rain, not booze," he replied. "I'm thinking Key West. I'd grow a white beard and take up the demon rum, maybe try to write a novel."

"You've thought about this pretty carefully. I'm even more worried now."

"Just covering the bases, Marie. See you soon."

Unloading his Tumi on a table in the bright and bustling front room of the pub, he was feeling bright and bustling himself. The energy of the week was still surging through him. He hadn't made that many phone calls with that much conviction in many a moon. His parched mouth was salivating, thinking of the first ice-cold Smithwick's as he searched the room for his lovely Molly. Nowhere to be found, a petite, strikingly pretty server in a red apron glided up to the table. "You look to be a happy man having a good day, sir," she said. "May I add to your fortune with something from the bar?"

"Why yes, thank you," he replied in a surprised voice. "Both for your astute observation and your kind offer." She curtsied and flashed an alluring smile. A wee curvy thing with full lips emanating the sweetest of brogues, her waistline couldn't have been half the size of his on his best non-pancake day. From his sitting position, he looked directly into a pair of seafoam green eyes partially obscured by lush black lashes. Her skin was fair, nearly translucent, like a cool silver mist in the early morning's sunlight. Her fragrance inspired an immediate flight to a more natural place, maybe a sunrise on a fertile seaside glen. With white-blonde hair tinged green, a St Paddy's Day thing he guessed, she was, in sum, a rare and delightful vision—a Celtic goddess gracing his presence. "I'll have a pint of Smithwick's, please," he said, returning the smile. "Are you new here?"

"I recently came from across the sea—County Antrim. But not so new, sir, that I haven't seen you before. I served you one afternoon over a week ago in the dimly lit back room. You seemed tormented and barely raised your busy head from your concerns."

"I remember," he said. "I apologize profusely; that *was* a tough day."

"No apologies with me ever, sir," she said gently while coming a step closer. "And thank you for such a generous tip. Even in distress, you are a sweet and thoughtful man. I'll get your Smithwick's now."

"Your name? May I ask your name?"

"I'm Maureen Finn. And you, sir?"

"Pat, er, Patrick—Patrick Seamus Connelly at your service," he said with a bow of his head.

"Patrick," she repeated dreamily, "I like that."

Marie arrived, and they enthusiastically shared drinks and stories of the week. How many "thank you for thinking of me" and "I love or hate Cracker Barrels" they'd heard. One client said he would never buy stock in a restaurant that didn't have a good wine list, never mind no wine list at all. Patrick laughed at his kindred spirit, countering with, "You're not dining there; you're just becoming a minority owner." But the client was steadfast. "No problem," he said, "when I find one with a good wine list, I'll give you another ring." He made a note to send him Darden Restaurants research, owner of The Capital Grille, Seasons 52, and Yard House, among others.

A few clients asked if they could deduct meals at Cracker Barrel now that they owned the stock. "I don't think so," Marie had said with a chuckle. "Unless it's a legitimate business meeting." She directed them to their CPA for further tax advice, following smartly with, "Hopefully, your biggest tax concern will be capital gains rather than deductions." All in all, it was a good week, a crazy good week, and if nothing else, it took their minds off the opportunists circling their business. In addition, the commission revenue they generated might quiet Saunders down for a few days.

When the stories were all told and glasses drained, they packed up to leave for home. Marie said, "Hey, Pat, I couldn't help but notice our waitress. She's drop-dead adorable and seems to have taken a fancy to you."

"Oh shucks," he said. "That reminds me, I'm 'Patrick,' in case you didn't notice."

"Seriously, *Patrick,* why don't you ask her out? How long has it been?"

"My God, Marie, you sure know how to pry open the wound. I don't think modern calendars go back that far."

"You could do a lot worse, Pat."

"Who's Pat?"

"Oh, spare me, *Patrick,* will ya?"

"Oh, Marie, get real—she's probably at least ten years younger than me." After a moment of silence, he said, "Will you accept fifteen?" Silence. "Can we agree on twenty and call it a night?"

"Do I hear twenty-five?"

"Sorry, Marie," he said with arched eyebrows. "The bidding ended at twenty."

"Ten, twenty, whatever." Marie reached out and held his hand. "Like it hasn't been done before? Don't you ever go to the movies?"

"I prefer movies about cougars rather than sharks," he said with a firm and grateful hug. "Good night, oh sweet Marie; safe home, get some rest this weekend, eat pancakes for dinner at Cracker Barrel—you deserve it."

When he moved to settle the tab, Maureen appeared from the clamor and stood so close as to cause a tremor to pass between them. His heartbeat gained the velocity of a long-traveled, overdue wave rushing to the shore. The resulting crash reverberated in his head, causing a shiver. With breath shallow now, lips tingling pins and needles, he faintly leaned in toward her. "Thank you, Maureen." He gave her arm a gentle squeeze. "It's been an unanticipated delight to make your acquaintance this evening."

"Yes, Patrick, I agree," she purred affectionately while resting her hand on his shoulder. "Will I see you again soon?"

"Yes, if you don't mind?"

"My heart would be broken otherwise."

18

FOR KEWPIE, WHEREVER
I MAY FIND HER

Patrick roamed the barren rooms of his house with the accelerated pace of a new or rediscovered purpose. Settling into his cozy den, he pictured Maureen nuzzled in his lap, a position she was custom-made for. Pouring a nightcap, he plucked a book from the library shelves. When he opened the dusty hardcover, he felt a void and immediately placed it back down. He'd neglected to tune Sonos to his favorite Celtic station. In the divorce, he hadn't fought for much, except his whiskey and wine inventory, his books and music, and his Sonos sound system—all equally cherished. Especially lately. The trio had a synergy to them and made for good company in his aloneness.

With a sad Irish lament piping lightly in the background [15], the first sip of port stoked the fire smoldering in his veins. Opening the hardcover again, he flipped to a random page and read from the bottom verse:

Though I am old with wandering
Through hollow lands and hilly lands,
I will find out where she has gone,
And kiss her lips and take her hands;
And walk among long dappled grass,
And pluck till time and times are done
The silver apples of the moon,
The golden apples of the sun.

Tears of remorse fell for his half-lived life as he paused to absorb the moment. Just this one moment when he felt so full. Full of friendship and culture and fine drink. Full of all of life's amusements wrapped in their familiar cloak of sorrow. Tonight though, he'd felt a redeeming purpose, even a glint of romance, however fleeting and fragile and impossible it may be. Immersed in the world's most noble of pleasures, he floated lazily in their current. How sweet the port; how sweet the verse of the master Yeats; how sweet the cry, and the wee sprite, the seductress. He would trade it all to lay with her this night. To feel her sweet embrace and the warm breath of her soft whisper. Just this one night. This one moment in time.

Drifting now in his snug leather chair, inflamed by this other-worldly creature, "Patrick" traveled through time to the only relatable memory he could conjure. One other moment in time.

☙

He was a young and vital twenty-five, despite his injury. And handsome, having been told often enough to allow for it. In the Pacific Northwest's mesmerizing Emerald City, he and his Irish buddy were enjoying carefree, high-energy days. He'd recently taken the training that would change his life's path, and these were his first few steps. They traveled with a mix of friends, including a not-so-threatening biker group. Not the lawyers and doctors by day, motorcycle enthusiasts on the weekend type so prevalent today. These were authentic bikers: leather-clad, kerchief-headed, tattooed, and lightly employed. One indication he was safe, though—they drank chardonnay from the Columbia River Valley, albeit from the same mason jars they drank everything else. Another was they welcomed the likes of Patrick into their circle.

One night, he met two of the group's girlfriends at McRory's Whiskey Bar, a downtown establishment nearby where the Sonics played ball. One of his biker friends said, "Pat, meet Donna and Donna—the two Donnas." He finished with, "They're great," sounding like Tony the Tiger raving about his Frosted Flakes.

"Pleasure to meet you both." He reached his hand out to a pair of adorable little bookends. All of five feet tall and a hundred curvy pounds, they were each clad in tight-fitting ripped blue jeans and time-worn, coffee-shaded leather jackets. One Donna had a thick mass of reddish hair to her mid-back and a sharper, more dangerous look to her face. The other Donna had shorter, wavier, honey-auburn hair and the disarming look of a round-faced, rose-cheeked cherub—like a kewpie doll all grown up. They both had a reputation for friskiness, said his biker friend. He said it differently.

When the evening at McRory's ended, the group said their goodbyes by a streetlamp in the puddle-sheened street. The Donnas leaned in close and quietly invited Patrick back to their home. Not the group—just him. He was quick to accept. He was a "giving, loving and accepting man," after all. What followed was one of the most memorable nights he'd ever had. It remains the case to this day.

No, that didn't happen. But he wouldn't have turned down the offer, as disappointed as they'd likely have been.

The drive to their home in Ballard was a pulsing blur through persistent raindrops until the bookends heroically tugged his wheelchair up three back steps and through their kitchen door. *God damn,* he remembers thinking, *there are at least three steps into every friggin' house in Seattle.*

When safely inside, dangerous Donna disappeared while kewpie doll Donna escorted him into her bedroom, saying, "I'll get a glass of wine while you make yourself comfortable on the bed. Is that okay, Patrick? You don't mind 'Patrick,' do you? I like that."

Her near-whisper caused him to tingle. "No, it's all just perfect, Donna; thank you."

Her bedroom was all fluffy and pillowy and lacy and girly. She returned with the wine, a smoky burgundy in the appropriate bubble stemware, and then closed the bedroom door behind her. Sitting next to him on the bed, landing like a baby wren, she leaned in with a soft kiss that deepened with each passing second. Her lips were as pillowy as her bed, more luscious than the burgundy. Merely touching her face, then her arm, then her full round breasts sent her into a feverish state of shaking, quivering, and moaning. They undressed and laid back into the cloud—kissing and touching and tickling and moaning in unison.

Wherever he stroked, her skin grew taut and goose-bumpy—especially her rose-shaded, candy-kiss nipples—and she shivered visibly. Her face radiated an internal heat as she tried to catch her breath, seeming nearly faint. He knew he wasn't this good at whatever he was doing and suspected Donna was more than just frisky. But he couldn't place the word. Whatever it was, she must have been the sweetest, gentlest, squishiest, most impassioned one in all recorded time. He was all that too this night, except maybe the squishy.

Patrick had little relevant experience and a shameful secret about to be revealed. The paraplegia had stolen his ability to maintain an erection. He'd get hard at times, but it would fade away too soon. Beyond that, the surface of his penis had close to zero sensation, like much of his lower extremities. So, whenever it was touched, stroked, or otherwise attended to, he would need to fake the expected physical effect, pretending it felt incredible. Propping his head up on a pillow to watch helped, but lacking sensation muted his overall immersion. Rather than released to spontaneous abandon, his mind was too often deep in analysis and worry, set on not disappointing his companion or embarrassing himself. His fire was at the wrong periphery of the nervous system, and he remained locked in this hideous prison his entire adult life.

More than even his sentence to the wheelchair, which didn't seem to dissuade a select group of attractive women from their amorous pursuit, this brutal affliction thoroughly destroyed his confidence. He knew ahead of time he was doomed, so he was reticent even to begin. He dreaded the intimacy, the act, the moment, the expectation, the disappointment, the explanation, and the soothing, "don't worry, it's okay" response. So, he serially avoided it. He'd turned down enough nights like this one to live with a stinging sense of regret. The debilitating "woulda, coulda, shouldas."

Of course, most girls weren't nearly as alluring or insistent as this teeny-weeny, grown-up kewpie doll had been on this night. And true to form, she expressed no disappointment when the desired response didn't turn up. Maybe it was just as well he couldn't go any further, given her uncontrolled shuddering that just petting had wrought. Intercourse may have killed her. Wishful thinking, he knew. Not the "killed" part. But this clearly wasn't her first spin around an unfamiliar set of six-pack abs. He had an acute desire, a crying need, to feel deep inside of her molten creaminess and to satisfy her every whim—that he couldn't was maddening.

In his mortification, he held her quivering squishiness tight to his chest, cradling her heated face so he could drink in her abundant drool. He did everything he could, would do anything she asked, but he still wished he were the one causing such ecstatic convulsion and expectoration rather than the idea of him. Alas, that wasn't how he rolled.

She woke him at the first light with a tray of rich Seattle coffee, fresh-baked muffins, and succulent, just-picked berries. Leaning in once again, she gave him a pillowy, trembling, breathless kiss. One he can still feel all these years later—almost. With her mouth still on his, she said, "Thank you for staying the night, Patrick. It was *so* much fun."

"My God, Donna," he responded, while kissing her honey hair with his grateful tears. "It was my pleasure. I'd love to see you again, anytime." There were a few more times, probably to confirm that he couldn't adequately fill her voracious need. But he would never again be invited to kewpies' sweet, fluffy bed, and he would never again experience anything that would rival this dreamy night—this moment in time. [16]

19

INTO THE MYSTIC

A flame had been lit. Patrick spent the next day opening boxes, dusting shelves, and organizing closets he'd ignored for months. Throwing open windows and doors wide to usher in the chilly February gusts, air that had grown squalid instantly freshened. He layered heavy cotton sweatshirts and worked his Keurig machine like a virtuoso while listening to Mozart's genius thrash clean the walls. [17] Pausing several times to take in another verse from Yeats, he finally cracked open that Joyce book he'd stared at for too long.

Somehow, with no physical evidence of such, he felt more alive than the day before. It was the energy of his newly inspired thoughts blooming, shifting a house into some semblance of a home. He thought of his crazy busy week, pancakes, his good friend Marie, kewpie, and the wee one. "The time to seize back control of my life is now," was his recurring refrain as he moved from room to room in a burst of productivity, even stripping the bed and reacquainting with the laundry room.

He called his two kids to check on them, hanging on their every befuddled word. "Everything all right, Dad?" they both asked suspiciously as he hadn't sounded this upbeat in a long while.

"Just want you to know I'm thinking of you, and I love you," he replied. "Let me know if you need any help."

"Okay, Dad, I will. I love you too." They each wondered if he'd gotten into the medicine cabinet.

He went grocery shopping; for what, he hadn't a clue. He ate most of his meals out, and most of those meals came from Murphy's. But sensing a need to fill up the fridge with milk, butter, eggs, English muffins, and sweet jam, he traversed the unfamiliar aisles at Publix. After stocking the much happier-looking fridge, he organized his old record collection on the den's open shelves. Jethro Tull, Led Zeppelin, Joni Mitchell, Cat Stevens, the Allman Brothers, the Beatles, the Boss, Van the Man, The Dubliners, The Chieftains, Eva Cassidy, and on. Like long-abandoned *Toy Story* toys, a warm smile dressed his face as he reacquainted with old friends.

Needing to fill a few glaring holes in his collection, he hopped back into the bullet and motored a few exits down the highway to bohemian Lake Worth to visit his favorite vinyl shop. On the way home, he was caught in the lineup at the Southern Boulevard off-ramp and saw a familiar sight. A disheveled man came lumbering toward his van with an erratically crayoned sign saying, "Lost my Home" and "Will Work for Food" and "God Bless." Like the hopeless strippers and downtrodden patrons at the local clubs, the faces here changed often, but the attire, the grime, the despair, and the labored gait never did. The ghost of a man passed vehicles with windows shut tight while their drivers anxiously wished for the red to turn green.

Patrick opened his window and reached into his Tumi, blindly fumbling through his wallet for whatever cash was there. He held out the folded bills, saying, "Please take care—get yourself a good meal and some shelter tonight."

"God bless you, sir. Your kind generosity will not be forgotten." He was squinting one watering red eye against the bright sunlight.

"Bless you too, my good man. I wish I could do more." He let go of the leathered hand to accelerate with the traffic. "Stay warm tonight," he called out.

When he did this in the company of others, he'd often hear he's being duped, that the money will just go to support the man's drug habit. One time he was riding to a company meeting with a few passengers, including Ian King. "Are you kidding me, Connelly," he chastised. "Really?" His tone grew accusatory: "Why not just inject that loser with a needle?"

"Don't you think that's a little harsh, Ian?" Patrick replied. "The poor man needs to eat, too, and besides, look at his life. Even if it's a scam, he needs help. It's the least I can do."

"Good for you, Connelly—save the world. But he's not getting a nickel of my money. If you really want to save the world, get them off the streets and into rehab."

"Actually, I can't disagree with you," he said pensively. "I wish I had that power, but I don't." Knowing King was making sense, he pledged to prepare sandwiches ahead of time to eliminate the risk, but he never did.

In an odd way, Patrick considered the beggar and he as one—two outcasts doing the same tough job any salesman must do every day to survive. And this guy took rejection a hell of a lot better than he ever did. Whatever modest comfort he could give the man, even a high to forget his pain for an hour, he was grateful to do. And he didn't give a rat's ass what anyone else thought about it. "Rat's ass" was a piece of the weaponry he'd carried with him from Seamus, the tyrannical "Bronx Bard." *A powerful weapon too*, he thought, *because caring doesn't get much less than for a "rat's ass."*

Returning home, he put a newly-acquired Van Morrison album on the turntable and ignited the fireplace. In the old country, he imagined setting and lighting a turf fire might take half an hour of hard labor. Here in the new world of Florida's Gold Coast, the propane hearth was clicked on with a remote just like everything else. *No wonder we've all gotten so soft*, he thought.

Making his way to the bar, it was time for this softie to sample the fruits of reward for a good day well spent. He sorted through the various Irish whiskeys on his copper-clad bar top: Jameson 18 Year, Red Breast 12 Year, Cooley's Connemara Cask Strength, Middleton Very Rare, Knappogue Castle 1951. He was glad Becky didn't value that one, or it would be "gone with the wine."

He finally poured a Bushmills 21 Year into a small crystal glass. No surprise his mind was residing in County Antrim. He sampled the prize and dove head-first into the adventures of Stephen Dedalus. Soon, to the haunting sounds of Van the Man, his soul and spirit sailed off into the mystic, snug and safe with his imaginings. [18]

Prying open his sleepy eyes, he took in the tall ceiling and cobwebbed beams of the bedroom he'd somehow transported to during his wistful night. Sunlight streamed in through the lead casings drawing him beyond to the soothing melody of early morning. Breathing in deeply, he stretched his arms high until his shoulders complained while his legs jumped about in their own ritual of waking. To his left, he saw the half-made bed and thought of the kewpie doll of long ago, the early years of his marriage, and the wee one of this moment—how he yearned to reach over and draw on her heated nectar in a welcoming gesture to the glorious new day. Oh well, an Irishman is always a fanciful dreamer.

Glancing at the Keurig, he decided he'd rather have a rich cup of Starbucks to compliment the Sunday papers he'd gathered up from the driveway. His breath visible in the rare winter morning frost only added to his vigor. Sitting bundled on an outdoor patio sounded delightful. Packing up his Tumi, he grabbed a few extra layers and motored north to an already humming Clematis Street. After ordering his cappuccino and breakfast wrap, he spread the newspaper on the table with a view of the stir—the static observer of all the commotion.

The entrance to sleepy Murphy's was just a few short blocks to the west. Irish pubs were easy to spot from the street with their wooden panels and window frames painted in bright lusters of hunter green, golden yellow, and Guinness black. The cream-colored stucco inset with dark hewn beams provided the perfect contrast, the way a perfectly poured foaming head offsets the dark stout below. The front door, often painted in a deep red gloss framing small, beveled glass panes, offers only a glimpse to the magic that awaits inside—a sharp contrast to the oftentimes cruel realities of the streets. Vibrant flower baskets hang from wrought iron rivets well-spaced along the entire shopfront, with especially opulent baskets bordering the entrance, further projecting the promise of passing into a better place.

If this were Belfast or Dublin or Cork or Galway, every block would display such regale. But an ocean away in West Palm Beach, in Amerikay, he thanked God for the tiny Emerald Isle of Murphy's and the comfort it provided him.

Sipping his cappuccino and enjoying the cool air, Patrick recalled an earlier time when the wheelchair was brand new, along with all its shattering uncertainties. He was nineteen and living in an English pub. The basement of his parents' 1920s four-story, brick-and-slate Tudor had recently been converted to their dream party room, probably to celebrate their third child moving on to college or out permanently. After his injury, the only room even remotely at street level was converted again into his semi-private living space. He was still getting used to a term called "wheelchair accessible." It had never occurred to him before. Now, his last shreds of independence depended on it.

One morning, he woke groggily from the previous night's consumption and floated hazily in his king-sized waterbed. All the rage at the time, his was about reducing the risk of bedsores rather than enhancing his sex life. And it certainly wasn't built for hangovers. The kitchen door at the top of the steep staircase creaked open, as it did several times a day, and down into his lair came the newspapers carrying the stale aroma of his father's early morning Tiparillo. Next came the heavy sound of the pile slapping the sofa and the "Here are your daily rags, Paddy."

Holding his arm over his eyes to block out the intruding light of day, he grumbled, "Good morning," and "Thanks, Dad," before closing his eyes and praying for the sounds of departure.

"It's afternoon now," came the response. The tug-of-war had begun anew.

In those early days, he wasn't in the mood to hear about getting on with his life, rejecting his father's every thought about going back to school, job hunting, slowing down the partying, going to church. He didn't dismiss the easy things like season tickets to Yankee Stadium and Madison Square Garden, just the more challenging ones. He would use dismissive two-word harrumphs or express vehement anger and victimhood on cue. Seamus's own vicious brand of anger would soon surface, and the battle would rage. It was the same script day after grueling day.

One afternoon after a particularly vile outburst, his younger sister, then a vital cog in his life, descended the stairs for a private chat. "Everyone feels so bad for what happened, Paddy," she started. "And we all understand why you're so angry, but you still have no right to treat Dad the way you do." She continued with, "No one on earth loves you more, and no one is more damaged, more distraught, than Dad."

"Except maybe me," he said bitterly.

"Okay, we get that," she said more sternly. "But for once, we're not talking about you; we're talking about Dad." She had her brother's attention. "He hasn't gone to work in months, and he barely eats. He just sits in his bedroom like a zombie repeating over and over that he wasn't there when you needed him, that it's all his fault. He told Mom he wishes it happened to him instead of you, and he cries himself to sleep. I hear him every night, and it's breaking my heart." He sat in solemn silence as she continued. "You know, Paddy, in a way, he's lost even more than you have. It happened to his son; it seems to me that's much worse." Standing up, starting back up the stairs, she paused and turned to face the brother who was once her hero, saying, "I just thought you should know that, and think about it." Quietly closing the kitchen door, she left him to his misery.

In the next several hours, and days, and weeks, he did think about it. A light turned on—he wasn't alone in his distress anymore. He came to think of it as just another team game, and he was the captain. Only he could lead the effort to make the distress diminish, to save his father's life, and his mother's, and his own. His grieving soon ended, and his second life was unleashed.

He felt a pair of eyes on him, then another, and another. Not unusual. It happened wherever he went, especially when he was alone, which was often now. Children were fascinated with the spokes of his wheels as if he were a large rolling toy or a clown riding in a wagon. They'd innocently point and ask, "Mommy, what's that man?" before being quickly hushed by discomfited, apologetic mothers. Adults would extend looks ranging from curious, to kind, to pitying, to revulsion. When he'd glance up to meet their eyes, the curious would slowly remove their gaze unaffected, the kind would smile faintly and mouth a greeting, the pitying would shield their eyes and turn away, and the repulsed would hold their disdainful glare as if demanding his exit. Facial expressions as windows into the soul. Whatever their motives, the shared emotion was, "Thank God it's him, not me or my children."

Patrick understood and sympathized. He was a game-changer, plain and simple, shifting the emotional energy of whatever room he entered. A startling presence to some, like seeing an especially small or obese person, and a threat to others, like a beggar on a street corner might be. He came to realize none of it had anything to do with him. The world's myriad of emotional or analytical output would be careening with or without him; people's shit, or rather, playbook, forever running with his presence just a momentary trigger. Once he left the room, or they left the room, he'd flash out of their crowded minds as quickly as he'd flashed in, and they from his. The whole exercise was curious but simply unworthy of attention.

One of the supreme charms of aging is incidences that once bothered him, soured his mood, year-by-year faded to irrelevancy. In his youth, it mattered what people thought of him and how they behaved toward him, and it would affect his state of mind. He'd feel embarrassed, or afraid, or just plain sad to be out in public. Though he never was able to look at himself in the mirror, never a kind and patient look, he did become more accepting of his circumstances. And once he stopped feeling sorry for himself and developed a craving to be someone, to accomplish things regardless, he turned his focus to such pursuit.

In short, he didn't much give a rat's ass anymore.

Spreading open the *Post* on the patio table, he lazily flipped through the pages. The first section, the mushy brown peas, was always difficult to digest with its details of ongoing strife, hopeless destruction, and redundant political deception ongoing throughout the world. Nurturing his Starbucks in contemplation, he continued perusing the paper. The local sports teams win and lose—usually, they lose. What did it really matter? His thoughts swam away once again to the nights before, and the lifetime before. A spark had been aroused, and his body hummed to an accelerated vibration. Taking in a deep breath, he unconsciously massaged his right forearm, then his neck, then his temple, before dispassionately turning to the next section. The top of the business page snapped him awake with the hauntingly familiar headline: "Disney Buys Cracker Barrel." He fixed on today's date—it was February 10th.

His Tumi started vibrating, and he dragged open the outer pockets' zipper to find his buried cell phone aching for release. Nervously sweeping at the tingling screen, he saw Marie had been calling and texting for the past hour. Her last message said, "My God, Pat, the news. I'm afraid. Call me, please."

He quickly tapped out a reply: "Saw the headline, can't talk now, call you later. Relax and congrats to us!" Folding closed today's *Post* and reopening it, the headline was the same. The date was still February 10th.

Pulling out the paper he'd found at Murphy's two weeks before, he unfolded it and turned to the requisite page. The headline said, "Europe Sliding into Recession." Folding it over and opening it again, Europe was still sliding into recession, and the date at the top read January 27th.

Returning to today's *Post*, the first line of the article read: "After weeks of negotiations, Disney has agreed to pay Cracker Barrel shareholders $130 a share, part in cash and part in Disney stock." He jumped to the horoscopes and read his sign: *You've been on a roll this past week. Good fortune will continue to flow your way. Stay positive and excited about the future. The vastness of the ocean and the sky are yours for the asking.* There would be a crescent moon tonight, he noticed, about half full. Now it all made perfect sense. *Wait,* he thought, *nothing here makes perfect sense or any sense. In fact, it's insanity.*

But he *was* on a roll, wasn't he? And it felt good, so damn good. He wondered again what on earth was happening. Was it all just madness? Had he simply lost his mind? Why not—he's especially good at losing things. Too much to contemplate, impossible to process, so he tried to let it all go. He thought of Saunders and sent him a big smiley face through the ethernet. Not precisely Kay's sage advice, a little more noble, but it felt good anyway.

His mind now in a reel, he thought amorously of the scrumptious sprite. He just couldn't shake her. *Stop your frivolous dreaming you salty old dog,* he chastised. *Get real, will you? Such a turn of fortune is not typically written into the script.*

Then again, it was crystal clear that these were not typical times.

20

A LITTLE PIECE OF CUSHENDUN

Stuffing all his stuff into his Tumi, Patrick set off from Starbucks and proceeded east along Clematis. Through the waterfront park's latent foliage, the early afternoon sun played off the rolling Intracoastal's white crests sending up sparklers and beckoning him on. He rolled on by the silver bullet, past his toxic office building, the charming French restaurant's elevated patio, and on through sleepy gray oaks lining the triangular park. *Why not,* he thought, *what's the rush to go home?*

Crossing over busy Flagler, he dropped his Tumi on a vacant bench, kicked his legs up, cradled his head in his hands, and soaked in the soothing views. Breathing in deeply, the crisp air burned a good burn reminding him of a former life. The business day ahead will be crazy, he thought, busier than the entire previous week. Plenty of rest tonight is the plan. He opened his phone to call Marie.

"May I join you, Patrick?"

Abruptly craning his head to the right, his eyes set upon the wee one silhouetted in a bending light. "Maureen Finn? What a coincidence," he said in a startled tone. "I was just thinking of you. Of course, you may." He straightened up and gestured her to sit, moving his Tumi to make room on the bench.

"Not so coincidental, really," she said. "I live just up the way and spend most of my time by the water. If you want to find me, you've come to the right place."

Smiling broadly, he said, "I'll have to remember that." After a pause, he then said, "We are in the right place, aren't we?"

"Yes, Patrick, I feel that way."

They sat watching the water roll by, talking for minutes, then hours. She told him about growing up in Ireland, about her home in a tiny coastal village named Cushendun on the rugged Antrim Coast north of Belfast. He excitedly told her he'd passed through her village just more than a year ago, stopping for lunch at the famous Mary McBride's Bar. "The town was uncrowded if you don't count the sheep," he said with a grin, "and simply idyllic."

"Why, thank you," she said. "Yes, I miss it dearly." Then with a twinkle, she added, "including the sheep."

"My daughter's favorite place in all of Ireland," he continued, returning her twinkle. "We've talked about going back, maybe renting a house there."

In a way, though, he thought, *a little piece of Cushendun has come here instead. The best piece imaginable.*

He talked about growing up in New York: his injury, his marriage and children, his career and recent troubles, explaining his worried demeanor the afternoon they first crossed paths in Murphy's back room. She listened patiently, with interest, caressing him with her understanding. After sitting in silence for a time, he said, "I'd better let you go, Maureen. I don't want to hold you."

"Oh, I'm sorry to hear that, Patrick."

"Hear what?"

"That you don't want to hold me."

Scanning her earnest face, heart thumping wildly, he set on her Caribbean green eyes. "You're a sweet little thing, aren't you? And a wee bit naughty too." He managed to force the words out through his constricting throat.

"Do you want to find out, Patrick? Just how sweet and naughty I can be?"

"Yes, I do—very much." She slowly leaned in and kissed him, softly and deeply. It was pillowy, trembling, and breathless.

Sunday evening turned out to be anything but restful. It was more like a powerful nor'easter's gale had buffeted his residence. Neither Patrick, Pat, nor Paddy had felt so much an object of wanton desire in a lifetime. Maureen was like a giddy child insatiably slurping an ice cream sundae: banana, three scoops with chocolate, nuts, whipped cream, and a cherry on top. And he responded as best he could, exploring every desirable inch from her delectable face to her tiny little toes.

Then he rolled her over and began anew. Her small frame was roundly feminine in a firm and muscular way. "All the swimming I did growing up," she said. Her breasts were nymph-like, topped with the same addicting candy kisses he'd recently conjured from long ago, and he suckled her as would a famished newborn. Her fingers and toes had connecting paper-thin skin, and he lightly kissed every delicate cell. His rapt adoration of her diminutive, perfectly smooth body was heightened when he encountered a rough patch below her knees. "I'm sorry it's so rough there," she whispered. "It must have dried out in the recent cold weather."

"Every inch of you is adorable and delicious," he assured.

Truth was, any little imperfection he discovered comforted him, making her more human, less a goddess. Having glanced in a full-length mirror for just a moment that morning, he was reminded who was getting the better end of this bargain. It wasn't even a contest.

She made him feel nineteen and whole again, like in the unbridled months just ahead of his injury. If she was put off or disappointed with the uniqueness of his condition, his tight legs moving in random spasms rather than on-demand, it was news to him. Rather, she seemed delighted with the whole of him. She knew just where to touch and how to touch like she could read his mind, and she generated responses he hadn't expected. He was completely at ease, worries melted away, in a state of abandon, and together they reveled in the pleasure of it all. She told him her favorite musician was Van Morrison, her favorite poet WB Yeats, and her favorite author Tana French. She felt so at home in his home, she said, that she wanted to weep. When she did weep, he held her face close and sipped from her salty tears.

"Where did you come from?" he whispered in her ear with an embrace he wished never to release.

"From Cushendun, silly, remember?" she teased. "Sometimes people meet and feel an instant connection of their energies, an overwhelming attraction, like a kind of magic."

"I'm totally feeling the magic," he agreed with a smile.

"It's a rare and wonderful thing."

"Why, though?" He lifted her up and sat her on his abdomen, like he'd placed a weightless doll there. "Why do you think it happened for you and me? and why now?"

Leaning down for several gentle kisses, she said, "Well, for one thing, you're a sweet, handsome, and deserving man, Patrick. You deserve a magical life."

"Thank you, Maureen." He wiped at a tear beginning to tickle his cheekbone.

"And who knows," she continued, "maybe we were meant to be here together, like it was written in some script a long time ago. Maybe there's a reason we need each other right now."

"Will you stay tonight?"

"Of course, I will." She nuzzled into him in a sort of seamless merger. Something primal. He reached onto the nightstand and fiddled with the Sonos app until the soft sweetness of Enya, from the magical land of shamrocks, serenaded the lovers into their dreamland. [19]

21

OVER A BARREL

"**P**at, where the hell have you been? Why haven't you returned my calls? The phone's ringing off the hook."

"Sorry, Marie," he said, pausing at her desk. "I've been otherwise occupied."

"Otherwise occupied? With what? And it better be good, like you spent the weekend with that server from Murphy's."

"Okay, I spent the weekend with that server from Murphy's. Her name is Maureen, by the way."

"No, Pat, really?"

"Let's talk later," he said. "It looks like I have lots of work to do." He grabbed the pile of messages from the corner of her desk and barreled ahead into his office. Cracker Barrel had opened at $132 on the news. There were reports of a competing offer coming, maybe from Yum! Brands, maybe Pepsi, maybe Darden. *This successful stock-picking thing is exhausting,* he thought with a *"What, me worry?"* grin.

"It's all good," he said aloud so Marie could hear it. "Or in the words of the office sage: 'It is what it is.'"

After reading the latest news, he returned calls as quickly as he could. His clients ranged from hero-worshiping to ecstatic to worried. Some wanted to take quick profits, and he advised them to hold on, saying they could defer some of the tax hit by taking Disney stock in exchange for their shares. Besides, he told them, it looks like a higher offer may come in, and Disney would probably match or beat it. Most listened, some didn't, and he gave the sell orders to Marie.

A few asked how Patrick knew and if they could get in trouble for insider trading. He assured them he knew no one at Cracker Barrel or Disney and had no knowledge of a deal ahead of time. "It's just dumb luck, and there's nothing to worry or feel guilty about," he said with confidence. "This is capitalism at its finest, and you should relax and enjoy the fruits."

"Saunders is on the phone," Marie called out.

"I don't have time for him. Tell him I'm over a barrel right now."

"It's the third time he's called; he wants to see you in his office."

"I really don't have time, Marie—look at all the messages." He was leaning to the open doorway and waving the pink stack over his head. "Tell him he'll need to stop down for a minute if it's urgent."

His thoughts soared back over the past twenty-four hours, and especially the past twelve, to the sumptuous creature still nesting in his bed. He'd given her a dozen light kisses and a dozen more, telling her, "Please stay as long as you wish. I'll try to get home before you leave for work to make sure you're all cleaned up good and proper." He had refused to let fade his last glimpse of her delicate, sleepy, satisfied face as he left the room.

"Connelly," came the quick rap on the door. Saunders burst in accompanied by Jack Lawson, his chief compliance officer—the top cop on the beat. The door closed firmly, meaning slammed, and they each planted in chairs across his desk. "We've got to know right now, Connelly. What did you know, when did you know it, and where did you get the information?"

"What are you talking about, Jeff?"

"Your insider trading felony."

"Felony? Are you kidding? I positioned the stock for the long-term like I've done all my career," he said defensively. "The merger offer is just dumb luck."

"Do you really think we're buying that?"

Lawson interrupted with, "Patrick, the head of legal in New York is already on this. They took notice of your request for the large block, and now this happens a week later. They smell a rat."

"That's probably because they're in New York City," Patrick said good-naturedly.

"Nothing funny about this, Connelly!" blurted Saunders. "We're all under the spotlight. They're going to look into every relationship, every phone call, every meeting you've had in the last few months."

"Good, that should keep them out of our hair."

"If you tell us what or who you knew, they'll go easier on you," Lawson advised. "They'd prefer to take down the source at the company or law firm. I've seen them give the retail player immunity if you're truthful."

"My God, Jack, you've already branded me guilty without the benefit of a trial."

"It does look bad, Patrick, and they're going to look under every rock."

"Honestly, gentleman, I've got nothing to hide. It was just good timing for a change," he said while gesturing them toward the door. "I've got dozens of happy clients to get back to. I'd better keep at it."

"This isn't over, Connelly," Saunders growled. "I'm coming after the truth, and then you."

"Nice to see you, Jack, as always; you too, Jeff," he said to their backs as they exited his office.

Later in the afternoon, before rushing from the office to his other occupation, he sat in private with Marie. She was worried, unsure if she could trust him. "You've been under such stress lately, Pat. This all seems too coincidental, too suspicious."

"I can see how it does, Marie, but you know I've been speculating about a Disney-Cracker Barrel deal for a decade, and I've been wrong for a decade, until now."

"You never bought all these shares until now, and you joked a week or two ago about Disney actually buying them—about an article in the paper."

"That's true, but that's all it was—a joke. Maybe I finally drew some positive energy my way by visualizing an article ahead of time—yay for me."

"They're not gonna find anything?"

"Of course not, Marie," he insisted. "I don't know a soul at either company or anyone else related to the deal." He reached out and held her hands, looking directly into her eyes. "It was just a feeling I had after seeing how crowded the local store was. It's madness, I know, but I finally said screw it and jumped in with both feet. We got a little help from the stars, and let's face it, we needed it."

"You're sure, Pat? It was just luck—you promise?"

"Of course, I promise. How long have you known me?"

"Too long, I'm starting to think," she said with a roll of her eyes.

"Hey, watch it, you," he said, squeezing her hands. "Relax and enjoy the moment, will you? We have nothing to worry about. We didn't buy any shares ourselves, and we didn't sell any to family. We've done nothing wrong."

"Thank God."

"Yes, and Allah and Buddha and Tinker Bell too," he said with a smile while straightening up and packing his Tumi. "Our clients made some money; good for them, and us."

"Where are you running off to now?"

"Oh, I've gotta stop home for a quick shower. Too much sweat work in one day for an old dog like me. I'll call you later—if you want."

"No, that's okay, Pat. Have fun."

"I intend to, Marie. See you in the morning."

22

THE ANTIQUE DEALER

Maureen had left for work by the time he flew home. On a kitchen chair were a few of her personal items, including a work apron, a large scarf, and a cap with a feather stitched into each side. They were each prominent for their shades of red, from cherry to black. Holding them to his flushed face, bathing in her intoxicating scent, he was immediately transported once again to the water's edge in another place and time—meaning to his bed the previous night. He tucked her things away in an empty drawer in the master suite, hoping they had found their permanent home. When he returned to the kitchen, he saw a note she had left which read:

Patrick, dear,

Thank you for inviting me to stay last night. It was so much fun. I had to leave before you arrived home but trust your offer to give me a good scrubbing still holds? Maybe I'll see you later at Murphy's? I'm there until 10.

With love,
Maureen

He released the breath he'd been holding since discovering the note, replaced with a broad smile. It sounded like the perfect plan.

Monday was typically quiet at Murphy's, and tonight was no different. Molly was off, but he was in good hands with his new friend. He liked being *Patrick* and feeling doted on, even pecked on when it appeared no one was paying attention. Sipping his Black Bush, he considered the events of the past two weeks. He *was* on a roll, as his horoscope had said, and it was about time. But how, and why, was this good fortune suddenly coming his way? Things had changed so quickly, the contemplation of it all was confounding and a bit overwhelming.

He thought of his meeting with Saunders and Lawson. Should he be worried? Talk of an SEC investigation is a serious threat, he knew. But what would they find? After looking a dozen more times, he felt certain the newspaper's date was January 27th, once and for all, and that Europe was sliding into a recession, unfortunately for them. He'd decided that no harm could come, so felt at ease. But the head-on assault to his dignity, his livelihood, his very freedom, was inflaming a rising hostility. Bullies can do that to an Irishman. One fortuitous stock pick wasn't going to keep them away, so what was he to do, especially with Saunders?

Glancing across the room at Maureen's miniature curves made such debilitating thoughts melt away. She was a stroke of luck even more mystifying than the enchanted newspaper. Earlier, he'd scanned the empty booths and tables but found nothing. Christ, what was he expecting, Samantha Stephens to wiggle her nose and give him next week's big news again?

A fan of the sitcom *Bewitched* in his youth, he vaguely recalled when Sam or Endora, or maybe it was wacky Uncle Arthur or zany Aunt Clara, zapped the next day's newspaper a day early. They were all legitimate suspects. Naturally, Darrin saw the paper, noticed the date, skipped work, and raced off to the track to bet on the winning horses.

Damn, I forgot about that, he thought with a smirk.

Anyway, Larry Tate, Darrin's overbearing boss—his Saunders— happened to be at the track with their biggest client. What were the odds of that? He catches Darrin gambling during work hours and fires him. That kind of thing happened to feckless Darrin about every other show. Having access to Sam's magic never worked out well for him. Kind of a morality tale for the kids. If magic was misused selfishly, for one's personal gain, only harm would come in the end. It was the same for astronaut Tony Nelson and his buddy Roger in *I Dream of Jeannie,* another childhood favorite. Jeannie's blinks got them into more trouble than they could handle.

The enduring message of both shows was nothing comes easy—greed is a vice and never pays off. Instead of depending on magic, you'd need to work hard for everything you get in life. Kind of a buzzkill as Patrick contemplated what may be coming next.

Looking to close out the tab, with Maureen nowhere in sight, he decided to hit the facilities. Moving through the dusky, desolate back room, he came upon an elderly man hunched over a table sipping from a jar. "Good evening, sir," the man said to his passerby.

"And to you," Patrick replied while applying the brakes. "You seem lonely back here all by yourself."

"If you think so, then sit a minute and keep me company."

"If you insist," came his friendly reply. Spread over the frayed mahogany tabletop were disordered papers, pencils, legal pads, file folders, a calculator, and a battery-powered lamp. The man had with him a complete mobile office. "You're not so alone after all," Patrick said, looking admiringly at the familiar though enhanced workstation.

"No, I'm quite occupied with my responsibilities," said the man. "There are a few too many thoughts careening around my skull, and this is where I come to sort them all out."

"I know well the feeling," he said, extending his hand. "Patrick Seamus Connelly, a pleasure to meet you."

"Kerry O'Connor—likewise." His grip was heartier than expected, given his small frame and advanced years. He wore several days of scraggy white facial hair framing ancient creases and a nose as red as his dowdy vest. From the back of his tweed cap fell a complementary coil of white fleece. An unlit wooden pipe in his left hand, a jar of whiskey poised to his right, you'd have mistaken him for one of those poor souls with the signs at the highway ramp except for his apparent industry.

"What is it that keeps you so busy, if I may ask?"

"Oh, you may, you may." He placed the pipe on the table. "I have a little antique furniture business just west of town."

"That sounds fascinating," he said with sincere interest, having an affinity for antiquities.

"It's a living, Patrick. And what occupies you, my lad?"

"No longer a lad, I'm afraid, but a hearty thanks just the same," he answered with a chuckle. "I've been helping people hold onto their hard-earned wealth with my investment advice for nearly three decades now. My office is just a few blocks east of here."

"A fine business," he answered. "A fine, commendable business."

"Thank you again, Mr. O'Connor, nice of you to say. I take pride in what I've accomplished all these years."

"As you should."

Patrick went on to say, "my profession isn't held in the highest regard by some—it's not as trusted as it could have been." Perhaps the whiskey had inappropriately loosened his lips in the company of this total stranger? Such is the curse of the ever-gregarious Irishman. "It's like our armed forces," he continued. "The vast majority of the foot soldiers in the field perform magnificently and with great honor. But the elitists back in DC making the decisions set them up for failure time and again."

"That's very true," Mr. O'Connor agreed.

"With rare exception," Patrick continued, "the elites running my industry a decade ago did the exact same thing. They had mixed up priorities—too fond of their mansions, penthouses, and yachts—while too many fighting their battles in the trenches were smothered in debt and hopelessness—set up for failure. Some of these Wall Street titans made monumentally bad decisions destroying countless careers and lives, just like their counterparts in the nation's capital. Entire companies went up in flames, and it all came with zero accountability. Even worse, I'm worried there may be more of them on the loose today."

"You've described much of the world condition, Patrick," the man answered. "The rich getting richer, the poor poorer, while misbehaviors, intended or otherwise, and ill-gotten fortunes are sanctioned. Meantime, the truly desperate are laid to waste."

"It's so tragic."

"But there's some good news, I think," Mr. O'Connor continued.

"And that would be?"

"It all evens out in the end before the eyes of God. Don't you think?"

"That's what I was taught in grade school," Patrick said. "I pray you're right."

"Keep up your prayers and your noble work, my friend, and I'll put in a good word myself."

"Thank you, Mr. O'Connor. I could certainly use the help."

Extending a card held between his fingers, he said with a glint, "Come visit my shop one day, and perhaps your faith in humanity will be a tad restored."

Laughing, he took the card, saying, "That's a tall order you take on, but I'll come by—you can count on it. Now I'd better take care of the business I came back here for and leave you to yours. It was a true delight to meet you, Kerry O'Connor."

"And you as well, Patrick Connelly." With that, he dashed off to the men's room.

When he passed back through a few minutes later, the room was deserted, the old man's table bare except for a small burgundy leather pouch. *He must have forgotten it,* Patrick thought, scooping it up and tossing it into his Tumi. Meeting the antique dealer had been interesting but cost him the chance to invite Maureen back to his home. Settling his tab, the bartender told him she'd just left. Disappointed that he'd neglected to get her cell number, he made off for home in a shadow of remorse.

Nestled in the den sipping his nightcap, he put The Chieftains on his Sonos and considered the night, and especially the night before. [20] The conversation with Mr. O'Connor had him thinking about the time, not long ago, when Wall Street's greed almost cost him everything. Suddenly exhausted, his thoughts faded and he slowly drifted off with the winds.

23

A SMOKING CAULDRON

"Take a message, Marie; tell him I'll call him back."

"He wants to sell everything, Pat. He doesn't want to wait."

"Oh, for Christ's sake. I just told him yesterday to hold on, that we're closer to the end of this than the beginning."

"It's a full-blown panic. Are you gonna pick him up or not?"

"Damn it, yes, yes. I'll speak with him."

It was 2008, and Wall Street firms were going down like third-world dictators before an angry mob. *There he is—kill him!* Bang. *Crash. Burn.* Just six years before, they'd gone through this same shit, and now the siege was on again. Mark Twain said, "History doesn't repeat itself, but it often rhymes." True enough. It *was* different in 2008. It was worse—much fucking worse.

He remembers watching the fiery towers collapse in 2001, over and over, knowing two of his closest friends were on the 104th floor trapped in the smoking cauldron. It had taken him four separate elevators to get up there when he'd visited them a few years earlier. Did they run to the roof expecting rescue? Did they finally hurl themselves through a broken window and plunge to their deaths? Or did they just curl up under their desks and burn alive? Did they suffocate? Or were they still alive when the building came crashing down? He had the same desperate questions as so many others and didn't want to know the truth, he couldn't bear it.

It turned out they were calling their wives to say goodbye, to say how much they loved them, and to please tell the kids daddy loves them. It took the families weeks to finally accept that their husbands, fathers, brothers, sons, and best friends weren't coming home. To bear the funeral ceremonies—the official goodbyes—was torturous. It was too final. "Let's give it just another week, please. Maybe they're lost or in a hospital somewhere?" Along with thousands of others, his friends left behind dreadfully grieving young families to fend for themselves in a newly cruel world.

He didn't let his own young children see the devastation, trying to preserve their innocence a while longer. The next day, September 12, 2001, he drove himself to the emergency room thinking he was having a stroke or heart attack, or both, leaving five hours later with his first script for Ativan. "It'll take the edge off," they told him.

The dot-com bust had been going on for more than a year, and the terrorist attack redoubled the market's bloodletting. By early 2003, stocks had fallen 65 percent from their peak, give or take. Mostly take. Those who owned all technology stocks, "new era" stocks they were called, were effectively wiped out. He was smarter than that, only losing a decade's worth of wealth accumulation. But it was over, thank the Lord, and he'd never again have to witness anything as bad.

About five years later, in the fall of 2007, the market averages had fully recovered. Patrick's heart never did fully recover. As new highs were printed day after day, he told worried clients they should avoid undue residential real estate speculation, but another stock market crash as bad as 2000-'02 was unlikely. "Bear markets that severe are generational," he said. "They come around once every twenty or thirty years to clear out the excesses."

Yeah, right.

By late 2008, it was more brutal than he'd ever seen. There was no place to hide. Stocks large and small, blue chips and otherwise, were down at least 50 percent from their peaks of just a year earlier. Investors were 'in the soup,' in other words. Corporate bonds and preferred stocks, traditionally safe investments, were also trading at half their value of a few months ago—if they traded at all. The global markets, unable to properly value or trade securities, had largely shut down. Government agency paper was going totally kaput. Wall Street firms were falling like the towers once did.

"Christ almighty," he fumed. "Could this really be happening again?"

It was the same bleak question he'd bring home night after night for days, weeks, and months. Coming of age in the first decade of the new century, his two kids had made only one sure decision. They would never do what their father did for a living. He was killing himself trying to survive in a business that wasn't to be trusted.

According to news reports, the primary villains for all this butchery were Wall Street's latest robber barons—the CEO's of several leading financial firms including his own. That was true, to a degree. The severely overpaid titans running these shops had been authorizing idiotic mortgages to real estate speculators and unsophisticated, would-be homeowners for a decade. Many were "low-income" or "no-income verification" loans mandated by the equally culpable federal government.

Corporate and government elitists fresh from their fancy management schools and consulting firms—Dumb and Dumber.

With suitcases full of ill-conceived cash, their dumb-ass disciples queued up in Miami, Phoenix, and Las Vegas to buy brand new condos and single-family homes. You know the scene: the grand opening of a sales office is greeted by frenzied lines wrapping around the block like it was a Beatles reunion concert—when four Beatles still existed. The guy at the front of the line sells his option to buy a two-bedroom, two-bath unit with granite countertops and a water view to the guy at the back of the line for an instant $50,000 profit—just rewards for having no job and a sleeping bag.

Late in the game, a client in his eighties instructed Marie to wire a quarter of a million to a bank in Las Vegas for a real estate investment he claimed would double his money in less than a year. Patrick held up the wire and did his best to talk sense into him. A few minutes later, the cash left for Vegas never to return, the latest version of "what happens in Vegas, stays in Vegas." When the last buyer was in and the tide started pulling out, the thimbleful of home equity was instantly wiped out in record numbers. Residential real estate values nationwide plummeted 40 percent and more from their insanity peaks, taking every other financial asset down with it.

To make the party punch even more potent, the elitist titans packaged millions of these flimsy residential loans into thirty-year securities, stamped a government-backed AAA rating on them, and sold them all over the world. "Come and get it, right here—safe income," cried the blue pinstriped vendors. "Come and get your safe income." Institutional investors and municipalities "got it" all right, with many teetering on the edge of insolvency. Whole countries, including Ireland, were brought to their financial knees. Iceland was bankrupted. Add in the poorly timed government regulation called "mark to market," meaning securities must now be valued at today's perceived market prices, even in chaotic plummeting markets. "Perceived" means they had no friggin' idea. But they did know this: Wall Street's balance sheets were destroyed, along with hordes of innocent companies and their employees.

"Christ," Patrick would say, "I thought we were in the *advisory* business."

By Thanksgiving 2008, a meaningful number of the biggest banks, mortgage purveyors, insurance companies, and brokerages were technically bankrupt. Without government bailouts or Treasury-managed mergers they probably would have collapsed. A few handfuls did collapse, further fueling the tsunami. Sharks circled the bloodied waters, and there was no public sympathy for the alleged perpetrators of all the carnage. An entire generation learned the game was rigged, or run by incompetents, or both. And with their exceptional work completed, these greedy-ass corporate and government geniuses—*yeah, right*—stole off in the night to their retirement castles on private islands and golf courses with hundreds of millions of shareholders' and taxpayers' dollars. No different than Jesse James holding up a bank and making off with the loot. Only they never even sent a posse out after this notorious gang—too much like looking in the mirror.

And with the totality of that shit sandwich sitting on his desk, Patrick showed up at his desk and picked up that phone every business day, feigning confidence while dispensing investment advice to scores of panicked clients. Many had depended on him, had been his friend, for more than two decades. Now they didn't know whether to hug him or sue him.

The feared "Second Great Depression" never happened—unless you were that Vegas client, or you lost your home, job, retirement account, or all three.

Patrick's performance-based retirement plans, brimming with mandated company stock, were in the toilet—down over 90 percent from the '07 peak. He had once voiced sympathy for the employees of Enron and WorldCom for losing their entire retirements in the previous greedy-assed debacle. Just a few short years later, he and his veteran colleagues across Wall Street *were* Enron and Worldcom. To this day, he'd never heard the first word of contrition from any one of the perpetrators.

The rest of his balance sheet didn't look so hot either. The only value that had stood firm was his home mortgage. It also hastened the eventual end of his marriage. If a crisis of this magnitude doesn't bring a couple together in compassionate support—nothing would. When the time finally came, he and Becky split the crumbs remaining in the retirement accounts.

Retirement? Ha, ha! he thought. *What's that?*

In the aftermath of the 2007-'09 devastation, profoundly hypocritical government officials punished Wall Street with excessive litigation and onerous new regulations. A small army of legal suits invaded the industry with their textbook knowledge and tedious lists of "don'ts" and "better nots." The guilty brass telling the innocent foot soldiers how to run a clean business. Absurd. Then, the latest procession of Ivy-educated Wall Street saviors went into overdrive.

For the breadth of these two historic financial crises, advisors at Patrick's firm, and across the industry, worked and fretted day and night to protect and prosper their clients. In many cases, they did heroic work. Highly trained and honorable, these advisors and their support teams earned the entirety of their portfolio management commissions and fees, and frankly, much more. Just ask their clients. In the most severe market conditions imaginable, not knowing if they'd even have a job the following week, they held tight to the ship's wheel and kept their clients calm, invested, and focused on the more prosperous days sure to come. They were the true leaders, and the chain of command who employed them, on balance, were equally steady and honorable, providing the critical support needed during the darkest days, as they'd always done.

However—except for a lonely few—the so-called "industry leaders," those who reside at the tippy top, meaning their penthouse suites in Manhattan, failed miserably. Their primary job was to gaze intently to the horizon and identify the warning signs, the potential storms ahead, and then navigate their companies, employees, and clients to a safe port. Slow down, think, be prudent and humble, and protect financial lives. Instead, apparently focused more on their ridiculous compensation packages than their compasses, they went full speed ahead until steering their entire industry directly into the rocks, and in some cases, the ocean's bottom.

The American story has always been one of resiliency and renewal. In the years ahead, both the economy and the securities markets recovered from this second collapse too. The latest collection of "leaders" looked to be a different class too—more humble, less self-focused. That can happen after a near-death experience. But the lasting damages at home and around the world were extensive.

Millions lost their homes and livelihoods, some ending up on the streets, and while none of that happened to Patrick, another piece of him had been permanently severed and left to rot. His view of the financial industry and capitalism—the interplay between government and corporate elites, and the common folk—had forever shifted. There were "haves" and "have-nots," as there always were, but the delineation had grown ever wider. He listened to politicians make their endless pledges to "raise up the poor" by spending "only a few hundred billion more" of our tax dollars on their doomed giveaways. Empty promises spewed with feckless words. The only communities benefiting from the massive waste were the already rich politicians and their cronies in business and lobbying and academia and media and entertainment. The "haves."

Watching the Bentleys flow east across the bridge to opulent $30 million manors, knowing they'd just passed by the torn and tattered beggars at the I-95 ramps and street corners to the west, he was certain they'd kept their frosted windows shut tight to the heat, staring the red light to green. The injustice of it all made him nauseous.

"Patrick, wake up, my darling."

"What? Who's that?" With a start, he raised his head in the faint light of the room. The Chieftains' magical winds were still adrift.

"It's me, Maureen," she said with a gentle stroke of his face. "You were having a bad dream, I'm afraid."

"I'm sorry I missed you tonight, sweetheart. I was so sad. How did you get in?"

"I knocked on the door—you didn't answer, but you left it unlocked, silly," she said with a little pinch of his nose. "I hope you did that for me."

"I have to give you a key," he said drowsily. "Hi, baby face." His arms wrapped around her and drew her in. "I must have fallen asleep. I missed you at Murphy's. I'm so glad you're here."

"I am too, beautiful man," she said with a soft kiss. "I locked up the house, and all is safe. Come to bed now, okay?"

"Yes, to bed. I'm so glad you're here."

24

SEEDS PLANTED

Patrick whistled and scatted the prehistoric tune from the Chairman of the Board. *Got the world on a string. Sitting on a rainbow.* [21] A tune he hadn't thought about since he was a little boy perched on his father's knee. Okay, not exactly on his knee; that never happened. Rather, when they were in the same room together. Okay, not in the same room, but the same house. That happened for sure. Today though, all of that was in its proper grave. He was indeed "sitting on a rainbow," and he was "lucky and in love" to boot. *Custom-made lyrics,* he thought with a smile.

It was early, he knew. Pathetically early. Yet, he couldn't imagine life without his new companion. He and Finnie—Maureen Finn's new pet name—spent every possible minute together, listening to music, reading aloud from books, sipping one libation or another, and otherwise tending to each other's every whim.

Is this how good life is meant to be? Come on, you're joking. It can't really be this good—could it? He was suspicious. Where's the punchline?

Taking a measure of things, he allowed a few drops of pride to seep in. He'd produced two smart, kind, and happy kids. With a little help from Becky—95 percent, give or take. Mostly give. Together they'd provided the best of everything, especially education, setting the kids up for a bright future. That alone made for a proper tombstone epitaph. There were no villains, really, in the Paddy and Becky story. Just two innocents who were mismatched and doing the best they could to survive from one day to the next. *Jesus,* he thought, *this is starting to sound a little too much like a Billy Joel song.* "Paddy and Becky had had it already by the summer of two thousand five." [22]

In all, he considered Becky to be an extraordinary young woman who, along with the usual blessings and challenges of marriage, had voluntarily taken on all his limitations and frustrations. *Is she batty?* he sometimes asked. "For better or worse," went the contract; until "worse" got too painful, went the caveat. Their "worse" had finally gotten too painful. Released from her self-inflicted prison cell, with his sincerest gratitude and blessings, and a little too generous an alimony check, in his humble opinion, Becky was off to reclaim her joy while he pushed ahead in pursuit of his own—both finding their own way to get by.

Patrick was suddenly doing a lot more than just getting by, though. Instead, he was in a sort of remarkable flow, feeling a sense of childlike euphoria. But he wasn't existing in a blind naiveté. Really, no joke, he was keeping his head screwed on straight. His life's experiences required him to retain a modicum of adult knowing that such states of bliss are vulnerable to passing in their due time. It never goes in a straight line in either direction, up or down. That's true of the stock market, certainly, and it's true of our states of emotion too. Within the volatile pathway forward, it all eventually returns to the mean—neither ecstasy nor despair. Somehow, we strive to retain our bliss in the mundane middle.

Whatever lay ahead, he was grateful for his good fortune, his bliss, on this day, and determined to revel in it despite the creep of his skeptic's voice.

The office continued to be a whirlwind of activity with Connelly in the eye of much of it. Disney raised their offer to $140 to fend off other suitors, and Cracker Barrel was officially added to their menu. Several unfamiliar blue suits fresh out of law school were roaming the passageways, spending most of their time behind closed doors with Saunders and Lawson. In their one interview with the primary suspect, they carried a dubious tone throughout. As if it were impossible to contemplate that he was telling the truth, that he'd simply gotten lucky. "We're on the same team, Patrick," they said. "It's a preliminary internal investigation, that's all." They assured him that if he cooperated, they were prepared to help. But if they caught him in a lie, they'd hand-deliver him to the Feds with no second thoughts.

Maybe he should have been more worried, but he couldn't fathom how they'd find anything. There wasn't anything to find. It was just a spate of good luck, he'd convinced himself. The incomprehensible kind. "And no one deserves it more than my clients," he told the detectives confidently.

They asked about the lunch he'd had at Cracker Barrel just ahead of the news. "Who is Larry Devlin?" they wanted to know.

"Just an old friend from bygone days. I asked him to lunch to catch up," he told them. "Since I was considering positioning the stock, we met at the local Cracker Barrel. It was jam-packed, and the food was delicious. I got even more excited about the idea."

"What's the point, Connelly?" Saunders blurted impatiently while putting his fingers together to form a point. This was something he'd do in office meetings to shame the imbecilic person who dared to speak.

A good way to forge loyalty, Patrick would think.

Flashing back the same derisive sign language, he said, "The point is, Jeff, the lunch bolstered my feelings about the stock, and the very next week, I got your approval and went to work on it. You remember me telling you about the lunch, don't you?"

"I remember warning you this better be on the up-and-up, and at the end of the day, it better be."

"At the end of the day?" he repeated snidely. "At the end of which day, Jeff? Do you mean the end of today or some future day? And if it's today, do you mean the end of the working day, like at six? Or once we've shut down for the night, maybe at nine? Or do you mean precisely at midnight?"

"It's an expression," snarled Saunders.

"Oh, thanks for clearing that up," he snapped back. "At the end of what day is making money for our clients a problem?"

"When it's done illegally."

"We're certainly in agreement there," he said. "By the way, has anyone tried the pancakes at Cracker Barrel? They're to die for." No one at the luminous faux-mahogany conference table was smiling.

"You should be taking this much more seriously, Connelly," Saunders warned. "This is career-ending stuff we're discussing, at the least."

"Please don't misunderstand, guys," he said in a serious tone now. "I'm sorry for all the bother, I really am. But I've done nothing wrong. And I feel good for my clients; they made some money."

"Not for long," cautioned Saunders as the legal team exiting the room pulled him along.

Soon after, Patrick called Larry Devlin to alert him. "Thanks for the head's up, Pat, but the blue suits can't touch me," he said. "I didn't buy a share of the stock—I'm sorry to say it completely slipped my mind."

"Thanks a lot, Larry. I should be offended," he said with a hearty laugh. "That's how much you value my stock ideas?"

"I've never been much for stock tips," he confessed. "But I've never had one work out like this either. Are you sure you're okay, Pat? You're clean, not in any trouble?"

"Of course, I'm clean; unless they take me down on some trumped-up charge, which I suppose is possible. They've been trying to get rid of me anyway."

"Stay safe, my friend. If I can help you with anything, let me know."

"You know I will. *Sláinte*, Larry."

He talked all of it over with Finnie: the newspaper, the merger, the compliance visit—and felt sorted out. Most importantly, she didn't think he was nuts regarding finding the future newspaper. Not able to explain it either, she no doubt believed in a magical universe. "I often rely on the stars to guide me," she told him. "Besides, anyone who wants something badly enough can attract it."

"So, in the same few weeks," he said. "I attracted the newspaper and the likes of you?"

"Anything's possible, dear. Good fortune comes from seeds planted years ago." She was lightly stroking his temples. "Now rest your weary mind. You think much too much." Her sharp fingernails raked across his skull to reinforce her point.

From the clench of his new companion, advisor, and confidante, he responded as best he could: "Those were some fertile seeds I must have planted."

"Speaking of that." She stood up and walked purposefully toward the master suite. Hot on her heels, he nearly ran her over in the endeavor.

"Would you wipe that shit-eating grin off your face, Pat?" said the other woman he spent most of his time with. "At least when guys who want to put us in jail are around?"

"That's not a very nice reference, Marie," he said through his shit-eating grin. "Maybe you should change that to 'pancake-eating grin'?"

"Schlemiel-schlimazel."

"Did someone spill soup?"

"What?"

"Nothing. I can't help how I feel Laverne, I mean Marie—*I'm sitting on a rainbow, lucky, and in love*," he crooned.

"And you can stop with all that crap too—you're making me gag." Her index finger was projecting into her open mouth, but in truth, she was thrilled to see the ebullient Paddy she hadn't seen in years.

The compliance officers camped out in the office were keeping everyone on edge. Even though it was Connelly in their crosshairs, everyone stayed out of the saloon when the sheriff was in town, busily cleaning up their own backyards. Or, in this case, their file drawers. Even the daily procession past his corner office had ceased—proving every ordeal has its blessings. But Saunders, or one of his sycophants, still had their methods to intrude on his brief period of repose. A caricature prominently posted in the lunchroom showed a guy in a wheelchair—*wonder who that could be*—sitting behind bars in an old country jail, strongly reminiscent of a Cracker Barrel storefront jailhouse. It was nicely done, including a sparkling Tinker Bell hovering over Cinderella's Castle in the background. The caption read, "Welcome to Connelly's Magic

Kingdom where Cheating isn't a Strategy." One redeeming thing he could say about Saunders, or whoever provided his graphic art, they certainly could draw.

Passing through enemy territory, Patrick saw King and said, "Hey, Ian, I saw Jeff's handiwork in the kitchen. Excellent job. Tell him I said he missed his calling by a country mile."

"How do you know it wasn't me? I minored in art at college."

"Jeez," Patrick replied, "another starving artist selling financial plans to put food on the table. What a heart-wrenching tale."

"Spare me your tears. By the way, I'm impressed—you sound cool and collected for someone about to crash and burn."

"I wouldn't be so sure, Ian," he said, glancing to the dozens of cardboard boxes stuffed with files and other junk lined up near Wolfe's desk. "You'd better lock up those files, Mia. I'd hate to see you get nabbed by compliance."

"Got it handled, Connelly," King shot back before she could open her mouth. "They'll be safe in their new home in a matter of days, we're guessing."

"Good luck with that," he parried. "By the way, as a special dispensation to the KW Group, I'm offering stock-picking advice for only two and twenty."

"How about if we get back to you on that? Once you're out of the slammer, that is."

As he moved on, Patrick's gloat was evident. Kind of a "pancake-eating" gloat.

Eager to be getting home, he bid Marie a good evening and headed down to the parking garage, stopping first in the public restroom on the lobby floor. Perched in the stall, he heard the door to the hallway swing open. The usual sounds of dress shoes tap-clapping across drab gray ceramic tile toward the urinal were absent. Oddly, there was no sound at all until the room suddenly filled with a low, slow hiss.

"Hello, who's there?" he called out. No response came, except for the hiss increasing in velocity to a resounding whoosh, like a jet taking off. "Who's there?" he called with more urgency.

His tunneled view under the ratty stall door revealed nothing as another more rapid whoosh filled the room. With no discernible smell of gas, he wondered what in hell was happening out there—a fire extinguisher, faulty air conditioner, a burst pipe? Breathing rapidly now, his fight or flight mechanism in full gear, he hoisted himself off the commode, leaned on the safety railings, and fumbled with his clothing to make himself decent. His problem, one of them at least, was when his self-protection instinct kicked in, he couldn't instantly take physical flight. Instead, his body moved in slow motion while his anxiety level soared. Another low, slow hiss was followed by another. He cried out a "Hello?" one last time before the fluorescent lighting snapped off, sending the room into pitch blackness. Propped awkwardly on his spasming legs, he slammed open the stall door and blindly groped for his locked and waiting wheelchair. Reaching in all directions, he found only air. Unsure what to do next, his decision was made for him when the lower body rigidity holding him upright released, causing his knees to buckle and sending him tumbling to the cold stone floor.

Lying prone, feeling panicky, he tried to remain calm and clear his head. "What the fuck is going on?" he roared, falling just short of calm. His elbow and wrist were signaling the hard landing, while his limited sensation below the waist made the distress he felt in his right hip and knee even more alarming. He wouldn't know until later the seriousness of his injuries. *For now, though, I just need to get the fuck off the floor.* He was practicing the art of prioritization.

In the dead quiet, a faint glow from inside the vacant stall seemed to intensify, allowing him to scan the room. *My cell phone?* he wondered. Several strides away in the far corner of the room, he saw his wheelchair pushed up against an industrial wash basin and tall waste basket. Rolling onto his left side, using his undamaged arm, he grabbed at tile as slick as the surface of an ice rink and inched his body towards the chair. Reaching the closest wheel, he spun the chair around to face him, gripped the front of its frame with both hands, and pulled up onto unsteady knees. *Relax,* he said to his racing mind, *you've done this a million times.* Then his shredded but still powerful shoulders took over, hoisting him up until he twisted his torso hard and landed safely in his seat, earning a 9.8 from the judges.

Flicking on the wall switch, shading his eyes against the sudden brightness, he pushed back towards the stall to recover his Tumi. The meaning of all the hissing and whooshing became immediately clear. His wounded wheelchair was sporting a flattened air cushion and four completely flattened tires.

25

ANCIENT TREASURES

Maureen was horrified to hear the story of the men's room assault as she tended to his injuries. There were no broken bones, just superficial bruises, and he had no proof of his assailant, so they decided to take no action. Not yet anyway. But Patrick well knew his accoster's identity, and those appalling few minutes in the dark, and his disabled wheelchair, would be seared into his psyche until some future time when he'd exact his revenge. He had no choice.

To ease his concern, take his mind off the incident, Finnie suggested he pay a visit to Kerry O'Connor's furniture warehouse. "He invited you, after all, and he'll appreciate the return of his pouch, I'm sure." While ancient and a bit eccentric, she considered him friendly and trustworthy. With a teasing turn, she then said,

"Besides, maybe it's time to fill this beautiful home with a few new treasures other than me."

"I just may do that," he replied with a laugh. Although his budget was tight, there were gaping holes to fill in his décor, and he loved the idea of perusing an old-world shop for just the right gift for his new, old-world beau. Not having courted a woman in decades, he hadn't the foggiest notion what that might be. But maybe he'd know it when he sees it.

It was Saturday, his favorite day of the week, in the early days of March, his favorite month. Finnie was working the lunch shift leaving him free until evening. It felt like the perfect time to pay Mr. O'Connor a visit. With the intriguing man's burgundy leather pouch and business card nestled in his Tumi, he motored away from SoSo.

The aesthetics deteriorated noticeably as he drove just a few blocks west along Southern. Bright tropical colors faded to chalky white on decaying buildings splattered with black mold and graffiti. "For Lease" signs were posted in clouded, barren, storefront windows above lifeless sidewalks. Stopped at a light, he signaled to a man in an oversized army green coat sitting with his back against a building. Clinging to the brown paper bag containing his entire world, he boosted himself off the ground with his free arm and ambled towards the van's open window. "Here," Patrick said while handing folded bills to him. "Please accept this, my good man, and enjoy a hearty meal."

"Why bless you, sir. Your good deed will not go unnoticed."

"Thank you, that's kind of you to say," he said, while gripping the man's hand. "I only wish I could do more."

The weather had become seasonably warmer, returning to the mean. *One less thing for the poor man to suffer this nighttime,* he thought. As the light turned green, he rolled forward with a wave to the innocuous figure returning to his hunched repose.

Glancing down at the business card in his lap, he crossed a set of rail tracks and made the first left into what looked like a warehouse district. Slowly winding past nondescript industrial buildings, he noted auto-repair and collision shops, swimming pool contractors, plumbing supplies, tractors, and riding mowers, and miscellaneous other businesses, before pulling in front of the pertinent address. Parking in the only wide blue guy spot, he made his way carefully across the broken, pebble-strewn blacktop. Large red letters painted on the gated window matched the card—*Antique Furniture Refinishing and Resale, Kerry O'Connor, Proprietor.*

The front door was locked, surprising given the noon hour, with a series of knocks finally bringing a small, white-haired man to the door. "Coming, coming, have you no patience, man?" he grumbled, fumbling to unlatch three bolts and pulling open the sturdy door. "Ah, Patrick Connelly, it's you. You've paid me a visit after all."

"Mr. O'Connor, it's a pleasure to see you again," he said with a warm grip of his hand.

"Kerry. My name is Kerry."

"Why, thank you, Kerry," he replied. "I've intended to come for a visit, and my good friend, Maureen Finn from Murphy's, gave me a little nudge this morning. So here I am, full of apologies for my lethargy."

"No apologies necessary, Patrick, you're here now. Maureen is a fine young woman. You are blessed to call her a good friend."

"I agree," he said, loosening his grip.

"Busy beating off the vultures, were you?"

"Well, yes, in a manner of speaking. I've been working to protect my interests, certainly—and enjoying some leisure time too, I must admit." *There was nothing wrong with the craftsman's memory,* he thought.

Moving through the doorway, he blinked rapidly while adjusting to the dusky space. Candlelight afforded a dull amber glow to the dark-trussed open ceiling and wide-planked wooden floor. And all the in-betweens. There was a workbench filled with artisan tools against the far wall. A black trestle table—Irish peasant design—sat in front of a massive stone hearth. A thick black chain hanging at its center held a large round iron pot. Nick-nacks galore were piled up on long shelves lining the walls. The only evidence of a retail shop was a glass-encased cabinet with an old-style cash register on the countertop positioned to his right, adjacent to the front door.

Kerry ushered him over to the hearth-front table, where several multi-hued clay jars were animated by the dancing candlelight. As the gentle sound of a piper warmed the medieval space, Patrick was reminded of the eighteenth-century thatched roof cottage he'd seen in Bunratty's folk village. His Celtic heart was once again captivated. Reaching for two cut crystal stemmed glasses, Kerry offered his guest a pour from the taller clay jar, which he readily accepted. The glass was heavy, and the golden brown drink viscous with a toasty nut finish. A fine whiskey of some sort, he guessed. A loaf of crusty bread and a bowl of butter were put out to accompany the drink.

"Delicious—thank you, Kerry. The glass is Waterford?"

"No, Patrick, not as famous, but equally useful."

He raised his glass, toasting his warm host and the beauty of the crystal with its tongue-coating nectar. Kerry told of his modest upbringing in a farmhouse outside Sligo, north of Galway on the Wild Atlantic Way. "Yeats Country," he called it. "This room harkens back to my family cottage—a bit of nostalgia, I suppose—and a connection to a simpler, happier time." He learned the craft of furniture restoration from his father, he said, and it became his life's work.

Patrick spoke of things he hadn't thought about in years, or at least since their first engagement in Murphy's: his early years in the Bronx and its northern suburbs; his brilliant and loving tyrant of a father, Seamus, and his blessed mother, Eleanor; his sports, the injuries, the emotional recoveries; his marriage and children; his tremulous career; his love of culture and all things Irish. He touched on it all. "Damn it, Kerry, the whiskey has loosened these pitiable lips once again. I'm boring you with too many tales of long ago and far away."

"Nonsense, my boy. I'm enraptured with every word."

"You're much too kind." *This man was also a damn good listener,* he thought. Remembering the pouch, he pulled it out and said,

"You left this at the table the night we met. I've been eager to return it."

"Why, thank you, Patrick. A rare breed you are—a man of honor; and an unintended thief, I'm afraid." He was rocking back and chortling while giving his knee a vigorous slap.

"Thief!" he cried out. "What do you mean?"

"The contents of the pouch were intended as payment for my night's consumption. On my next visit, I was informed I'd skipped out on the bill, so took care of it then."

"Oh, for Christ's sake," he said, turning burgundy to match the pouch. "I am so sorry. Well, here, at least you have it back now." He reached to put the pouch in the old man's hand.

"No, no," he insisted. "Please keep it as a small token of my esteem."

"I couldn't, Kerry."

"I really do insist," he said with a raise of his thick white eyebrows. "See here?" Patrick's eyes followed his finger to the side of the pouch. "My business is engraved into the leather."

"Ever the crafty businessman, I see." He laughed and slipped the pouch back into his Tumi saying, "Thank you again, my good friend."

"It's nothing, Patrick."

"Speaking of the business," he said, straightening up in his chair. "May I see these antiques and fine furnishings I've heard so much about? I have empty spaces to fill at home and a new love to consider as well."

"Oh yes, I should show you around the plant, shouldn't I," he said matter-of-factly while jumping up to begin tidying the table. Latching the front door, he motioned for his guest to follow him to the dark corner behind the fireplace and through the low passageway.

Entering a room set alight by a dozen iridescent chandeliers mounted high from exposed trusses, Patrick stopped in his tracks. "Oh, my word, Kerry," he exclaimed. "*This* is your 'little antique business'?"

He was gazing around a space five times the size he'd imagined from the exterior of the building. As cavernous as Harry Potter's Great Hall at Hogwarts, it was filled with layers of furniture from golden oaks to deep browns to charred reds to blacks in showroom settings as far as his eye could see. They began to move methodically through wide aisles, with Kerry narrating a kind of centuries-old tour. There were grand poster beds and sleigh beds with decorative headboards; nightstands and bedside tables with white marble tops; tall, mirrored wardrobes, stately armoires, and Scotch chests. Many pieces were elaborately carved with scrolls and vines and shells, majestic animal heads and masks, and grotesque-looking goblins. The base of one dresser looked like a powerful animal poised to charge forward. "Eagles and lions and ghouls, oh my," Patrick mimicked lyrically.

"These pieces are mostly from the 18th century and uniquely Irish," Kerry said. "Much of earlier Irish antiquity was destroyed."

"Destroyed? How?"

"By the never-ending occupations in medieval and later times," he answered. "Our forests were ravaged, destroyed by greed, and our homes were looted and burned to the ground. The finest surviving manor houses and castles were bequeathed to English or Scottish settlers, along with the farmland."

"How heartbreaking."

"Yes, the suffering was incalculable, and the history lost can never be recovered."

"Shameful."

"No doubt. But human resilience always wins out, Patrick. A new generation of notable furniture makers and wood carvers emerged in 18th century Cork, Dublin, and Limerick: Kirkhoffer, Houghton, Kelly, Booker, Wisdom, Hearn, Pearce, Cranfield, Strahan, and Locke are some of the more notable names."

"I'm ashamed to say not even one rings a bell."

"You're not alone. Most of Ireland's best craftsmen worked in obscurity. It was different in the kingdom, where a golden age of artistry was well underway, and the great Georgians were becoming famous around the world."

"Georgians?"

"The reigns of the Georges—I, II, and III—make up the Georgian period. Its influence on architecture and design is without parallel. Names such as Chippendale, Heppelwhite, Adam, Shearer, and Sheraton remain much sought after today.

"Even I've heard of Chippendale," he said with a gleam. "Aren't they a team of male dancers?"

"Unfortunately, yes." Kerry had an exasperated look. "But before that, Thomas Chippendale was a fine cabinet maker. Because of him and other masters, remarkable pieces were being crafted with a distinctly Irish flair. Most are in private collections and museums, and a few are sitting here before your eyes."

Trying his best to extinguish the image of Chris Farley auditioning for a Chippendales dancing role, Patrick said, "Why are there so many carvings of animals and otherworldly creatures?"

"Ah, the Irish flair." Kerry lit up. "More than their counterparts, these craftsmen, or their commissions, were interested in the natural world, the mysteries of the forest, and the unseen world. Some of the figures are from popular mythology and tell stories of courage and heroism, others pay homage to mysticism, and some were just playful. But each artist was reaching for something magnificent."

"They certainly hit their mark," his guest said with admiration.

Continuing the tour, they came upon dining tables, chairs, sideboards, and bread and tea cabinets. One long banquet table came with enough slat-back upholstered chairs to seat at least thirty. It was set with tall candelabras and serving trays of silver and pewter, woven china tableware adorned with shamrocks, and fine diamond-cut crystal glassware as if an elegant state dinner were about to take place.

"Expecting the prime minister?"

"One never knows, my boy," Kerry said with a glint. "Staging helps the buyer see the piece in their own home."

"You mean mansion."

"Yes," he agreed. "This piece is destined for the Isle of Castles across the bridge to the east."

"Isle of Castles. Clever—I like it," Patrick said with a nod. "Why is so much of the furniture so dark? Black even?"

"Many started their lives with a tawny color—yew or oak—or a rich mahogany red," Kerry answered. "Think of the times, though. The open hearths were the center of family life where bodies were warmed, children were taught their lessons, and meals were prepared and eaten. Later in the evening, it's where the music, the stories, the whiskey, and the laughter resided."

"First the whiskey," he countered. "Then the music and stories and laughter. Then more whiskey."

"Correct," he said with a knowing wink. "The hearth was the center of family life from sun to sun."

"Food and light and heat. It makes perfect sense."

"So, to your question: the furniture surrounding the hearths would be coated in black smoke and soot, especially in the days before chimneys were properly designed. Layers of varnish and wax would seal in its chronicle for perpetuity. Thus, black is a consistent feature of Irish furniture and an apt companion to its troubled history."

Patrick listened now in thoughtful silence. Next came tall secretaries and fine-looking writing desks with soft leather tops, framed by giant ornate bookcases filled with old books. He was immediately smitten, saying, "Any one of these would certainly enhance a home's library."

"Ah, Patrick—you have a good eye. The writing desk is considered the Rolls Royce of Irish ingenuity and craftsmanship."

"Why is that?"

"With their love of all things literary, these were the most requested and honored pieces. The carvers took special pride in their creation."

"Who could afford these gorgeous pieces," Patrick asked, "then or now?"

"An aristocratic family," his host responded. "Everything you've seen, the lavish mahogany and rosewood inlay, the exceptional carvings, and other appointments, were only afforded by the gentry, who became less and less of the population."

"Ireland's 'one-percenters'?"

"So to speak."

"The rest were middle class or poor?"

"Follow me, Patrick. If I'm going to give you a brief history lesson, we may as well visit a pub."

Kerry zig-zagged his guest through the maze until stopping at a square pub table in dark, distressed mahogany. Moving aside one of the chairs, Patrick soaked in the setting. It rivaled anything he'd seen in the Temple Bar district in Dublin.

A burnt oak-paneled bar centered the space, with high relief carvings of grapevines and festoons highlighted by a Bacchus mask. By his count, there were a dozen stools, allowing would-be patrons entry to the variegated copper bar top. Whiskey bottles, jars, and assorted barware filled shelves lining the mirrored backing. To the side sat large cabinets and wine coolers stacked with vintage French and Australian wine bottles, pewter tankards, and other accouterments. It was a fully decorated Irish pub room including game tables, a dart board, and an Irish National flag.

"This is astounding," he said. "Impossible to fathom." With a laugh, he added, "And it's making me thirsty again."

"It's not your fault. I shouldn't be teasing you so." Kerry moved behind the bar and reached for pint glasses. "What is your preference?"

"Insofar as?"

"Guinness, Harp, or Smithwick's?"

"Are you kidding? I'll take a Smithwick's, please." Kerry drew a perfect pint for his guest and one for himself.

"*Sláinte*, Patrick," he said, handing him the ice-cold red ale and hoisting himself onto a barstool.

"*Sláinte* to you, bartender," he responded while incredulously raising his glass to his fantastical host.

Taking a modest draw, Kerry began his history lesson with the telling of Britain's invasion of Ireland in 1160. Famed Irish king, Brian Boru, had finally defeated the Vikings near Dublin. The battle cost the king his life. Soon after, Great Britain put the thumb firmly down on their "homeland." For the next five hundred years, give or take a millennium, England ruled Ireland as a separate kingdom, especially along their eastern coast. Then, in 1603, Northern Ireland's kingdom of Ulster was finally conquered. The Catholic majority watched with venom as their rightful lands were parceled out to Scottish farmers and other invaders who'd supported the throne.

"How do you just give away what isn't rightfully yours?"

"It's called imperialism, Patrick," Kerry answered. "It's happened throughout all recorded time. Irish families were forced to pay rent for properties they rightfully owned, and they worked the land for a pittance."

"Brutal. Disheartening," growled Patrick. "I can't imagine." His mind awakened to the modest parallels in his own life—the ongoing invasion of his own homestead. He could imagine a smidgen of such brutality after all.

After freshening their glasses, Kerry picked up the tale just after the English Civil War of 1640, when Oliver Cromwell's army invaded Ireland. Needing money to pay his troops, he gave them Ireland's most fertile farmland instead, hanging the resistors and sending their children away to indentured servitude, meaning slavery, in Jamaica and elsewhere. This vignette only grazes the brutality of the heinous Cromwell, a nearly unparalleled war criminal. After the infamous 1691 Battle of the Boyne, where Protestant King William III defeated the Catholics, the English declared supreme rule.

"I saw it firsthand, Kerry."

"You're older than I imagined," he smirked.

"I feel like it some days," Patrick responded. "I mean when I toured Belfast last year—I saw the residual unrest up close. Every first weekend in July, the Protestants—the Orange Order, they call themselves—celebrate Boyne by burning huge bonfires and parading thunder bands, pounding percussion, through Catholic neighborhoods looking to incite a violent response. More than three hundred years later, for Christ's sake, they're still taunting their old foes."

"Old resentments die hard," Kerry said, as Patrick closed his eyes in dizzy contemplation of the day.

The 18th century didn't go any better for the Irish, Kerry reported. Many unfortunates were transported to the rocky, wind-whipped Atlantic coastland in Connaught, where they struggled to survive. Periodic revolts against colonial rule were put down in bloody fashion. The Acts of Union in 1800 created the United Kingdom and affirmed British control over Ireland. The largely Catholic population had their remaining freedoms and much of their lands stripped from them.

"Getting to the meat of your question, Patrick," Kerry said, "only those beholden to the crown owned the richest lands with their plentiful crops and livestock. These luxurious furnishings populated the finest manor houses which were no longer owned by Irish natives."

"That's so awful, Kerry—sickening. It sounds eerily like early American settlers routing the native people from their lands."

"The parallels are clear: the first Americans were largely European, many from England, I needn't remind you." Motioning it was time to move along, he said, "There's more to see, my boy."

"If most of these fine furnishings were owned by British invaders," Patrick asked, "why even trade in reminders of such humiliation?"

"It's more complicated than that," Kerry replied. "Many of these pieces were made by the hands of Irish cabinet makers and Irish-owned at one time, and many of the occupiers were honorable people who helped build the Irish culture. All through our history, we've been nothing if not a true melting pot."

"That's heartening to hear."

"And in any case, this furniture is a vital part of our history and in high demand by collectors of all nationalities." He pointed ahead and said, "Let's take a look at this same period in a sharp contrast."

As they moved deeper into the warehouse, Patrick thought of his drive west along Southern Boulevard. Block by block, leaving behind the finely crafted and decorated homes for those simpler, more downtrodden. Homes where function and protection against the elements trumped summer kitchens, guest cottages, and three-zone air conditioners hidden in the lush tropical landscape. Homes where the finest appointments had to do with survival and nothing more.

The furnishings they came upon told such a story: modest rectangular table and chair sets, low cabinets with keys dangling from locks, high-backed settles and settle beds, four-poster canopy beds, butter churns, and chicken coops—all made of simple woods in various shades of black with no hints of artistry. Sturdy and serviceable. In a way, Patrick found them more attractive than their elaborate predecessors. He was born in the Bronx, after all.

"Some of these were made for one and two-room thatched cottages," his guide instructed. "And some were servants' quarters furnishings in the basements of fine manor houses."

What these pieces lacked in lavishness was made up in their ingenuity, he was told. Careful thought was given to preserving the little raw material they had. Much of the wood was softer and more petrified, often recovered from the bogs, and the finished product had dual purposes: Canopy beds would protect against drafts and drips of water and bugs falling from the thatched roofs. Benches by day would convert into beds after dark. Three-legged stools somehow sat evenly on hard-packed, bowing mud floors.

Many of the pieces were made to fit along walls or in corners to preserve precious space. Cabinets were cleverly designed to protect perishable foods from the elements. Front doors could be taken from their hinges and used as a table or a dance floor.

"These are some of the rarest in the warehouse," Kerry informed him while pointing down the row. "In the worst years of the famine, the 1840s, most were burned for heat so they could stay alive for another day."

"Just heartbreaking," Patrick said, stifling welling tears.

Near the back of the vast warehouse, Kerry stopped at several rows of church pews facing what appeared to be a genuine marble alter. "Churches are losing favor in some places and gaining in others," he explained. "I'm an intermediary, and it's a surprisingly robust business."

"Well, thank the Lord for that," Patrick said, looking for acknowledgment of his unparalleled wit. It wasn't forthcoming. Feeling like a ravenous kid in Willie Wonka's Chocolate Factory, bloated with history, he continued, "I must say, Kerry, I'm at a loss for words, which I needn't tell you is quite the feat."

Resting in a coffee-speckled oak pew, Kerry spoke of his friends and relations all over Ireland and the UK and how he buys inventories from vacant farm homes, bed and breakfasts, restaurants, pubs, manor houses, and even the odd castle. "The smoking ban in public houses closed down half of the pubs," he explained, "and then the real estate bust hit Ireland hard; container after container of new supply has been rolling in the last several years."

"The bust was much worse than even here in the States," Patrick agreed. "I saw vacant buildings, shuttered pubs, properties for auction everywhere. The entire town of Lisdoonvarna seemed to be for sale; it was a lovely, picturesque village."

"It breaks my heart, it does," Kerry replied. "Not much use for the matchmaking business anymore, I'm afraid."

"It's all done online now. I was thinking Match.com should buy the whole town. It would be pocket change for them, and it would make a good promotion—combining the ancient ways with the modern. The annual festival could have their corporate name."

"Clever idea."

"Thanks. Becky used to call me 'the idea guy.' It wasn't meant as a compliment. It was code for, 'Will you please shut the blank up?' Or something to that effect."

"Ah, the blessings of marriage."

"Yes, a global challenge, it appears," he chuckled. "But the real estate market will come back—it always does. Especially a charming little village on the road from Galway to Killarney."

"You're a bit of a matchmaker yourself, Patrick, and I agree with your prognosis. There are signs of recovery everywhere."

"That's wonderful to hear," he replied. "So, who buys all your inventory?"

"I ship all over the world, but the vast wealth right here in Palm Beach and South Florida is never-ending. It's no different today than in the Gilded Age."

"I've said the same thing," he exclaimed. "There's no doubt we're in a modern-day Gilded Age. Astonishing wealth accumulating to just a small handful, fueled by technology, information, and free money."

"You're correct, Patrick," he agreed. "And too many have been left out of the miracle. Whether our prosperity is modest or great, we owe those suffering from lack our earnest attention—whatever we can do to lift their spirits and quality of life."

"Hear, hear!" he said, lightly applauding his host. "And first on the list is providing better educational opportunities to those shut out, so they can prosper without charity. If we don't, we'll meet with a severe day of judgment, I'm afraid."

"I couldn't agree more." Lifting off the pew and pointing wearily to yet another low door in a darker corner still, he said, "There's one more room I want you to see."

Using a set of keys to unlock the fortress-like entry, Kerry led his guest through yet another threshold. Moving quickly to the right, he flicked on a light switch to reveal the most splendid room yet. Before Patrick's disbelieving eyes was a living replica of a library and music room, like an old country manor house museum. The walls were lined with soaring built-in bookcases filled with impeccably kept leather-bound books. On an immense oriental rug of muted yellows, greens and burgundies sat the finest examples of furniture he'd ever seen. No less than those which populate Palm Beach's Whitehall mansion, Henry Flagler's turn-of-the-century home-turned-museum. But Whitehall sits on five acres of some of the most valuable waterfront property in all the world. This was a warehouse in a non-descript industrial district far west of the tracks.

Confounded, he blinked his eyes to take it all in. Finely polished musical instruments—string, wind, and percussion—were sitting on lustrous tables throughout the room. Among them were fiddles, mandolins, flutes, tin whistles, accordions, uilleann pipes, bodhrans, and a prominent baby grand piano. Half a dozen fine chairs and small sofas were set for sitting and playing or simply listening. One long table displayed antique gramophones with vinyl record albums lining the shelves underneath.

Closing his eyes, he dreamily imagined a scene from Yeats's Galway or Joyce's Dublin. "My good lord, Kerry, I'm flabbergasted—this is truly superlative."

Finally, his eye went to the far corner where an embroidered stool was poised next to an elegant green and gold harp nestled on a low table. They were all in miniature as if built for children. The rest of the room disappeared instantly, like when you encounter the finest piece of art in a museum—the piece you take home in your heart.

Imagining his diminutive Maureen gracing the stool and expertly strumming the strings, he knew then he'd be leaving this magnificent old-world warehouse with this magnificent harp. At whatever the cost.

26

THE CONNELLY REGISTRY

He hadn't planned on spending money on furnishings, especially money he didn't have in the discretionary bucket, but he couldn't resist. He wished the entire nineteenth-century Irish cottage could've been transported home. Besides, the prices Kerry quoted were beyond reasonable. Nearly incredulous. Several pieces were arranged for delivery the following afternoon, and Patrick wanted it to be a surprise. His home, so homey of late, would soon receive another injection.

The next afternoon, Maureen was called into Murphy's as an emergency replacement. Disappointed, with a big hug, he said, "Get home as soon as you can."

A Christmas Eve kind of anticipation adorned the day, and he knew Santa would soon be pulling up in his sleigh. Or rather, it was a mid-sized truck with a car trailing behind that slowed down and stopped in front of his home. Out jumped two young, burly, bearded elves in tweed caps, followed by a pint-sized version of Santa. The gang from the antique warehouse had arrived.

"Right on time, Kerry," he said while shaking each of their hands. "Hello, gentlemen. Thanks again for doing this on a Sunday."

"Pleasure to be of service, Patrick. Beautiful neighborhood. A step up from just so-so, I'd say."

"Damn it, man, its value descends with every reference," he retorted with a laugh. Showing them in, they proceeded to their work. "I was hoping Maureen would be here," he said to Kerry. "But she's been called into Murphy's."

"It'll make for a nice surprise when she arrives home." He was wielding a measuring tape and peeking around corners. "My, my; you are needing an infusion of character now, aren't you?"

"Are you speaking of the home or its owner?" He gave a light-hearted eyebrow raise.

"Just the home, Patrick," came his chuckled response. "We'll do what we can to elevate it to match its fine landlord."

"That shouldn't be much of a challenge," he said with a laugh.

Home designs inspired by Addison Mizner often featured one-room deep living areas with surrounding breezeways encouraging cross-ventilation, and the SoSo home was no exception. The doors and windows were thrown open to welcome in the mild Florida winter day. Leading his guest through tall double-doors into the oversized den, Kerry scanned the lofted, beamed ceiling before descending to the wide-planked, beveled wooden floor and all the in-betweens.

"Ah, the heartbeat of the residence is before my eyes," he said.

To his left were tall, decorative French doors capped by arching windows looking out through a breezeway to the lushly landscaped entertainment area, including a swimming pool, summer kitchen, and guest cottage. Defining the corner beyond the doors were built-in shelves filled with hardcover books, record albums, pictures of the kids, and fresh flower arrangements courtesy of his enchanting housemate. The far wall's centerpiece was a limestone hearth framed with bright tiles of turquoise and rose-yellow crowned with a substantial wood-carved mantel. The wall beyond the fireplace featured a bank of bright windows looking out to the front and balancing the French doors.

The social attraction was sitting across from the den's entrance: an oak-paneled bar with four complementary stools. Behind its hammered-copper bar were shelves lined with whiskey bottles and glassware. The smoky mirrored backdrop drew in natural light while seeming to multiply the collection. Below the counter sat a sink and two coolers holding an assortment of wine, craft beer, and anything else a guest might think to request. Two flat-panel TV screens were placed strategically so not to miss the games of interest from wherever your location. Nearby was a brown leather chair, cozy and worn, a brass reading lamp and side table. A quaint resting place for when the day had been accomplished. The various wood trims and moldings throughout the room were stained light chestnut, connecting these assorted entities into one synergistic living space—a charming pub room filled with his books and music and sports and memories.

"Why ever leave?" Kerry asked admiringly.

"To pay the bills, my friend," he said with an affectionate pat of his narrow shoulders. "What can I offer you from the bar?"

"Whatever the proprietor is serving will be delightful, I'm sure."

Moving in behind the counter, he sorted through the bottles and filled two crystal glasses with a golden brown libation. Handing one to his guest, he said, "I went straight to the top shelf for my good and generous friend."

"*Sláinte*, Patrick. Oh my, and a delicious shelf it is."

"*Sláinte*." Patrick paused to consider the assortment of oak and honey and spice flavors lingering on his tongue. "Wow, that is special; it's hard to fathom this Knappogue Castle has been alive longer than I've been; a true treasure with a history that can add meaning to life."

"I agree," Kerry said. "That's the fascinating part of the antique business, as we discussed at some length back at the shop; furnishings have their own history—a story to tell of the time-period, and especially the people who prepared the bread and stew on their tables, recorded their lives with quill and parchment at their desks, read books by oil-lit lamps, stored their clothing in their armoires, danced on their front doors, and slept and died in their beds."

"Any deaths recorded in, or around, the items I purchased?"

"Not to my knowledge, Patrick."

"Probably just as well," he said with a twinkle, wondering just how much of the previous owners come along with the furnishings. Nodding toward the men busy laboring with an especially large piece in the hallway, he asked, "I wonder if there'll be enough room on that one's registry for a Connelly?"

"I'm certain there will be, Patrick, and many happy times it will record," he said with raised glass, "I wish you all the best."

"Thank you, Kerry," he replied with a soft clink. "This is a good day."

To the percussive piping of The Chieftains [23], Kerry directed his men to move this piece over here, that table there, take this desk out to another room, burn that one for fuel. "But I bought it many years ago just before we were married," Patrick protested. "What about that history?"

"Its history will now include my dropping it off at a thrift shop where it will be well appreciated," Kerry said with a smile. "Frankly, I'm surprised it lasted this long."

"Ouch."

Historic specimens new to the Connelly registry arrived at a steady pace. A commanding oak wardrobe with scalloping mirrored doors and a harmonizing nightstand now adorned the once sparse master bedroom. It would soon be in service to the beloved lady of the house. Through the den doors came a walnut writing desk inset with rich green leather trimmed in gold leaf. This superlative piece was positioned so the writer could see in any direction of interest: to the den's entrance, the bar, the sitting area by the fireplace, and the prism of the natural world beyond the beveled and pitted glass. Choose your inspiration. It proved to be a seamless complement to the room. Also arriving was an old-fashioned phonograph he'd transported from the music room at the back of the warehouse.

A few pieces from the "peasant collection" now found their new home. One whose story he couldn't resist sat in the foyer: a long, narrow, double-leafed serving table from the 19th century. As the story goes: due to disease, lack of medicines, starvation, and conflict, untimely deaths were too common an occurrence. The table was designed to double as a serving space in happy times and a coffin holder in darker days.

While Patrick wasn't expecting a casket anytime soon, the thought of holding a memorial service for one especially noxious person did come to mind, followed by asking for God's forgiveness, which was a fairly regular practice.

The signature piece, the harp, came in last. In the far corner near the fireplace, an oval rug was rolled out over the bare planks. Then the embroidered stool was placed just so. Finally, the jewel-green, black-trimmed instrument was unwrapped and set on its accompanying mahogany black table. Patrick sat nearby, examining his prize. [24] The high-headed traditional Irish harp featured hand-painted clusters of gold shamrocks decorating the frame, ivory knobs on the column holding white gut strings in their proper place, and brass knobs at the top and bottom for an old leather strap. About three feet in height, Kerry had called it "a Royal Portable from the early 19th century—the romantic Regency Era when harp music filled the drawing rooms of Dublin, London, and country manor houses across the kingdom." A brass plate at the bottom was inscribed, "John Egan, 30 Dawson Street, Dublin."

He went on to say that in 1792, a Belfast Harp Festival generated tremendous enthusiasm for the instrument. Egan then made a revolutionary design change by retaining the shape of the ancient Irish harp but building his smaller and lighter with rounded back sound boxes and adorned with iconic Celtic images. His were gut-strung and tuned to E-flat to create a softer, sweeter tone meant to accompany the singing so customary to the people. Egan was named harp maker to His Majesty George IV in 1821, and even so, the instrument was gaining in popularity in middle-class homes for the first time. He constructed about two thousand harps in total, Kerry said, and only eighty or so were known to exist today, mostly in museums and private collections.

Hearing this and gazing at its splendor, Patrick said, "Jesus, Kerry, you sold me a museum-worthy piece of Irish history at a fraction of its value. Are you sure the price was acceptable?"

"Absolutely, Patrick. I paid a fair price, did a bit of restoring, and then sold it for a fair profit. That's my business." With a wink, he then said, "I do recommend insuring it at several times the price you paid, though, just to be certain."

They sat at the bar over a second pour of the Knappogue '51, drinking in the Irish history now replete throughout the room. The Chieftains' pipes and harp were enduring and lovely. Glancing up, he was startled to see his antique dealer friend with tin whistle in hand and mouth, deftly playing along with the reel. He sat back in silence, enchanted by the music, the room, the whiskey, the mysterious newspaper, and the fairytale turn of events that had delivered two such delightful sprites into his life.

In his mystical trance, Patrick had dismissed all matters of business, especially thoughts of his difficulties at the office. But a sobering glance at the clock warned that the typically disquieting Sunday evening was at hand, and the tangible threat came rushing in on a turbulent stream. He saw Saunders's face, heard his threatening voice, "Turn off that shitty music, Connelly, and roll yourself the hell out of our home. This all belongs to me and KW now."

"Patrick? You look quite troubled suddenly. Is everything okay?"

"Oh, I'm sorry, Kerry," he said woozily. "My mind drifted a moment to the business day ahead, re-engaging with my nemesis." Kerry sat silent, encouraging him to continue. "Too soon, it'll be back to the game of daily survival."

"It's the game we all must play," he agreed.

"No different, I suppose, than when this desk was crafted, and this harp." Patrick was pointing to his new furnishings. "With their stout spirits, our forefathers built sound lives until vicious barbarians came along and looted all they'd achieved—their land, their wealth, maybe even their lives."

"That's true, and people haven't changed much with the passing of time," Kerry added. "We're all made of the same stuff."

"But the more aggressive of the lot have the advantage, I think," Patrick said. "Or, maybe they're just the extroverts. They have no fear, it seems, and play by a different set of rules, or maybe no rules. They thrive in conflict and conquest."

"Predators do flourish in such a world," Kerry granted.

"Well, I certainly don't." His voice was agitated now. "I'm the prey, and I don't do aggression well. I'm not sure I can hold them off."

After accepting another short pour, Kerry said, "I understand your worries, Patrick. But I see a different person, one with all he needs to win the day. You've seen much worse in your time and risen above it all."

"Maybe," he said with a faraway look. "But that was long ago."

"Believe me," Kerry continued, "the quiet ones, the introverts, in their passivity often have the advantage. While the others are acting without thinking first, without considering the broader impacts, you're doing the opposite."

"Christ, Kerry, that's what Marie, my colleague at the office, says all the time. But she calls it something different. I think 'slothful' is the word I'm looking for."

"They can look the same," Kerry said with a chuckle. "But in your repose, your quick mind and eloquent tongue, and your valiant and kind heart—the Irishman's trinity if you will—are always at work, making you a formidable opponent. You just need to believe it, and hone the rust off your sword, sharpen it up,"

"Why, thank you, Kerry," he said. "I appreciate your kind words, and I think I'll write that down. It'll be my new affirmation."

"You do that, Patrick. Your greatest weapon, for or against you, is what you believe and say about yourself."

"Jesus, Kerry. I'm stealing that one too."

"And while you're doing that, I'll make my departure." With a final wetting of the lips, he moved toward the den's double-doors. "Thank you for a lovely afternoon and do enjoy your new treasures."

"Hang on a second, Kerry. Let me get you a bottle of water and accompany your departure with a suitable song." After handing him the water, he tapped on his iPad, and they both turned their attention to the rafters and the mass suffering of the poor and hungry, both across the globe and on their doorstep, praying it will come no more. [25]

Resting an elbow on his new foyer table, Patrick bid his delightful friend a good night with a promise to look for him at Murphy's and visit his shop again soon.

"There's one more thing I should tell you," Kerry said, pausing at the front door. "In the 5th century, under profoundly more difficult circumstances than ours, St. Patrick taught the children of Ireland a valuable lesson. One you should consider today."

"My pen is at the ready."

"Patrick taught that it is possible to be brave in the face of mortal danger, and yet be a person of peace." While the current day, non-St. Patrick leaned on the table scribbling away, Kerry continued: "In the worst of pagan times, Patrick neither feared death nor desired to harm another human being. Instead, his fearless courage had taken hold. Let us always seek to live in this great man's aroma of peace."

"Beautifully said, Kerry. But how do you stay peaceful when someone is out to destroy you? How would you survive?"

"A peaceful mind is a clear-thinking mind, *Patrick*," he said. "The Irishman's trinity is only accessible to the clear thinker; and remember this: If your heart is in the right place, as yours is, you will never be alone. I assure you, help will always be available."

"Thank you, my good friend. You are a true blessing—a gift from God."

27

MOJO RISING

Finnie came home after he'd gone to sleep and nestled in next to him, keeping his dreams graceful. The following morning, having no desire to rush off to the office, he lingered in her healing entwine. She was thrilled with the new wardrobe and nightstand, the full-length mirror, the fragrance of the wood, and the ancient nooks and crannies, while lightly chastising him for spending undue money on her.

"I needed furniture anyway, Finnie," he reasoned. "You can't keep living from a suitcase when you're here, and besides, Kerry's prices were too good to pass up."

"Since you're doing it mostly for you," she acquiesced, "I'll enjoy it."

"Maybe it'll be an incentive to move some of your things over here, you know, more permanently," he said hesitantly. "All you've left here are a cap, a sweater, an apron, and a few other things. They keep me company when you're away, but I could use an expanded inventory—particularly undergarments."

"You're so sweet, I think," she scolded.

"It's your fault, Finndoll; you've dredged my naughtiness from some deep, hidden bog," he said from his nuzzle. Releasing her suddenly, he headed down the extended hallway making the sharp left and into the den. "Follow me. I have something else to show you."

Trailing him, she hesitated at the doorway and fixed her eyes instantly on the prize sitting in front of the hearth. "Oh, Patrick, what a beautiful harp. Are you mad?"

"Well, in a word, yes, but the moment I saw it, an image of you sitting at it, playing it, came to me. Isn't that silly?"

She had already hurried past him and was sitting down on the little stool, extending her arms, lining things up with her hands, measuring her reach to the instruments' frame. Looking back at him intently, she said, "No, Patrick, it's not silly at all." With that, she began lightly strumming the strings, emitting a series of notes which enchanted the silence. The sound then scaled to something like the gentle beginning of a symphony. [26]

He moved closer, intermittently closing his eyes to match her melody, soaking in her mastery. When she paused, he hesitated, so not to interrupt the ensuing timbre of quiet, before saying, "Will wonders never cease."

Sitting in the kitchen later over their tea, she asked, "How did you know? How did you select the most perfect gift?" Her voice was that of a giddy child on Christmas morning.

"I didn't even think," he said from his dreamy state. "I just saw the harp and knew."

"Your intuition is genius—you should always trust it."

"I'll take that under consideration, Finnster."

Her mother taught her to play the harp as a child, she said, and in the evening, they'd gather around the hearth with their instruments and join in song until the fire waned. A detectable break in her voice surfaced as she recalled her youth. He could have held her hand all day listening to her sweet murmurings. But as it was nearing the noon hour, he reluctantly readied to leave for the office.

"And I'll be off to the den," she said with a smile. "Oh, I nearly forgot." Digging through her bag, she handed him a copy of *The Irish Times*, the national newspaper of Ireland. "This was left at Murphy's last night; I thought you'd enjoy it." With a sheepish laugh, she then said, "It's not quite the gift you gave me."

"Of course, it is. I'll enjoy it thoroughly, and I love you for thinking of me." After a kiss and a promise to get home early, he stuffed the paper in his Tumi and headed out the door.

"Well, look who it is. Good evening, Pat."

"Top of the afternoon to you, dearest Marie," he said while pausing at her desk. "Did anyone miss me?"

"Here are your messages," she said, handing him a small stack. "Things are pretty quiet. The compliance geeks must have left on Friday; The gnat pack is back to passing by every hour."

"I'm sorry to disappoint them by continuing to breathe."

"No joke, Pat. We'd better watch our backs. Saunders had a tech guy here this morning looking at the wiring, the outlets, measuring for a TV monitor, the whole deal. They're coming after our space and not even bothering to pretend."

"Bring it on, barbarians," he said defiantly.

"Barbara who?"

"Just an ancient name for evil bullies," he answered. "I promise you this, kiddo, I'm not going down without the fight of their lives. I've got a kind of mojo rising they shouldn't be messing with." [27]

"'Mojo rising'? Who are you, Val Kilmer?"

"Jesus, I wish. I wouldn't be slinging stocks for a living, that's for sure."

"Yeah, no kidding," she said. "Look, Pat, I'm happy for your mojo, but it's been a few weeks since we did any real business. Can some of that rising include your production?"

"I'm working on it, Marie," he responded. "Come into my office for a minute, will ya?"

Following him, she closed the door and slid into his client chair, saying, "What's up?"

"Not much. What's up with you?"

"Pat?"

"Sorry, Marie," he said in not so sorry a voice. "Listen, if I were to decide to join Larry's firm, or maybe one of the bigger broker-dealers—you know, the headhunters call almost every day—if I accepted an offer, would you come with me?"

"How much?"

"Christ, we're back there again?"

"Of course, I'd come," she said with a laugh. "You can't leave me here with the wolves. But Pat, you know I need certainty."

"I'd get you a raise, and a signing bonus, and a title. You'd be my partner, and we'd be world's better off than we are here."

"Where've you been all my life, big boy? let's get the show on the road then."

"Slow down, mojo girl. You know the work it takes to jump firms; we've seen it a million times."

"A million and one."

"Right. We'd be working like ravenous rookies for six months, a year, maybe more. On the phone all day, selling the new firm, pleading, calling in favors. And the reams and reams of paperwork. Are you sure you'd be up for it?"

"Up for it? When we pitched Cracker Barrel, we worked our butts off," she reminded him. "It was the most fun we've had around here since I don't know when. It's a hell of a lot better than sitting around twiddling our thumbs and worrying all day."

"Have you thought of becoming a motivational coach? You'd be great at it."

"Come on, Pat. I'm serious."

"Okay, serious," he said with an embellished frown. "You couldn't be more correct, Marie."

"How about you? Are you up for all the work? These are supposed to be your golden years, your reward time, when you get to nap at your desk even more than usual."

"Watch it, wise-gal," he said with a chuckle. "Tell you the truth, working like a starving rookie wasn't in my plans. But being a starving veteran isn't either, and worrying every day that they're coming after my financial freedom is fueling a fury." He looked at her with resolve and said, "We have to get the hell out of here, Marie. I'll start the search today."

"Good," she said. "But before you do, Mr. Fury, or Fuel, or whatever the hell you just said, could you please get on the phone and sell something to someone? Call Mr. Weaver; he'll buy anything."

"Hush now, Marie; good things are starting to happen. Let's not panic."

"Way too late for that."

Clearing the last of his messages, a handful of client proposals sat on his desk staring at him. He'd been meeting with referrals for the first time in a while, one of the good things starting to happen. New client relationships were the lifeblood of the industry, he knew, and spectacular stock-picking was one sure way to get the blood pumping again.

As he looked them over, his mind wandered back to his earliest days in the business. When comedian Steve Martin coined the phrase "wild and crazy," he must have been thinking about the stock brokerage industry in the early '80s. At Patrick's first brief stop, a penny stock firm out of Denver with an office on Okeechobee Blvd, his prospect list was the phone directory for Century Village, a middle-class retirement community located just across the busy eight-lane road connecting the coastline to burgeoning western communities. The average age of his target audience was eighty, and his pitch was "getting rich with high growth companies priced under one dollar a share—the opportunity of a lifetime." That's why his stay there was brief.

The one lasting memory of his penny stock days was the office's "big hitter," a guy named Freddy, snorting lines of coke off his desk on IPO day (the day a new penny stock came public). He'd "cross" the stock in his own book, meaning half his clients would receive IPO shares (the initial allocation) and sell them at the opening for a pre-determined 200% profit, and the other half would buy those same shares at the premium, destined to eventually lose their entire investment. Once Freddy had finished writing up the fifty or so transactions, with a large gold chain dangling from his open collar, he would lean over his desk and snort his lines of coke. He was celebrating his $40,000 in commissions, he said, about 20% of his client's investment on each side of the trade. A few days later, he pointed Patrick to his brand-new Cadillac, a pink convertible, parked in the steaming asphalt lot just below the second story window. The perfect reward for a job well done.

The longer-term game was making sure each client had a taste of the exhilarating IPO gains while slowly vomiting their capital in the other trades. Patrick wasn't willing to play and got the hell out of there as soon as a legitimate brokerage firm would hire him.

When one finally did, for the first year he inhabited a tiny cubicle and shared a boxy computer called a Quotron with the guy sitting next door (quotes and news headlines only, delivered in small, goldish-yellow text on a black screen). His desktop contained only one other piece of equipment—a telephone. When he needed to quote a stock or a bond price, he would grab hold of the swivel shelf between the cubicles and wrench the Quotron away from his neighbor, holding firm against the pressure to yank it back. It was a bad setup if peace and collaboration in the neighborhood was the objective. His first iPhone was still twenty-five years away from its birth, so that wasn't an option. But Patrick was in the big time, a stockbroker at a major Wall Street firm, and all he needed to do was survive until the next day, and the day after that.

Sometimes, the stars align, and good fortune comes your way. That's how Patrick saw it anyway. This was one of those times. That guy sitting next door tugging at the Quotron machine was also a new hire to the firm. A CPA before joining the brokerage industry, he was quiet, smart, and meticulous, just what you'd expect from an accountant. Patrick watched, listened, and learned from him—more than he'll ever know. Together, they found peace and collaboration in their neighborhood while learning their trade.

A few old maxims come to mind. Famous Wall Street commentator, Louis Rukeyser, once said: "The market will fluctuate. It will 'fluc' down, and it will 'fluc' up." It always raised a smile whenever

Patrick heard it. Warren Buffett said it another, perhaps more useful way: "Be fearful when others are greedy, and greedy only when others are fearful." The point was he was a value shopper, only and always. Finally, John Templeton laid out a roadmap for success in tracking the never-ending market cycle when he said: "Bull markets are born on pessimism (the fear stage), grow on skepticism, mature on optimism, and die on euphoria (the greed stage)."

Each of these well summed up the pendulum of investor emotions always moving between the two extremes of fear and greed. Sometimes the pace was gradual, playing out over multi-years, and sometimes it was hectic, playing out over months, weeks, days, and minutes. Patrick preferred gradual, but it wasn't his choice. It was basic human nature at work, and he took it as it came.

His early years were all about fear, both in the markets and in the rookie broker's head. Nonetheless, he slowly built his client book by showing up every business day despite the inherent uncertainty he'd be certain to face. As he said it: "Pretending I knew what the hell I was talking about, until I knew what the hell I was talking about."

When the market was at the fear extreme, like during and after the October '87 "Black Monday" crash, brokers fled the business in droves, and he'd take on a few new clients. When it was leaning too much towards greed, like in much of the '90s, he had a moral code, or some other kind of code, that helped protect him. It was also based in fear. He hated rejection, hated being so publicly wrong; and he hated when clients were angry or disappointed in him. At times, it was so painful he could barely pick up the phone when they called. He questioned his worth, why he was even in the financial advice business in the first place. Something like, "Who in God's name do I think I am?" or "Who the hell do I think I am?" or "Who the fuck do I think I am?" depending on how badly he'd screwed up.

He noticed that most successful salespeople didn't share these same emotions. The best in the trade, the highest producers, appeared to have no fear at all, and the consequences of their bad decisions didn't seem to bother them in the least. In that regard, Patrick was handicapped in more ways than were apparent. He almost left the business a few times, once nearly buying a marble floor polishing franchise. But he didn't. Instead, he showed up at his desk every day to pick up that goddamn phone. Maybe he realized running that enormous marble polishing machine from his wheelchair would have been an even bigger bitch?

Speaking of the stars aligning, in October of '87, he needed a temporary assistant to answer the phones when his regular one, some gal named Marie, went away on vacation. He'd recently met a nice young lady and asked if she was interested. "My phone rings about five or six times a day, max," he told her. "It'll be a piece of cake." She said "yes" and came in the following Monday. It was October 19th, "Black Monday." His phone rang about five or six hundred times, and panicked clients were doing everything but jumping out of buildings. At the worst of it, with the Dow Jones index down 23% by late afternoon, a broker working in Coconut Grove was shot dead at his desk by a newly destitute client. Patrick's manager locked the office doors and posted a guard outside. In sum, it proved to be a difficult first day at the office for the young lady who'd said "yes." Even though he hadn't exactly been truthful, or at least accurate, Becky said "yes" one more time and married him anyway.

His industry had plenty of other struggles in those early days. It had a way of getting into trouble, one way or another, especially toward the greed end of the cycle. A veteran once said it this way: "Every five years or so, when things are going too well, we shoot ourselves in the foot and need to spend some time in rehab."

The reason, Patrick speculated, was that financial services was about more than just retail client advisory. It was also a vast manufacturing machine—the creation and assembly of investment products the customers wanted, oftentimes demanded, using some perceived enhancement of the three main ingredients—stocks, bonds, and real estate. Regardless of the investment climate—fear, greed, or somewhere in-between—the customer always wanted the same thing: to make money, and not to lose it. But most investors only recognized money-making opportunities toward the end of the cycle, the greed stage, and they wanted nothing to do with investing in the fear stage. That's why Templeton further said, "To be a successful investor, you must act counter to human nature. Most people can't do it."

That's where the advisor came in. One of Patrick's most important jobs was to identify the stage of the cycle, try to control destructive behaviors, including his own, and then discern the diamonds from the coal—the least risky pathway to success. To attempt to do that, he borrowed from the Hippocratic oath: "When in doubt, do no harm."

The dawn of the internet in the mid-nineties brought increased transparency and competition across every aspect of the business, mandated primarily by more sophisticated clients. Brokers became advisors, and they focused less on products, especially crappy ones, and more on developing realistic financial and life plans. With tangible goals in place, they then guided their clients to making the best choices possible toward their main objective—the smoothest possible route to a prosperous retirement.

Patrick had witnessed a revolution, the information revolution, changing everything for the better—for clients, advisors, and the industry. A twenty-year bull market in just plain stocks and bonds, ignited by President Reagan and Fed Chair Volcker's inflation-killing policies, didn't hurt the cause, propelling his career to something honorable, enjoyable, and enduring.

In other words, Patrick Connelly had mojo—until the more recent years, anyway. But maybe that was changing before his eyes? Maybe his mojo was on the rise again?

28

DO YOU BELIEVE IN MAGIC?

After an hour or so of hard labor, so to speak, with another glance at the snail-like clock, Patrick put aside the proposals and picked through his Tumi, plucking out *The Irish Times*. It was an expanded Weekend Edition, he noted with satisfaction. Confirming first that Marie wasn't heading his way, he spread the paper open on his desk. It was time to kick back for one of those "golden years" moments.

The Irish Times was oversized and colorful with thick paper stock that didn't go limp against one's mere glance. Reminiscent of the grand old days of American newspapers, he felt a distant pleasure come rushing back.

The front page reported several examples of never-ending global strife, as usual. Prominent here was the conflict between the Protestants and Catholics, meaning the loyalists and nation-alists. A less violent version of the "Troubles" was still on the boil up in old Ulster. The priorities of some people hadn't changed enough in the fifteen years since the Good Friday peace accord was signed.

Has it only been fifteen years? Patrick mused. *That's the blink of an eye on the scale of time. Rather than burning Republic flags, the old farts in their orange clown costumes should be focusing on something a little more constructive, like how about quitting smoking? Or maybe they could improve their schools and local economy so their kids could have a fighting chance to get good jobs instead of just fighting?*

Gerry Adams's competing political party, Sinn Fein, appeared to have gotten its act together in a relative sense. However, by all reasonable accounts, and contrary to his creative reimagining of history, Gerry was quite the sinner in his more "troubled" days. Meanwhile, both sides were still painting murals on Belfast's walls and buildings as memorials to fallen heroes, and for other, more hostile political purposes.

"Grow up, people," he admonished aloud. "At the core, we're all Irish, for Christ's sake."

Flipping forward, article after article promoted writers, poets, libraries, schools, museums, and theaters all around the country. James Joyce and William Butler Yeats festivals, Samuel Beckett awards, Oscar Wilde and Seamus Heaney readings, new productions of Bram Stoker's famous blood-sucking aris-tocrat, and the like.

What a rich cultural history, he thought with admiration, *and they sure do honor it.*

Jumping ahead, he landed on the sports section. "Jesus, Mary, and Joseph," he said aloud, allowing one of his mother's well-worn expressions to surface. He was referring to the Irish being mad for any game with a ball and a place to throw it, kick it, smack it, or carry it over a goal. Especially if there are hordes of bodies to slam into along the way. Every few weeks, there's a "match of the century" in one sport or another setting the island nation's hearts ablaze.

"Bring home the cup for us, boys, make us proud now," would come their smoke-trailed pleas from the wrought iron-framed, red slat benches lining alleyways outside the endless smoke-free pubs. There, the ancient would sit stoically beneath colorful flower baskets spinning misty yarns while crushed stubs smolder in the gray cobblestones below amidst their tarnished dress shoes.

"A passionate bunch, these Irish," he muttered aloud. St. Patrick hadn't quite eradicated every last drop of warrior blood. Speaking of the patron saint, the paper included a separate pullout section devoted to his annual celebration, still a couple of weeks off. He'd be sure to nurture it as the big day approaches.

He'd slain enough of the clock to placate Marie, he figured. It was past time to go home. Mindlessly packing up his Tumi, the old habit of never leaving a newspaper unspoiled cover-to-cover reared its unspoken influence. Just a few pages to go.

Disappointed to find neither comics nor horoscopes to cap his dawdling, he settled on the last unconsumed section titled

"Business Today." A portfolio of commercial buildings, primarily in Dublin and Cork, had been bought by a public REIT. Good news—the tepid recovery grinds forward. A new hotel is being built in Belfast, once again excellent news for the reascending capital of Northern Ireland.

Maybe they should get that underutilized port humming, he thought, *get the shipbuilding business going again. So what if the Titanic didn't work out so well? Come on, for Christ's sake, get over it already; where's that old Irish 'get up off the ocean floor and get at it' spirit?*

They'd better work at something to hand their children a more flourishing future, he knew, so they would be among the "haves." Through all of time, Patrick believed, most conflict is really about the "haves" versus the "have-nots." It's not as much about religious affiliation or allegiance to a certain government as the leaders would have us imagine. Instead, those who are suffering in poverty and hopelessness desire, and deserve, a larger piece of the pie. Not handouts, but opportunities. And it's in everyone's best interest to productively spread the wealth: in Ireland, in America, and across the world.

The more there are of "haves," the less there would be of "want-someone-elses," resulting in less power for the government and corporate elites who depend on the dependent. That was simply a non-starter in many of the executive suites. Could it be that they were willing to trade a rising tide of peace, prosperity, and contentment across the globe to keep and grow their power?

Yes, it could, he lamented, *and they should be damned to hell for their selfishness.*

One last page separated Patrick from the Marie-guarded gateway home. Glancing past her desk, he tamped down that *Monty Python and the Holy Grail* scene where the knight seeking passage across a bridge is dismembered—his four extremities severed one at a time—by a surprisingly savage bunny. If Marie turned so ferocious, which wouldn't be as surprising, he'd have none of the knight's courage, he knew. Instead of taking the risk, however minimal, he instead watched patiently for any indication that she was off to the mailroom, the copy room or the ladies' room so he could steal away unscathed.

As he corralled the paper to put away, he noticed a small headline on the last page, lower right. It slammed into him like a big-bodied rugby player in a fierce scrum: *Disney To Buy Competitor Cedar Fair.* "Oh, for Christ's sake," he said out loud. "They're at it again—and so soon?"

Quickly scanning the article, he straightened up in his chair and typed Cedar's symbol, FUN, into his desktop. The closing price was $39.50 per share, nowhere near the reported $70 Disney had agreed to pay. The news scroll showed business as usual for Cedar Fair: announcing the dates of theme park openings, dividend payments, and the like. Nothing about Disney or the reported merger agreement.

The events of the last month came rushing back. Blood surging, breath narrowing, perspiration building at his pulsating hairline, the brightly flashing screen ramped up his sudden sense of vertigo. Hesitating, he deepened his breath and picked up the paper, searching its unfamiliar front page. The large banner at the top said *The Irish Times Weekend Edition.* To its right, in contrastingly small print, he read, "Saturday and Sunday, March 16 and 17." Shielding his good eye from the light with his free hand, peering down to the lower right of the computer screens, he squinted hard and focused in on the vitals.

It was 4:15 p.m. on Monday, March 4th. Disney's takeover of Cedar Fair would be nearly two weeks from today.

Marie shut down her terminal, locked her drawers, and sped from the office with a "see ya tomorrow" wave. Before her Jersey cackle had dissipated, limbs secure, Patrick was on her heels.

Nearly plowing down the door from his garage into the kitchen area, he called out, "Finnie, where are you, sweetheart?" The delightful sound emanating from the den provided his answer. Planting a breathless kiss on her cheek, he asked, "The paper you gave me, *The Irish Times*, where did you get it?"

"I told you—someone left it at Murphy's. Why? what's wrong, Patrick?"

"I'm not sure anything's wrong. I'm just trying to understand."

"Understand what?"

"Well, you remember the other newspaper I told you about, and how it was dated February 10th, but it was only January 27th, and it said Disney was buying Cracker Barrel, but they hadn't bought them, but then they did buy them?"

"I'm following you, I think," she said with a laugh. "Yes, of course, I remember you telling me. Why?"

"I think it's happening again. The paper you brought home isn't last weekends. It's dated two weeks from now."

"It can't be. Are you certain?"

"Oh, Jeez. I'm not certain of anything," he said with a tremor. "The last time, when I showed it to Marie and then Molly, they only saw the date January 27th. And they saw a different headline, something about Europe and recession. Same with me when I was with them. It was only when I was alone that I saw the future date and the Disney headline. And then it came true, which means I wasn't nuts. But it could mean I'm nuts anyway, right?"

"Yes. I mean, no," she answered. "I mean, relax, please." Stroking his face with the back of her hand, she said. "Let's look at the paper together."

"Right, good idea." Reaching into his Tumi, he pulled out the folded-over paper. Moving to his freshly polished walnut desk, he spread it open and looked cautiously over his left shoulder. "Okay Finnie, ready? What does the front cover say?"

"*The Irish Times*, Weekend Edition."

"And the date?"

"Well, heavens above," she said. "It says Saturday and Sunday, March 16 and 17."

"You see the same dates that I do? Thank you, Jesus—I mean, Finnie." He was leaning back for a one-armed embrace. "Okay, okay. Let's flip to the business section now, last page, lower right." His excitement was growing—more a feeling of nausea. "Okay, here it is, lower right, right here," he said, pointing his finger. "Read that headline, please."

"'Disney To Buy Competitor Cedar Fair.'"

"You see it—you actually see it!" he cried out. "I'm not crazy. But why? why do you see it?"

"I don't know, Patrick. I just do."

"What's happening, Finnie? Why is this happening?" He was confused, and relieved, and dizzy, all in the same whirl. But he wasn't alone in the madness. *Thank God,* he thought, wiping away a tear. *I'm not alone anymore.*

Later, they talked about magic and sorcery, heaven and hell, good and evil, and God and the devil. Maureen was as bewildered as he, having no good explanation for what was happening or why. The entire episode was a mystery to her. When he asked again, she repeated that she'd found the newspaper in the empty back room of Murphy's, the same as how he'd found the last paper. His mind was in a quandary reel: *Why Murphy's, and why me? Is this good, like magic, or evil, like witchcraft? Am I being tested? Should I throw the paper out or burn it, or should I use it again for personal gain?*

"Those are difficult questions to answer," she acknowledged. "I suppose the same information can be magic to one and sorcery to another. It depends on the intent of the user."

"I really don't know what I intend, Finnie."

"For starters, let's go to bed. A rested mind makes better decisions."

"That sounds like a good plan." His impish smile was pressed into the warmth of her neck. "Better than good, really."

Once settled in, she lowered the light and dropped her nightgown to the floor, saying, "In Ireland, we were raised to believe in magic."

"Speaking of magic." He paused while scooching to the middle of the bed within range. "I like the new look."

"Why aren't I surprised?"

"I can't speak to that." He wore a grin—you know the kind. "Growing up in New York, there was no such thing as magic, just mundane daily living."

"That's a shame. How dull."

"Well, except maybe Tinker Bell and Mickey on Sunday nights; and Peter Pan, *The Wizard of Oz*, and Santa Claus once a year; and *The Hobbit* and Gandalf, and then Harry Potter came later. Oh yeah, and there's Superman, Batman, and Spider-Man— kind of. Superman for sure, but Batman and Spidey may have just been extraordinary athletes. And then there's *Bewitched* and Jeannie and *Mister Ed*. No one can tell me a sarcastic talking horse isn't magic. And the *Miracle on Ice*, of course." He was reeling off lost fragments of his youth as they surfaced.

"That's a lot more magic out there than you thought," she said with a chuckle.

"Jeez, you're right," he agreed. "But they were just stories, you know, fairytales. Especially beating Russia in '80. In real life, though, whatever we got we worked for, nothing was handed to us."

"Magic isn't about handing things to people, I don't think," she replied. "It's a power that's available to anyone who's paying attention; and it's so ordinary, sometimes, it's easy to miss."

"Such as?"

"Well, such as a stranger's kindness, a smile, or a hopeful word; or maybe a random message or chance meeting that changes a life's direction; or a coin tossed into the cup of a hungry man or woman which brings good fortune." He was watching her sweet face and listening intently as she continued. "And think about all the bad things that might have happened—that haven't. Who's to say a little magic didn't intercede to keep us safe?"

"Wow, that makes perfect sense, Finnie," he acknowledged. "It's all in the meaning we attach to these things."

"That's right," she replied. "If you've worked a good day, done a good deed, had a good laugh, and your loved ones are all safe in so uncertain a world, now that's a bit of a magical day. Don't you think so, Patrick?"

"Why, yes, I do—when you put it that way. It's all that really matters and a wonderful thing to believe in."

"We have to believe in something," she went on, "so why not magical days?"

"I'm sold," he replied. "I hate being redundant, but what's happening to me seems more complicated than that—it's in-your-face supernatural."

"I can't disagree," she said. "But maybe it's happening to the right person at the right time—an honorable man who will use it wisely. Does that make sense?"

"Sure, I guess so," he said with a gentle squeeze of her hand. "But in a weird way, a very weird way, I'm trading stocks on advanced information, which doesn't seem so honorable."

"But don't you see—your guilt is what makes you honorable. You could also see it as something being directed from a higher source and an opportunity for your career."

"I suppose I could," he said. "And that brings me full circle to the primary question. Why me? And why now?"

After letting a note of silence resonate, she said, "I can only reference again all the seeds you've planted—the large pot of goodwill you've stored up." Then, she reached over to her brand new ancient nightstand and flipped off the lamp. Leaning back in again, dragging her nails slowly along his lower belly, she purred, "You must be the right person, darling, and this must be your time."

Patrick closed his eyes and allowed the magic and the music to set him free. [28]

29

FUN DAY AT THE OFFICE

This time he didn't need approval from Saunders to solicit Cedar Fair. The firm had an analyst's opinion, deeming the stock a "Neutral," neither a buy nor a sell, but rather a hold. The dividend was considered "Secure," which mattered because this was an investment generally bought for income. The stock symbol was FUN, custom-made for the Palm Beach retired crowd.

"Marie, I think I've found a home for our Cracker Barrel profits—a new stock idea."

"Well, gee whiz, glory be, as I live and breathe."

"Are you done with the overwrought clichés?"

"Hells bells and Jiminy Cricket. Be still my heart."

"I guess not."

"Knock me over with a feather."

"I'll wait."

"Good golly, Miss Molly. Pray tell."

"Go on."

"'Pray tell' means that's it."

"In sum, I suspect I'm being called lazy?"

"That would be an understatement."

Once his embellished sense of personal affront had run its course, he said, "Have you saved any time to hear my idea?"

"Sorry, Pat, whaddya got?"

Hearing the word "sorry" come from her mouth was so rare, he lingered in its tenor before saying, "It's nothing as exciting as the last one, believe me. But it'll keep us busy while we're deciding where we go from here." He handed her the bullet points he'd written up. "Cedar Fair, LP, based in Ohio. They operate eleven theme parks around North America; they've been around forever."

"Theme parks, again? What, you've still got Disney on the brain?"

"I've been looking at the industry with more interest, that's for sure," he replied. "But Cedar is a grain of sand compared to the House of Mouse. Most of their parks are only open in the summer months and draw a local crowd. The CEO is a former big wig at Disney. They pay a 5 percent dividend, so it's mainly an income play—perfect for most of our clients. They can hold it the rest of their lives and collect the cash flow."

"Could you repeat that? I couldn't hear you—I was too busy yawning."

"I said it wasn't exciting."

"That's okay, Pat. Your job isn't to entertain me."

"I'm relieved to hear that."

"Seriously, I went to one of Cedar's parks in Pennsylvania a few years ago when I was home visiting family. Dorney Park, I think. People from Jersey drive there all the time."

"What did you think?"

"Clean, well-run, *Peanuts* characters everywhere; my nieces had a blast. I had fun too."

"Charlie Brown and Snoopy were there? Even better." After a momentary visit to his lost youth, he said, "It's funny you mentioned 'fun,' Marie, because you'll be saying that a lot in the next week or two. That happens to be their symbol."

"Whaddya mean, '*I'll* be saying that a lot?' Aren't you the salesman around here?"

"Oh, Marie, you know better than that. This is much too big a job for just one person, no matter how awesome that person might be. And remember how much *fun* you had pitching Cracker Barrel? Well, I'm handing you another ticket to the funhouse."

"Whoopee."

"I figure we'd do the same script. I'll call the top fifty; you'll call the rest. I recommend calling Mr. Weaver first. He'll buy anything."

"Funny," she said, with an emphasis on fun. "Okay, you're the boss after all."

"Say again?"

"Forget it. What about Saunders and compliance?"

"We have an opinion on Cedar, a 'Neutral,' so we don't need their permission for anything. Besides, it's a safe, boring, income play. What can they say?"

"I guess you're right. But they worry me anyway."

"Anytime your boss wants to can you, it's a good reason to worry," he agreed. "I'm sure we'll hear from our buddy as soon as the orders start dropping."

"Can't wait," she grimaced.

"Okay, Marie, let's get busy. Ready? Break. You get ready, and I'll take a break." Her stern look indicated he should put off his break until later. As she was leaving his office, he said, "By the way, would you do me a favor?"

"I've got a lot to do, Pat, thanks to you. What's the favor?"

"Can you tell me what date you see on this newspaper?"

"Did you leave your readers home, grandpa?"

"Nice, Marie. Just tell me the friggin' date, will ya?" He was pointing to the top right of the front page he'd just unfolded.

"It says, 'Saturday and Sunday, March 2 and 3.'"

"Excellent, Marie, excellent."

They pounded the phones that day just as they'd done the month before. The fledglings fluttered past his office, curious to see the rarest of sights—a stockbroker's factory buzzing at full capacity. Not one client responded with a "no" or a "maybe" or a "let me think about it," and the orders flowed. By market close, more FUN shares were on the books than after a week of pitching Cracker Barrel. Even the oenophile who'd said no the last time popped his cork for Cedar. The ancient stock jock had acquired an element of street cred.

Maybe that was one of the reasons so many investors lose so much money in the stock market? They get lucky once or twice, get frothy, and let their defenses down. They're all financial experts. Investing is fun again. They can't wait to take another ride on the roller coaster. Eventually, the law of averages, the return to the mean, reasserts itself, and their luck runs out. On the next sizeable decline, shaking and retching, they bail out, vowing never to hazard another ride. Being a successful long-term investor is akin to figuring out how to enjoy the theme park on a lifetime pass: take it slow and easy, ride the bumper cars and teacups and kiddie coaster, enjoy all the grand shows and other pleasures. Stay far away from any upside-down adventures with names like "Cannibal" and "Fury" and "Gatekeeper" and "Top Thrill Dragster."

They warned their clients not to expect another thrilling ride, saying, "Lightning doesn't strike the same portfolio twice; just enjoy the steady income and pride of ownership if you ever take your grandkids to one of their parks." Eager clients queued up even so.

Patrick had no intention of stopping there. "Tomorrow, we'll blow the dust off that list of prospects rotting in our file drawer since forever," he told Marie. "Let's see if we can't build the business a little." For any number of reasons, he was feeling more confident this time around.

Saunders was in his face at the first sniff of stock accumulation. "What are you doing now, Connelly?" His friendly greeting disrupted the elevated spirit.

"Working, Jeff. I'm a financial advisor, advising my clients on how to invest their money. Pretty common stuff, really."

"Why Cedar Fair? Why so many shares? Why now?"

Handing him a copy of the bullet points, he said, "Just looking to park some of the Cracker Barrel profits. Get it? 'Park' the profits? Theme 'park.'"

"I'm not amused, Connelly. The calls from New York are already wrecking my day. They're asking all the same questions."

"Tell them it's a safe income play, perfectly appropriate for our clients. We follow it, we don't hate it, end of story."

"Are you a leisure industry specialist now? you have expertise in restaurants, theme parks, hotels, and cruise ships?"

"You sound like a prosecutor, Jeff. Do you need to be a 'specialist' to follow an industry? The Cracker Barrel success has me looking at hospitality more closely, that's all." He went on to say that Cedar raises its distribution almost every year, making it a good inflation hedge. "Perfect for retirees, and my clients have no problem with the partnership status. It's all been covered. Makes good sense, don't you think?"

"I don't know what to think. I'm just trying to stay ahead of the curve. If you go down, I go down. No one, especially you, will be taking away my golden shovel."

"Golden shovel?"

"My chance to make a fortune in this business—to own a place across that bridge." He was making the expected gesture east from whichever finger wasn't glued to his cell phone. "Unless an anchor like you sinks me, this job is my ticket to riches." As he gazed out the eastern window adoringly to the barrier island, Patrick's eyes mimicked the white crests' arch and descent.

"Speaking of that," he continued, "I'm not approving the size of your commission discounts. It's ridiculous."

"What are you talking about?"

"I'm talking about you giving away the store, as usual," he said. "I've instructed New York to adjust the commissions back up to something more doable."

"That's thievery. Why should they pay so much for us to push a frigging button?" He was seething now. "The standard commission schedule is obsolete, and you know it."

"You're obsolete, Connelly, and you're forgetting all the other expenses of keeping an old curmudgeon like you at this desk."

"How do I explain the increase to my clients? Tell them my greedy boss wants a bigger cut of their action?"

"Careful, Connelly. You're standing on the line. Oops, sorry, I mean, *sitting* on the line."

"Screw the politically correct bullshit, Jeff," he steamed. "What do I tell my clients?"

"You can tell *our* clients we're not the Salvation Army, and we don't do soup kitchens. They should be in a fee-based format anyway, then there'd be no commissions, and you'd have to work harder to earn your pay. It's in their best interest, and yours. Try that on for size. If they give you any lip, put them through to me. Maybe I'll introduce them to King and Wolfe."

Staring harshly, Patrick said, "Are we done?"

"Almost. There's one more thing. I'm making some changes around the office, moving people around—to keep things fresh."

"Don't do this, Jeff."

"It's already done. On April 1st, the KW Group is coming down to this corner. I'm not certain yet where you'll wind up. It depends if I get a team from the competition I'm working on."

"I've been in this office for ten years. I've earned it."

"'Earned' is past tense," Saunders snapped. "This is a dog-eat-dog, what-have-you-done-for-me-lately business. We eat what we kill around here. You ain't doing enough killing, and I ain't doing enough eating."

"Brilliant stuff, Jeff; you are one world-class jackass."

"Tsk-tsk," he said while standing up. "There's that potty mouth again."

"As long as you're up," he said, pointing his finger, "there's the door."

"What? Are you jealous of tall people or something?"

Ignoring him, Patrick said, "By the way, we don't give a crap what you do on April 1st. Marie and I will sit anywhere you put us."

Passing through the threshold, Saunders grabbed the door's frame and did a half turn. "Oh yeah, thanks for the reminder. I'm making some changes with the staff too. Your assistant will have a new assignment on April 1st, supporting me and KW. You'll get some help too; not sure who yet."

"You can't do this!" he raged. "I won't let you, and Marie won't work for you anyway." He was red hot now, nearly hyperventilating. "I'll take this to New York."

"First, I'm the manager. So, I *can* and *am* doing this. Second, by all means, take it to New York. You're on thin ice as it is, and they *will not* be thrilled to hear from the likes of you. Face it, Connelly, you're an over-the-hill producer in legal jeopardy, and this just isn't your choice."

"You're declaring war, Saunders. You know that."

"Bring it on, Ironside, bring it on," he said with a grin.

Temples bulging, soaked in perspiration, Patrick was barely able to breathe. "Get out of my office, you thief."

"You mean King's office, don't you?" he taunted, then added, "You know, one way to make all this go away is to sign the partnership papers with KW."

"Screw that," he railed.

"Think of it this way: they'd teach you how to be successful again; you'd get to work with Marie, and who knows, maybe Ian would even consider letting you keep this office, although I can't speak for him. Frankly, I don't see any downside."

"Not in a million years, you son of a bitch."

"Tsk-tsk. I'll email you the partnership papers, just in case you change your mind."

30

A HOPEFUL STRATEGY

Fuming, nearly out of control, Patrick raced from his office, afraid of what he might do had he stayed. Marie too erupted in a rage as soon as she heard the news and took off for Saunders's office.

Ian King, clued in to the unfolding turmoil, was peering from his bank of cubicles. He flashed an exaggerated smile and wave while Patrick waited for the elevator door to open, calling out, "How's your day going, Connelly? Good, I hope. Remember though, hope is not a strategy."

Patrick's middle finger was all that remained visible when the elevator doors began to compress.

"Calm down, sweetheart," Maureen advised when she heard his agitated account. "There's no need to do anything rash. April 1st is still a few weeks away."

"It's outrageous, Finnie; not just my office being snatched, but Marie too? It's unacceptable, the end game."

"They're pushing you to the edge," she agreed, "and you're going to have to act, but with a level head after you've cooled down."

"The obvious move is to get the hell out of there now, before all this goes down."

"Yes, you may have to, but that could be just what they want. Didn't you say it's like handing them your book of clients and then having to spend day and night for the next year trying to win them all back?"

"That's exactly what I said, and the thought of it makes me sick."

"So then, do your homework, in case that's how it goes, but keep all your options open."

"What other options do I have?"

"Well, remember all the good things that are happening. The newspapers, for one, and the people who support you: Marie, Larry Devlin, your new friend, Kerry O'Connor, just to name three," she said. "And I'm with you, Patrick. You're not alone anymore, dear."

"You're right, Finnie; thank you." He recalled Kerry's similar advice. "I've got to stay peaceful, clear-headed, not react from fear or rage."

"Exactly." She gave him a lingering hug before finishing dressing. Belying her peaceable exterior, Maureen Finn was even more infuriated than her dear Patrick. In fact, she was flaming red molten rock ready to engulf everything in its pathway.

Working from home the next day, he called several headhunters he'd known over the years, telling them he was seriously considering moving. "What took you so long, Mr. Connelly?" one asked. "The deals have never been better," said another. "You've picked a perfect time to make a change. Let's meet for lunch," was the chorus.

"We can skip the lunch," he replied to each. "But let's get together on the details as soon as we can."

He then called Marie on her cell. "Let me go outside. I'll call you right back," she said, on the edge of tears. "That creep is really doing it, Pat. He's forcing me to work for them."

"We'll complain to New York," he said. "We've been here five times longer."

"He offered to dial New York for me, said I'm lucky to have a job at all."

"I want to slaughter that monster, I swear," he despaired. "All the higher-ups we used to know are long gone anyway, cleaned out after the last crash."

"I'm so screwed, Pat. I'm losing the extra comp, too—that's my mortgage payment. He said a year-end bonus will depend on my performance." She was crying now. "What am I gonna do?"

"Take a deep breath, Marie. Let's be calm, rational. April 1st is still a few weeks off," he said, mimicking Finnie's counsel. "First of all, you're not losing the comp. I'll keep paying it—happily; and second, I've made appointments with the other firms, and I'm calling Larry Devlin next."

"Leaving's our only choice now, our only way out. Isn't it?"

"It may be, but it's not over yet." He had a steely, bolstering tone. "This is our home, Marie. We always talked about being lifers—how proud we were to be among the few not jumping firms for the bonus money. Remember?"

"Yeah, I remember, but that seems like a lifetime ago. It doesn't matter anymore."

"I know it doesn't," he said.

His therapist Kay's face flashed into his mind, her plump lips saying, *"Tell them to go fuck themselves."* He tried to hold the image as it slowly faded, finally disappearing. Lips last.

"Pat? Are you still there?"

"Yes, I'm here, just thinking."

"About what?"

"Luscious lips."

"What? Who are you?"

"I'm not sure anymore," he replied. "Seriously, Marie, I'm really thinking I want to make those bullies sit and spin. They're jeopardizing our business, our careers, our goddamn freedom." Sour bile churned in his gut threatening an unplanned visit north. "Do we just hand them our clients and then fight like dogs to get them back? Where's the justice in that?"

"They'll come with us, Pat, the ones we want."

"Probably, but you never know," he said. "Some of them are in their eighties, and the only moving they're hoping for relates to their bowels."

After a pause, she started laughing, then he started laughing, and together they laughed and laughed. "Oh crap, Marie, we'll figure this shit out," he said through streaming tears.

"You shouldn't say 'crap' or 'shit' right now," she forced out, "or I'll be changing my underwear." That started their uncontrollable laughing again.

When they finally composed themselves, he asked, "Are you okay? Sanitation all in order?"

"Barely."

"Good enough. Listen, Marie, let's be patient, not get ahead of ourselves. It's too early to be surrendering to those assholes."

"Assholes, Pat? Really?" She was giggling again.

"Sorry, Marie," he said through his own cackle. "Let's just see how this plays out for the next few weeks. Whaddya say?"

"You sound almost confident, like you have a plan."

"I absolutely do. I'm planning on the Lone Ranger riding in on Trigger to rescue us while Tonto takes a few scalps along the way."

"I was hoping for something a little more realistic."

"Did you just say 'hoping'? You know what our eminent thinker, King Ian, says about 'hope,' don't you?"

"Don't keep me in suspense, please."

"Okay. But fair warning, this borders on profound. Maybe you should write it down."

"I'm ready. Give it to me."

"Are you sure you're ready?"

"Pat?"

"Okay—drum roll, please. King says, at every opportunity, 'Hope is not a strategy.'"

"That's it? What the hell does that mean?"

"I'm guessing it means we shouldn't hope," he explained. "Or at least we shouldn't use hope as a part of our daily plan, like as a replacement for a strategy."

"Can we ever hope?"

"It may be okay to hope in private," he responded. "Like late at night, hoping we can fall asleep, or hoping we get laid, or hoping we don't die in the middle of the night—that kind of thing." He was trying to keep a serious tone as he continued. "But it's much better to have a strategy. Like if you want to get laid, for example, your strategy would be to have someone in bed with you who feels the same way."

"Oh, I get it," she said. "So, if you *hope* you don't die tonight, that's okay, but a strategy would be better, like losing weight or stopping smoking."

"Precisely," he said, enjoying their repartee. "And under no circumstances should you sing Cat Stevens's song 'But I Might Die Tonight.'" [29]

"That's a given," she said with a chuckle. "Or how about that prayer we used to say at bedtime, 'And if I die before I wake, I pray the Lord my soul to take.' What the hell was that all about?"

"It falls into the category of child abuse, I'm guessing, so that's definitely out."

"I think they've softened it a little anyway," she said. "Too many kids wetting the bed."

"One more small step out of the Dark Ages," he smirked. "To be clear, I've never asked Ian for clarification on what he means—it never seemed important enough. But I'm guessing we should only hope frivolously and never during business hours. Office time is for strategizing only."

"This could be the end of hope," she said. "I hope not, but just in case, would you shoot me now?"

"Is that a strategy? Or are you just hoping I shoot you? Don't answer that."

"I wasn't going to."

"Smart lady. Marie, here's an idea, a strategy, if you will: Why don't we keep saying our prayers, believe in a little bit of magic, and just see what unfolds. Okay?"

"Got it, boss. One little thing, though. Aren't prayers, and even magic, based on hope?"

"Jesus, that's a really good point. Maybe we should ask Ian for a ruling?"

"Let's say we don't."

"Good strategy."

"Pat?"

"Yes, Marie?"

"Thank you."

"You're welcome, honey. See you tomorrow—I hope."

"Not if I see you first. That'll be my strategy anyway."

"Magical, Marie. Simply magical."

31

CONVERSATIONS IN THE GARDENS

Arriving in the parking lot of the low-rise office center, thirty minutes early for his appointment, as usual, Patrick sat a moment admiring the sharp, contemporary design of cream-colored stucco clad in reflective blue glass. A decade earlier, Larry Devlin had purchased one of the several compact, eye-catching buildings nestled snugly in "the Gardens," the suburban enclave half an hour's drive north of the city. It would become home to his independent financial advisory practice.

The quiet, woodsy area he remembered, now anchored by a popular regional mall, was bustling with shops, restaurants, medical facilities, and office complexes. Every building was tied together cleanly by sun-bleached, brick-paved pedestrian walkways and oak-shaded patios with decorative stone fountains. This little slice of commercial heaven-on-earth was balanced by Canary Date and Royal Palm trees keeping watch over walled gardens filled with glorious, multi-hued flowerbeds. The symmetrical precision of the landscape architect, he noted, rather than the indiscriminate hand of nature. Both had their place. Just outside this canopied haven was never-ending traffic hustling by in all directions.

Wrapped in floor-to-ceiling glass and filtering sunlight, the first-floor lobby featured red rock-bedded tropical gardens and trickling waterscapes. *This place is true to its name*, he thought. While looking around the busy workspace with a discerning eye, he concluded that Marie would be happy here. Larry seemed to have the gift of peering into the future and drawing sound conclusions before making decisions—a helpful skill for anyone, especially a financial advisor.

When the office door swung open, Larry strode towards him with that urgent step indicating the markets were open and trading. Extending his hand, he said, "Hey, Pat, great to see you again."

"Pleasure's all mine," came his reply while being led into his old friends' office.

After they settled in, Larry began, "It sounds like things aren't getting any better down there."

"Not unless being raped and plundered is an improvement," he replied before bringing Larry up to date. "I'd still prefer not to go through the hell of moving, to be honest, but I'm running out of options."

"Why haven't you reported your boss to senior management or human resources?" Larry asked. "It sounds like he's breaking every rule in the book."

"I've considered it, believe me, but someone up there picked Saunders to lead Palm Beach, so I'm worried there are others cut from the same cloth."

"Probably right."

"Besides, he can argue he's simply following the firm's strategic plan by pushing me into their full-service model, and I've flat out refused. It's pretty much the truth, and I'd lose that argument all day long. The other stuff, his unfriendly behavior, let's call it, that's all 'he said, he said' crap. Besides, I couldn't give a rat's ass what he calls me. At this point, I should just get the hell out of there."

"I agree, Pat." He went on to say, the small independents don't pay "crazy transition bonuses" like the bigger banks, but he'd make it up over time with the higher payouts. "There are no long-term contracts so you're not locked in. Just manage your clients' assets with either commissions or an annual fee, your choice, and start earning the higher percentage."

"That sounds ideal," Patrick said.

"Everyone's welcome here, regardless of how they choose to do their business," he assured. "If you want to be an old-style stock-broker—we're happy to have you."

"What a relief," he said. "But my main worry is Marie. We'd be working long hours in the first few months, mostly selling the move, and transferring assets. That's a huge mess of paper-work for her. And we wouldn't be earning much of anything for a while."

"That's true. We do pay a modest bonus to tide you over, but you'll need to have staying power."

"Now hold on a minute, Larry. You never said anything before about my needing 'staying power.' That's what my last girlfriend said just before slamming the door in my face."

"Funny, Pat. I'm talking financially."

"She was too, I'd like to think," he said with a laugh. "Hey, just keeping things light."

"Much appreciated, as always."

"Seriously though, I'd be okay financially for a time, but I'm not sure about Marie. I promised her a bonus, a higher salary, even a title and a piece of the business if she came with me."

"Whoa, slow down, big spender. Can you live up to all that?"

"I'd have to," he replied. "I need Marie more than she needs me." Then with a roll of his eyes, he added, "Do me a favor, will you? Don't ever mention I said that."

"Like she doesn't already know?"

"I wouldn't have been sure," Patrick said, "except she tells me every other day."

"My kind of lady," Larry said with a smile. "And you're right, Pat, most assistants in this business have no idea how important they are. We'd all crater without them."

"No kidding." He'd met with two "big dog firms" earlier in the week, telling Larry, "They've agreed to everything I asked for. I could bank substantial money upfront and keep all my promises to Marie. It's a tough call."

"Tough call? Seriously? Do you really think it's any better at one of the clones?"

"No, I really don't."

"Damn right, it's not. You'll sign a seven-year contract, minimum, and there'll be pressure every day to justify the bonus; you'll be on the same treadmill you're on now, with the speed turned up a few notches."

"Damn it, I know you're right. The managers I met look and sound exactly like Saunders, on his best behavior, schmoozing their asses off."

"Just think about it, Pat, and be careful. Don't do anything for a quick gain you'll regret later. The best in life comes in time—slow and graceful. There are no quick fixes."

"Understood. Thanks a million, Larry."

With the business portion of the conversation completed, Patrick leaned back, breathing easier, asking, "When are you clearing out of here for Dingle?"

"As soon as possible," he responded. "Probably in early May."

"Good for you, Larry. Let me ask you another question."

"Proceed."

"At the pancake emporium," he said with a grin, "you mentioned studying Irish mythology and mysticism and that you believe in it. How do you know? Do you have tangible examples?"

"That's not how it works, Pat, I don't think." His mood transitioned to something more contemplative to match the subject matter. "You have an experience, you can't explain it with logic, it makes no sense. It's more about belief."

"Like religion?"

"Maybe a less scary word, like spiritualism," Larry said. "Much of the universe, our very existence if you stop to think, is beyond our ability to comprehend. We take a lot of it on faith."

"Or we just make it up."

"That too. We do need a story to explain it all."

Patrick paused while a pitcher of iced tea was brought into the room, then asked, "So, my friend, what's your story?"

Shifting in his chair, a look of vulnerability replaced his usual certainty. "Things happened around the time I left the firm, things much too personal to discuss. I'd rather leave it in the past where it belongs."

"Of course."

"But I can tell you this: some type of help, something otherworldly, was there to guide me. I've thought about it over and over, and there's no other explanation. Since then, I've been paying more attention and tapping in more often. Why are you so interested?"

"My Irishness, for one." Patrick collected his thoughts before continuing. "And frankly, strange things are happening to me that I can't explain. I'm trying to understand: is it good or bad, and what do I do with it? Or maybe I'm just losing my mind."

Larry jogged over to his bookshelf and plucked out a small pile of books. "These are a few of the books I've read. They've helped me understand."

"But that's just it—understand what?"

"Well, for me, it's that most things we call magic are just illusions, sleight-of-hand, the stuff magicians do to entertain."

"I follow you."

"Then there are things we call coincidences. We're amazed and wondering if something else is happening."

"Like what?"

"Well, maybe you think of someone you haven't seen in years, and the phone rings, and it's them."

"Check."

"Or you run into just the right person at the right time, and they have important information for you."

"Double-check."

"Or maybe, out-of-the-blue, you have an overwhelming feeling to go a certain place. So, you go and meet a perfect stranger who becomes a friend for life, maybe even a spouse."

"Checkmate," he said with a grimace.

After a brief respite to return a phone call, Larry continued: "Here's another example, Pat. You open a book to a random page, and a message is there. Something that helps you solve a problem or understand better." He leaned forward and flipped open one of the books on his desk to a page, and read the chapter title out loud, "'The Fear Gorta.'"

"Fear Gorta? What does that mean?"

"Probably nothing. It's just a mythological figure in Irish lore." He closed the book, saying, "The point is, usually it means nothing, or maybe we take the information and make it something."

"I've been doing the same thing for years," Patrick said. "Reading horoscopes, scanning books and magazines, always looking for a message. I've run into people randomly who have something to teach me."

"Then you understand."

"Absolutely, but like you said, it's hit or miss. Why would any of it be considered magic?"

"That's just a loose term for it. Call it a coincidence, luck, timing, serendipity, intuition, cosmic energy, kismet, a hunch, a miracle, destiny. Call it whatever you want."

"Got it," Patrick said. "There must be something to it. After all, humans have been describing the phenomena forever."

"No doubt," Larry agreed, "and before the age of modern communications, people depended on it."

"You mean the pre-Google era?"

"Even a little earlier than that," Larry said with a laugh. "It's an interesting point, though. Just think about all the information floating around out there. Google figured out how to put a kind of magnet, a human intuition, into their software to search, gather and organize it all; it's like a piece of our brain is in our hands."

"Creating billions of dollars of magic right out of thin air." Patrick had a passing thought of how many shares of Google he didn't own.

"Hundreds of billions by now, maybe trillions," Larry said to his friend's deepening frown. "Before such amazing technology, our minds were receivers and organizers of information. We read, observed, listened, and learned. Collectively, I think we've gotten lazy, less educated, in that regard."

"Agreed," he said, "and we're all faux geniuses."

"I've never met so many," Larry concurred.

"Well, regardless of how information is gathered and organized, we still have to process it and decide what to do next. Humans are as flawed as ever in making good decisions."

"Probably more than ever," Larry agreed. "Too much information, not enough focus."

"Say again?" Patrick was glancing down at his phone.

"I'll pass."

Sitting back a moment, waiting for Larry's elongated eye roll to abate, the conversation shifted once again to the heart of his initial inquiry—understanding the essence of unexplainable events.

"On rarer occasions," Larry began, "something happens that rises above the extraordinary. It's a complete mystery, and you can't explain it with any other word than magic."

"I think that may be happening to me right now."

"I recognize the pale look on your face, Pat. I thought I was crazy for a long time. I wasn't, and you're not now."

"What a relief to hear. It's so confusing, though."

"I can't tell you what to do, except go slow, trust your intuition, and stay open to all possibilities. And read up on the subject—start with these books here." He pushed the pile across the desk.

"Thanks a lot. I'll get them back to you before you leave for Dingle."

"I know where you live," he said with a grin. "One thing about magic: if justice for all is served by its practice, good over evil, then there's nothing to worry about."

"That's helpful, Larry. Thanks."

Two of the most important people in his life now, Finnie and Larry, were living from the same playbook and handing him a copy. He felt part of a winning team again.

"What is it about Ireland that has you so hooked?" Patrick asked.

"It's in my blood, just like in yours. It wasn't that way when I was young, but the older I've gotten, the more I'm drawn there, like going home again."

"Maybe we get a little lost, disillusioned, so we go on a search for our roots, trying to understand the meaning of it all."

"I think you're right," Larry said. "The Lucky Charms leprechaun and four-leaf clovers weren't doing it for me, so I started to look a little deeper. I realized folklore and magic were a big part of our history."

"Along with oppression, tragedies, and triumphs—overcoming it all," Patrick added.

"Undoubtedly."

"Isn't a lot of the lore just made up? Like leprechauns, rainbows, pots of gold, faeries, dragons, giants, headless horsemen, ghosts? Isn't it just for entertainment?"

"Certainly, there's some of that; the Irish do love to spin a yarn. But the stories are often intended to teach important lessons."

"How so?"

"We're talking hundreds and thousands of years ago," Larry said. "The people worked the land and the sea, and their survival depended in part on nature: the sun, the rains, the tides, the seasonal cycles. Most of their information came word-of-mouth from travelers, and they discovered their skills by trial and error. Their stories are about survival, heroism, honor, the value of all human life, including women and unfamiliar people, which was uncommon at the time, and trying to explain the unexplainable."

"It was all so uncertain," Patrick said, "like America's Wild West days; competing for scarce resources, sometimes viciously, just trying to make it through to the next day safely and build their lives."

"Are you talking about our first few years in the business?" Larry asked.

"Christ, it sounded that way." Patrick was frowning. "We can call it *our* 'Dark Ages.'"

"True enough," Larry said. "But seriously, many poor souls around the world, billions really, still live there. They have next to nothing. We're truly blessed in comparison, and oftentimes take it for granted."

"You're so right," Patrick agreed. "Our basics—food, shelter, education, jobs—are covered. We have leisure time to search for meaning and complain constantly about how unfair life can be. Christ, we haven't a friggin' clue."

"And in our security, and our certainty, we've lost the magic," Larry lamented. "It's usually hiding in the uncertainty."

"How do you find it? The magic?"

"Lots of times it finds you if you're tuned in."

"That's what Finnie says. But how?"

"Well, you start by dropping the all-knowingness, quieting the mind, getting comfortable with not knowing; embrace it, learn to enjoy the adventure, and keep your mind, and especially your heart, wide open."

"A lot to consider."

It was getting to be time to wrap things up when Larry asked, "Didn't you tell me that you kissed the Blarney Stone?"

"I did," Patrick replied.

"You said it changed your life, gave you the Irish gift of eloquence and wit."

"Did I say eloquence and wit? That may have been the 'blarney' talking."

"I was thinking the same thing," Larry said with a laugh. "But do you really believe kissing the Blarney Stone made a difference in your life?"

"Yes, I do—without a doubt. Last year, I insisted we drive three hours from Killarney to Cork just so the kids and Becky could kiss the stone. I wanted it for them too."

"So, you believe kissing the Blarney Stone has made magic in your life?"

"Absolutely, yes. I don't even have to think about it. I just know it."

"How?"

"Well, when I was eighteen, after months of saying no, at the very last minute, I agreed to hitchhike around Ireland with my high school buddy. Strange things fell into place to make it possible—like the stone, or something of the old country—was arranging for me to come. Of course, I didn't know my injury would happen so soon."

"We don't get a copy of the script ahead of time," Larry said softly.

"Just as well," Patrick responded. "I'd do too many rewrites."

"Talk about needing certainty," he said, smiling.

"Jesus, you're right. Spontaneity has never been my thing. I make plans to make plans." After a pause, Patrick continued.

"Anyway, something pulled me to visit Ireland, and there I was, a red-haired, freckled kid from the Bronx, in Ireland, in Blarney, standing on the ramparts of the 15th-century castle, and then leaning backward down a deep well kissing the iconic stone. It was the day I became an Irishman, inheriting a power I'd soon need for my survival. I had no idea it would be my last chance—that the clock was ticking so urgently."

"It's always ticking," he said. "It runs out on all of us."

"Thanks for the uplifting message, Larry." He was checking his watch.

"Always here to help. So, Pat, your story of embracing uncertainty and folklore, and finding the magic in it, sounds pretty concrete to me."

"Actually, it's limestone."

"What?"

"The castle," Patrick answered, "it's made of limestone." He agreed wholeheartedly with his Irish friend's spinning eyes.

Packing up his Tumi, he was jotting down notes as Larry offered a few takeaways: "Let's slow down our minds, stop with all the analysis, our need to be certain. Instead, get quiet and listen without judgment. Get away from all the modern communications, all the 'Googles,' and out into nature. Tune in from somewhere else. If we can do that, we can still connect with the magic."

"Like tuning in with our feelings, our senses, our emotions?"

"Yes, tuning in with our hearts."

"Become like a child again."

"Precisely, Pat. Live in uncertainty and wonderment and discovery, just like a child."

"That sounds like a hopeful strategy."

"Hopeful strategy?"

"Just a newly coined expression. Thanks for everything, Larry."

32

THE CALL OF FREEDOM

St. Patrick's Day was due to arrive this coming Sunday. Starting with Irish Fest along Flagler's waterfront, Patrick's week-long celebration was never over the top. It was more nuanced, sublime even, mimicking his everyday life except for a heightened awareness of all things Irish. [30]

He'd ramp up the Celtic music to 24/7, visit Murphy's even more often to count down the hours, move up a shelf on his whiskey bar, dig into various readings from Irish authors, listen to Bing croon "Too-Ra-Loo-Ra-Loo-Ral," just this one time a year. He'd even stomach the deplorable leprechaun movies on cable until shame overcame his poor judgment.

The big day itself, the 17th, was his least favorite of the lot—more ordeal than celebration. Mid-morning, the green-clad authentics would have their parade, corned beef and cabbage, and pints of Guinness. As they drifted away, satiated and sleepy, Clematis would bolster the barricades for the after-work crowd, soon to be as thick as their brogues were thin.

Plastic cups would replace pint glasses, so the excessive drinking for any old excuse mob pouring in wouldn't leave the streets littered with their shards of disregard. Menus would be cut to just a few of the standards, rushed from kitchens half-cooked on greasy paper plates as if the annual tradition included eating like swine. *Worst of all,* he thought, *traditional Irish music would be replaced by loud, crass rock and roll to perfectly match the swarm.*

In 21st-century Amerikay, Patrick's national holiday had been hijacked, including at his own Murphy's, which he wouldn't go near on the 17th.

The more his Irishness emerged, the less any of it mattered. Especially this year with his own homeland under siege. His new Sligo friend, Kerry O'Connor, had invited him to a "different type of celebration" and he jumped at the offer. "Pleased you can make it, Patrick," he said. "Let's meet at the warehouse on Sunday in the noon hour, and we'll see where it goes from there."

Finnie couldn't join them because it was all hands on deck at Murphy's for the insanity. While she and her colleagues were happy to make the extra money, she said, it was their least favorite day of the year. Same as the poor souls in retail who endure the month-long Christmas rush. Frozen smiles on frazzled faces.

He met offsite with Marie and gave her the plusses and minuses of moving the business, as he'd discussed with Larry. "I trust your decision, Pat," she said. "Just get us out of here."

She was working overtime at home organizing boxes of client transfer documents he'd gotten from the other firms. He was also busy copying client files and lists and keeping an eye out for his oppressors. They well knew the drill and surely had their prey under surveillance. The big news around the office was no longer the imminent changes. It appeared the rout was worsening. King and Wolfe were opening a "huge account," according to Saunders. "The largest in the history of the office."

The walls said they'd met an heiress to a family fortune from commercial fisheries across several Scandinavian countries. She'd recently put a binder on an oceanfront mansion on the island and was moving a dollop of her chowder across the seas. On the day she opened her account, the red carpet was rolled out, including an appearance by the big pooh-bah from Miami. The only thing missing was a pipes and drums greeting.

Saunders had the gall to walk their new catch to the entrance of Patrick's office unannounced. With a dismissive turn, he pointed to the eastern view and said, "This will be Ian's new office next time you're in."

Lingering just a moment on the view, clearly discomfited by the intrusion, she turned and stepped back into the corridor, saying, "Please excuse our interruption."

Tall and lean, extremely attractive in a mature Lauren Hutton sort of way, she was dressed exquisitely in a two-piece beige suit with an elegant red blouse and matching shoes direct from the windows of Worth Avenue. Her outfit included a feathered hat with a sheer veil to protect her cream-colored Nordic face against the mid-day sun. Head to toes, she looked every inch the heiress. From out in the corridor, King made certain to flash Patrick a huge grin and snarky thumbs-up.

Marie had been called down to Saunders's office and introduced as the client associate who will be servicing her account. "Her name is Erica Salmberg," she told Patrick. "She's very polite—gracious even."

"I can't say the same for King," he grumbled. "He can't even be dignified in his winning. She deserves so much better."

After her highness had departed, Saunders made a point to stop back over to torment him further. "Hey, Connelly, your prospective share of KW's growing empire just got cut in half. Better not dilly-dally much longer; it'll only get worse from here."

"Thanks for the update." He didn't bother to lift his eyes from his desk. The time for talk had long since passed. He'd be leaving for greener pastures soon enough.

Trying his best to put all this aside, to stay peaceful, he focused on the good while continuing his preparations for the coming St. Patrick's festivities.

The pre-party started Friday evening at Murphy's with Smithwick's served in a proper pint glass, a superb meal served on proper dinnerware, Bushmills Irish Coffee served in proper crystal, all enhanced by proper traditional live music. It was a properly lovely evening all around. [31]

On Saturday, St. Patrick's Eve, he took Finnie south to Delray Beach to enjoy a change of scenery. After a fine dinner, they held hands and clanked glasses and sang traditional Irish drinking songs until a yawn and glance at her watch signaled it was time to close it down. It was a routine he well recognized: the instantaneous shift from party mode to work mode.

On the drive home, they stopped for a brief period of reflection at their favorite bench along their favorite waterway to watch the stars sparkle and the moon enchant. With his arm gently cradling his sweetheart from Cushendun, Patrick sat by his Atlantic sea contemplating the days ahead. Gazing northeast toward the miraculous Gulf Stream, flowing in the general direction of the old country, he felt the call of freedom in his breast. [32]

33

ST. PATRICK'S DAY, COUNTY PALM BEACH

U p early on Sunday, Finnie was getting ready for the all-day battle while Patrick was busy preparing for Kerry's warehouse affair. He was a wee bit more ebullient. *This green shirt, or this one? Maybe the Guinness rugby jersey? Or maybe both?* His tweed cap was a certainty whichever direction he went. The news had broken on Saturday: "Disney has agreed to acquire Cedar Fair Entertainment Company for $70 a share." It hadn't slipped his mind this time, and the news was far less startling. With their imminent departure from the firm, what client wouldn't follow him to greener pastures now? Across an ocean, if he asked.

His cell phone had been buzzing all the previous evening which he'd blissfully ignored. Now though, as it step-danced frantically across the kitchen table, he wrestled it in and hit the accept button.

"Geez Louise, Pat, what the hell is going on?"

"Good morning, Marie. What's shaking, besides my phone?"

"Every inch of my body. Crap, we're going to jail. I don't want to go to jail."

"Relax, honey, please. We're not going anywhere. I'm as surprised as you are. I've never been this lucky in all my life."

"Come on, Pat, this can't be luck. They'll never believe you anyway."

"You're right about that. One success is bad enough. But *you* need to believe me, Marie. I know no one at Disney, Cedar Fair, Cracker Barrel, or anyone who knows anyone. This is all just dumb luck."

"I want to believe you; I really do," she said with a tremor. "But holy moly, this looks bad. Real bad."

"I'll talk to anyone who wants to talk to me; I'll take a lie detector test if they ask. It's on the up-and-up. I'm like a poker player who's gotten a couple of royal flushes in a row, that's all."

"What are the odds of that?"

"Pretty low, I'm guessing."

"Crap, what are we gonna tell the clients? Monday will be crazy."

"How about if we tell them the truth—that we've had a once-in-a-lifetime spark of good luck, a bit of magic, and they should relax and enjoy it?"

"Okay, Pat, but things aren't getting any easier, I'll tell you that."

"Happy St. Patrick's Day, Marie. I love you."

"Sweet talking's not helping. Crap—" She was still saying "crap" when he ended the call.

Patrick was having more fun this time around, feeling lightheaded, otherworldly. King's face, then Wolfe's, and especially Saunders's militaristic profile came to mind. He saw the incredulous disgust at his good luck, heard the vile accusations.

Kay's venerable face interceded, this time floating in a pink bubble overhead, overseeing the entire landscape in a "Kay the Good Witch of the South" scene. In super slow motion, she drifts in closer, looking a little pasty from too much makeup. Her still sumptuous lips form and then expound the words: *Tell them to go fuck themselves. Nobody fucks with Patrick Connelly."*

"As you wish, my dear," he says with a laugh. Not very Oz-like, but he liked the rewrite, nonetheless.

He opened *The Irish Times* Weekend Edition one more time. It read, "Saturday and Sunday, March 2nd and 3rd." The news articles were all different, and the St. Patrick's Day festivities pull-out section was absent. Folding the paper back up, he stuck it in a file drawer along with the January 27th 'Europe Sliding' paper. "Keepsakes," he named the file.

"You know, Finnster, I was thinking, maybe we should have checked out the racetrack results, played a few winners—just the long shots." Her deep frown expressed her opinion meticulously. "Just a joke, sweetheart," he assured her.

Damn, he thought, *maybe she'd seen the same* Bewitched *episode.*

They shared a traditional Irish breakfast, sans blood any-thing, and by request, she accompanied The Chieftains on her harp. Gazing around his homey den, watching his sprite pluck-ing on the strings, he imagined his old buddies from the Bronx saying, "Oh for Christ's sake, Paddy, will ya wipe that shit-eating grin off your face before we do it for youse." He wouldn't need to correct them to "pancake-eating." In the context, "shit-eating" worked perfectly.

When it was time for her to leave, she said, "Please give Mr. O'Connor my warmest St. Patrick's greeting and have a grand time," followed with her usual warning, "Remember to drink plenty of water, a bottle an hour, and drive carefully, please. Call a cab if you need to."

With a grateful embrace, he said, "You know I will, Finndoll. Best of luck at the rugby scrum."

As he drove west on Southern, calls were storming his cell from both Jeff Saunders and Jack Lawson. "These can wait for-about-ever," he muttered, turning off the volume and zipping the phone into his Tumi. The man usually inhabiting the corner of Dixie and Southern was nowhere in sight. *Too bad,* he thought, tucking away his special green treat. *I'll catch him the next time.*

Arriving at the antique storehouse just ahead of noon, a sign taped to the front door read: "Happy St. Patrick's Day. The Door is Open—Please Enter." He gave a heavy push and passed into the dimly lit front room, once again visible by candlelight and the glowing hearth. Not a soul in sight, he made his way into the shadowed far corner, through the open door, and back in time.

The chandeliers' amber light shimmered, casting a cathedral-like quality to the long, high-raftered room. Hearing a mild din down the way, he pushed on toward the "Temple Bar district," as he'd described it to Finnie, where his host was serving drinks to several figures sitting on stools at the bar.

"Patrick, you're here," Kerry called out. "Good to see you; come and meet my other guests." He was introduced to three men and three women, each dressed in drab brown clothing resembling something a monk might wear.

"You didn't tell me to arrive in period costume," he scolded.

"Oh nonsense, my boy. You're looking very dapper in your Irish cap—and ready for a match if one breaks out."

Settling at a low bar table, he was handed both an Irish coffee and a pint of Smithwick's, both in authentic glass and crystal vessels. A good sign there'd be no crowd of rowdies pouring in here any time soon. "You read my mind, Kerry. This is how I always begin the big day."

"I've no such skill, Patrick, but my memory still serves on occasion," he said. "I picked up on your tradition in one of our chats."

Patrick raised his glass to the group and toasted, "Happy St. Patrick's Day to all. *Sláinte.*" The greeting was returned all around. After a period of amiable chatter, wherein he took note of several deep brogues, a distant piping came in the direction of the back of the warehouse. Kerry informed his guests this was their cue to fill their glasses and proceed down the way.

Trailing the group along the antique-lined parade route, he soon came upon a lighted chapel gaily adorned with fresh flowers. A small man in an oversized jacket and cap sat alone on a stool clinging to his odd-looking wind instrument. When everyone was settled in the pews, Kerry gave a nod. Moving only his right arm and fingers, the man began playing a haunting wail that Patrick recognized from Riverdance's seemingly never-ending tours. He'd seen the show at least once whenever it came to the Kravis Center. As the piper emitted his melancholy sound, the audience sat perfectly still until the last notes cascaded through the vastness, and their hushed tears spilled into the tragic beauty of it all. [33]

The spell was finally broken when the piper began to speak in his native tongue from under a tweed cap tilted low. Wishing there were subtitles, he discerned the piper's name as Paddy, of all names, the instrument uilleann pipes, and the piece he performed the lament of Cú Chulainn. An exalted hero of medieval Irish mythology, Chulainn had mistakenly slain his only son in battle after being duped by the jealous mother.

No wonder the intensity of the cry, Patrick thought, while his only son Liam's precious face flashed in his mind. He wished Liam and Erin were here this very moment to embrace—and to share in his grief and savor such splendor. He missed his children terribly, especially at times like this.

Kerry stepped to the podium to announce a short ceremony in honor of "the only true Celtic nation remaining on earth" and the endurance of the Irish spirit and culture. As one of his guests approached the front, Kerry said, "This is a day meant for solemn gratitude and contemplation, in sharp contrast to the wild, drunken street brawl it has become in America. And so, we treat it here as such."

"Amen," Patrick said.

The woman standing at the podium referenced *How the Irish Saved Civilization*, Thomas Cahill's seminal book, as a meaningful source before relating the following story: "Born in Great Britain in the late 4th century, Maewyn Succat, who would one day become St. Patrick, was a lowly shepherd boy enslaved in the northern hills of Antrim for six years. After escaping and making his way home, he found faith and joined the clergy. Years later, legend says, the voice of the Irish people begged him to 'come and walk among us once again.' At age forty-seven, Patricius heeded the call and spent his final thirty years converting Irish pagans to Christianity.

"A larger-than-life man of courage, steadfast in his compassion and generosity, he profoundly loved and worried about his flock. His temper would flare whenever he perceived an injustice, especially against women. The Irish came to revere women for their courage, determination, and intellect, which was revolutionary in the barbarian world. Although his flock still loved a good fight, Patrick decreased violence and fostered a more peaceful culture of spiritual courage. By redirecting their intensity, the warrior-children of Ireland became more humane and noble. He taught them it was possible to be both brave and nonviolent. He was the first human known to speak out unequivocally against slavery, bringing an end to the Irish slave trade."

She paused for the eruption of applause to abate before continuing:

"In a time when barbarism swept over Europe and destroyed much of its heritage, Patrick's monumental efforts led to monasteries sprouting up all over Ireland and Scotland, and eventually England and elsewhere. These became the first population centers and places where Irish and Europeans, poor and rich, women and men, were fed and educated for no expense. Irish monks and converts followed in Patrick's footsteps and accepted seekers from all walks of life. By the time he died in 461 AD, the Roman empire was nearly extinct, while Ireland, in sharp contrast, was emerging from chaos towards peace and literacy. The Apostle of the Irish nation, the first missionary bishop in history, Patrick became Ireland's first patron saint."

The next speaker focused on two worthy heirs who followed in Patrick's footsteps: Columcille, or St. Columba, and Brigit of Kildare, or St. Brigid. "These two heroic leaders exhibited extraordinary faith and charity," he began, "and their boundless compassion spread over Ireland and beyond. They taught that prayer and hard work could overcome avarice born from previous sufferings, and with enough adherence, they could be like joyful little children again."

Holding up an extraordinary example of an ornate leather book cover, he continued: "As just noted, Patrick and his

successors inspired the building of stone monasteries throughout Ireland and Scotland. In these spiritual and scholarly colo-
nies, Irish monks preserved oral traditions, manuscripts, and the
world's greatest literary works, saving much of it from extinc-
tion. Working tirelessly, they delighted in their literary endeav-
ors, playing with the language, developing it, forever seeking to
enhance their skills. They considered the shapes of letters and
the sequence of numbers magical, particularly the number three,
which represented the Trinity.

"Replacing sheepskin with vellum, they produced the Irish
codex—early Christian gospels—the most illustrative and magical books the world had ever seen. The most famous of these is
the *Book of Kells*, a priceless masterpiece on display at the Library
of Trinity College in Dublin. It has been called 'genius,' and 'the
work of angels, not of men.'"

As he held the book aloft again, flipping open to a few
pages filled with colorful words and designs, the group
expressed their appreciation of this great achievement. Becky
and Patrick Connelly had spent time in Dublin with their children the year before. When he wasn't too busy pub crawling,
they freed up some time to tour the Trinity College grounds.
After waiting an hour in the rain and being slowly herded into
a dark narrow room, they briefly glimpsed two pages of *Kells*
displayed inside an impenetrable glass case before being ushered along. It felt underwhelming. Afterward, they descended
a floor to the famous cylindrical ceilinged library where all
would be forgiven. In this most enthralling room they'd ever
had the good fortune to visit, every other tourist seemed to

disappear as they lingered on benches for an hour or more in its serene magnificence.

"With early medieval Europe in ruins due to German barbarism," the speaker continued, "Irish monks fanned out to colonize bereft peasants left in squalor. In their safe communities of learning, they engaged in the freedom of discussion, passed on habits of the mind, and encouraged independent thought. Tying books to their waists where severed, blood-drenched heads once dangled, they were now cultural warriors bringing their love of learning and bookmaking skills to wherever they went. Because of their heroic efforts, literacy was reestablished in exhausted Europe, and at the same time, Christianity was introduced into Ireland without bloodshed, which was a first in history. Combined with Roman literacy, they helped lighten the Dark Ages, at least for a time."

Once again expressing debt to Thomas Cahill for writing one of the great books of Irish history, the speaker departed to enthusiastic appreciation.

Kerry stepped back to the podium to further the fascinating story: "Patrick and his ancestors had, in effect, designed an 'Irish Code of Honor,' and those who carried it would be under the influence of a higher power. The code included three traits: First, courage under fire—always seeking the promotion of peaceful outcomes, which is true bravery. Second, compassion and generosity—extended especially to the weakest and those in urgent need. Third, a love of learning—seeking the advancement of literacy and culture to all peoples of the world.

"However, as throughout history, change, and upheaval were approaching. The 8th century brought Vikings attacks which ransacked much of Ireland, largely destroying the monasteries. This began a relentless period of invasion and occupation, including the 12th-century Normans and the British from the 16th to 19th centuries. The great famine of the mid-19th century was a flattening blow to the Irish culture, causing mass death and migration. By then, nine million island inhabitants had shrunken to three."

The room paused a moment in silence to absorb the depth of their bitter history before Kerry continued: "The formerly lush and fertile land could no longer feed their people, one of the great tragedies of barbaric occupation. Too many died, and too many others left for Australia and America desperate for a better life. The remaining great families of Ireland, the educated and prosperous landowners, fled in all directions and became known as the 'wild geese.' They left behind a generally impoverished and bitter nation of uneducated peasants."

Kerry's guests sat in rapt and reverent attention, unable to hold back their tears.

A final presenter brought the Irish story across the sea to America's shores:

"The massive Irish immigration during the famines, the 1840s and '50s, changed the face of the emerging nation forever," she began, "particularly the cities of New York, Boston, Chicago, and Philadelphia. Industrious and loyal, the immigrants answered rampant discrimination and poverty by working long hours for little pay, gradually grinding their way up the chain in such fields as public service and soldiering. The Irish populated as much as 40 percent of these northern cities by the time of the Civil War, and nearly 170,000 served on both sides of the conflict to end slavery.

"In the north, one way to show their loyalty and put an end to the 'No Irish Need Apply' signs was to enlist in the Union army in all-Irish brigades. In earlier decades, the Irish migrated south to Charleston and Savannah to build canals and railroads. Sympathetic to the Confederacy's desire for independence from an overbearing government, they also raised Irish brigades to fight in the war."

If they hadn't heard enough pitiable history by now, she added another blow: "Known for their courage, ferocity, and toughness on the battlefield, the Irish led the charge at such notable battles as Potomac, Antietam, Fredericksburg, and Gettysburg, where they were slaughtered like sheep. One of the heartbreaking tragedies of the war involved Irishmen fighting bloody battles against Irishmen. Once they understood the desperately poor were being used to fight a rich man's war and they were being used as cannon fodder, particularly by the Union army, the Irish ceased volunteering."

Aware of what happened next, Patrick felt a rising mixture of anger and shame. In dire need of soldiers, the Union Army targeted poor immigrants by drafting any able-bodied man who couldn't pay $300 to avoid service. The anti-war sentiment across the teetering nation skyrocketed, and the Irish violently protested their conscription. During the infamous 'NYC Draft Riots' of 1863, they conducted themselves deplorably by any measure, effectively ending their organized participation in the war.

In closing, the speaker said: "On this 150th anniversary of the American Civil War, it is important to remember the Irish brigades who fought so valiantly and suffered as much as 60 percent casualty rates, with tens of thousands killed and wounded. We must also honor the important role women played in the effort, where countless Irish wives, daughters, and nuns served the war effort as nurses and in other ways. They behaved with typical Irish grit and courage."

Stepping forward one last time, Kerry said, "Many thanks to each of our superb presenters. We will now make a brief bestowal before getting back to the festivities." Handed a folded brown garment and a scabbard with a long handle extending from it, like a medieval sword might have, he said: "In honor of his authentic Irish spirit, and his dedication to the same precious code of honor our brothers and sisters have carried forward throughout the tumultuous centuries, we present this robe and sword to our newest guardian." When the light applause ceased, he continued, "In the name of three spiritual luminaries of peace and generosity, St. Patrick, St. Columba, and St. Brigid, and the brave warriors throughout history who gave their lives on battlefields protecting the homeland and adopted lands, we now present these symbols to Patrick Seamus Connelly."

Patrick bolted straight up in his chair with a flummoxed look and began breathing in rapid flutters.

"Patrick, when you recover your ghost," Kerry said with a chuckle, "would you approach the front of the room, please?" He quickly motored to the podium to blithe laughter. Handing him the robe, Kerry said, "This humble robe symbolizes your never-ending pursuit of learning and literacy and the humility, kindness, and generosity you impart to all you touch." Extending the sheathed sword, he said, "This powerful symbol of your undying fortitude and quest for justice has been infused with magic from long ago. Consider it an invaluable weapon in the protection of the weakest, aligned only with your highest values." Now he faced the group and, in a raised voice, declared, "Patrick Seamus Connelly, as you are elevated to the lofty status of the druid, may the noble champions of spirit, light, and truth continue to guide your every decision."

Patrick accepted his gifts to rousing applause and thanked the group. "I'm . . . touched, humbled, grateful for the honor. I hope I can be worthy of your trust." He donned the monk's robe and carried the considerable weapon on his lap as he returned to his place. The only thought that rose in him was, *Christ, did I just say 'hope'?*

"Now it's time we repair to the dining table for our traditional feast," Kerry said, and with a mischievous glow added, "Please stop at the bar for a refill, or three, on the way."

The sound of the pipes rose once again, this time with a more cheerful tenor accompanied by percussion and whistles. [34] As the group proceeded along the wide aisleway, they came upon the half-dozen musicians sitting between the bar and the festal dining table. Patrick accepted his host's gracious invitation to visit the bar—three times—before settling into an open place at the long table. Blinking his eyes two or three times, it didn't change what he thought he saw. If he wasn't crazy, which was still eminently possible, he believed the entertainment for this St. Patrick's Day afternoon, direct from Dublin, was provided by The Chieftains.

With all the guests now seated at the table, another twenty or so chairs remained unoccupied. A clamor soon arose from the direction of the warehouse entrance where a procession of men and women advanced towards them, led by the two burly bearded men who'd delivered his furniture. Those who followed were directed to the open seats by another figure in the famil-iar hooded brown robe. When everyone had taken their places, the cloaked person sat in the last remaining chair. Drawing back his hood, Patrick was stunned to be sitting across the table from Larry Devlin. They exchanged looks but didn't speak as the focus had turned to the new arrivals. The two sitting on either side of Patrick seemed familiar, but he couldn't quite place them.

The band quieted, and Kerry introduced his newest guests as "Prominent people of great courage, who although down on their luck continue to fight every day for a better life." Now raising a glass, he toasted, "Today, in the true spirit of St. Patrick, we pay tribute to each of these distinguished men and women. The very best we have. *Sláinte.*"

"*Sláinte!*" came the chorus, and the celebratory music rose in unison.

On this most historic St. Patrick's Day, the best he'd ever had, Patrick the Druid was feasting with old and new friends, listening to the most iconic Irish band of all time, in the prestigious company of the homeless men and women from the various crossroads of County Palm Beach.

34

MONDAY FUN DAY

The next morning arrived much too soon. Cedar Fair Monday was bound to be lots of FUN. He reluctantly jumped up and raced groggily from the house while his exhausted Finnie slept soundly.

Arriving at the office just as the market was opening, he saw his latest bit of "dumb luck" had zoomed to $70 with a record number of shares trading hands. The headlines asked, "Who's Next for Disney?"

"May as well ask Connelly," was the answer circulating around the office.

"Happy day after, *Paddy*." Marie was cradling the phone while pointing to the stack of messages already piling up. "Ready for a crazy day?"

"What's the general tone?"

"Most are thrilled," she replied as she put another caller on hold. "A few think you should run for president, but they want to hear it from you—that it's just a hot streak you're on."

"I can do that," he said. "Because that's all it is."

Exploding past the cubicles with the entire compliance staff trailing him, Jeff Saunders bellowed, "What? You don't return urgent phone calls from your boss? Really, Connelly? Really?"

"Boss? I was always told the office manager works for the producers," he responded impatiently. "That would make me your boss." Marie had turned her head down and away, fumbling nervously along her desktop.

"I left four messages!" Saunders lashed. "I don't care what you call me, but I do expect my calls returned." His underlings gathered behind were shifting uncomfortably in their silences.

Breathing deeply, Patrick counted to three and said, "It was the weekend, Jeff, not to mention my national holiday. Even God rested on Sunday."

"You don't get the gravity of this, do you?" He plowed past him into King's future office.

"Gravity of what? Getting lucky twice? Making money for my clients? It should happen to everyone."

Hastily dragging in extra chairs, the flock nested, and the door slammed shut. Jack Lawson spoke first. "Patrick, we had no choice but to contact the SEC and ask them to take over the investigation."

"You've called in the SEC?" His expression turned incredulous. "What evidence do you have?"

"You tell us, Connelly," Saunders barked out. "My patience has run out, buddy-boy."

"Like I've said, this is just a streak of good luck I'm on. It's never happened to me in thirty years, so I'm just trying to enjoy it. Can't you do the same?"

"Enjoy it?" barked Saunders. "I'm taking you down, wise-ass."

"Enough, Jeff!" cried Lawson.

"Enough?" he screamed back. "My whole operation's in chaos because of that felon."

"Felon? Again?" Patrick repeated. "That's quite the creative leap."

"He didn't mean it that way, Patrick," replied Lawson. "But the circumstances are concerning, I'm sure you understand. Listen, it seems clear you have a source at Disney, or investment banking, or one of the involved law firms. It'll do you a world of good to tell us who it is now."

"I wish I could help you, Jack, I really do," he countered, "but I'm clean. It's just dumb luck, or maybe I should say Dumbo luck—like a kind of Disney magic?"

"Dumbo luck? Disney magic?" Saunders yelped. "That's the story you're sticking with?"

"We have to believe in something, Jeff. Why not something fun like Disney magic?"

"Okay, criminal, you've left me no choice." Saunders was growling while stampeding around the room. "This office is closed, off-limits, evidence for the SEC. Your assistant's area too. I'm reassigning her today, and you're suspended without pay until we get to the bottom of this."

"Suspended? without pay? Can he do that, Jack?" Patrick's hands were raised in a befuddled, shrugging manner. "Who is he, Roger Goodell? Did I fail a friggin' drug test?"

Saunders was up and leading his scrambling followers into the corridor while Lawson remained sitting. "Patrick, your desk and file cabinets are the firm's property," he said. "Let's step outside; I've got to lock the door."

"This is insane," he reasoned. "I've had a clean record for a quarter-century."

"Who else did you speak with about buying Cedar?"

"No one, besides Marie and Jeff. Why?"

"There was an inordinate amount of buying throughout the office in the last week. Nearly every employee owns shares, present company excluded. Some of their clients too."

"I didn't tell a soul. Like I've said, it's just a boring, conservative income play. There was nothing to tell."

"My problem is the 'boring, conservative income play' was involved in a merger a week after our office loaded up on the shares."

"Ask our boss about that. 'The walls have ears,' he likes to say."

Packing up his Tumi, Patrick glanced around his former office. Gathering framed photos and other personal items from the bookshelves, the entire past decade rolled through his mind—the good, the bad, the ugly. The yin and the yang. Slowly, reluctantly, he moved away towards Marie's desk. Lawson followed and turned to lock his office door.

"You're going down, Connelly." Saunders was again striding towards him. "And I'll be the first to say 'bon voyage.'"

"Nice, Jeff," Patrick uttered. "Will you at least be bringing the champagne?"

"Fat chance." As Marie's rigid face surveyed the grim scene, Saunders called back over his shoulder, "Report to my office for reassignment, Maura."

"It's Marie," she said to no one.

Lawson had stayed behind. Looking at Patrick's steaming red face, he said, "You're telling the truth, aren't you?"

"Of course, I'm telling the truth."

"Okay," he said with a nod, adding, "I'm sorry, Patrick, about the personal attacks. It's inexcusable."

"It's not your fault, Jack," he said. "I've seen guys like him before, and I honestly don't think it's anything personal. I'm just the latest obstacle in the way of his big dream—living across that bridge by next year." Patrick was pointing east from his window to the magnificent panorama beyond, probably for the last time.

"He does seem in a hurry," Lawson agreed.

"A hurry? Christ alive, Jack, he's riding a bullet train. He reminds me of the town hall meetings with our ex-CEO, the guy in charge before you came on board. 'Don't tell me your problems,' he would say to the poor guy who dared ask him a question, 'give me your solutions.' He got his 'solution' when they sent him packing."

"I didn't know him."

"I don't think anyone did," Patrick said. "But I was always nervous listening to him. Jeff's kind of the same—serious, self-focused, hyper-intense—like a walking, talking nervous breakdown.

When he's done with me, it'll just be on to his next hurdle. Wouldn't you say so, Jack?"

Lawson turned away slowly, silently, and began to lumber down the corridor into the wake of his brutish boss.

His new antique desk would become his mobile office until further notice. Assuring Marie their move was in the works, he told her, "Keep preparing and keep smiling; this nightmare is almost over."

"I'll try, Pat," she said stoically. "But they're already giving me the new rules: how to answer the phone, how they like their coffee, and lots of other nonsense. Saunders made copies of our client contact lists. This is hard to take."

"For Christ's sake, Marie, just don't get yourself fired. Their time is coming, I swear; I don't know when or how, but it's coming. In the meantime, keep your cool and keep me informed."

Then he dialed up his clients, one after another, telling them, "Marie will be working on another project temporarily, and I'll be working from home." Answering their questions as best he could, he confidently said, "There's nothing to worry about, so please, relax and enjoy the profits; our success came from solid research and lucky timing."

Most were ebullient, never having had instant success like this in the stock market. Several asked, "Any more ideas, Pat?"

"Not this moment," he replied with a laugh. "I think we'll just let this one simmer for a few weeks."

"Not a good idea to walk away from the table when you're on a hot streak," one client added.

"Haven't you heard Kenny Rogers's gambling song?" he responded. After singing a verse, it was suggested he keep his day job. [35]

Keeping his day job was Patrick's strategy—or at least his hope.

35

THE PALM BEACH CYCLE

Enjoying a quiet Chieftains reel, he poured two splashes of whiskey and settled into the den with Finnie. [36] Their lives were a whirlwind of late, and they each sat jiggling their ice in tranquil reflection, welcoming the shared silence.

"Was St. Patrick's Day really just yesterday?" Patrick finally asked in an exhausted voice. Silence. When he asked how her day at Murphy's went, Finnie just rolled her eyes in response. When she asked about his suspension, he said, "Let's not spoil the evening, and besides, there's nothing much left to say." So, they each sat jiggling their ice in tranquil reflection, welcoming the shared silence.

After a time, he recounted the festivities at the warehouse: the guests, the brogues, the speeches, The Chieftains, Larry Devlin's appearance, and dining with the homeless. "The man sitting to my right said he recognized me, that we'd met in Dublin many years ago when we were kids. That's not even possible, but Christ, why the hell not? I'll believe anything these days. Anyway, it was the most amazing day I've ever had."

"More amazing than the day we met," she teased, "and every day since?"

"Well, The Chieftains are pretty tough competition," he teased back. "I was wishing you were with me the entire time, Finnster. You're like an appendage—I wouldn't know what to do without you."

"Thank you," she said with a smile. "I've never been referred to as an 'appendage' before."

"That reminds me." Leaving the room briefly, he returned with the leather-sheathed sword straddling his lap. "Take a look at this bad boy."

"You're an official druid now. See that, Patrick? I told you it was your time."

"Time for what, though? It still confuses me, all that's happening. I can't even imagine what comes next."

"This comes next," she said, leaning in with a vacuuming kiss imprisoning his lips.

"It's the sword, isn't it?" His words came clumsily through lingering pins and needles.

"Undoubtedly," she concurred.

Finnie unsheathed the stunning weapon and wrapped both tiny hands around its engraved, leather-bound hilt, which included a jeweled cross guard and open ring design. Struggling with its heaviness, she raised it aloft, saying, "It's absolutely magnificent—it looks a thousand years old."

At just that moment, a lone dusky ray of light peeked through the window illuminating its diamond-shaped, double-sharpened edges. Sitting a spell in the glint, noticing the coincidence, Patrick said, "It must be a replica. Don't you think? It would be worth a fortune otherwise."

"Probably," she answered, carefully sliding it back into its scabbard.

"What will I do with it?"

"You can't go on a mass murder spree, slicing up all who oppose you, if that's what you're asking."

"I was thinking just a mini-spree."

"Sounds charming, but I suspect there may have been a more peaceful message in the ceremony."

"Unfortunately, I believe you're right. But I could use a little *Game of Thrones* action right about now."

"Those were brutal times," she rebutted. "I think you may have a few better options today."

"Bummer. I miss the good old days."

Shifting the subject to something a drop less bloodletting, she ran her hand along its length, saying, "A sword is so rich in symbolism."

"Like, don't be messing with me?"

"That's one, for sure," she answered. "But medieval metalworkers were considered sacred, not only for the protection their weapons provided but also for the beauty of their artistry."

"It is gorgeous," he agreed. "For a killing machine, that is."

"It was more than that," she said with a hint of displeasure. "The sword was of earth and water, often imbued with magic."

"Just what I need, more magic."

"The more, the merrier," she countered. "The sword evokes the owner's will, spirit, and resolve, and it aligns with a higher purpose and set of values. I suspect that's why it found you."

"Found me?"

"Yes, remember we've spoken about magic finding us? If we suspend our disbelief and keep our eyes open, sometimes it comes along just in time."

"But why a sword?"

"Well, it can be used for evil, to slaughter and conquer, or for good, such as protecting the innocent. It's the intent that matters, what's in your heart."

"Then you're saying I can slice them into ribbons, if that's what's in my heart?"

"Sure, if you want to spend the rest of your life in a dark little cage with a guy named Sal."

"Jesus, my skin is crawling at the thought," he said with a shiver.

"Then you'd better keep your sword sheathed, dear."

"This disappoints me greatly to hear, Finnster."

After refreshing their drinks, the conversation turned to the greatest Irish mythological heroes of battle. "The most revered warrior of the Ulster Cycle is probably Cú Chulainn," she started. "He's still adored by both Irish nationalists and unionists."

"Something they actually agree on?" he asked incredulously. "Christ, that's not easy to find. What do you mean, 'Ulster Cycle'?"

"The second of the four great cycles of Irish mythology—the Ulster Cycle centers around the 1st century AD. In legend, Chulainn protected Ireland against foreign invasion, and he also defended the ancient northern kingdom of Ulster from conquering armies to the south. The stories of his power and fearlessness have been re-told throughout the years, even by the likes of Joyce and Yeats."

"The lament Paddy Moloney played at the ceremony," Patrick recalled, "about Chulainn mistakenly killing his son on the battlefield. It's heartbreaking."

"You know what's been said about the Irish: 'all their battles are merry and their songs sad.'"

"It sounds like most of their battles didn't turn out so well."

"They rarely do," she agreed. "One of the most powerful women depicted in literature came from these early stories, Queen Mebd, also known as Maeve."

"What made her so powerful?"

"Her name means goddess of intoxication."

"Nice start," he said with a lift of his glass. "Go on."

"She was called the warrior queen of Connacht—famous for her renowned beauty. Men would fall to their knees at the sight of her."

"Probably not a good pick-up move," he said with a smirk.

"You're right," she said. "Strength was Maeve's aphrodisiac. She displayed all the passions usually attributed to men: accumulating property and wealth, prowess on the battlefield, and especially in the bedroom. It was said her sexual expertise was unparalleled, and her bravest warriors were often granted access to her willing thighs."

"I'm feeling a little faint," he said, fanning himself. "Are you a descendent, perchance?"

"I think not. Sorry to disappoint you."

"You couldn't disappoint me in a hundred cycles."

"You notorious charmer," she said with a smile.

After a short Maeve-inspired break, Finnie continued his latest Irish history lesson. "Next came many of Ireland's most beloved folk tales: the Fenian Cycle stories dated from the 3rd to 5th centuries AD, give or take a century."

"What's a century when you're in the Dark Ages?"

"A little early for the Dark Ages," she corrected. "The Fenian stories centered on the Fianna warriors, especially Fionn MacCumhaill, better known as Finn MacCool. Many were written in verse by his poet son, Oison."

"I've been to Fionn MacCool's in Jacksonville Beach. Great pub. It was St. Patrick's Day about a decade ago."

"I'd appreciate you not mentioning that cursed day for a while, at least until my feet feel better."

"Sorry, Finnie. Want a foot rub?" She immediately popped her distressed dogs up into his lap.

"Ooh, that feels divine," she cooed, and continued her story. "Fionn was a gentle, benevolent giant, just like you, Patrick. Only he was fifty feet tall with size forty-seven shoes."

"Slight difference. Can you imagine what his—I can't even say it."

"Thank you," she scolded. "He grew up in Ballyfin, County Laois, which translates to 'town of Fionn.'"

"I like that. I think it's time to change the Bronx to Ballypatrick."

"Why don't you write a letter, start a campaign?"

"Maybe I will, as soon as I get through this losing my career thing."

"Good idea. Anyway, Fionn was a beautiful boy with thick, flowing, white-blond hair. He spent his youth in the Slieve Bloom Mountains in Ireland's midlands. It was mostly forestland, and that's where he was trained in war, hunting and poetry; by two women incidentally."

"That seems to be a consistent theme in Irish mythology," he said. "The power and influence of women."

"Absolutely," she agreed. "Women had equal rights to men, owned property, and had positions of high power. Ireland stood alone at the time."

"It makes me feel pride."

"Yes, me as well," she said. "So, we'd read the stories and take to the forest, both the boys and the girls, for a day of hunting and battle."

"We watched a World War II show called *Combat*," he said, "then went out to the woods to kill the enemy. Same thing, in a way."

"In our stories, the forest was the source of magic," she recalled, "with druids and gypsies and faeries and other magical creatures living there."

"Our woods were crawling with Krauts—that's what our soldiers called the enemy." Receiving no feedback, he quickly shifted battle plans. "The woods still feel full of magic, don't they? The shadows. The mist. The echoes. The creeks and waterfalls. The strange creatures. All the creepy beauty."

"We should go to the forest someday, Patrick."

"I'll put it on our list."

"That would be fun," she replied. "In one famous Fionn story, he was training with a druid named Finnegas near the river Boyne, north of Dublin. They caught the magical salmon of knowledge in the river. While cooking the salmon, Fionn burned his thumb and put it in his mouth to ease the pain. In doing so, he acquired all the world's wisdom."

"Talk about the power of Omega-3."

"Funny, it sounds logical now that you mention it," she said. "Fionn eventually traveled north to the glens and rocky coastline of Antrim—the land of the giants—where massive stones covered graves no human could possibly lift. In legend, he protected the people from Scottish giants and built a stone causeway to bring the battle across the sea to Scotland."

"I was there—Giant's Causeway, the miraculous six-sided stone pathway to the western isles."

"They look magical, don't they? Fitting together like a honeycomb from the cliffs out into the sea."

"Well, to tell you the truth, guys in wheelchairs don't do so well on rocky coasts. I dropped the family there and went to Bushmills just up the road."

"Not a bad alternative," she laughed.

"I agree. Bushmills definitely had its magic too."

"Fionn used his powers reluctantly," she continued, "to fight invaders and giants and goblins from the underworld. He defended the homeland and its good people from rape and pillage and certain death."

"How did he become a giant?"

"Stories about shapeshifting were common. In a battle for survival, I imagine, a great warrior's heart and courage would grow to something beyond human. That may have been one way. And I'm sure as his deeds were passed on, they would magnify, his legend growing with each retelling."

"Isn't that called exaggeration? Or blarney?"

"Maybe. But Fionn's courage and heroism on the battlefield weren't in question. And he had a clever wife too. In one story, Oona used trickery to drive off a Scottish giant who was too large and powerful for her husband to defeat. Without her giant mind, Fionn might have perished that day."

"There's the power of Irish women again," he said. "And I've been lucky enough to experience it firsthand."

"Thank you, dear Patrick," she said, giving his hand a squeeze. "Because of Oona's shrewdness, Fionn had the courage to chase the retreating giant back to Scotland. He scooped up a huge handful of earth to throw at him, and the hole became Lough Neagh, Ireland's largest lake. The earth he threw into the sea became the Isle of Man."

"That's quite a handful," he said with a smirk. "I was at Lough Neagh, just north of Belfast. It sure is gigantic."

"I'm in pun pain."

"Do you want a head rub?"

"Yes, I need one badly."

"As you command, Queen Maur," he said while gently massaging her temples. "Do people really believe these tales?"

"We sure did when we were children. Did you believe in Peter Pan, Santa Claus, Gandalf, Dracula, Snow White, Cinderella, the Little Mermaid?"

"Absolutely, I did, and I'm starting to believe in them again. My druid friend, Larry Devlin, says, 'You gotta believe in something. Why not fun things like that?' And you've said the same."

"The problem with adults is we apply our logical minds to everything. We grow up and leave all the wonder and magic behind in the woods."

"Sad."

"Yes, it is. When Fionn was mortally wounded in battle, he strapped himself to a rock so he would die standing up."

"What a picture of valor," he said in contemplation. "It gives me chills."

"Since Americans love their conspiracy theories," she added. "You'll be happy to know we have one for Fionn."

"Let me guess—two archers killed him, one from a grassy knoll? No? How about—a spaceship came and took him away?"

"Nothing so grand," she said with a chuckle. "Our question is: did Fionn even die, or is he sleeping in a cave beneath Ireland? According to legend, he and his army, the Fianna, will someday awaken and defend Ireland in their moment of greatest need."

"Too bad the Fianna weren't an army of accountants," he said, batting his eyes. "They could have risen up last decade to slaughter all those ridiculous bankers and real estate speculators before they wrecked the economy."

"Don't remind me," she said glumly. "It destroyed a lot of hope."

"Did you say, hope?"

"Don't you start with that again, King Patrick," she warned. "Unfortunately, I've read nothing about the Fianna having calculators. They were nomadic warriors, hunters, and poets."

"Sounds a lot more interesting. Anyway, the legend is a good metaphor to describe the spirit of the Irish people. To protect the homeland, they'll rise up with courage and resolve, like modern-day MacCools and Chulainns."

"Not a bad story; how do you think of such things?"

"I kissed the Blarney Stone, remember? And I'm a druid now—licensed to embellish."

"So I've heard," she said with a kiss from her enchanting eyes.

"Lastly," Finnie continued, "there's no doubt Brian Boru was a real man living in County Clare around 1000 AD— a part of the Historical Cycle. The 'Lion of Ireland,' as he's remembered, is considered our greatest military leader and the last great High King."

"I've been to Brian Boru's Pub in Lake Worth," Patrick said. "Forgive me, but however legendary a king, Boru is clearly not a great restaurateur. Murphy's is much better, especially since you started working there."

"Good to hear." After receiving the expected fist bump, she said, "Brian defeated Irish kings in Limerick, Leinster, and

Dublin, uniting the south. Then he turned back Viking invasions and restored Irish rule to the nation. A ferocious warrior, he always sought first to avoid fighting and settle matters peacefully."

"Peace through strength, just like our last American Lion."

"Who was that?"

"Ronald Reagan—1980s. He, too, united a divided country and kept us safe from attack."

"Was he slain in battle like our Brian?"

"Almost," Patrick replied reflectively. "I'll tell you about Ronnie sometime. But continue, please, I'm fascinated with Brian."

"Thank you. He was called 'Brian of the Tributes' because he collected fees from defeated rulers and land barons and used the money to restore monasteries and libraries destroyed in the invasions."

"Interesting, our lion was 'Ronnie of the Riches.' He lowered taxes and slayed inflation, leading to a stock market boom and a rising middle class. Kind of the same thing—in a way." Her silence got him back on point quickly. "I love that Brian sought to rebuild the culture and spirituality of the war-torn nation. He sounds like a benevolent man, rather than just a warrior-king marauding around the countryside."

"Yes, Brian was one of a kind," she agreed. "By the time he won the infamous Battle of Clontarf near Dublin, he was elderly. A retreating Viking stumbled into his tent and killed him while he was on his knees in a prayer of gratitude."

"Ouch," he said with a grimace. "Kind of the antithesis of a prayer answered."

"I'll say," she agreed. "His body rests in St. Patrick's Cathedral in Armagh, northwest of the capital city. Buried in the church built by St. Patrick himself."

"Jesus," he said. "That kind of brings the story full circle, doesn't it?"

"Yes, it does."

After splashing each glass with a modest nightcap, he said, "Thank you, sweetheart. I can add brilliant scholar to your many other talents."

"You're welcome, Patrick. I'm proud to pass on some of our history to a true Irishman."

"A common theme in all the stories of your military and spiritual leaders, real or imagined, is they each possessed fearless courage, a deep connection to nature and spirituality, and a love of learning."

"Correct—and they had an uncommon humanity," she added. "Always kind and generous to those unable to fend for themselves. There was a higher purpose to their actions, a heroic moral to the story—the Irish Code of Honor manifest."

"Absolutely," he affirmed. "By the way, Finnster, you only mentioned three of the four mythological cycles. What was the fourth?"

"It was actually the first cycle, called Mythological," she answered. "It came before the Ulster stories."

"Too bad," he responded. "I was thinking the fourth cycle was going on right now, maybe called the 'Palm Beach Cycle.' Maybe we're even writing one of the stories?"

"Let's go with that," she said with a smile.

"I think I will," he replied through a stifled yawn. "Thanks, Finnie, my courageous, spiritual, learned, and generous Irish lassie." Taking the sword in his lap and moving toward the door, he turned and added, "I think it's time I put my sword away."

"I know just where you should put it," she said, standing up to follow him.

"Be careful," he said. "I understand it can cleave a person in half with one swift blow."

"That will be perfect."

36

TO THE FOREST WITH QUEEN MAUR

If you live in South Florida and take a nap in April, you may miss the entirety of the spring season. In a matter of an hour, the prevailing winds will shift to southerly, ushering in warming squalls with stifling tropical humidity. There's an upside. This is the day the winter population, swatting haplessly at the "no-see-ums," make their plans to decamp. In the Passover-Easter-Mother's Day corridor, the procession of cars leaving temple or church services, or brunch at the club, migrate to Palm Beach International or the I-95 and Turnpike northerly on-ramps.

"Bye-bye for now," the locals exalt. "Don't let the egregious, non-resident property tax bills hit you in your collective asses."

It was early April. Patrick was sitting out back, reveling in the comforting air when he made the mistake of dozing off. He woke an hour later in the steamy soak of a sauna bath. The abrupt shift to scorching came too soon, and he longed for the Emerald Isle, or the Emerald City, or the mountains, or the forest, or anywhere else where he could bathe his brain cells in a reasonably enlivening climate.

With his suspension from the firm in force, he was too hot a compliance risk to move his business. In limbo, he was feeling out-of-sorts, not to mention out of cash flow. When you do something every working day for more than half your life, something that defines you, and it's taken away, a new routine comes on clumsily. Less structured, less certain, bewildering at times. The search for meaning begins anew.

He wasn't grieving like when he lost hockey or when his marriage ended. This time, so much else was so good that his cool smile never faded. This wasn't an end to his relevance, he believed, but more an intermission. *Stretch your torso and shoulders, have a good yawn, go to the restroom, freshen up, and get ready for the next chapter.*

He checked in with Marie a couple of times a day, both to bolster her spirits and get any new scuttlebutt. "They're introducing themselves to our clients as 'your new advisory team, likely on a permanent basis,'" she told him. A part of the script they made her type read, "Your old advisor, Patrick Connelly, is under suspicion of insider trading and has been suspended by the firm. Any action taken will not affect you or your account. We will protect you under all circumstances. Your well-being is our one and only concern."

"Is 'well-being' a synonym for 'assets under management'?" His tone was unmistakably snarky.

Marie shrugged, saying she was strictly forbidden from discussing the issue with their clients. Even while under the same restriction, Patrick was answering non-stop cell calls and explaining his side of the story. His attorney and old friend, Justus Fredericks, was looking into whether Saunders had acted within his legal rights. All the while, Kay's delectably defiant lips flashed through his mind, saying, *"Tell them to go fuck themselves."*

The battle was clearly engaged.

Taking seriously Finnie's request to be spirited away to the forest, he made plans to visit the closest one he could find, Ocala National, located four hours to the north in the rolling hills of Central Florida's horse country. He booked a nearby B&B called the Shamrock Thistle and Crown Inn, naturally. When the day arrived, he loaded a few bags and a cooler into the silver bullet and whisked his Queen Maur away to her summer retreat in the countryside—as far from the sweltering state of affairs in their homeland as was required.

Emerging to the north of the vast Orlando metro area, things began to change quickly: the traffic thinned, the air lightened, and the drearily flat earth began to undulate up towards the sky and down again towards the netherworld. Majestic oak tree limbs became laden with verdant mosses hanging lazily in the drifting air. The colors of their new world were energized with the seasons once again in attendance.

"Are you familiar with The Byrds?" he asked.

"Any particular breed?"

"Yes, politically inspired folk-rock; listen to this." Patrick was playing both pilot and entertainment director on this cruise, masterfully managing the craft and his iPod against all AAA and law enforcement warnings.

"I'll take over the music from here, okay?"

"Good to have the smart one on board," he said, handing over his magic music box. As they listened to the revolutionary rock classic, a peace settled in, and together they watched the seasons turn before their eyes. [37]

A myriad of unfamiliar autumnal colors swept over the landscape. Formerly lush greens turned golden brown nestled in the shadows of thickening groves varied in their cycles, some still discarding and others in rebirth. Arriving in horse country, elevated grazing lands and training rings were sectioned with white picket fences, barns, and stalls. Grand southern colonial homes crowned the palatial properties speaking to both commerce and family.

"You're not in the tropics anymore, Dorothy."

"Who's Dorothy?"

"Just another frivolous reference from my youth."

"Ex-girlfriend?"

"I wish. It's a famous line from maybe the most beloved of American folklore—*The Wizard of Oz*—made during the World Wars and Great Depression Cycle."

"Not everything is a cycle, Patrick," she said. "The typical cycle can last several centuries."

"Excellent news," he said with a grin. "Then we're still early in the Palm Beach Cycle."

Soon enough, they were pulling in front of Shamrock Inn's three-story stone and clapboard house. Perched amidst stately oaks in long-abandoned citrus and guava groves, the enchanting Victorian-style structure built in 1887 was authentic to its bones—from its exterior of corniced gables and dormers with transom windows to its welcoming portico with rounded columns and dentil moldings. Inside were intimate northern-style rooms with cozy fireplaces and decorative plaster ceilings. Lustrous original heart pine moldings and floors secured its century-old charisma. A few decades before the recent climate warming phase had taken hold, persistent wintry winds killed off Central Florida's citrus industry. In 1994, the house was turned into a B&B by Annie, the resilient owner from County Antrim.

In the cooling shade of sprawling oaks, they checked into a separate lodging called Annie's Cottage, advertised as the honeymoon suite. The romantic picture-book setting included a small cabin faced with rounded yellow clapboard and white trim, a small porch, and a yard separated from the swimming pool by a charming white picket fence.

After a thorough inspection of the ground-level accommodations, Patrick took note of the rarest of circumstances—a thoughtfully designed and accessorized floorplan so blue guys and gals would have their complete independence. Rather than his typical check-in routine of calling the front desk with a long list of inadequacies and broken promises, he instead cracked open the cooler in celebration and gratitude. After clinking glasses with his queen and wetting his lips, he let out an elongated "Ahhh."

The forest was everything they'd anticipated, a complete change from their familiar subtropical seaside environs. On the scenic drive through hilly clusters of longleaf pines and misty ponds, barely visible in the fog-shrouded scrubland, the bullet's windows were open to the early morning chill. Finnie played tour guide, reading aloud from the national park guide.

"This forest is three hundred and eight-four thousand acres—that's massive."

"Think we can cover it in one day?"

"If you keep driving this fast, we'll be done by noon," she admonished. "Slow down, Speed Racer."

"Right, sorry. How do you know about *Speed Racer*?"

"There are televisions in Ireland, dear."

"Yes, I know, but I thought they only showed football matches and *Benny Hill*," he said with a Benny grin.

"That's not far from the truth."

"Ocala was proclaimed a national forest in 1908 by Teddy Roosevelt," he said, showing off his preparation. "He was responsible for preserving much of the American wilderness and creating our national park system, including the Everglades."

"Impressive," she said while her head circled to the views. "Wasn't he a cowboy?"

"In a way, yes," he answered. "His wife and mother died of illnesses on the same day. Can you imagine that?"

"No, it's awful. Hard to fathom."

"Well, it happened, and he needed to get away, to take a break from New York politics. He left his infant daughter in his sister's care and rode into the uncharted west to manage a cattle ranch. That's when he came to appreciate the vast natural beauty of the country."

"Then he was elected president?"

"First, he led a band called the Rough Riders into a silly battle in Cuba. Then he was a mayor, a police commissioner, the vice president, and finally, he became president when President McKinley was assassinated. Roosevelt was the youngest and—many consider—the best president we've ever had."

"He certainly understood the value of nature and preserving wilderness for future generations," Finnie said admiringly. "That makes him heroic."

"No doubt," he agreed. "What an incredibly courageous and vigorous guy."

"Just like a Celtic warrior," she said with pride.

"Absolutely," he said, meeting her smile. "A giant in the company of ordinary men."

"This is the oldest and southernmost national forest in the US," she continued. "And the first east of the Mississippi." They pulled over and gazed upon thick, cooling canopies of tall pines, bald cypress, moss-draped live oaks, and rare Florida willows. The shaded forest floor was abloom in the pink and lavender colors of rose-rush and rosemary amidst ancient, browning, palm-laden bush. "It says an Indian tribe named Timucua settled here between 1100 and 1300 AD."

"Not long after Brian Boru's time," he said.

"That's right," she concurred. "Little by little, thirty-five chiefdoms with nearly two hundred thousand tribe members, living from Southern Georgia to Central Florida, were destroyed. First by Spanish explorers and missionaries and the diseases they brought in the 1500s, and then by British invasions in the 1700s. The tribe was extinct by 1821, the year the United States purchased Florida."

"How shameful," he lamented. "The poor natives here fared no better than Middle Age Celts."

"The parallels are undeniable," she agreed.

They stopped at one of the several natural springs meandering its way through the forest in tributaries of the St. Johns River, the largest river in Florida and one of the few in the country that runs north. "I'm not surprised," Patrick said. "It's trying to get as far away from South Florida as it can—just like us."

From an accessible boardwalk, they observed snowy egrets and blue herons wading in turquoise ponds and sandhill cranes navigating the scrub while a large predatory bird soared above. "They look similar to bald eagles," he said, pointing to the imposing wingspan in the hazy blue sky. "But it's probably another osprey." Creature sounds interrupted the silence as an owl hooted a greeting, and a red-headed woodpecker nosily hunted its squirming prey.

"These little bluebirds scooting around are scrub jays," Finnie said, referring to the guide. "They've been nearly wiped out, and this is their last safe haven."

"Let's try to capture one; it would make a good pet." To her stern look of disapproval, he said sheepishly, "Hey, some work, some don't." He decided to drop the humor and scare her instead. "Did you know that alligators are the fastest creature on land for the first twenty yards?"

"No, I didn't," she said, looking down from the walkway to one sizing her up. "That's not good to hear,"

"If one comes at us, we're supposed to zig-zag away. Not run in a straight line."

"I'll try to remember that. How are they at leaping?"

"About as good as I am, so that's a break. Speaking of fast, I understand these woods are full of bobcats. They're pitch black, have thick, powerful hind legs, and they can run a mile at high speed."

"Wonderful."

"Oh yeah, we're also supposed to be on the lookout for black bears. If you see one, do not run, whatever you do. Just lie on the ground and pretend you're dead."

"Okay," she said tremulously.

"So, to summarize: run from a gator, but not in a straight line; don't run from a bear, lie down on the ground, and close your eyes; if it's a bobcat, just say your prayers, unless you're an exceptionally fast miler. Got it?"

"Got it, Patrick. All good to know."

"One last thing, there are loads of snakes in these wet prairies," he said while sweeping his arm in front of him. "One species called water moccasin is extremely poisonous. So, we should be hyper-aware of that too."

She moved in a little closer now and put her hand on his broad shoulder, gripping tightly. His tactic had worked well. Meanwhile, if they really did encounter any one of these scenarios, he'd freeze in his tracks and pee his pants, at the least. He'd brought a fresh change with him, just in case.

As the day warmed, Finnie dangled her feet in the crystal-line water—a thimbleful of the eighty million gallons gurgling up from the earth every single day. Sitting in the hypnotizing stillness, browsing the full theater, a sense of an ancient, misty-white, wooded bog overcame him. Filtering sunlight played with the water, setting his little companion's feet on a kind of illuminated step dance.

"This is so perfectly lovely, Patrick," she said in a hushed tone. "Thank you."

"It was your idea," he responded, tenderly cradling her slight shoulders. "I've never been happier; it's you who deserves thanks." Leaning down, he brushed her fine white-blonde hair with a kiss, saying, "You're my little miracle, Finnie."

In the distance, a large speckled gray creature rustled the placid shoreline waters as it ambled towards them, pausing to munch on mossy grasses along the way. As it neared, she didn't move her feet, seeming to know instinctively of its gentleness. "It's a manatee," he whispered. A magnificent sea cow twice her length and many times her girth paused at her now quiet feet with one eye trained on her. She gazed back intently while letting the creature explore her toes. A glorious calm ascended. It felt like he was watching two old friends from another time and place reconnecting.

Later, they opened a book of poetry WB Yeats had written more than one hundred years earlier in a place very different yet very much the same. "The wild west coast of Ireland, near Sligo, was the inspiration for his most beloved works," she told her beloved. "He detested Dublin and especially London, craving his next visit with family and friends near Slish Wood."

"Slish Wood?"

"Yes, a stunning natural area of ancient oaks, ash, willows, and alders on the southern shore of Lough Gill, near Sligo Bay. Yeats just adored it there, especially the tiny Isle of Innisfree."

"'Innisfree' is one of his famous poems, isn't it?" He was thumbing through the charmed tome as he spoke.

"Maybe his most famous," she answered, going on to say that Sligo was a land of ancient families and troubled spirits. More than anywhere else, this was where Yeats discovered delightful mysteries and embedded them in his rich Irish folklore. He was eager to hear the faerie stories of traveling bards and gypsies, legends of terrifying giants, frightening ghosts, fire-tongued beasts, and headless women.

"Headless women? Gnarly," he grimaced. "Well, at least they can't yell at you and call you ass-wipe."

"Actually, they can," she said. "They hold their severed head in their hand while it spits out blood and venom."

"That sounds eerily familiar," he said. "Other than the severed head part." Then he added, "Although, we were both pretty close a few times."

"Hush now, my fierce little warrior."

"Right. Sorry."

"Back to Yeats?"

"Please."

"So anyway, in the solitude of the woods," she continued, "he would tune into the spirit world, the mystery of the otherworld, and let his imagination and dreams take flight. Just the way Thoreau did before him."

"I'm sure you've read it a million times Finnie—but listen to this:

"I will arise and go now, and go to Innisfree,
And a small cabin build there, of clay and wattles made:
Nine bean-rows will I have there, a hive for the honeybee,
And live alone in the bee-loud glade.

"And I shall have some peace there, for peace comes dropping slow,
Dropping from the veils of the morning to where the cricket sings;
There midnight's all a glimmer, and noon a purple glow,
And evening full of the linnet's wings.

"I will arise and go now, for always night and day
I hear lake water lapping with low sounds by the shore;
While I stand on the roadway, or on the pavements grey,
I hear it in the deep heart's core."

"Thank you, Patrick. How simply delightful," she purred while brushing his lips with the back of her hand. "In one of his poems, Yeats says, 'The innocent and the beautiful have no enemy but time.' Isn't that poignant and so true?"

"Absolutely," he agreed. "And his ability to say something so timeless, with so few words, is pure genius."

"I agree. Yeats is one for the ages."

"Speaking of time," he said with a flash of his watch, "it is now *our* enemy. We must depart from the woods and proceed to our evening feast."

"Have you picked a place? As if I need to ask."

"Ocala isn't a fine-dining mecca, I'll admit. But we have a few solid choices. I thought I'd run them by you."

"Run away."

"One is called Tilted Kilt. It offers traditional Scotch-Irish pub food, an okay wine list, and live music, depending on the night."

After an extended pause, she asked, "What are the others?"

"They didn't sound as good."

"Hmm. May I ask you a question?"

"Of course, you may, Finnster."

"Isn't Tilted Kilt that chain restaurant featuring sexy waitresses with ridiculously short kilts and fake boobs bursting out of their low-cut bustiers? Kind of a Celtic version of Hooters?"

"I hadn't heard that," he said while glancing to a distant cloud. "I was focusing more on the quality of the food."

"Would you pass me your iPad, please?" Her tone was disbelieving.

He reached into his Tumi and handed it over. After a minute of sliding and tapping, which seemed to him an hour, she held up the screen to show him the web page. "Holy Jesus, will you look at that," he said with embellished surprise. "You were right, Finnie."

After hesitating a moment, she smiled and said, "I wouldn't mind seeing some of that action myself." And with a solicited fist bump sealing her tenuous blessing, they were off to dine at the Kilt.

The next day, they awoke with the cock's crow and enjoyed a sumptuous breakfast of fruits and fresh-baked scones with ample jams, cheeses, and Kerrygold butter. A variety of teas and lively storytelling around the communal table accompanied the banquet.

"This is so much better than my burger at the Kilt last night," he groused, flashing a sour look on his face.

"Don't remind me," she replied, matching his grimace.

"At least the service was good."

"Yes, world-class." Finnie's hint of derision weakened his glow.

As it was already time to depart the woodlands, they settled the tab and thanked the proprietor profusely—promising to return. Reluctantly packing up the bullet, they pulled away from a most extraordinary place etched in an earlier and largely forgotten time.

On the ride home to West Palm Beach that afternoon, they quietly ruminated about their magical weekend: the Shamrock Thistle B&B, the enveloping forest, the warm springs, the myriad of fascinating creatures, and the poet Yeats. The Tilted Kilt was formally placed on Finnie's "do not discuss" list. He had no reasonable defense.

In all, they concurred that their summer retreat to the countryside, however brief it was, and certainly not a memorable culinary experience, had been worthy of scribing into the growing archive of the ongoing Palm Beach Cycle.

37

LOOKING FOR SPACE

Home and feeling as refreshed as he had in years, Patrick set upon the difficult tasks at hand. He needed to get an income stream flowing again, and if it meant moving his business, so be it. Most importantly, he needed to restore his reputation and good standing with regulatory agencies and his clients. Without the latter, there'd be no former. His first step was meeting with Larry Devlin again to firm up plans to relocate the business, and in the meantime, better understand what the hell was going on in his life.

Driving just twenty minutes north this time, he took a sharp turn west to Larry's marshlands home bordering something called the Loxahatchee Slough—the eastern edge of the Everglades. It had a pioneering feel not so different from the mystical woodlands Queen Maur and her entourage of one had just visited. The unpretentious Devlin manor was nestled in canopying oak tree groves amidst tiers of taller pine trees, lower clusters of booted palmetto palms, and other native species in the underbrush, including a dozen or more errant golf balls on any given day.

They sat for lunch on his back pool deck in a steady breeze, enjoying long panoramic vistas of pine-shadowed, bottle-green lake waters. Upon closer inspection, Lough Devlin abounded with vibrant green lily pads, golden reeds, and yellowing marsh grasses, all nesting in a browning porridge of fluorescent green algae blooms—courtesy of the prioritized golf course maintenance policies. Groaning frogs provided the backbeat for a chorus of joyful noises from the multitude of water birds busy in their varying pursuits. Larry pointed out an imposing wood stork, white with brown trimming, traversing the near shoreline as a great blue heron gracefully circled here and there, collecting wispy branches for its newest family home. They both sat still for a time, allowing their senses to be overtaken with the symphonic magnificence of it all.

"Very impressive, my friend," Patrick finally said.

Observing a horizon of scrub pine woodlands set against the sun-paled blue April sky, breathing deeply, he tried to extinguish his exhausting worries and angers and judgments and opinions. At this gateway to the natural world, a sense of peace and perspective seemed available—a richer contentment here for the asking. By opening his eyes and ears and heart, stopping the cursed motor in his head from whirring, anything seemed possible. He could be Thoreau, or Yeats, or Larry, if only for a brief time. He needn't take four-hour drives to rolling forestlands and natural springs to find such a retreat. They are everywhere: in a woodland marsh, by a seashore, in an urban square, and in the darkest recesses of his mind.

Seek, and ye shall find.

They settled on the first Friday in May to move his business, expecting his licensing to be restored by then. Friday at four—the traditional departure day and time. Larry agreed that his friend's suspension from the firm would complicate the move.

"Yeah, no kidding," Patrick said.

"Besides that, Pat, the surprise factor is clearly gone. They're watching Marie's every move, I'm sure. And your clients have already been contacted by the new team, which gives them a huge head start."

"Which is illegal."

"What did your attorney say?"

"He said because I'm being investigated by the regulatory agencies, it's a gray area."

"Sounds right."

"So, the bossman threatens me, calls in the cops, suspends me, and takes away my book *and* Marie. All with zero evidence of any wrongdoing."

"Pretty clever."

"More like diabolical, and believe me, they have nothing on me. I'm completely innocent."

"I believe you."

"Thanks, Larry. But will the SEC?"

"Well, we can only pray. You can be certain though the firm won't stop there," he cautioned. "The day you're free to move, they'll file a suit preventing you from contacting the clients, and they'll hold up the transfer of your license."

"I'm sure you're right," Patrick bristled.

"Try to relax, Pat. Let's plan on the first week in May; it's still a few weeks away—anything's possible."

"Sounds good."

"Whatever happens, we'll deal with the consequences together. I've delayed my travel plans until you're settled.

"Thanks, Larry. You're a true friend."

"My pleasure," he said with a smile. "It's not often I meet another druid."

Larry's comment shifted the conversation markedly. "Speaking of that," Patrick blurted back. "I have so many questions I don't even know where to start."

"Fire away."

"How long have you known Kerry O'Connor? How long have you been a druid? Who the heck is Kerry O'Connor anyway? What does it even mean to be a druid?" He paused to catch his breath. "I mean, I've read about druids in one of your books, but why are we druids?"

"That it?"

"Not even close. How did Kerry get The Chieftains to appear, and on St. Patrick's Day no less? That's nuts. And who were the others in the monk robes? A few of them seemed like they were right out of the Middle Ages. And how long have you been feeding the homeless?"

"Anything else?"

"Yes, plenty else, but that's a good start."

"You sound like me a long time ago," he said with a laugh. "First, you should be proud, Pat. Very few are named druids by Kerry's group, so it means you've already been living the code of honor for years."

"I'm no angel, believe me. How do they even know how I live?"

"Word gets around, I suppose. Listen, there's still a lot I don't understand all these years later. I've learned not to ask; it just feels right."

"You told me certain things happened about a decade ago," Patrick said. "About the time you left the firm. Is that when it all started?"

"Yes, I'd hit a crossroad, a crisis. I kept it private from you and everyone else. But I was in real trouble, Pat."

"I'm sorry to hear that."

"Don't be sorry. It all happened just as it should, and I'm a better man for it. I've never been happier."

"That's the way I'm feeling now. Even with all the chaos, I've never felt more engaged, more vital, like I'm a part of some great adventure."

"And here's the best part," Larry followed, "the adventure never ends if you stay awake and tuned in."

"Jeez, I don't even need to tune in these days."

"Your receiver does appear to be on auto-tune," he agreed. "The disarray you're feeling now, I promise, will change for the better;

and it will keep changing, like the ebb and flow of the tides, the turning of the seasons; the more you accept the change, embrace both the good and the bad, the happier you'll be."

Patrick thought for a moment and said, "The higher the uncertainty, the higher the potential for happiness."

"Exactly. We need uncertainty to feel alive. We need to take some risks. Waking up to a new challenge is better than waking up dead."

"I sure am grateful I'm not dead," he said with a search of his friend's eyes. "Get it? *Grateful* I'm not *dead*? *Grateful Dead*?"

"How does Finnie put up with you?"

"Honestly, I don't know," he answered. "She must be a kind of magical creature."

"Or maybe she's just hard of hearing?"

"A selective listener, let's say," he said with a laugh. "Speaking of Finnie, her favorite poet, WB Yeats, said, 'the more difficult pleasure is the nobler pleasure.'"

"I like it."

"Yeats certainly embraced uncertainty; he was forever exploring the unknown, and he worked damn hard at his craft."

"One of the most exceptional bards who's ever lived," Larry agreed.

"His poems are so succinctly written," Patrick added. "Every word so thoughtfully chosen. How in hell can he be Irish?"

"Good point, Pat," he said. "Maybe he wasn't a drinker?"

"Like I said, how in hell can he be Irish?" After a good laugh, Patrick said, "Yeats gets right to the heart of what really matters—wisdom for those who are ready."

"I agree," Larry said, "and you'll have access to more wisdom now as you move along on your journey."

"Where?"

"Well, you saw some of it on St. Patrick's Day. A pretty amazing group, wouldn't you say?"

"Amazing doesn't do it justice."

"True," Larry concurred, "I still blink my eyes sometimes to make sure it's all real."

"And?"

"It's all real, Pat."

Patrick looked at his friend and dwelled a moment, then said, "So Finnie's real. Kerry and his warehouse are real. The Chieftains were real. And you're really a part of all this. Honestly, I'm still pinching myself."

"Keep pinching," he replied. "It helps you stay awake."

After lunch, Larry suggested taking a drive around his neighborhood. It wasn't very different than driving through the national forest, other than the few dozen luxury homes stationed amongst woods, lakes, and golf course vistas. They pulled over at a remote spot on the western edge of the community with a mile-long view of the wetlands.

"There are a few things to see out here," he said, "if we're lucky."

He helped push his friend's chair along a sandy path and onto a narrow wooden boardwalk before continuing out into the marsh. Stopping where the uneven, weathered-gray pine boards widened,

Larry took a seat on a bench, holding tight to a camera dangling from his neck. There wasn't another human as far as the lens could see. [38]

"Man, Larry, if you're looking for space, this is it—like sitting in the middle of a bird sanctuary," Patrick said, shading his eyes and peering out to a variety of water birds busily proceeding with their day. Some stepped purposefully through the river of grass in pursuit of sustenance; others were in various stages of takeoffs or landings; still, others posed spread-winged on dry banks warming in the sun. The same opus he'd heard on Larry's back deck played more intensely now as an abundance of new performers joined the orchestra.

"I come here sometimes to think, and other times not to think," Larry said. "About the time I left the firm, I sat right here trying to sort out the turmoil."

"Great," Patrick grinned. "You come here, and I go to the darkened backroom of an Irish pub. It explains a lot."

"Oh, I've spent plenty of time in the pubs too."

"How did you meet Kerry?"

"Speaking of Irish pubs, just before I left the firm, I ran over to Murphy's in the middle of the afternoon for a whiskey or two, you know, to lower the stress."

"Sounds familiar."

"By evening, I hadn't accomplished much, except the whiskey, and was ready to go home. On the way to the men's room, sitting alone in the back, busy at work by lamplight, was an older, kind of elfish gentleman." Patrick suddenly felt like he was listening to a ghost story. "He introduced himself and asked me to keep him company, which I did. We chatted for quite a while. He's a very engaging guy."

"That's precisely how I met him, to the word. Did he give you his business card?"

"He did. I went to visit him at the warehouse soon after to do some antique shopping, and we became friends from there."

"That's when everything started changing?"

"Yes."

"And one of the changes was leaving the firm?"

"That's right," Larry said. "Kerry helped me realize there's more to life than money and pursuing prestige."

"But you stayed in the money business. Why?"

"The money business wasn't the problem. It's an honorable profession, and good people will always need good financial advice. But I had to reclaim my freedom, do things my way."

"Freedom. What a concept."

"Right. For instance, I was able to be a stockbroker again, an old-style customer's man, not herded into some robotic army of homogenized, fee-only wealth advisors."

"Christ, welcome to my world," Patrick agreed. "I understand the need for order, a consistent process the firm and the clients can depend on, but it's not for everyone."

"Not me, that's for sure," Larry chimed in.

"I have my own method of achieving a client's objectives," Patrick continued. "I learned it the hard way, by showing up every day in the depth of several crises and doing the required work. Mainly, I learned that being educated and prepared, being patient, and especially, avoiding the two emotional extremes—fear and greed—is a pretty good template."

"Well said, Pat; nothing beats those experiences. One of the things I enjoy most now is looking after the smaller accounts, thinking of more ways to help them, instead of the constant pressure to hunt for multi-million-dollar relationships. Since the move, I've been serving people who really need my help. They're grateful and it feels good."

"I understand completely."

"God bless the wealthy and mega-wealthy," Larry continued. "In most cases, they're wonderful people who've earned their success; they pay most of the taxes and keep the economy going. But they don't need my help to buy their third or fourth Lexus or Mercedes. Focusing mainly on them, I was shriveling up in my insignificance."

"You were courageous to make the move when you did. I feel like a deaf, dumb, and blind idiot for not joining you then."

"It's impressive, Pat, how many special needs categories you can offend in just one sentence."

"Oops, just a mindless expression," he said with a laugh. "Did I mention I've felt like a slave at the firm ever since?"

"No, you left that constituency out."

After their reticent smiles faded, Patrick asked, "What other changes happened in your life besides going independent?"

"Everything changed; just look around at where I live." They each paused and scanned the vast marshlands. "I've seen otters leaping in and out of my lake; sandhill crane families cutting through my yard; roseate spoonbills scouring the shorelines for their dinner. There are dive-bombing hawks carrying away bass twice their size and jet-black bobcats gingerly stepping through this marsh right out there," he said, pointing his finger. "Then taking off in a sprint after their prey."

"Did they get them?" He nearly gripped Larry's shoulder for comfort.

"Never failed," he replied. "You do not want a bobcat chasing after you."

At least he was telling Finnie the truth, he thought.

Just then, a large shadow moved steadily across the marsh. They cast their eyes to the sky where a prominent brown and white wingspan circled overhead several times before compactly landing at the top of a tall, nearly bare Australian pine. It soon climbed into a tightly wound sphere. "Osprey?" Patrick asked.

"No, that's a bald eagle." Larry's voice was a reverent whisper. "She comes back every year to that same nest. I've watched her fledglings take their first flight."

"Amazing. I feel like I'm in a John Denver nature song. I dream sometimes of soaring in the sky like an eagle—and I'm disappointed when I wake up here on the ground." [38]

"Never stop dreaming, Pat. These marshlands are like my dream materialized—it's where I rediscovered the magic."

"Who wouldn't want this," Patrick said, "it's a better life."

"I'm operating more on emotion, less on intellect, trusting my heart instead of analyzing everything and worrying myself to death. I've learned how insignificant we are in the greater order. It's helped me take things in stride, the good and the bad."

"That's the way it's been for me lately, especially since meeting Finnie. I should be a basket case with what's happening in my career, but oddly, I'm not."

"Rediscovering love can do that," he said. "It orders our priorities. The less I focused on money, the more on being lighthearted and trying to help people, which I think means love, the more money flowed my way."

"Nothing wrong with that. I could use a little more flow myself."

"Keep the faith, Pat, and keep looking for the adventure; Oh, yeah, and keep picking takeover stocks—and I'm sure you'll do just fine."

"Cute, Larry. That's what I'm talking about—it's been one crazy thing after another. In the old days, I couldn't pick a take-over stock if Martha Stewart called me personally."

After sharing another hearty laugh, Larry glanced at his watch. "We'd better wrap this up. Maggie will be getting home soon—it's almost time for our chardonnay sunset."

"Gotcha," he said, straightening up in his chair.

As they strolled along the pathway back to the bullet, Patrick reached into his Tumi and pulled out the burgundy leather pouch he'd found the night he met Kerry. "Does this look familiar?"

Holding his glance an extra moment, Larry reached into his front pocket and pulled out a mirror-image bag. "It hasn't left my presence in ten years."

Saying nothing, they each put their pouches away. After all, what was there to say?

Dropping his friend back at his driveway, Patrick had one last question: "As an experienced druid, how would you deal with people like Saunders and King, besides getting far away from them? Would you ignore them, you know, just let it all go? Or try to change them, or even understand and forgive them?"

"Oh no, Pat. None of the above."

"What then?"

"I suspect that's why you were given the sword. Just in case."

38

FESTIVAL TIME APPROACHES

Whenever he wanted to locate his glorious companion, he simply needed to follow the glorious sounds emanating from the den. This time, he had an important question to ask. "Finnster, why is there a mug of milk on the kitchen windowsill?"

"To ward off evil spirits," she said from her little stool by the harp.

"Is it working?"

"Do you see any evil spirits around?"

"No, I don't. But if they're spirits, then I wouldn't be able to see them."

"Excellent point, Patrick," she laughed. "But you'd feel them. You'd definitely know they were here."

"How?"

"Well, maybe a chill will sweep by you, or you hear a loud noise from another room that makes no sense. Or maybe a bad or evil thought occurs to you, or you might suddenly feel sad or depressed. Or, out of nowhere, you feel an abrupt pain in your head or your neck. Those kinds of things."

"That sounds like a normal day for me," he smirked. "Until the last few months, that is."

"You must have had a lot of evil spirits about the place."

"No doubt; I think you cleared them all out."

"See, the milk works."

"I've never thought about physical pain or shifting emotions in that context before," he mused.

"The mug of milk can be used as a reminder, so evil spirits don't take over your thoughts."

"Like a metaphor or a positive affirmation."

"Yes, a reminder to let only the good thoughts in."

"I like it," he said with a warm embrace."

The cup of milk was an old family tradition in Northern Ireland, she told him. Her mom would put it out whenever she felt danger lurking about the family or during festival time.

"Festival time?"

"Yes, dear. May Day is nearly here."

"What's that all about, other than being the first day in the merry month of May?"

You were just calling March the 'merry month of March,'" she reminded him.

"I'm feeling merry these days; what can I say?"

"You covered it," she said with a smile.

"The Irish are big festival people," Finnie continued, "and May Day is one of several we celebrate every year."

"Sounds like another good excuse to go drinking."

"Yes, for some." She frowned. "But each festival represents something important, the same as Christmas or Easter, for example. They hearken back to another time, connect us with our ancestors."

"The way we celebrate Memorial Day, Labor Day, and July 4th."

"No," she said. "Those are just your excuses to barbeque and go drinking."

"You got me," he said, reaching out for a deserved fist bump.

"Many of the festivals are from pagan times and celebrated the changing of the seasons," she continued. "They'd pray for their loved ones' safety and for the protection of their crops and livestock and the salmon in the rivers. Without these resources, the people couldn't survive."

"That's the way I'd feel without Publix."

"It is similar, I guess, in an odd way," she said with eyes screwed. "On the eve of May, there'd be a big celebration to mark the end of the dark winter. The seeds had been planted, and summer was on the way. The faeries are especially active, in a merry mood, and they take the size and shape that pleases them. They feast, fight, make love, and the most beautiful of music and dance."

"That pretty much covers the entire gamut, doesn't it? I mean, what else is there?"

"Well, we could probably do without the fighting."

"To everything, there is a season," he reminded her. "Without fighting, we wouldn't be human. The world would be some type of utopia, like the Garden of Eden or Woodstock."

"That didn't turn out so well," she grimaced.

"You're right. They barely had any food or bathrooms, and it poured rain; Max Yasgur's farm was a muddy, litter-strewn wreck after it ended. Not to mention, it almost killed the Dead's career before it got started." [39]

"I meant the Garden of Eden."

"Oh, right," he said with a bat of his eyes. "That too."

"At home in Cushendun, we'd get ready for May Day with bouquets of yellow flowers everywhere: in doorways, on window-sills, on the dining table." Her eyes revealed a faraway look. "We'd have a Maypole, and they'd light bonfires and dance till their shoes were worn out."

"Jesus, not bonfires again," he said with a frown. "You grew up in a country full of pyromaniacs. I hope you had competent fire departments."

"More than one thatched roof went up from flying sparks, I'll tell you that," she remembered. "But the whole town would pitch in with water from their wells to douse the flames."

"What good souls the Irish are. For pyromaniacs, that is."

"The smoke from the bonfires was said to protect the crops, the livestock, and the people from supernatural forces."

"Except the people whose homes burnt down, of course."

"Yes, may God bless those poor souls."

"So, how should we celebrate May Day, Finnster? It'll be my last chance to party before we move the business, Christ willing. Who knows what'll happen next—I may be in jail by then."

"I'll visit you every chance I get." She gave him a less-than-tearful embrace.

"That's so sweet—my moll will be waiting loyally while I'm doing my time."

"Let's not get carried away—I have a life to live."

"I would understand."

"Thank you. So, in the meantime, Murphy's is having a May Eve celebration with flowers, live music, dancing, poetry readings, fresh salmon. It should be fun."

"Salmon?" he protested. "No offense, but I've had enough salmon recently that I've become too wise."

"You can't be a May Day Grinch now."

"Familiar with the Grinch too, are you? I shouldn't be surprised. How do you feel about Beetlejuice?"

"Loved him." She had a peculiar look of reminiscence on her face.

"Do you have to work on May Eve?"

"Yes, but I'll have time for you and my work. May Day is a bit of a relic, along with the woods and faeries and family farms. It'll probably be quiet. They're doing it to drum up some business and to humor me, I think."

"I'll humor you, dear, by leaving you to your instrument of sweet magic." With that, he leaned in with a soft kiss on her sweet lips, which always left him feeling the magic.

As May Day approached, the mug of milk became a windowsill staple, a yellow wreath marked the entrance to the festive home, spring flowers filled vases, and salmon was on the menu a little too frequently. Aside from Patrick's noticeably oily complexion, there was a sweet, warming sentimentality to such ritual. The home in SoSo, which had felt so suffocating for so long, had the rich air of a loving enclave again.

While his feelings of contentment were lush, no doubt, they were sullied by the slightest nuance of separation. Just the normal progression in every seasonal cycle of love, he reasoned. Smooth sailing eventually shifting to choppier seas had been a hallmark of his romantic relationships. He was disturbed by the trend, of course, and it exacerbated his worry now. But whatever he was sensing with Finnie had more the effect of a silent ripple than a thundering wave. Her kind and supportive demeanor never diminished; her immutable femininity and sweetness were sprinkled everywhere.

Maybe it was the look in her eyes, not quite as enveloping, as if she weren't "all in" anymore. Maybe she looked away at times to prevent him from reading her? If so, the look away was appraisal enough.

In those very first minutes following a harvest moon, when the moon is no longer precisely full, can one even say for sure it isn't? Certainly, it remains a thing of grandeur. He would gratefully accept Finnie at whatever her phase, praying the waning crescent never arrives.

Glancing at the mug of milk on the windowsill, unable to eradicate this one evil spirit lingering in his thoughts, he wondered just where in the world his sprite's heart resided. Here, in County Palm Beach, or there, across the vast Gulf Stream, in County Antrim.

39

A GOOFY COVER-UP

The call came abruptly, turning his morning coffee to acid. He'd been summoned to the office for a meeting with FINRA enforcement representatives. The morning paper was reporting an early-season tropical storm blowing in from the south, and raindrops were already drumming on the flower-draped window-panes—a bright yellow foreground to a dark and rumbling sky.

While only a month had passed since he'd last donned a suit and tie, it felt unnatural and constraining. His forced time away from the office had unleashed the free-spirited Paddy of his youth: more lighthearted, taking things as they come, looking for space. He'd taken a breath of the life Larry was living and liked the aroma. But here he was on the last Monday morning in April dressed once again in polished black shoes, pressed gray slacks, starched white collar, tie still dangling in disarray, motoring up Olive in the silver bullet, late for a meeting he had no interest in attending.

With his windshield wipers slapping time, he reacquainted with a few old friends: sweat droplets beading on his temples, anxious thoughts swirling in his mind, and a bluesy classic tune meant to ameliorate the other two. [40]

Entering his old office building was like passing into a world recognizable yet distant, like visiting the old neighborhood where you spent your formative years. The once vivid picture of the theater that staged your earlier life has faded, the scenes populated now with strangers. Feelings wash over as you try to recall it all, looking for the familiar: the delicatessen, the bakery, the ice cream shop, the five-and-dime, the ball fields, Three Ponds, Kelly's house, the train station to Grand Central, the bus station to the Bronx, the parish schoolyard and church, Albert's downtown domain, the tall, red-brick Tudor in the outskirts. The battlegrounds and sanctuaries.

Where did those woods go? When did they build that monstrosity? Where is all the open space I remember?

Befuddled, you look for the one or two old friends who will bring it into focus, and he's not there, and she's not there. The phrase "you can't go home again" comes to mind. You can't articulate what you're feeling except that this isn't your life anymore—it isn't home.

Patrick paused behind a pillar and watched the one old friend who brought it all into focus. Marie was at her same old desk in the same old corner doing her same old daily routines. But it was Ian King running her show now. There he was racing from his office—*screw that, it's* my *office.* King interrupted her, dumped a pile of papers on her desk saying something caustic that caused her face to scrunch. Then he raced away to the sound of a sharply slamming door.

Just the day before, she'd said, "Pat, I don't know how much longer I can take this. King's really an okay guy, not what you'd think; he seems more worried than excited. But Saunders is such a damn bully."

"We're nearing the finish line, Marie," he'd responded. "Just hang in there another week or two."

"We'd better hurry. I think he's planning to merge his business with KW and ours. I saw something about 'The Saunders Group' on his desk."

"Naturally."

"Mia doesn't seem to be a part of it. I heard Saunders tell her to keep her mouth shut and just do her job."

"But she's the W in KW," he flared. "That makes her a part of it."

"Maybe you're right, but it's all happening so fast, I don't know what to think. How are we going to move with all this going on?"

"We'll move, don't you worry. Larry's ready to help us."

"I hope so."

"Hope?"

"Shut it, Pat."

"Noted. Try to relax, Marie, please. Hang in there—we'll make this right." He was searing with rage when they ended the call.

※

It was past time to meet with the Feds. He turned away from Marie with a silent pledge to get her the hell off that desk or die in the effort. But what happened next was out of his hands. It wasn't his choice.

When he reached the appointed conference room, he shook hands with his attorney waiting just outside. "Thanks for coming, Justus."

"I'm always here for you, Pat. Good to see you."

The sight of the distinguished, Paul Newman-handsome Justus Fredericks brought back memories of the early days. Young and ascending in the local business community, considered among the "movers and shakers," they were regulars at all the happy hour business card exchanges. Besides collaborating to build their respective careers, they'd spent time watching their kids play ball and dance ballet, and they'd spent more than a few nights kibitzing in the pubs. Now they met up when they needed each other's services. Justus was still the "mover," having moved across the bridge, while Patrick supposed he was the "shaker," needing his old friend's legal services to save both his reputation and his livelihood.

How the mighty dreams of youth have fallen, he thought.

Together, they pushed open the conference room door to the scene of pinstripes snaking around the table, with Saunders at the head. "Hey, Connelly, long time," he hissed. "Take a seat, um, I mean, pull right in."

Ignoring him, Patrick rolled up to the open place at the table. He noted the discomfort in Jack Lawson's eyes. Fredericks sat in the chair to his right, placed his briefcase on the table, and handed around business cards.

"Let's dive right in, shall we?" Saunders said. "The regulatory team here has discovered some pretty damning evidence against Connelly." He was pointing an accusatory finger while investigators looking as young as Patrick's kids sat in silence, nodding, scribbling on legal pads, seeming to be more minions than persons of authority.

"Jeff," interrupted Lawson. "I'll take over here."

"I like your style, Lawson." Saunders looked around the table beaming. "It's all yours, executioner, render the verdict."

Ignoring his gloating boss, he put two file folders on the table in front of the accused and said, "Patrick, these are copies of documents found on your computer and in one of your file drawers. Can you explain them?"

He grabbed one folder and slid the other over to Justus. They both scoured the typed notes of alleged discussions he'd had with an investment banker code-named "Goofy." According to Saunders, the notes documented Connelly being tipped off and aware of Disney's acquisition plans and offering "Goofy" a percentage of the take.

"Justus, these are bogus, total fiction, like a really bad spy novel." He was furious. "I didn't have contact with anyone, and I certainly didn't code-name anyone Goofy." He pointed to a passage in the notes and read aloud, "'I told Goofy we could each make a good chunk of change if we do this right; we need the money bad; at the end of the day, that's what divorce does to you. It is what it is.'"

"You divorced, Connelly?"

Ignoring Saunders's snarky question, he said, "First of all, Justus, there was no 'chunk of change' made. I didn't buy a share of the two stocks."

"We don't know yet what side deals you may have made," Saunders interrupted. "We're still looking at that."

Ignoring him again, he pointed Justus to the document and continued. "Second, I don't use idiotic phrases like these, but I sure know who does."

"What are you saying, Patrick?" asked Lawson.

"I'm saying I didn't write this garbage. It sounds like I'm listening to Saunders and King talking. I'm surprised there's no mention of my 'golden shovel.'" Glances of puzzlement waved around the table. "And come on, Jack, even if I had, why would I keep it on my computer at work?"

"Because you're lazy, Connelly," laughed Saunders. "In addition to being desperate."

"Keep it professional, Jeff," warned Lawson.

"You're even more shameful than my client described, Mr. Saunders." Fredericks had a look as threatening as he'd ever allowed in public—a mixture of professional and personal outrage at what he was witnessing.

Rumbles of thunder and electric flashes interrupted the proceedings as hard rain began to pelt the windows. The conference room lighting flickered, causing the table to erupt in activity unrelated to Patrick's fate. The minions were scanning their phones for weather updates—especially the ones with flights out of town a few hours hence. The reports didn't look promising.

When order was restored, Fredericks turned to his client and said, "This crap doesn't even make the grade of circumstantial evidence, Pat. It wouldn't hold up in a kangaroo court, never mind a court of law."

"This is my court of law," Saunders snarled, "and it's holding up just fine. Your client's a crook, and we've got the goods on him."

"Crook? The goods?" Patrick growled. "Who is this guy, Jimmy Cagney?"

"Mr. Lawson," Fredericks finally said, "you seem like a sensible man. I assume that you, Mr. Saunders, and maybe others had access to Mr. Connelly's office and computer since he was suspended, correct?"

"Yes—just the compliance team."

"Which includes Mr. Saunders?"

"Of course," barked Saunders. "I run this shop."

"So then," he said, glaring at Saunders, "you, or someone else, could have placed this information in my client's computer and file drawer."

"And why would someone have done that, Mr. Barrister?" Saunders challenged.

"In an effort to set Mr. Connelly up. Wouldn't you say that's possible?"

"I guess anything's possible," Lawson said.

"No, it is *not* possible," Saunders contradicted angrily. "The computer and file cabinet have been sequestered."

"Our experts will have no trouble determining that the computer files were tampered with," Fredericks said to the room. "It'll probably take half an hour tops; expect a subpoena later today." Turning to Lawson, he said, "Do you have anything else connecting my client to insider trading allegations? Anything in his handwriting? Phone or email records? Physical witnesses with statements? Testimony from this alleged Goofy character? Anything at all—"

"We're working on all of that," Saunders interrupted. "We'll have it all if you decide to take any further action."

"What do you mean, 'further action'?" Patrick shouted. "Give me back my job, and my office, and Marie—and I want back pay too. That's the only 'further action' you need to take."

"Yes, sir. Right away," Saunders saluted derisively.

"You're not getting away with this, you despicable thief," he replied, shaking with rage. "It's a complete hoax, Justus. Totally fabricated."

Fredericks reached over and placed his hand on his client's shoulder. "Relax, Pat. This is patently ridiculous; there's nothing to get riled up about."

He asked for a five-minute break to allow his client to cool down and to get the ball rolling on the subpoena. It gave the FINRA brat pack a chance to scramble for new travel itineraries. A glance at the brooding skies suggested that no one in their right mind should voluntarily leave the ground in Palm Beach County tonight.

When the meeting resumed, Saunders launched right in: "Here's the thing, Connelly. There's nothing to give back to you. Your employment at our firm has been formally terminated as of today."

"Justus—for Christ's sake," cried Patrick. "He can't do this."

"Jeff, what are you talking about?" asked an agitated Lawson. "We didn't discuss any of this."

"We didn't need to. It's my decision, and I got the go-ahead from the regulators."

"Do tell." Lawson's stern face looked directly at the boy band from New York. The rail-thin one with a face full of acne sitting a full head below Saunders cleared his throat to speak.

"Um, we have found probable cause here," he began. "The volume and timing of the purchases were, um, suspicious; the fact that Disney was involved with both mergers too; then there's Mr. Connelly's divorce and his apparent financial distress; and these documents detailing the entire timeline of events. It's all pretty, um, compelling."

"What are you talking about? I'm in no financial distress. Where are you getting this garbage?" Patrick's face was red, his eyes intense.

"Don't speak directly to them," advised Fredericks. "Please tell us about my client's financial distress, if you would?"

"Um, well," began the watchdog. "We were given records of Mr. Connelly's divorce settlement, and um, the assets he shipped out; his monthly expenses, such as his mortgage, taxes, college tuition, and the alimony—they all far exceed his monthly income.

This type of behavior is not uncommon in the industry, and divorce is a big red flag."

"Christ, Justus, this is an invasion of privacy."

"Of course, it is," he replied. "It's inappropriate and illegal."

"Just protecting my golden shovel, gentlemen," Saunders said.

"What the hell is he talking about?" Fredericks asked as shoulders again shrugged throughout the room. Then he faced the little pod of regulators and asked, "Are you aware that Mr. Connelly didn't personally purchase a share of these two stocks in question? And are you aware he discounted his client's commissions meaningfully until Mr. Saunders here modified it? How do you explain that? Those aren't the actions of a distressed rogue broker. They're quite the opposite."

"That is unusual, I admit," the young man responded. "Perhaps he had friends purchase shares away on his behalf. We've even seen customers give kickbacks after the fact. All of that is, uh, under investigation."

"Have you taken a look at Mr. Connelly's twenty-five-year record in the industry?" asked Fredericks. "Never even a customer complaint, never mind criminal behavior."

"We've looked at all that, yes. Very impressive. But, uh, Mr. Saunders told us he's been a changed man since the divorce: worried, short fuse, uncooperative, depressed."

"He's a psychologist now too?" Patrick was seething. "It's all a lie."

"Mr. Saunders' opinion of my client's state of mind is irrelevant, of course," Fredericks said. "Has it even occurred to you that these documents may have been planted by a person or persons who would benefit from Mr. Connelly's firing?"

"Why would anyone do that?"

"You must be joking." Fredericks's voice turned gentle now, paternal even. "How long have you been with FINRA, young man?"

"Why is that relevant?"

"I'm interested to know, that's why."

"Uh, six months."

"How many cases have you investigated?"

"This is my first time in the field."

"Thank you."

"What's the point of all this, Mr. Fredericks?" Saunders barked with his triangled fingers making their inevitable appearance.

"It'll all be relevant for the litigation," he replied, glancing at Patrick to acknowledge the threatening finger triangle in their faces.

"Justus," his client said, "I've got to get out of here, or I'm gonna level this jerk."

"Big talk from the sitting man," countered Saunders. "Come on, Connelly, take your best shot." He was standing now, looming over his target.

"Back off, Jeff." Lawson had moved between his boss and Patrick and was leaning against the sturdy table for support. He wore a disgusted look on his face.

"Let's go, Pat," said Fredericks, packing up his briefcase. "I think we're done with this circus sideshow."

"Enjoy your retirement, Connelly," chided Saunders as they left the room. "I'll send your watch in the mail."

Marching double-time through a series of gawking plebes, they took the elevator down to the building's lobby. Justus assured his friend not to worry. "We'll reverse this travesty in court, no problem, and we'll sue for damages and knock him on his bullying ass."

"How long will it take?"

"It could be weeks. That's if I can get a judge to fast-track it."

"Weeks? They've stolen my livelihood, Justus, destroyed my reputation. It's already been a month. I can't wait much longer. I'm supposed to move the business this Friday."

"I wouldn't recommend it, Pat. You have no license to transfer. Your clients are being told you're a cheat and a liar. We have to get this resolved first."

"Son of a bitch," he said, on the verge of hopeless tears.

Promising to get busy filing their action, and warning that his cell phone records would probably be subpoenaed, Justus Fredericks proffered a confident handshake, opened his umbrella, and pushed through the heavy glass doors into the intensifying maelstrom.

40

MAY EVE TUMULT

All that next day, menacing clouds and rain-drenched winds battered County Palm Beach with a ferocity that filled the glades and ponds and lakes. The kind of soaking that reverses a multi-year drought in twenty-four tumultuous hours. The kind that floods the western-most enclaves with their poorly designed drainage systems. And the kind that kept Patrick fixed firmly inside his stucco and clay asylum.

After giving Finnie the details about his goofy meeting with FINRA, she said, "It sounds juvenile, really. I'm certain your attorney will get it all straightened out and win back everything they've stolen."

"Thanks, Finnster. You're like a high and dry island in a sea run rampant." She smiled at the reference.

Reports came of local flooding and abandoned cars and school closings when there were reports at all. The power flickered on and off throughout the day as the local utility struggled to keep the connection. Anyone who experienced the three monster storms a decade earlier, hitting one after another after another, had installed a power generator if they could afford one. Patrick was in that club and spent half the morning trying to get through to the propane delivery company.

"We apologize—your call is very important to us. Please hold for the next available service agent." They neither answered the phone nor delivered the fuel.

"That's a monopoly for you," he complained. "Always ready to serve until you actually friggin' need them." With a helpless shrug, Finnie continued readying for the May Eve event at Murphy's, in the unlikely case the storm broke early. "This is your first taste of May Day in the tropics," he said. "Shouldn't Murphy's just cancel and close for the night?"

"They still may," she answered. "But we have several reservations, mostly regulars who will probably show up. So, they're holding out a while longer."

"Man, that's optimistic," he said.

"This is a mere rain shower to the Irish—a non-event," she said. "And anyway, you know what they say about an Irish pub."

"Tell me."

"It never rains inside."

"True—until they play one of those sad laments, that is; then the place fills up with the blubbers." [41]

"It wouldn't be Irish without the blubbers," she agreed with a peck on his cheek.

"Stay dry, Finndoll. See you later, alligator."

"In a while, crocodile."

"How do you know of such cultural oddities?" he asked, watching her cute little tail disappear through the threshold.

"I work in an Irish pub," she called back over her shoulder.

May Eve is on! came Finnie's happy text.

Such resilient souls, he thought, as he searched his closet for a waterproof jacket. Paddling the silver bullet slow and easy up the River Olive, he veered here and there to avoid the severed limbs strewn about. The only lights he saw up and down Clematis came from top floor windows in his old office building. "Sure," he scowled. "The capitalist's pursuit must never rest."

Pulling into an open blue guy spot by the waterfront triangle, he donned the only covering he could find—a Disney character poncho. They'd bought the paper-thin plastic straitjacket at one of the Disney parks during a cloudburst long ago and far away. One of those emergency purchases where you pay fifteen dollars for about fifty cents worth of product. A good lesson in demand and supply economics.

Funny, he thought, *this is the second time in two days I've been involved in a Goofy cover-up.*

After waiting a few minutes for the torrent to subside, he surrendered and dashed up the hill towards Murphy's, dodging in and out of storefront awnings and getting pummeled along the way by their gathered drippings. He finally saw the familiar yellow wreath on the front door of the public house welcoming their seafaring guests. The mood inside was festive, with fresh-cut spring flowers all about, pints of Guinness lining the bar, and a dance reel playing as servers flitted around the room dressed in varied imaginations of faerie attire.

Finnie had been right—it wasn't raining inside the pub. By the loud pattering on the roof, that could change at any moment.

Rumbles and flashes added context as his old friend Molly approached with open arms. "We don't see enough of you these days, Patrick Connelly," she said with a welcoming hug.

"And I miss you most of all, Molly, O Molly," he said from their embrace. "You make a very sweet faerie, may I add."

"Faeries aren't always so sweet, you know; they can be quite temperamental. So, keep your eyes wide open."

"That they'll be, dear. I suppose I have become quite the homebody."

"And I don't blame you for that," she replied as they both watched a glowing Maureen glide by with a pints-filled tray. "You've brought a wee bit of Murphy's spirit home with you now, haven't you?"

"I certainly have," he said with beaming pride. "The best of it, I imagine."

"Oh, yes," she agreed. "Maureen's undeniably one of the good faeries. Follow me, sir; your table awaits."

The seeds had all been planted, and the fertility festival was pulsing. Shoes were being worn out from the non-stop dancing. He enjoyed it all, especially the occasional dart-by kisses. There were no moldy lips on May Eve, he learned. The whole evening had been Finnie's creation, and it was a brimming success. He'd never seen her so brimming. He passed on the "Fionn's Salmon of Wisdom" dinner special, instead ordering a burger smothered in Irish bacon and cheddar. With a side order of fries—extra crispy. It felt like a guilt-free, comfort food kind of night.

Later, the music quieted, the dancin' fools rested, and the room hushed. Professional actors and dancers from the local Dramaworks and Palm Beach Ballet companies took the stage for a performance, beginning with a poetry reading from the magical prose of WB Yeats:

> Let us go forth, the tellers of tales,
> and seize whatever prey the heart long for,
> and have no fear.
> Everything exists, everything is true,
> and the earth is only a little dust under our feet.

A rapturous opening, he thought. They had the crowd's attention. A flute and mandolin played softly in accompaniment as they continued:

> There is another world, but it is in this one.
> The world is full of magic things,
> patiently waiting for our senses to grow sharper.

The mystical life is at the centre of all that I do,
and all that I think and all that I write.

Such as:

A daughter of a King of Ireland, heard
A voice singing on a May Eve like this,
And followed half awake and half asleep,
Until she came into the Land of Faery,
Where nobody gets old and godly and grave,
Where nobody gets old and crafty and wise,
Where nobody gets old and bitter of tongue.
And she is still there, busied with a dance
Deep in the dewy shadow of a wood,
Or where stars walk upon a mountain-top.

Where do I sign up for some of that? he was thinking as he sipped from his jar of Bushmills. On this May Eve, he had all the delights Yeats had yearned for: a hearty meal, a dewy drink, a convivial home, and a magical love to share it all with. He was a youthful man again radiating in the wonder of it all.

Come away, O human child!
To the waters and the wild
With a faery, hand in hand,
For the world's more full of weeping
than you can understand.

He lamented his own world full of weeping—like getting canned and possibly spending time in the slammer for securities fraud. *Great*, he thought sardonically, *from SoSo to Sing Sing*. His glimmer dimmed a tinge in the contemplation.

> *Come, faeries, take me out of this dull house!*
> *Let me have all the freedom I have lost;*
> *Work when I will and idle when I will!*

'Yes! Freedom!' he jotted on his notepad. 'I'll choose when I work and when I idle! No one else chooses my fate.' Then he scribbled, 'I crave my freedom, need it to survive. These disgraceful thieves will not snatch it away without a fight to the death. That, I promise!'

> *Faeries, come take me out of this dull world,*
> *For I would ride with you upon the wind,*
> *Run on the top of the disheveled tide,*
> *And dance upon the mountains like a flame.*

'Yes! Yes! Yes!' his busy pen decreed. 'It is my time to ride the wind—run on the wave—dance upon the mountains. I am the flame! Why not me?' In unison, the troupe rhymed:

> *Wine comes in at the mouth*
> *And love comes in at the eye;*
> *That's all we shall know for truth*
> *Before we grow old and die.*

I lift the glass to my mouth,
I look at you, and sigh.

He looked around the musty old pub room, his pub room, with fond reflection. And he watched the faeries buzzing about gaily; watched the smiles they raised. Then he spied the sweetest faerie in the land, the sprite, and lifted the glass to his mouth, and sighed.

O body swayed to music, O brightening glance,
How can we know the dancer from the dance?

A gentle ballet ensued. "Such elegance," he said. "Such beauty." Watching the lithe, muscular bodies lift and sway, here and there, in a graceful expression of restrained freedom, he caught a gathering tear with the swipe of his hand.

Suddenly, the lights wavered in deference to an external surge. On stage, a bodhran percussion instrument joined a deep-voiced actor who boomed with a startling urgency:

Out of Ireland have we come.
Great hatred, little room,
Maimed us at the start.
I carry from my mother's womb
A fanatic heart.

As a foreboding shift in the narrative swelled inside the pub, the storm outside amplified, its full brunt now fierce upon the city.

Lights again were flashing as if choreographed, and the room was growing more restless. Patrick imagined he was in McGurk's Bar in early '70s Belfast while loyalist thunder bands roared down the main drag taunting nationalists and threatening bonfires were aflame all about the city. He looked warily to the front windows wondering if a Molotov cocktail would come crashing through at any moment.

The thickly bearded face with the deep voice began to read from darker passages still; these, he said, were from the Nobel Prize-winning Irish poet Seamus Heaney. In a disconsolate timbre, he spoke of suffering and torture inflicted and endured which could never be made fully right. An agitation prickled through Patrick's spinal column like electric shocks. Kay's imagined admonition seared his mind. *"Sounds like you're the loser, Patrick; sounds like they told you to go fuck yourself,"* came her derisive succulence.

Why had the evening turned so gloomy? Isn't this supposed to be a celebration?

The dark bard was now warning against hope, saying it's a waste of our time. *Did Heaney just say "hope"?* Patrick thought with a sneer. While the deep voiced one thundered on, his reverberating words heated the whiskey fermenting Patrick's blood. He was listening now as never before with tears streaming and limbs twitching and jumping. Scrawling madly on his pad, here's what he wrote:

'The poet speaks of tidal waves and sea-change; justice and revenge. He speaks of a sympathetic ear in the volatile sky, and miracles and healings.' *Fuck it! I tried the miracles and healings and it's all bullshit!* But Heaney seemed to be saying that in the rarest of times—like once in a lifetime—justice can prevail. *That's pretty fucking rare. But I must believe this time. After all, I have no other choice.*

'Here's my choice,' he continued writing, 'Will I be timid or bold? Will I seek glory one last time before I die?' Then he nearly cried out, "Is this God shouting down at me from the violent sky? Is this my time for vengeance, my time for renewal? Please God, say Yes!"

Just as the actor was bidding the disturbed room "a safe home," a charged thunderclap landed severing the remainder of the evening. In the ensuing blackened chaos, ghostly shadows shrieked their urgent exodus, battering open the front door again and again to a lone streetlamp's golden ambiance. Out into the troubled city in a state of emergency they poured.

As he grabbed hold of Finnie's extended hand and moved toward the sporadic mad misty glow, William Butler's voice interceded one last time:

> *Bolt and bar the shutter,*
> *For the foul winds blow:*
> *Our minds are at their best this night,*
> *And I seem to know*
> *That everything outside us is*
> *Mad as the mist and snow.*

41

DAY OF RECKONING

It was early afternoon when the cell phone rumbled him madly from his timeless slumber. Marie's message was, "Pat, where in heaven or hell are you? This place is crawling with Dick Tracys. FINRA's here, the SEC's here, even the FBI, I think. Call me, please!"

Still feeling completely wiped from his May Eve outing, he groggily returned her call. "How goes the battle, Marie?"

"It's a slaughter, Pat. These guys aren't the kids; they're the grown-ups. You'd better get in here or outta there. Head to Key West, or Ireland, or back to the forest. Whatever it is, you'd better do it fast. We're screwed, really screwed."

"Hold tight, Marie, and don't speak to them without an attorney. I'm calling Justus now, and then I'm coming in."

The note Finnie left said she'd gone out, there was leftover salmon in the fridge, and she loved him. He gobbled it up cold from the container, even sucking the oils off his thumb, figuring he'd need all the wisdom he could conjure. Then he showered off the night's residue and put on his pinstriped prison garb once more.

The storm had abated—the sky clearing, the winds down, the humidity oppressive. He tossed his Tumi over to the passenger seat, hoisted his chair into the open back, hopped into the silver bullet, and slalomed up an Olive still strewn with debris from the historic May storm.

This is it, he assumed. "Assumed—ha, ha," he muttered, seeing Felix Unger at the courtroom blackboard writing out the word "assume" for the judge, then circling "ass," "u," and "me." His message was obvious—never assume. But this wasn't a sitcom, and the circumstances here were clear cut. His career was over, no doubt, and maybe his days as a free man. Saunders had pinned the insider trading charge on him, and the Feds must believe all that trumped-up bullshit he called evidence. He was about to find out what public humiliation felt like, not to mention the inside of a jail cell. The day had arrived when he would face his greatest fear, his nightmare made tangible, his good life in ruins.

The newspaper headline flashed in his mind: "West Palm Beach Financial Advisor Patrick Connelly Guilty of Insider Trading, Sentenced to Prison." He was afraid to put the number of years in the headline. He could wait on that.

His mind turned to his beautiful, accomplished children. Would they be ashamed of him once they heard the news? Would they keep their distance? A lot had gone wrong in the past few years; they may decide to wash their hands of him for good. He thought of their mom. "Ass-wipe" would be a compliment compared to what was coming next. He thought of Marie. Was she implicated in the fraud? Had he taken her down with him? What would become of her? Will she ever forgive him?

Such misery cascaded throughout a skull still spinning from the activities of the previous night. How had the May Eve celebration turned so dark, so ominous? Had the vicious storm shifted the tone of the performance or vice versa? Either way, it was certainly not the carefree festival he'd expected, more like his thatched roof cottage had caught flames, forewarning the coming day. He hadn't had a chance to catch up with Finnie, so the fuller context would need to be left to another time. When the battle remains furious, the damage assessment waits.

As he headed north toward his imminent fate, the anxious tremors and sweat droplets were oddly absent, replaced with a sense of calm and a swelling confidence. Leaving the radio off, he instead enjoyed a silent presence unlike anything he'd felt in years. The team he'd assembled, or they'd assembled, or someone had assembled: Finnie and Kerry, Marie and Larry, Kay and Justus—while maybe not "Murderers Row," they were quite a remarkable lineup. And in the oft-murky world where the separation between right and wrong can be razor-thin, there was no ethical dilemma here. The good versus evil chasm was as large as the Atlantic, and his team was holding the moral high ground.

Putting aside his insider trading, that is.

Oops.

The sphere Patrick moved in his entire adult life, a privileged class where humility was rare, nearly everyone believed they're right, and others be damned. Baby Boomers and Gen Xers, especially, include vast populations of elitist know-it-alls—most without enough successes on their resumes to justify any of it. In their wake, he was feeling enormously humble this day. He didn't know a goddamned thing anymore. A part of him was accepting that he had crossed the line, broken the law, and had to pay for his sins. A part of him felt relieved.

Gratitude welled for everything he'd been given along the way: the opportunities and the challenges; the good influences and the bad; the joys and the sufferings. They all added up to who he was this moment—a good man who meant well—and a man who did his best given the trying circumstances. A 'giving, loving, and accepting man' who only wanted what was rightfully his, just like Charlie Brown's little sister, Sally. And he wanted the same for everyone else, too. Justice manifest. Work hard, do your best, keep your nose clean, and you'll get what you deserve—your just reward.

That was how the game was set up, wasn't it? *No,* he knew, *that's not how the game was set up.* He thought of William Blake's time-honored truth:

> *Man was made for joy and woe;*
> *And when this we rightly know,*
> *Thro' the world we safely go.*

Joy and woe are woven fine,
A clothing for the soul divine.

Despite it all, he still believed life was not a zero-sum game where one person benefits at the cost of another. With plenty of joy and woe to go around, humanity hadn't yet achieved an ideal plan to distribute it equitably. *In fact,* he thought, *the system is so breathtakingly broken that it seemed hopeless at times.* He grieved for those born into abject poverty, disease, broken families, and inept educational systems—those with no real chance to reach their potential or realize even their most modest dreams, those whose tapestry was woven with little joy and much woe.

Speaking of woe, it was time to come to terms with his and put his house in order.

Unloading his wheelchair, he positioned it just so, pushed it open, and tossed the air cushion in place. When the spasticity in his knees began to unlock, he forced his body down into the chair—another safe landing. The sole passenger applauds. Straightening himself, he lifted one frozen leg, and then the other, onto foot pedals vibrating from the rarely absent clonus triggered at the balls of his feet. Leaning left and then right, he pulled at the taut cloth and aligned his suit pants, zipper over crotch, to look as normal as possible. Maybe people wouldn't know he was crippled. Then he donned his suit coat, pulling the tails away from the wheel's spokes, tucking them in behind his back, to keep them as free of the parking lot's filth as possible. Finally, pulling his tie's knot straight and tight, he hoisted his loyal, ever-present Tumi onto his lap.

Slowly pushing away from his beloved silver bullet, beloved for its utility, not for its sex appeal, he thrust directly into the face of his earthbound day of judgment.

A day we all must one day face.

42

BEWITCHED, BOTHERED
AND BEWILDERED

Rolling through the parting elevator doors, he immediately entered what seemed a hornet's nest. "Are you Patrick Connelly?"

Pointing to the wheelchair, he said, "How could you tell?" He was thinking of Joe Pesci in *Goodfellas* for some odd reason, thinking he may as well be a full-of-bravado wise-guy as they throw him in the joint: *"What the fuck are you doing? You're hanging around my fuckin' neck like a vulture, like impending danger."*

A buzzsaw of blue suits scurried toward him, the lead guy saying, "Come this way, Mr. Connelly—this way, please." Saunders was nowhere in sight. No King or Wolfe either. His mind was so numb it may as well have been day three of Woodstock. He was in a kind of purple haze and couldn't even think clearly, never mind defend himself. [42]

Several advisors he barely knew were standing at their cubicles with jaws-dropped, earnestly watching the proceedings. This was more entertainment than any young salesperson could ever hope for—so much better than the day-to-day drudgery of dialing-for-dollars, however that's done these days. He knew exactly what they were thinking, too: *I wonder if I'll get any of his accounts?* That passed for camaraderie in the money business.

He saw Marie sitting in a small, glass-wrapped conference room surrounded by a blue throng pressing in with microphones and legal pads. Veering quickly to the right, he pushed open the door. "Marie, say nothing until Justus gets here." Her drooped face looked like she was next in line to the gallows. If she said anything, he didn't hear her in the ensuing frenzy.

"Mr. Connelly, you can't go in there—Mr. Connelly!" Two tall men lunged from both sides and grabbed hold of his shoulders, jarring him backward and out of the room.

"Get your hands off me!" he yelled while flailing his arms, almost tipping over his chair in the scuffle. "I said let go of me." He was warning the one holding back his arms while the other pushed him down the hallway and into Saunders's corner office.

Startled by the commotion, half a dozen strangers were shuffling around the kingly desk, but no Saunders or Lawson. Red-faced and breathing heavy, he said, "I'm not saying a word without my attorney present." Just as he spoke, Justus Fredericks burst through the door. "Justus, they're questioning Marie in another room. She has no attorney and needs your help."

"Okay, Pat, sit tight for a minute, and don't say a word." He turned and strode quickly from the room.

Patrick sat squinting against the bright lights. *As bad as Kay's office,* he was thinking, *with not nearly the compensatory décor.*

Encircled in the same blue probe as Marie, a pack of ravenous hyenas, the most daring darted out for a piece of his flesh. "Mr. Connelly, what is your current status with the firm?"

"I'm sorry," he huffed. "But we'll have to wait for Mr. Fredericks to return."

"We understand you've been suspended for suspicion of insider trading. How long has it been?"

"Did you not hear what I just said?" His voice was tinged with animus.

Glancing around the table, he was feeling enmity unlike any time since the days and months after his injury. These compliance guys were just doing their jobs, he knew, same as the rehab doctors and nurses were doing theirs a lifetime ago. Glaring faces with zero invested emotion. Why should they? It wasn't their lives on the line. It was just another day, and he was just another criminal to these cops, same as he'd been just another cripple to the medical staff. Dispassionately going about their jobs before going home to their safe and normal lives—neither cripples nor criminals.

His life had somehow spun completely out of control, blowing in the wind, and what happened next simply wasn't his choice. Or maybe it was? Maybe he'd stoically admit his guilt, confess that he had information ahead of the merger announcements, and get it over with? He didn't need his attorney present to tell the truth. But what the hell would he say? There was no informant, no Goofy, and no written notes stored in his files. It was all made up. They'd never believe the true story in a million years.

What would he call it, the "Darrin Stevens defense"? "Sammy twinkled her nose, and I had the newspaper a couple of weeks in advance—twice."

If he were lucky, he'd spend time in some type of mental hospital instead of prison—an indolent acquiescence to something less ambitious, more dawdling. Three squares a day and an afternoon of *Ryan's Hope* and *Days of Our Lives* sounded pretty good right now, just like at the rehab center post-injury. No expectations. No pressure. Everyone pretending there's hope of recovery except that prick, Dr. Ernst. He knew there was no hope, and he told the truth or at least inferred it, and that made him a prick. An honorable prick.

Paddy had refused to believe Ernst. He tried to walk again—digging deep and giving it all he had. Seeking out dozens of healers, from doctors to therapists to nutritionists to charlatans, he pushed himself to the limit, fasting for a week at a time, and sticking acupuncture needles in nearly every orifice of his body. He went horseback riding in the Netherlands for a month at one of their handicapped programs near the German border. He was promised only that he'd feel a warmth and flexibility in his torso and legs, like a deep tissue massage, while experiencing a unique sense of freedom and movement again. They were right on both counts—it was totally cool. Another time, he got the literal crap

Rolfed out of him, and he went back week after week until he couldn't stand the suffering any longer. It was not totally cool. These were the years before kinder and gentler Rolfing, probably mandated by lawsuits. Besides, he didn't know there were so many nutjobs living in Seattle.

In the early hours of the morning, alone in the dark, he'd pray that if he got it all back, just this one small miracle, he would never take a moment of his life for granted—ever again. "Please God, I'm begging you," he would begin. "If you give me one more chance, I promise to honor every sensation: the firing of every nerve, the turn of the hip, the contraction of the quad, the bend of the knee, the flex of the ankle, the position of the foot, the stretch of the toes. I promise, God, I will never miss another moment of its glory. And I'll give you all the credit, tell everyone that you created this miracle. And God, whatever I did to deserve this hell, I'm very sorry. Please forgive me and grant me one more chance. Please, God." (He left out that he wanted to feel his sexual organ again, figuring that might blow the deal)

It wasn't to be. God must have known what he was thinking.

From his anguish and trials he'd ascended in some ways, though never out of the goddamned wheelchair. But he had a life to live either way—walking or rolling—and it was past time to give up the dream and the prayers and get moving forward again.

"And where does the power come from, to see the race to its end? From within."

That was a long time ago. Maybe he was finally ready to stop fighting all the bullshit? What did any of it matter anyway? He'd be happier sinking passively into his eternal insignificance. It would be a hell of a lot easier than the world he'd strived in all these years. Maybe it was time Patrick skated away on the thin ice of his new day? [43]

❧

"Okay, let's get started," he said suddenly. "Let me tell you about the newspaper first." The blue suits sprung to attention.

"Go ahead, Mr. Connelly—we're taping the conversation."

"Well, this is going to sound crazy, but here goes."

"Pat, hold off on making any comments." Justus had dashed back into the room at that moment and sat down next to him. "Let's hear from them first. Just answer their questions."

"How's Marie?"

"She's fine—she'll be fine." Then Fredericks turned to the mob and exchanged business cards. He looked the pile over for a few moments and finally said, "Okay, gentlemen, go ahead with your questions, please."

"What were you about to say regarding a newspaper, Mr. Connelly?"

"Pat, be careful."

"Don't worry, Justus. I have to get this off my chest. Regarding the insider trading, I—"

"Pat," Justus said sternly. "You don't need to go there. Just answer their questions."

"Justus, it's okay," he said. "I'll feel better." Then he turned back to the pack and said, "Back in January, I found a local newspaper, a *Palm Beach Post*. It was dated about two weeks into the future.

At first, I didn't believe it; but I kept checking, and the date of the paper was February 10th, but it was only January 27th, and I was the only one who could see it."

"Pat?"

"It's okay, Justus," he insisted. "The paper had a story about Disney buying Cracker Barrel, so I acted on it. And then it happened."

"Pat?"

"Then I found another newspaper in March, this time an *Irish Times*, and again it was dated a few weeks in the future. It was a St. Patrick's Weekend Edition, and the last page had an article about Disney buying Cedar Fair, so I acted on it again. I'm sorry I did it, and I apologize for all the trouble I've caused."

The lead cop exchanged blank stares with his team of investigators while light chuckles started around the table. He finally said, "That's it? Future newspapers?"

"Yes, that's it," Patrick replied. "And I'm really sorry I acted on them. I don't know what I was thinking."

One of the older investigators, struggling to muffle his giggling, asked, "Didn't that happen once to Darrin Stevens in an episode of *Bewitched?*"

"Yes, it did," said another. "But the paper Sammy zapped was only one day ahead, I think. And Darrin didn't buy stocks; he went to the track and bet on the horses."

Another chimed in, "That was the Dick York Darrin, wasn't it? He was a much better Darrin than the guy who replaced him."

"Dick Sargent, I think," another guy said. "What a let-down he was." There were grimacing nods of agreement around the table.

"I don't think Samantha ever zapped a future newspaper," said another who was checking his iPhone. "It might have been Aunt Clara. She was totally losing it, making mistakes all the time, and she was into horse racing, if I recall."

"That does seem simpler than risking insider trading charges, Mr. Connelly," the lead guy said. "Why didn't you just go to the track?"

"Well, for one thing, I'm a stockbroker," said Patrick. "Also, didn't Darrin get caught at the track on a working day by Larry Tate, his boss, and get fired? so that didn't work out so well either." Now they were all roaring with laughter.

The head guy finally stifled his and forced out, "That Larry Tate was a total jerk; he was firing Darrin like every other show."

"He was!" howled another. "Until Darrin produced another winning advertising campaign to save the day."

"Tate would never get away with that in today's workplace," another added. "He'd get his own butt fired instead."

After the latest outburst had quieted, the head guy said, "Well, thank you for your honesty, Mr. Connelly; we really appreciate it."

"You're welcome," Patrick said, not quite sure what had just happened.

"But we're not here for insider trading allegations. We did take a look after Mr. Saunders brought it to our attention. But all we found was a lot of suspect evidence, which is a whole other matter. The stock buys you made appear to have been just a wee bit of good luck, Mr. Connelly. Twice."

"And now we can add a layer of blarney on top of that," said another with a smile. "Thanks for that—we needed a good laugh."

"You're welcome, again," Patrick said through his reddening face. Turning to Justus, he asked, "So why are they here?"

"If the entertainment portion of the program is over, Pat," replied Fredericks, "they'll get to that now."

"Sorry," he said sheepishly. "Please go ahead."

"We're here on an extremely serious matter, Mr. Stevens; oops, I mean, Mr. Connelly." Muted giggles were discernible but dissipated quickly. "What do you know about Erica Salmberg?"

"What? Who?"

"Ms. Erica Salmberg—the largest account in the office. Certainly, you know who she is."

"I believe she's KW Group's new client," he said after collecting his thoughts. "I had nothing to do with her account. You may have heard King and I weren't the best of friends. I met her briefly when Saunders walked her entourage into my office, the day they onboarded her."

"Onboarded?"

"Opened her new account."

"Phew," the questioner said. "I thought you were talking about airlines."

"I did too, for the longest time," he replied. "Anyway, Saunders told Ms. Salmberg he was kicking me out of my office, that it would soon be King's. He showed her the view of Palm Beach, and then they left—less than a minute total. That's it. You can ask Marie."

"They already have, Pat," said Fredericks.

"Why? what's going on?"

"Jeff Saunders has implicated you in her disappearance and the disappearance of the money."

"What do you mean, implicated me? What did he say? What disappearance? What money?

"It's in your best interest to cooperate, Mr. Connelly," said one of the regulators. "The truth is always better—it'll help you later; we'll be more lenient if you make our job easier and tell us what you know. Do you know the whereabouts of Ms. Salmberg?"

"How on earth would I know?"

"He's told you everything he knows, gentlemen," Justus said coldly.

"Besides," Patrick added, "what hasn't Saunders implicated me in, for Christ's sake?"

Justus Fredericks put his arm around his client's shoulders and, with a little pat, said, "Blarney aside, this man here is nothing if not truthful. He lives by an ethic that despicable people like Jeff Saunders wouldn't even recognize. And with that, gentlemen, Mr. Connelly's presence is no longer required here. I'll stay for however long you need me."

Walking Patrick to the elevator, Justus said, "I never knew you were so damn funny."

"Believe me, Justus," he replied. "I'm as surprised as you are." [44]

43

GOLDEN SHOVELS TURN TO LEAD

May Day at the firm's Palm Beach location turned into a prolonged episode lasting late into the evening. Counselor Fredericks sat for hours with the enforcement agents getting a full rendering of all they believed had transpired. Saunders, Lawson, King and Wolfe had been taken to separate locations for questioning.

"At the end of the day," as some prefer to say, not only were Marie and Patrick cleared of insider trading allegations, but the regulators were preparing charges against Saunders for attempting to implicate "Connelly" falsely. That he hadn't bought any shares of the two stocks himself, or for family or friends, had helped his cause. It showed a lack of greed, they said, unlike everything else happening in the office. The authorities believed Saunders's accusations in the Salmberg case were spurious as well.

"Just blowing smoke out of his ass," Justus reported with a grin. "Their words, not mine."

In addition, they were interested in any recent portfolio changes in Patrick's former accounts, promising to follow up diligently.

"That's great to hear, thank you," Patrick said. "But what Salmberg case? What in hell is going on?"

Marie had been correct. In addition to FINRA and the SEC, the FBI was in house and on the case. The primary reason they'd all descended on the firm's Palm Beach office was the activities around Erica Salmberg. "A big problem," they called it.

Although the investigation was preliminary, Justus reiterated what they knew or suspected: Ms. Salmberg was anything but an heiress to a fortune, although she did deal in big money, apparently shilling for a company that runs fisheries in Scandinavia and the Baltics as a facade for illicit activities. They operated worldwide, allegedly funding money laundering schemes, sex trafficking, drug trafficking, delivering weapons to extremist organizations, and other wholesome things like that. The EU had been monitoring the network of companies and recently opened a formal investigation, but hadn't yet informed America's intelligence agencies. Breakdowns in communication channels between international law enforcement agencies, unfortunately, were commonplace, Justus was told.

Arriving in town during Palm Beach's high season, Salmberg canvassed the market looking for vulnerabilities, waiting for the perfect opportunity. When she met Ian King and Mia Wolfe at a seminar, and then their boss, she apparently had found her marks: young bankers hungry for success, or maybe just anxious to keep their jobs. Either way, the investigators said, bankers fixated on building their businesses sometimes act without a full vetting. They may even operate autonomously. After all, it's often a zero-sum game they played.

Fastest guy across that bridge is the winner, Patrick was thinking.

It happened more often than one would think, they said, because the financial business was a prime target of professional scam artists. Once Salmberg identified her foils, she simply had to be smarter, more patient, and more devious than they were. As it turned out, it was a piece of cake. In this case, maybe a crab cake. In March, she called her bosses for the funding and opened several accounts. That was the day Saunders flaunted her around the office. In the next six weeks, in addition to running tens of millions of dirty funds through the accounts to wash them clean, she availed herself of various ancillary services the firm offered. Although she hadn't purchased stocks or any other investments, she promised that was coming once things settled down.

But she did borrow money—lots of money. She agreed with her new advisory team, effectively Saunders, that spending her own cash on the Palm Beach mansion under contract was unnecessary when tax-deductible interest rates were so attractive. She was thrilled when they secured her ultra-high-net-worth jumbo mortgage in record time. Saunders pulled every string he knew, and a few he didn't know, and the funds had been wired the previous Friday afternoon, just in time for the closing.

The problem, among others, was that Salmberg asked them to wire the funds to *her* attorney's escrow account. "We're trying to keep control of the transaction until the inspection is sorted out," she had said. "You can't be too careful these days." The money trail ended there, never making it to the seller. There was no closing. The imaginary buyer was happy to lose her deposit given the loan proceeds were about fifteen times that. If that weren't enough, she quickly maxed out two new credit cards for "tooling around town" money.

By Monday, the firm's legal team in New York was frantically searching for the wired funds while Saunders and King, in various states of shock and panic, prayed that their computer screens were wrong, that the Salmberg account balances weren't really hovering near zero. By Tuesday, yesterday, it was confirmed the entirety of the cash had vanished, along with Salmberg and her attorney. They fell off the face of the map without a trace, the money and the perpetrators gone—*poof*—like magic.

It appeared to be a classic example of money laundering and financial fraud where the all-too-eager advisor acts as an unwitting accomplice at each step along the way, Justus was told. Saunders had allegedly abetted the entire scheme by skipping over Jack Lawson and his legal chain of command at every opportunity. These are typically complex cases that would take many months, years maybe, to sort out. The cash was already long gone, they lamented, and Salmberg may never be found either.

Along with King, Wolfe and Larson, Saunders had taken up residence in the office penalty box, the "suspended without pay" club recently vacated by the terminated Patrick Connelly. Pending a full investigation, there were several "golden shovels" at severe risk of turning to lead, the latest version of "fool's gold."

"Oh well," Patrick said to Marie when they finally met up the next day. "It's a dog-eat-dog world, after all, and we eat-what-we-kill around here."

"At the end of the day, Pat, it is what it is," she replied with an exhausted smile, after which they both leaned in for a hug. The long, teary-eyed variety of profound relief.

44

BRAND NEW DAY

The notorious Palm Beach money laundering mess made the national headlines as one of the largest fraud cases in the firm's long and storied history. The senior crisis control team from Manhattan had taken temporary residence in the vacated palatial corner office, bringing along at least a dozen fire extinguishers.

One of the first actions they took was to reinstate Patrick Connelly to his former wealth management position with a formal and very public apology. Returned were his book of clients, with any upended portfolios restored, back pay, and the deed to his old corner office with the view across the bridge—a lease, not a bill of sale, with conditions, to be clear. Oh yeah, they returned his assistant too. He took the opportunity to negotiate a modest raise for Maura, er, Marie. They even inherited a few select clients from the account distribution, those who were content with an old-style stock guy. They would be living under a new set of rules. For one, referrals were a choice—not a mandate. Dale Wampler humbly asked his old friend and advisor for forgiveness. Patrick thought about it for 1.5 seconds before opening his arms. With one caveat—the next few rounds of drinks at the club were on Dale.

The wiring of a client's money, in or out, would typically have been Marie's purview. Had she been an unwitting participant in the laundering scheme, her job would have been at grave risk. But Saunders wouldn't let her near it, saying, "I need this done yesterday, so I'm doing it myself."

"Knock yourself out, jerk-face," she'd muttered to herself. And that he did.

Jack Lawson's hands were apparently clean of the whole debacle. Besides skipping such trivial steps as running his activities by local compliance, Saunders also allegedly forged several signatures along the rocky road, specious approvals Lawson never signed off on. He was moved from the penalty box to "paid leave" while it was all being tidied up.

The grand total of the scam: the home loan, the cash washed clean, the joy ride credit spree, and other incidentals was allegedly in the fancy neighborhood of thirty million. The possible sanctions, fines, and other damages would add to that total. Saunders was lawyered up, so was King, and they were getting ready to point their middle fingers at each other. The W in KW, Mia Wolfe, remained on an extended leave of absence. She was said to be more a victim of bullying than an accomplice to any of the disastrous proceedings. Marie's statement of her time with KW was supportive of this notion.

Distribution day, late Friday evening, when the "free agent" client accounts would be spread around to the remaining advisors, was the most exciting day in the life of a young salesperson. In the money business, being handed something for nothing was as close to socialism as they'd ever come in the entirety of their careers.

***

The moment the scandalous news broke, Larry Devlin called to check on his friend. He was relieved to hear neither Pat nor Marie were an unwitting part of the unfortunate happenings. He knew that honorable advisors get caught up in questionable, or even illegal proceedings on a regular basis. That was just one of the many reasons why compliance guys like Jack Lawson existed—to save management, advisors, and their support staffs from the myriad opportunities to sink their careers. Saunders never gave Lawson that chance.

"Hey Larry, remember the option income and government plus funds we were hawking back in the '80s," Patrick asked his old friend.

"I'd rather not," Larry answered.

"I hear you, but it's too late." Patrick was grinning. "What a disaster that was—plenty of clients lost their money, and brokers lost their clients, and then their careers. We were newbies, thank the Lord, so we didn't have enough assets to do any serious damage."

"Speak for yourself," Larry grumbled.

"Oops, sorry."

"Are you really?"

"Umm."

"That's what I thought." Larry joined in the grinning. "Well, it turned out that 17% annual income comes at a cost—like half your capital. You forgot to mention the emerging market debt funds, Pat. When '94 rolled around, the worst bear market in bonds we'd ever seen, most of the 'emerging' countries submerged, along with the mutual funds buying their debt."

"True—just another example of greed, or at least poor judgment, winning out for a time," Patrick added. "But when the last buyers finished piling in, that's when the bottom fell out."

"It happens over and over," Larry agreed. "You can almost set your watch to it."

"How about all the limited partnerships on our menu back then," Patrick reminisced. "With marginal tax brackets as high as 70%, some of the deals were offering three and four to one write-offs. Invest $100,000 and write $400,000 off your taxes. You'll be way ahead on day one, and it won't even matter if you get your original investment back (which they didn't). I think that was your pitch, wasn't it, Larry?"

"Yeah, sure, Pat. I learned it from listening to you if I'm not mistaken. I can't think of a reason why the IRS ended up shutting them down."

"No, me neither," Patrick said with a chuckle. "How about the Hawaii Fund? I'll never forget that roll-out meeting in Boca. Pretty girls dancing the hula, giving us leis and Mai Tais, and then the godfather of partnerships, "the don," I think he was called, spun our heads with dreams of pineapples and macadamia nuts and condo units with ocean views, along with 15% annual returns."

"I remember," Larry said with a grimace. "They never did get those condos built, did they?"

"Not even the first spade hit the dirt."

"Even so, how do you lose money in Hawaiian farmland?"

"Maybe the annual expense ratio, something like 20%, explained it?"

"That sounds plausible," Larry concurred. "How about those movie partnerships? Our clients could be Hollywood moguls, own a sliver of the next series of hits coming to the big screen from Paramount, Twentieth Century, and Disney. How exciting."

"Yes, it certainly was, and supremely ignorant," Patrick said. "Who knew that only one movie in ten makes any money? I must have missed that in the prospectus."

"Funny, so did I."

"A few years after they all flopped, went down the tubes, so to speak, a *Forbes* magazine article said it best: 'If you want to invest in Hollywood, you should come in through the front door, not the back.' Meaning, simply own the stocks of the media companies making the movies instead of complicating your life with high fee, high maintenance, illiquid rubbish."

"Good advice, Pat. Have you ever thought about going into the advisory business?"

"Once or twice."

"You should give it a shot—I think you'd be good at it."

"Maybe I will, Larry, thanks for the idea. Well, that pretty much covers our early days in the biz and brings us into the 21st century, which kicked off with the 'dot com' crash, and then the 'mortgage and derivatives' crisis which nearly brought down the entire global economy. We can probably let those go for now?"

"Excellent idea. The wounds are still healing."

"No one ever promised us financial advisory would be easy," Patrick said, "but we survived all of it. We're stronger for it, better advisors, and the entire industry is wiser and heartier for the experiences too, I think."

"I agree," he replied. "Our financial markets are the best in the world, and the advisory industry is the soundest it's ever been."

"Very true, Larry, the Wild West days are long buried. On balance, today's advisors are highly trained, ethical, and dedicated, and they really do focus on providing clients with a consistent, exceptional experience. Not to mention, no junk products need apply."

"So true," Larry agreed. "Keeping it simple always works the best."

"Even Saunders cared about the clients." Patrick's tone was more somber now. "It was the advisors, I think, the people he was supposed to lead, where his caring tank ran a little low. And something about me *really* rubbed him the wrong way."

"You are an acquired taste, Pat."

"Gee, thanks Larry," he said, trying his best to sound offended. "But anyway, he sure got weeded out quickly."

"Weeded out?" Larry repeated. "I'd say it was more a total excavation."

"Good point," Patrick agreed. "It's really a shame. I feel bad for him, for all of them."

"Well, it's over, Pat, and you can take a deep breath and relax now; maybe you'll get to be a lifer at the firm after all."

"Maybe so." Patrick expressed his gratitude to his druid friend, suggesting he hop into the Gulf Stream's miraculous current bound northeast for the Emerald Isle at his earliest convenience. They agreed to meet up on the magical Dingle Peninsula as soon as feasible.

The muckety-mucks from headquarters had other plans for Patrick Connelly, though. Saying he was "an important part of our reputation restoration strategy," they asked him to consider managing the office on a temporary basis, "just until these disappointing circumstances are behind us." He asked for a few days to think about it, let it all simmer, and he'd get back to them with a decision.

"Christ," he said to Marie, "I feel like the entire past decade has been one long restoration project." He rattled off the usual laundry list seared into his nervous system.

"That's a pretty depressing summary, Pat, and just when things were getting back to normal, this had to happen," Marie said. "It's like, here we go again."

"True," he said. "But it's more an isolated incident this time, and it will fade away, as they all do. Our clients are whole, the markets are solid and recovering, and the future looks superb."

As optimistic as he sounded, Patrick was uncertain he was the right man to begin stitching a piece of the firm's reputation back together. Very uncertain. Especially since he had no management skills that he could think of, never mind his work ethic, which was never considered Herculean, or even MacCoolean. "One thing's for sure, Marie, it's been a long century so far, almost like an entire cycle."

"Cycle?"

"Never mind."

Patrick was thinking about Dingle in the summertime. It sounded rather alluring. Not to mention the few-hour drive northeast to Finnie's Antrim Coast. Moving the business to his own shop, setting the more relaxed pace and tone he craved, might allow such a formerly frivolous dream to unfold. On the other hand, managing the local office for a while, a short while, trying to set a more positive one-for-all tone, felt like a pretty good option too. It might even be fun, he dared to think. Was that even possible in the 21st century money business?

That may be the most incredulous dream of all.

Nonetheless, he was safe, in charge, and he had choices. The dark clouds had rolled away, and the brand-new day included a sense of freedom he hadn't experienced in a long while. It all felt perfectly delightful. [45]

But he needed to have a talk with the one person that this decision hinged on, the most important person in his life, whether she knew it or not.

45

THE BAND PLAYED ON

Sitting in his den amongst his many treasures, his thoughts were accompanied by a heightened appreciation of the things that mattered the most. So much of it, he ascertained, was right here within his grasp, with the most precious of all being his Finnie. Placing one of those treasures, a Van Morrison vinyl, on the turntable, he poured another treasure into a short glass and engaged in his favorite pastime—contemplation.

As one of Van's many masterpieces haunted the nooks and crevices and soul of the room—if "many" is even possible in the context—Patrick considered the artist in the house. [46] The loner from angry Belfast was called "aloof, eccentric, and moody" by music critics. Artists, including rock stars, were often considered all the above, different from the rest of us. But Van took "aloof" to a higher level. He was a classic introvert, busy engaging within his mind more so than the world around him. Patrick saw it firsthand when he attended a concert at Hard Rock in Hollywood not too long ago. In a dark suit and tie, with dark sunglasses under his dark fedora in the darkened arena, Van stood onstage at a microphone stand looking down at his dark shoes while performing his one-hour set. The superstar didn't even once attempt to connect with his audience. His music was jazzy and poetic and brilliant that night, as usual, and when he finished, he finished—the cheering crowd calling lustily for an encore were summarily dismissed.

Decades earlier, in the summer of 1968, Van was tasting global stardom at the fresh age of twenty-three after releasing his classic, "Brown Eyed Girl." Seemingly disinterested in repeating such trivial "pop" success, he instead went into a New York City studio with a masterful jazz trio and in short time produced *Astral Weeks*, considered today among the greatest works ever recorded in the genres of rock and jazz.

Like much of the work of genius, it was a commercial failure and not given its appropriate status until many years later. Amidst the clamor of the times, neither music critics nor fans understood what they were hearing from the peculiar young man from Ulster. They wanted the next "Brown Eyed Girl" and instead got *Astral Weeks*. Van took care of the commercial side when he knocked out the mega-hit *Moondance* album in 1970. Even he had to keep the bosses happy and pay the bills.

In '68, Paddy was a little too young and distracted with typical coming-of-age challenges to notice much of anything, never mind an obscure fusion album from a Belfast rock musician. But with age came wisdom, and he'd grown to savor the perfectly spun charm of *Astral Weeks* while seeming to grow a fraction younger with each spin. Today's spinning precisely mirrored his mood. [47]

Patrick's introduction to music was eclectic and included Herb Alpert (because of that notorious whipped cream album cover and his father wearing out the vinyl); Vince Guaraldi's piano jazz from the *Peanuts* holiday specials; then there were the Temptations R&B, Franki Valli's high school crooning, and Judy Collins's weeping. After that, he got into Van's commercial hits; Cat Stevens and Joni Mitchell's rock-based introspections; Simon & Garfunkel's contemplative, inspirational ballads; Bob Dylan's "Blowin' in the Wind" and other protest songs; rock bands Dave Clark Five, the Beatles (of course), Jethro Tull, the Stones, the Doors, Pink Floyd, and others of that ilk.

Oh yeah, and the Monkees, although he'd prefer that not be relitigated. "Christ," he would say, "I had to listen to something until the Partridge Family came along."

The national tone in the late '60s was unruly, colored primarily by the Vietnam War, racism, civil rights, poverty, and the very public assassinations of President John F. Kennedy, civil rights leader Martin Luther King Jr., and Senator Robert F. Kennedy. The latter being the one politician he revered above all others. Having once seen Bobby Kennedy up close at the Bronx Zoo, when Patrick was ten, and watching him deftly handle the thronging media, was unshakeable. He later understood what he'd witnessed to be the senator's extraordinary confidence, eloquence, and charisma on full display.

On that sweltering early June morning in '68, when news broke that Bobby had been murdered at a presidential campaign appearance in LA, Patrick cried tears of outrage mixed with hopelessness. *My God,* he thought, *the world is just one big "ball of confusion."* But, as always, the band played on. [48]

There's a concept in finance called "opportunity cost." It means whenever you make an investment decision, by choosing the one, you are choosing against any number of others. You've picked Microsoft as your technology stock, for example, instead of Google or Apple. You've chosen Macy's as your retailing stock instead of Amazon. *Ugh!* You've decided against buying a rental apartment building, instead keeping the capital in stocks or cash. The investments you eschew represent opportunity cost—the potential returns you've given up by your choices. To gain a fuller understanding of any investment decision's impact, or any life decision, really, your choices should be measured as such in the months and years ahead. Whatever the assessment, though, you plow ahead undeterred. The band plays on.

In this same light, he often thought about the murders of those three revolutionary leaders: JFK, our first and only Irish Catholic president; MLK, the seminal voice of the oppressed who spoke primarily of peace and love as the magic formula for overcoming prejudice; and RFK, the youthful, handsome, champion of the people, of *all* people, and the promise for a better tomorrow.

What would our country, and the world, look like had all three been allowed to see their shared missions to fruition?

When assessing the alternatives, and the societal conditions since, Patrick suspected the opportunity costs of their hateful exterminations were extraordinarily high. [49]

Trying to piece together all that had happened in the last few days, weeks, and months, he told Finnie he felt like he'd been living in the latest JRR Tolkien fantasy.

"Interesting," she said with a raise of her eyes. "I didn't realize he was still writing."

"Am I misinformed?"

"Probably; he died in the UK sometime in the early 1970s."

"Maybe he has a ghostwriter?"

"Clever comeback."

"You know what I mean, wise Finnster."

"I do," she consoled. "Apologies for behaving a little too much like you."

"Burn," he said, noting the similarity.

Nesting in his lap, silky head warm to his chest, she said, "It's been an incredible ride, that's for sure."

"One I never want to end. On that note, I have a quick thought I want to run by you."

"What's that, my dear Hobbit?"

"Well, I'm not sure how I feel about the business, staying or moving, but either way, I think my financial worries will be a thing of the past."

"It sounds that way," she concurred. "And it's a wonderful thing. No one deserves it more than you."

"Thank you, sweetheart, that means a lot," he said. "What I'm getting at is, well, it means this will change things around here too. If I have more security, financial security, then so do you."

"You are always so sweet and thoughtful," she said, turning her face up to express her appreciation.

"Whoa," he driveled.

Long removed from his truncated youth, he still wished to be like the young lovers in Van's song. Silly of him, he knew. But once upon a time, he'd gone from being a strapping nineteen to a decrepit senior, nearly overnight. A teenager's mind entombed in a retiree's arthritic body. While he couldn't have his physical youth back, he wanted another shot at one of its greatest blessings—a less serious, more playful, dream-like existence. He wanted to forget the pain, and never, ever grow so old again. [46]

All he had left to strive for, he'd concluded, was someone special to non-strive with. He wanted to feel the sweet, unhurried simplicity of new love, enduring love; he wanted it to envelop and lift him to some sort of heavenly state. It happened once with Becky, and in the early years it was delightful. With Finnie, he'd tasted those early years once again, coating his tongue in sweetness, filling him to a peaceable satiation. All he wanted was tomorrow to be just like today, and the following day to be like tomorrow. He didn't need any big wins, but please God, no more losses.

"What I mean to say, Finndoll, is you don't need to work at Murphy's anymore if you don't want to. If you want to—great, but you don't need to."

"What would I do?"

"Anything you want," he responded. "Follow a dream or a passion. Play music, start a business, get married, have a child, have another child." Then, after a clumsy pause, he said, "If you stay by my side, I promise I'll love you and take care of you, forever and ever."

"Thank you, my love." Tears rolled off her lids like tiny ripples cresting in the shallows.

Considering the opportunity cost of going any further, he decided to stop there—to lighten things up. "One caveat though, if you marry or have a child with someone else, I'll have to renege on the 'forever and ever' offer."

"That sounds like a reasonable qualifier," she said with the giggle he always managed to raise. Well, maybe just short of 'always.' At least not 'never.' In a more serious tone now, she said, "I guess we both have important decisions to make."

"No, Finnie, that's not what I mean," he said. "If you're happy with things just as they are, that's plenty good enough for me. Then, there are no decisions to make. We'll just let the band play on."

"I'm so lucky I met you, Patrick."

"The luck is all mine, dear." [50]

46

SANCTUARY KAY'S HAT TRICK

Patrick Connelly accepted the firm's offer to preside over office operations for the time being. Knowing she'd be doing most of the work, Marie wasn't thrilled with the news. Until she saw her new paycheck. Jack Lawson was cleared of all wrongdoing and back running compliance. None of the typical chatter was coursing around the office, meaning the walls no longer had ears. Yet, he learned in conversation that Lawson had smelled a rat's ass and called in the Feds—a day too late as it turned out. They made a good leadership team, Lawson and Connelly, meaning Lawson and Marie, and the decorum around the office changed palpably. Most of his clients treated Patrick as a decorated hero returning from battle. It was a pleasure to be in the money business again.

With the breadth of his new office duties, he came home late and mentally spent many nights. As the weeks flew by, he and Finnie settled into a satisfying domestic routine, yet a silent unsettledness had taken residence in the home. He'd driven out to Kerry's warehouse a few times for a visit with a wise old friend whom he missed. Each time, the door was locked with a "closed for vacation" sign posted. He reasoned that maybe Kerry had gone on a furniture buying tour around Ireland. Florida's winter season was over. It was common for business owners to shorten their hours, take a break, and flee to the Georgia, North Carolina, or Tennessee mountains or anywhere else beyond the broiling peninsula. Ireland certainly fit that description. Wherever in the world Mr. O'Connor had fled, Patrick was disappointed not to have been informed of his plans.

On other occasions when his mind twisted in uncertainty, he paid a visit to his therapist, Kay. While he hadn't seen her in the flesh in a few months, her wise and plump lips, and the saucy language he smartly provoked, had continued in their important advisory role. It was past time for an image refresh.

Kay was like an unchanging sanctuary in a volatile, ever-changing world. The sparse, too-bright office populated with the sizzling, sharply dressed therapist was intact. The one thing that did change, as promised, was her hourly rate. So, the money man in him cut out the small talk and got right to it. Like if a bartender started charging for her time to engage in droning, meaningless conversation—you'd nod a hello, order the drink, and move on, saving the hollow blather for a less costly venue.

Nesting in his usual spot, she closed the door behind them, saying, "I'm glad to see you, Patrick. It's been a while. Tell me what's been going on."

"Great to see you too, Kay," he answered. "Going on? Not much, really."

"Why are you here then?"

"So much is going on I don't even know where to start."

"That's what I thought," she said, smiling. "What's the primary reason you thought to make the appointment? Let's start with that."

"I was wondering what you were wearing, to be honest." He'd missed her eye rolls. "Seriously, it's all good. I just thought I'd update you on a few things and get your feedback." He caught her up on the events around his career and his recent spate of good fortune.

"I read the articles in the paper about the big scandal in your office," she said. "I was worried about you. But your name wasn't mentioned, so I figured you were okay."

"Thanks, Kay—I appreciate the call."

"Sorry about that," she said with a grimace. "I can't charge for outgoing calls of concern; that falls into the category of pro bono work, and God knows, I have more than my share."

"Very magnanimous," he smirked. "I'm impressed." Their smiles met.

"Seriously, I'm so happy to hear all this news. It looks like the good guy came out on top."

"Sure, I guess so," he said with a shrug. "Do you remember the last advice you gave me?"

"Help me."

"What you said to me the last time I was here. We were talking about the risks of my business being poached."

"Do you mind if I glance at my notes?"

"Of course not," he said. "I feel your pain." He watched patiently as she flipped through her three-ring binder. He was willing to wait all evening if he had to.

"I think I've got it."

"Let's hear it."

"I said to tell them to go fuck themselves; nobody fucks with Patrick Connelly."

"Bingo," he said, taking note of the two F-bombs—an excellent start to the session. "And you know what, Kay? I did it—I told them to go fuck themselves, metaphorically speaking, of course."

"I'm so proud of you, Patrick," she continued. "You're the champion of the world."

"Jeez, Kay, I'm really sorry, but that's a layup," he said, as the Queen in him came out. [51]

When he'd finished singing a few lines from the stadium anthem, Kay said, "So, this is how you want to spend your time here?"

"Where else could I get an audience to listen to me?"

"In the bus station—with an open guitar case sitting in front of you?"

"Nice, I appreciate that," he chuckled. "Instead of tossing coins, maybe you can lower my bill at the end."

"I was thinking of raising it, you know, throw in pain and suffering."

"Let's call it a draw then. The truth is, Kay, all this success is kind of unsettling. I've never been one to revel in good news without wondering, where's the punch line? what's coming next to say 'gotcha'?"

"Are you sure you're not Jewish? We spend our lives looking over our shoulders."

"We Irish are the same; oppressed throughout history, a chip on our shoulders, abounding skepticism, our hearts bleeding for all those who've suffered a similar fate."

"Victims in arms," she said with a nod before continuing. "Seriously, Patrick, maybe this time it's only good news. Have you considered that?"

"Sure, I have, but that would defy the world order, at least from my experience," he replied. "Speaking of good news—I'm in love."

"That's fantastic. Tell me about it, about her. It is *her*, isn't it?"

"Do you really have questions about that? Christ, I guess I haven't slobbered over you enough."

"Nothing surprises me these days."

"I hear you. *Her* name is Maureen, and she's perfect in every way. I know all young lovers say that, but that's how I feel, like a young lover. Isn't that pathetic?"

"No, it's sweet. Young is in the mind."

"It had better be because it ain't out here," he said, gesturing up and down his exterior. "Anyway, Finnie, that's her nickname, is from Ireland and quite a bit younger than me. But she has an old soul, and she's a knockout, a sweetheart, and really smart. We read Yeats together, listen to Van Morrison and The Chieftains—she even lets me listen to Bob Dylan. I mean, what woman lets you listen to Bob Dylan?"

"I certainly wouldn't."

"See what I mean? It's like letting me watch *Benny Hill* or *The Three Stooges*. It's incredulous."

"Are you *sure* she's not a guy?"

"We're back on that?"

"Sorry."

"No problem. I've seen her in the shower—she's definitely not a guy. And really, we laugh a lot, all the time. She actually thinks I'm funny."

"Now I'm worried for her."

"Me too," he said with a smile. "But she keeps me in my place, believe me. And she's quiet and patient and a great listener too—the only one left on earth, I think. Who's not being paid to listen, I mean."

"Touché."

"She's also my chief advisor—wisdom delivered with love. From you, I only get the wisdom."

"It's the best I can do. It's all over the licensing paperwork."

"And it's enough, believe me."

"Phew," she said with an exaggerated wipe of her forehead. "This is wonderful news, Patrick, I'm so happy for you. And seriously, she is one smart lady for reeling you in."

"Thank you, Kay, I appreciate that. But here comes the punch line."

"Oops—go ahead."

"It's just that . . . she seemed to come out of nowhere, just when I really needed her. Like she was sent from heaven to answer a prayer. And now, there's nothing wrong, she's sweet and kind and loving, and we spend all our free time together. But my gut tells me she's drifting away a little. Like she came in with the tide, and one day she'll leave with the tide. Does that sound weird?"

"No, it's a common concern in new relationships. But it sounds like you're letting your fear take over. You're analyzing too much instead of just enjoying the moment."

"Probably . . . No, I'm sure you're right," he said. "I've enjoyed everything immensely. But I've talked to her about meeting my kids, hinted about something more permanent. She gets quiet, doesn't respond, like she's avoiding the subject."

"How long have you been together?"

"Three months, thirteen days, three hours and twenty minutes—give or take sixty seconds."

"But who's counting," she said with a laugh.

"Not me, I swear. I happened to be checking the calendar today—pure coincidence. But really, I get feelings sometimes, and they turn out to be accurate. I'm a Cancer—me and the moon are tight. What worries me—"

"Worry, worry, worry." Kay had uncrossed her legs and was sitting up straight now with both hands holding her head, pivoting side-to-side with each "worry."

"Hey, if I didn't worry," he said with a smile, "I'd have too much free time. I might get in trouble."

"More than already?" she responded in kind. "But really, Patrick, maybe it's time to put away the worry."

"I'm working at it, Kay. I've been working at it my entire adult life."

After a brief break to take down a few notes, Kay looked up and said, "Let's talk about that – your tendency to worry. Why do you think that is?"

"Well, when I was young, like nine or ten, I worried that my father, or my oldest brother, or both, were going to kill me. They were like Frankenstein and Dracula monsters hiding in the walls around the next corner, ready to grab me."

"Wow," came her exclamation.

"I wish I were exaggerating," he said. "Later, when I was playing hockey, even if we had a 6-0 lead in the third period, I'd worry that something would go terribly wrong, and we'd lose the game."

"Did it often go terribly wrong?"

"No—never. Until the day it went terribly wrong." He paused his uplifting trip through the archives for a sip of water.

"Go on," she encouraged, "when you're ready."

"Thanks," he said. "After I left for Florida, I guess I blame most of my anxiety on my career choice. All the industry upheavals we've spoken about ad nauseum. Also, being wrong and losing my client's money really sucks—it's brutal. And then there's the wheelchair."

"I understand job anxiety—that's a common problem we've been dealing with, and we'll keep working on it. But tell me more about the wheelchair, so I understand."

"Well, there are always extraneous things to think about. For instance, most people decide where they're going to dinner, get dressed, and go to dinner. I decide where I'm going based on available parking, front steps, how close the tables are to each other, are they high tops or lower tables, access to the bathroom; and if there *is* an accessible stall or separate bathroom, it's always taken by a walking guy—either a patron or a kitchen staff guy. They love to camp out in there, like it's a rental; and believe me, I've run into more than my share of disgusting slobs."

"Gross," she said. "Thanks for the image."

"Sorry," he said sheepishly. "At least you didn't get the scent."

"I did now. Let's move outside the men's room if we can."

"Jeez, Kay, sorry again; I think I'm done in there anyway." His wise-guy grin was prominent before continuing. "I've sat in hotel lobbies with my family for hours watching everyone else check in because my promised accessible room, the only one in the hotel with a roll-in shower, was given away to someone else. I've checked into 'accessible' rooms to find everything wrong: a bath-tub instead of a shower, doorways too narrow, the A/C controls too high to reach, the carpet too thick, and how do they think I'll be getting into that pedestal bed at shoulder level—by helicop-ter? I've scrambled dozens of times to find another hotel in town while my kids and Becky sat on lobby sofas, nearly in tears. *Here we go again,* they're thinking, *this is what's called a vacation?*"

"Unbelievable," she said with a dropped jaw. "I had no idea."

"Most people don't," he replied. "It gets worse."

"Not worse than the men's room stall?"

"Well, no, but close, and it does involve another bathroom."

"Can't wait."

"Do you need a bathroom break?"

"No, thank you; please continue."

"Got it," he said with a grin encore. "So, whenever I fly on an airplane, I dehydrate myself for two days because once I'm carried to my seat, there's no way to get to a bathroom. A nine-hour flight to Dublin watching everyone else eat, drink, and be merry while I'm sitting rigid like a corpse. I wear an external urinary device, of course, but what if it leaks, which it often does. Or what if, God forbid, I need to go number two? I've sat for several hours in anxious discomfort, trapped, unable to think of anything but impending doom, praying for the flight to end—meaning to land safely, of course. And when it does land, my prayers shift to hoping my wheelchair is still in one piece when it comes out of the plane's belly. That's about a fifty-fifty shot."

"That's ridiculous," Kay groused. "The airlines, the entire travel industry, should be ashamed."

"Yeah, sure—don't hold your breath," he said. "And that's just scratching the surface of the potential issues; every day is a new surprise. Christ, it's no wonder Becky hit the road. Sometimes I wonder what took her so long."

Kay sat a moment, considering what exactly to say. This wasn't her typical patient's laundry list of complaints. "I'm sorry, Patrick, but please don't be so hard on yourself; you've had more challenges than most could ever dream of having."

"Probably better described as nightmares."

"Yes, I suppose you're right," she responded with a hesitant chuckle.

"Sometimes I feel the acid churning in my gut, especially after meatballs and pasta," he said with a bat of his eyes. "I've been a worrier my entire life. It's my inheritance. My Irish father from the Bronx, Seamus, worried himself to death—literally."

"Well, isn't there a resonant message in that for you?"

"Yes, I guess there is," he said. "If it's 'don't be Irish and from the Bronx,' it's a little too late for that."

"Maybe something else?"

"I hope so; there's only so much Prilosec one man can take."

"Fourteen days, max."

"Thank God you're not my gastro guy." He couldn't help but notice the latest undulation of her large, exquisite eyes.

Settling back in after his requested bathroom break, Kay began, "You've had a long marriage, good times and bad, like nearly everyone, fabulous kids, home, and job, and now you have a new 'knockout' girlfriend. It seems to me you've done better than most able-bodied guys."

"Thanks, Kay. You make it sound better than I remember. I'll hire you to write my memoir someday. I'll call it: *The Awesome Blue Guy.*"

"Blue guy?"

"It sounds better than cripple."

"Got it," she said with arched eyebrows. "Well, bad news on the memoir writing front. I charge 250 an hour, 350 if it involves a lot of whining."

"Maybe I'll take a first whack at it before bothering you."

"Good idea," she said. "So, Patrick, your anxiety is normal, understandable, and we can continue working to manage it. But when will you finally accept that you're an attractive and desirable man and just decide to have fun in this relationship instead of worrying?"

"I could probably do that," he said. "It does feel like I have another shot at love, like a kind of redemption, but what if the same old pattern emerges? Passionate beginning, an extended period of malaise and drifting apart, and she finally exits stage left."

"Now she's Snagglepuss?"

"How in the hell do you know Snagglepuss?"

"I'm a bit of a Hanna-Barbera freak," she said. "Listen, Patrick, if that happens, it simply means you're human, for fuck sakes."

Holy fuck, he thought, *there's 'fuck' number three—the hat trick.* A rare feat and so perfectly fucking delivered—a touch of spice on the tongue and innocence on the lips. This has been a very good day insofar as inciting her sauciness. He glanced around the room for a hat or two tossed onto the ice. Unfortunately, no fans were in the building. This achievement would be his alone to celebrate.

"Patrick? Are you there?" she asked while waving her hand.

"Sorry, Kay, just lost in thought for a moment."

"How long did your marriage last?"

"Twenty-five years, give or take, but it seemed like at least thirty."

Glancing at the ceiling lights one more time, she said, "If this new relationship with Minnie—"

"Finnie," he interrupted. "It's her last name made cuter."

"Minnie, Finnie, Shminnie," she continued. "If this relationship lasts another twenty-five years, give or take, would that make you happy?"

Counting out his perceived remaining years on his fingers, he said, "Yep, that would pretty much cover it."

"Oy Vey! Clearly, you haven't been reviewing your session notes."

"Oy Vey? Is that a Jewish curse word?"

"No, but it should be," she snapped. "The fact is, Patrick, no relationship of any length will make you happy. Only you make you happy by deciding to be happy, regardless of the circumstances."

"That does sound familiar, Kay. Hold on a minute." He reached into his Tumi for his notepad. "I can see we're entering the note-taking stage."

"Good," she said with a glance at her watch. "Then write this down: Three months is simply *not* a long time, and then there's your age difference. Older men, especially, tend to be more in a rush to secure their future—meaning their comfort."

He smirked. "You sound biased against men."

"Sorry, but it's a fact—you all want your mommies back."

"That is so repulsive," he said.

"Look it up—under Oedipus."

"Do you mind if I don't?"

"Suit yourself," she said. "But don't you think this is a lot simpler than you're making it? It's just way too soon to get so serious. Maybe you should slow down a little, lighten up, enjoy what you have with no expectations."

"That's great advice, Kay—it really is." He broke into song once again, this time about dropping all the worry and living for today. [52]

"Is everything a song to you?"

"You know what Jethro Tull said about that, don't you?"

"I suspect I will now." [53]

After finishing a mercifully brief verse of Tull's "Life's a Long Song," he said, "I can't help it—I grew up in a very musical time. It's like my life has a soundtrack to it just waiting to be recorded. Crap, that's actually a good idea," he enthused. "I'm going to put that on my to-do list."

"Good idea," she said while stirring in her chair. "And while you've got your pen out—our session is over for today."

"What a friggin' mercenary," he said.

And with a stroke of the pen and a grateful hug for both her fertile wisdom and consistent support, he delivered her well-earned bounty at whatever the hourly rate. The hat trick of fresh material he'd deposited in his mental bank was icing on the spoon, a valuable resource for future consumption.

With a promise to visit again soon, Patrick bid Sanctuary Kay adieu and rolled off to the remainder of whatever would be his story.

47

THE SEA-GREEN MIST

"Finnie, I'm home, sweetheart. Finnie?" He paused a moment and listened for her enchanting harp to brush his cheeks lightly, raising a shiver. Instead, a ghostly silence clutched at his throat. His pace quickened as he dashed from room to room, his voice turning more desperate with each "Finnie?"

The master suite's bed was neatly made—everything tidied and in order. He sat frozen amidst an aroma of finality. Just hours before, they lay together in an embrace reminiscent of the first night they'd met—and reminiscent of what was so good about his world. The wardrobe she so adored loomed before him. Drawn to the oak antiquity from the day it arrived, she tearily expressed reminiscences of home. He approached it and pulled open one of its massive doors to reveal a chest of drawers closed tight. Hesitating, afraid to look inside, old feelings of panic began to rise. Backing away, he looked up at the tall, mirrored front panel. Staring back was a person markedly older than the one who'd been there earlier that morning.

Breathing shallowly, he moved in again and slid open the top drawer. His heart emptied into its cavernous space, and into the salty mist of her lingering fragrance, his teardrops fell.

The room so warmed by Finnie's presence turned instantly harsh and ugly in its barrenness. Every one of her personal belongings was gone, including the things he'd tucked away so dearly after that first night too few months before. The apron, the cape, and the peculiar cap with its two feathers—each in their unique shades of red. He'd prayed that wondrous night would be a beginning, and his prayer had been answered. Her little treasures had been stored in the musty oak repository on the day of its arrival, and there they'd rested. Until today.

Following Kay's "lighten up and enjoy the moment" advice from their last session, he had stopped speaking of the future. And they laughed and played and doted as they always had, the same as young lovers do. In the quiet of the evening, he'd look for any hint of her deeper commitment—the most minimal sign of something more enduring than just that day. If she'd shown any, he'd missed its nuance. So, he put his fretting aside as best he could and lived from moment to glorious moment. It was all he had, and it was enough.

Jumping into the silver bullet, he shot up to Clematis, landing at Murphy's. Moving around the familiar room with its unfamiliar people, it felt like he was visiting that old neighborhood again—looking for the mile markers, the connections, and that one person who could bring all the tender memories flooding back. She wasn't to be found. He asked the bartender, "Maureen Finn? Is she working this evening?"

From behind the grand mahogany bar, he said, "Maureen? She gave her notice last week, just left in the last day or two." If his heart could sink any further, these words provided the ballast.

"Do you know where she went?" he asked the floor manager.

"No, I'm sorry—she didn't say," came his response from the cramped backroom office by the kitchen. "But we'll sure miss her. A true pleasure to have on staff, and such a hard worker. She'd have been running the place soon enough had she stayed."

"Yes, I understand. Thank you." Turning away quickly to shield his shame, he moved toward the heavy door and pushed it open to the stifling thoroughfare beyond. Glancing down to the threshold, he spied the specter of a better time. Visible in the indomitable twilight was the desiccated residue of formerly bright and festive May flowers.

As his mad busy hands drove him down the hill toward the bullet, his disquiet became nearly unbearable. He felt more alone in that moment than at any time before. The compounding of all the loss over the years cascaded down on him. When the fifth-grade punks squinted and called him "one-eye." When the last visitor had left his hospital room, and only his battered body and tortured mind remained behind. When his mother lay in grace in her splendidly polished mahogany coffin. When the divorce papers were signed, and his home officially became a hollowed-out house. And the day every parent dreaded most—when their all-grown-up child stands in the driveway waving goodbye, promises exchanged, hugs rendered, watching the car window's reflection for a fleeting image until the taillights finally vanish.

Left with only tears commencing their inevitable descent. Tears spent in recognition of the impermanence of it all.

For the first time in a long while, there was no reason to go home. Sitting still on the sidewalk, feeling desperate, he stopped searching his Tumi for his keys, instead continuing past the bittersweet patisserie and the dark theater before angling south through the oak-shrouded waterfront park. Crossing over Flagler Drive, he stopped at the marina's edge and dropped his bag on the vacant bench. Kicking up his legs and cradling his head in his hands, he soaked in the unsettled waterway and the Isle of Castles beyond, spending some alone time with only his distressed mind as company. Glancing up and down quiet Flagler, the famous Luke Kelly song "On Raglan's Road" occurred to him. He knew it by heart, knew it was an old man's ancient lament for having lost his young love. He adjusted the lyrics as necessary to fit the moment, as he always did. [54]

Just as he got to the final verse, the one about old ghosts meeting on quiet streets, and having loved the wrong way, he was startled back into the moment.

"May I join you, Patrick?"

"Oh my God—Finnie!" he cried out. "Yes, of course. You came back." Wrapped in her shawl, holding her feathered cap, his love was standing on the white concrete sidewalk an arm's length away. He straightened up and reached out to touch her, to hold her, only to watch her recoil. It cut to ribbons whatever cloth of hope he had remaining. He had no strategy for this.

"I'm here to say goodbye, my dear man."

"Why, baby? Why? What have I done?"

"That's why I came. I knew you'd be here. I knew you'd remember the right place."

"I didn't think—I can't think, Finnie."

"You're so smart, Patrick; so beautiful a mind and heart, and so worthy of love. But you can be self-punishing too. I had to be certain you didn't misunderstand."

"Misunderstand?"

"You've done nothing wrong, sweet man. All you've done is love me—genuine, sweet, pure love. And really, you can't love someone too much, or in the wrong way, if your love is pure."

"Why then, Finnie?" His voice was sullen, pleading. "Why are you leaving?"

"I came a long way from home to see to something, and I did see to it, and now it's time to go home. I miss my home."

"To Antrim? I'll come with you. I'll open a little pub, and we'll live in a cottage on a glen, and we'll play music and read books and tell stories and laugh and cry together. We'll love each other, and I'll take care of you, sweetheart."

"That sounds lovely, Patrick—it really does. But it's not that simple."

"What do you mean?"

"I wish I could explain it better. I want you to know I love you, and this isn't easy for me, and I will never forget you. I'm leaving despite my love for you."

"I don't understand."

"See? I told you it wasn't simple."

"It's never simple," he moaned. "Why can't it be?"

"A world with too many minds and hearts colliding, maybe," she said. "Too many people in need of help, some desperate, and too many others either indifferent or intent on doing harm. Does that make sense?"

"No. I don't want you to leave, Finnie. I need you more than anyone in the world."

"No, Patrick, you don't. You have everything you need. You're handsome and strong and courageous. You possess the Irishman's trinity, and you live by the code. You are a formidable man, and God knows the world needs many more just like you."

"I'm so much better with you, baby. I need to love you."

"You will love another. It won't be long, and your life will be brimming with love—I just know it."

"You don't know that." He was weeping openly. "How could you?"

"I read your horoscope."

"What day was it?" He met her feeble smile. "I'd better clip it out."

"If you need to talk with me or ask me something—just talk with me, ask me. I won't be far away."

"That's so hard, Finnie, it fades away so quickly. It's so lonely. The house is so lonely without you."

"You don't ever have to feel alone again, Patrick," she said, holding out her hands to his. "I'll always be with you—in the poetry and in the music."

They each sat in silence and watched the now sleepy movement of the water, her little hands imprinted in his. After a time, she said, "It's time for me to go."

"How? Do you need a ride to the airport?"

"It's all arranged."

"What about your harp? You forgot to take it. Do you want to come home to get it?"

"Oh no, dear sweet Patrick—always so generous. The harp is already home—it's meant to stay right where it is."

"The harp means nothing without you playing it, sweetheart."

"Remember—fearless, peaceful courage, just like St. Patrick." And with that, she trained her Caribbean green eyes on his, leaned in slowly, and kissed him. It was pillowy and trembling and breathless.

When he opened his eyes, Finnie was gone. His love was gone. He swirled around in all directions, but there wasn't a trace of her. Except, maybe, when he looked east over the waterway, where a sea-green mist hovered in the fading light of the day. [55]

48

LAMENT: HEALING WATERS

Patrick tried his best to stay resilient, but the days ahead were various degrees of torturous. If he slept at all, it was fitful. His true love was no longer waiting, no longer lying beside him, and every tomorrow was such a long time. [56]

In his fidgety solitude, he settled in the den for a time, then paced the halls, and then settled in again. There was nothing settled about it. He strained to quiet his mind, turn his thoughts to the good, but it was futile. There was an all-too-familiar grieving process to get on with, and he knew well the drill.

He plucked the top from a bottle of Smithwick's and a book from the shelf, spinning it open to a random page. "Oh goodie—my old friend Yeats," he said aloud to no one, speaking his thoughts to the air once again. His prickling eyes landed on a poem called

"September 1913," nearly a century ago to the month. One pulsing word—"Romantic"—jumped off the page, and he read on from there:

> *Romantic Ireland's dead and gone,*
> *It's with O'Leary in the grave.*

Not so removed from Patrick's middling age when he wrote the poem, Yeats longed for an earlier Ireland without all its pomposity. The focus of merchants was too much on money, he raged, thinking them greedy and destructive of his beloved Ireland's courage.

Christ, if he wants to see world-class greed and destruction, Patrick thought, *he should take a gander at the last few chapters of my life.*

Yeats was particularly upset that in an Irish nation so ravaged by famines and occupations, the nationalists' cause had gone awry. Violence had replaced good sense. Many were dead and rotting needlessly in their graves, along with a true Irish separatist hero, John O'Leary, who died in 1907. And now, there was nothing left of the nation to save.

Who was the yellow-haired woman later in the poem who "so maddened every mother's son"? he wondered.

Tapping away on his iPad, he learned it was Maude Gonne, the love of Yeats's young life, who'd shunned him to marry another man. Old man Yeats grieving while his beloved lay in the arms of another man. *Apropos,* Patrick thought while taking another sip of the bitter. It didn't escape him that across time, one notable old man's disillusion well-matched his own on this gravest of days.

Tossing the book on the bar, he poured himself a Bushmills Black, made from the malted barley and pure waters of the one and only County Antrim. "Happy day, WB," he toasted aloud ruefully. "And to you, Patrick," he said to the shadow in the smoky mirror. "And you as well, dearest Finnie."

As the day slogged on, he found himself splashing in healing waters attributed to St. Brigid. Dribbling some on his forehead, his belly, his legs—always his legs—he prayed for its promised higher consciousness. Brigid, one of Ireland's two revered patron saints, was legendary for her kindness and charity—two attributes he sorely needed this day. He needed to raise the vibration in his mind, eradicate the evil spirits bounding all about the place. He needed a kind of healing—a wrapping of his arms one more time around his youthful vitality. In Finnie's wretched absence, he needed Brigid.

He wasn't interested in some unattainable miracle, like the one he'd begged for after his injury. It doesn't work anyway, all the begging bullshit, he'd concluded. *You work your ass off, and it's either in the stars or it's not.* In that other time of abject misery, he wanted it all back, but it proved too much to ask for. After a few years, he'd toned it down to a more sober appeal. "Please Lord, let me move one toe, just one toe, and I'll take it from there." No such luck. Bullshit.

Today, he was humbler still. He simply wanted a return to his youthful days of the previous week. "Just last week, dear Brigid," he moaned aloud to the echoing emptiness. "Is that too much to ask?" Through a wash of Irish Whiskey, holy water, and tears, he wished to wrest the sweet memories of Finnie from their archival burial in some recent mythical Palm Beach cycle. He wished to make her tangible again.

Whatever man he was the week before, he'd been halved—again. Now, all he wanted was his other half back.

Holy wells reside across the island nation of Ireland like franchises do in America. During his trip to the old country, Patrick visited St. Brigid's Well in Liscannor, County Clare, just down the hill from the Cliffs of Moher. The well was a quiet respite compared to the hectic cliffs. He couldn't descend into the dusky grotto where the spring-fed, healing waters flowed, which he thought ironic, so he sat in the parking lot in not-so-reverent silence. On his behalf, his spry son Liam rumbled down the steep stairs and into the gray stone abyss, emerging twenty-five minutes later holding a plastic bottle filled with water deemed holy by three separate denominations: Christianity, Paganism, and Druidism. Patrick was a member of all three constituencies depending on the circumstances of the day.

On the same trip, they'd sought out Yeats's churchyard gravesite in Drumcliff. And there, under bare Ben Bulben's head, he "Cast a cold Eye on the Life and Death" of the great poet. The poet's words and spirit as coldly alive as ever, Patrick's "Horseman soon passed by" the ancient cross.

You had to be there.

In this case, Patrick's "Horseman" was the driver of the Mercedes Sprinter wheelchair accessible van he'd hired to tour the country. It would soon carry them south to the medieval town of Sligo, which Yeats loved so well.

Patrick planned to love Sligo, too, especially its ancient public houses Hargadons and Thomas Connolly Bar. He understood they were crawling with history and hoped to become a minuscule fraction of their register. Upon arrival, he found a congested seaport town of colorful, multi-tiered stone and brick buildings with gray stone churches pious under steep slate roofs. The centuries-old structures framed narrow, winding cobblestone streets rolling along and crossing over the royal riverfront. This typical European mosaic, more sooty working-class than flag and flower basket festive, bustled under the western shadow of Knocknarea, the Hill of Kings and eternal home to Queen Maeve. His heart fluttered momentarily at her conjured image.

If Patrick had to summarize his brief Sligo visit, he would say: A guy in a wheelchair would last about fifteen minutes in the town before hurtling himself off one of the stone bridges to his everlasting salvation. The good news was that fifteen minutes was twice the time he'd last in bed with Queen Maeve before she'd dismember him and feed his parts to her more virile warriors. So, he swallowed his bile and took the half-assed, fifteen-minute van tour of Yeats's beloved Sligo. Before moving on, he peed in a jar for want of locating a blue guy bathroom. He didn't consider it holy water worth saving, so it was flung to the lush countryside at his earliest convenience. Evidence he'd been there, though not in any permanent registry.

The same afternoon of his Sligo non-tramp, they visited Knock Shrine in County Mayo. In a reasonable brood when they arrived, he was finally able to break from the Sprinter's shackles, brush off the gathering cobwebs, and roam freely on cured white concrete walkways. A minor miracle itself across the old world. The lore of Knock's holiness was an apparition in 1879 where Mother Mary herself gave a two-hour performance on the church wall to fifteen witnesses standing in the pouring rain. He believed the story wholeheartedly. The part about the pouring rain. He was less certain of the rest. Times were tough in late 19th-century occupied Ireland reeling from yet another famine, and the pubs were open for business that day in the tiny, impoverished village of Knock.

Oh well, he thought, as he topped off his Black Bush, *what's another decade in Purgatory?*

Whether the Blessed Mother made a rare appearance that day, or perhaps it was her tribute band, he did believe the shrine was holy ground, including its water, and that was enough. The visit to Knock, dousing in its waters, served to soothe and repair his vigor on what had been an otherwise humbling day for a modern blue-guy monolith sitting amongst ancient dwellings requiring vigorous mobility for their whole enjoyment.

A common stream that cut across every culture and religion throughout history was the veneration of water. Fragile humans had forever sought disease cures from magic-imbued waters. It made perfect sense. A human's brain and heart were comprised of over 70 percent water. Without water, a human could survive for about three days, depending on certain factors. Such as if a cooler full of Smithwick's were in the house, it could be meaningfully longer.

Patrick took to his iPad in search of more information on healing waters. Why not? He had unexpected free time on his hands. He learned that some four hundred years before the time of Christ, Alexander the Great described a healing "river of paradise." Christ himself—the person whose name Patrick took in vain incessantly to his deep regret—baptized his followers with water. As did his innumerable disciples to follow. Pilgrims poured into Lourdes since God knew when. Greeks, Hindus, Buddhists, Muslims, and any number of other reverent communities forever cleansed spiritually with some sort of immersion into holy waters. Each with their own spirited mythology.

Fast forward to the sixth century and Spanish explorer Juan Ponce de Leon. He arrived in the Western Hemisphere searching for a Fountain of Youth located somewhere north of Cuba. While he was more likely seeking territory and wealth, it was said that King Ferdinand of Spain had married a woman thirty-five years his junior and asked Ponce to keep his eyes open for the miraculous fountain.

"Christ, the more things change!" Patrick blurted out loud. "Even a rock star like Ferdinand was worried about disappointing his woman."

Ponce apparently found the miraculous waters he was seeking in St. Augustine, Florida. It sounded fishy, of course, given how many old people lived on the peninsula. *With the fountain's convenient location and plentiful parking, you'd think there'd be fewer walkers, oxygen tanks, and early-bird diners in the surrounding area.*

Nonetheless, the famed explorer evidently discovered the fountain before traveling south through the Florida Keys and into the Gulf of Mexico. After a float-by in Puerto Rico, he sailed for home. Eight years later, per legend, he returned to Southwest Florida, in the Naples-Sarasota vicinity, where he intended to start a colony. *Unfortunately, when a realtor took him around to view property, he died of a heart attack at the asking prices.* Patrick was pretty sure someone on Wikipedia made that last part up. More plausible was the poisonous arrow which struck his thigh in a battle with Calusa natives. Ironically, he was searching for fresh water at the time. Taken to Cuba for treatment, he died soon after. Ponce wouldn't be the last whose dreams died in Cuba.

In earlier times, before modern sanitation, medicines, and air conditioning, a doctor's prescription for recovery often included leaving the grimy city in favor of the seashore's cleansing, salt-infused ocean breezes. Such advice drew wealthy oil tycoon Henry Flagler to Ponce's same St. Augustine in the late 19th century—Yeats's time. Flagler's attempt to cure his first wife's ailments failed, but he was smitten with Florida and decided to build railroad tracks, hotels, and other infrastructure down the peninsula's east coast, thereby helping invent modern-day Florida, including West Palm Beach and the Isle of Castles.

Yeats himself needed such respite away from the stifling soot of industrializing Dublin and his most despised London. His visits to Ireland's west coast, its "Wild Atlantic Way," inspired poetry often describing the healing nature of the woods, lakes, and seaside around Sligo and Galway.

At the very same time, America's most famous humorist and writer, Mark Twain, fell in love with a specific body of water, the magnificent Mississippi River. His passion motivated not only his greatest novels but also such profound thoughts as: *Water, taken in moderation, cannot hurt anyone*, and *The solution to our water problems is more rain.* He accompanied those with, *Until I came to New Mexico, I never realized how much beauty water adds to a river.* When he was in a more serious mood, Twain called water *an individual, an animal, and alive.* In comparing the miraculous combination of oxygen and hydrogen to deity, he essentially wrote, *Here was mute Nature explaining the sublime mystery of the Trinity more luminously than any trained master of words ever had.*

In honor of the grand master of American literature, Patrick topped off his crystal while reading another of his H2O-related thoughts: *Whiskey is for drinking; water is for fighting over.*

"*Sláinte*, Samuel," he said while raising his liquid crystal. "Thanks for the excellent advice."

Speaking of crystal, across North America and the world, natural springs have forever been associated with spiritualism and healing. When Patrick spirited his Queen Maur away to Ocala's National Forest, they discovered an endless supply of crystal-clear water bubbling out of the earth at precisely 72 degrees. Native Americans logically believed the springs miraculous, supernatural even. What other explanation could there have been? By his proximity to the national forest's silver springs not so long ago—forever ago—he felt connected to a higher source.

Thinking back, he strained to recreate every step, imagine every conversation, every touch, every creature—one especially. He could still see her reflection in the beauty of that "silver, singin' river," as Dylan so presciently wrote, and he could still hear her voice, but the touch wasn't coming so easily. [56]

Since the beginning of time, "blue guys" like Patrick and Franklin Delano Roosevelt, to name two notables, would seek out such springs for healing. Although crippled by polio, FDR was blessed with a brilliant mind, boundless courage, an even smarter and more courageous wife, and a cute girlfriend to boot. Talk about a grand slam, other than the cripple thing.

It was okay to call Franklin Delano an "invalid" or "cripple," Patrick thought, *because that was what he was in the language of his day.* Politically correct jargon like "handicapped" and "disabled" weren't all the rage back then. They were a little busy trying to survive the Depression and the attempted annihilation of western civilization by the latest wave of barbarians, this time from the scourges of Nazism, fascism, and imperialism. Only the soft and entitled had the luxury to concern themselves with political slights such as a label they consider offensive. Unless it was hateful and meant to demean—certainly those needed to be buried—but some softies even consider "disabled" too harsh and pushed for a more sensitive term like "in-other-ways-abled" and other such euphemistic bullshit.

"I'm definitely in-other-ways-abled," he'd chide, "like I'm 'ways-abled' to pee all over myself at any moment—and that's on a good day."

The weaklings trying to shame others for such nuanced language should be pushed off the Cliffs of Moher and plunged out of their misery, he was thinking flippantly. *That's what they'd have done a century and two ago with all the aggrieved complainers and their pain-in-the-ass advocates—and are still doing today in dark places all around the world.*

FDR, on the other hand, wasn't a passive complainer—he was a man of action. One of those was to travel to Warm Springs, Georgia, often with his nurse and companion (meaning his girlfriend), to seek out its healing waters. It seemed a good restorative strategy, regardless of the physical outcome. Patrick visited the same springs once to see FDR's "winter White House," although he didn't bring a cute nurse girlfriend along for the ride. When he arrived, there wasn't a drop of water to be found—bone dry. He evidently neglected to make a spa appointment ahead of time. Even though he left Warm Springs the same blue guy and a little parched, he was vacationing away from the money business with his young family. The best kind of healing.

Of course, water's power cut both ways: healing and destruction. Hurricanes, tsunamis, floods, drownings, chemical poisonings—the countless victims of nature's wrath and human malfeasances, intended or otherwise. Every loss carried with it a degree of permanence, and those who suffered such tragedy would never be convinced of the healing nature of water. He grieved for every victim of loss throughout the planets' checkered history, wishing for universal healing. *Christ,* he thought, *the human story is always the yin and the yang, isn't it?* Every element had in it both light and dark, good and evil. Amniotic fluid bringing life and dreadfully diseased fluid drowning a cancer-stricken lung. Same body. Creation and destruction. Joy and woe.

Running his fingers lightly over the smooth, oddly configured, green wicker cross honoring Brigid, lost in thoughts of healing waters and blue guys and resiliency and whiskey and Finnie, drooping eyes signaled that his lament had drawn to a close for the day. He didn't give a rat's ass if Brigid's powers were real or a figment of mythology. If they were real to him, they were real. Healing the heart and mind was at least as important as healing whatever vehicle lugged it all around.

"Thank you, dear Brigid," he whispered with a kiss on her cross.

Proceeding to the desolate master suite, he immersed himself in a healing shower to freshen and revitalize. Tomorrow was nigh, and there was still more grieving to accomplish.

49

LAMENT: TO HAVE LOVED AND LOST

When you are old and grey and full of sleep,
And nodding by the fire, take down this book,
And slowly read, and dream of the soft look
Your eyes had once, and of their shadows deep;

How many loved your moments of glad grace,
And loved your beauty with love false and true,
But one man loved the pilgrim soul in you,
And loved the sorrows of your changing face;

And bending down beside the glowing bars,
Murmur, a little sadly, how Love fled,
And paced upon the mountains overhead,
And hid his face amid a crowd of stars.

Patrick was at it again. The continuation of his never-ending lament. Or so it seemed. Pulling the Yeats book off the bar top one more time, probably not the last time, he pulled on his oft-present crystal, undoubtedly not the last time. In contemplating that most exquisite verse, he was looking back some one hundred and twenty years and into the soul of this perennially remorseful man. Or so it seemed. Yeats had loved, and he had lost. His girl, Maud, was gone. Maud Gonne was gonne. Funny. And Finnie was *fini*. Not as funny.

But Christ, only two days into my lament, he was thinking, *and it feels like I'm making reasonable progress. Poor Yeats never got over his young Maud's betrayal. Who the hell was she, the next coming of Queen Maeve?* It was oddly comforting to know the torment he was feeling was nothing unusual. Rather, it was universal and infinite. Especially for friggin' Yeats. Same durable script, different characters. The agony was his to suffer today, another's to suffer on another day, and Yeats's to suffer in perpetuity. And on throughout history. Every human would suffer lost love in their own time and way—if they were so lucky.

"Hey," he said aloud while taking another quaff of the stinging brown. "I'm one lucky guy." [57]

Evil spirits eradicated by Finnie's sweet presence had come rushing back in. His fidgeting grew madder still as he navigated the length of the house and back again. Wherever he roamed, he soon ventured back to his "fountain of youth," the centerpiece of his cozy den—the bar.

Smartly realizing he'd consumed more than enough whiskey in the past two days, he decided to open a bottle of pinot noir. After a satisfactory sampling, he moved to the kitchen where he filled a mug with milk and placed it on the windowsill. Nothing about the dark mood changed. The mug on the windowsill lacked its once protective powers, becoming just another unwelcome memory of loss; so he splashed its contents into the sink—or maybe it was into an Irish coffee.

Finding himself in the kitchen, he took the opportunity to check the fridge for any leftover salmon to pair with his pinot. Thankfully, there was none to be found, so he broke out the sharp Irish cheddar, toasted up some sourdough, and meandered back to the den—the location of the bar.

Will Finnie ever grow old, he wondered, *like I have? When I'm rotting in my grave, along with O'Leary and the others, she'll still be a youthful beauty gracing another man's bed, showing him all her naughtiness.*

"Don't do this," he implored aloud. "No self-persecution this time, Paddy boy. You deserve better." After all, he'd done nothing wrong; Finnie even said so. And she had done nothing but bless him with her devotion and fiery love until it burned away. Where's the crime in that? *Welcome both the fire and the burning away,* he thought with a toasty toast, *and never stop looking for the next kindling just waiting to spark into flame. It's all a part of the adventure.*

"How heroic of me," he growled derisively. "Fuck me—it's all just bullshit, anyway." He hadn't figured out how to work in a "rat's ass."

Focused now on "bullshit," he decided to soften his disdain to "blarney," thinking it a good first step toward lightening up and feeling better. He was wondering who wrote "bullshit" —oops, "blarney" —like "it's better to have loved and lost than never to have loved at all?"

He proceeded once again to his miracle machine—the great equalizer in the pursuit of all knowledge and myriad superficialities. The internet was genius, he knew, but also brimming with rubbish and worse; in some cases, much worse. *The bad—all degrees of it—is forever intertwined with the good and splendid, isn't it?* The human condition in digital form. The challenge placed before every developing mind was parsing the degrees of good and bad into appropriate categories and then making choices, understanding that every choice came with both opportunities and costs.

> *I hold it true, whate'er befall;*
> *I feel it, when I sorrow most;*
> *'Tis better to have loved and lost*
> *Than never to have loved at all.*

It turned out Alfred Tennyson, England's poet laureate during the reign of Queen Victoria, had written his enduringly splendid words half a century before Yeats's corresponding anguish. His sentiments were not about a woman but a best friend lost early to illness.

'Tis it really better to have loved and lost?

You scoured her with your eyes until every crevice and fold and freckle was made familiar. You held her near, tasted her every salty excretion. You nurtured her, as she did you, and together you laughed and cried and loved and aspired. It was all so blessedly divine. But now, moment-by-frozen-moment, it all began to fade: her taste, her touch, her image. And the laughter too withered, leaving you with only the cry. By the tick and the excruciating tock, it all would go numb and blurry. And then one day, you would wake up, and Tennyson's HBB is gone, and Maud is gone, and Finnie is gone.

Was it all a dream? Did I really love like that? Am I really the better for it? Or is the resulting void, the suffering, just too unbearable?

What if you'd been relegated to spending your life as a store display mannequin, with its empty, faraway look and frozen plastic smile, rolling around on some sort of trolley? What if you were Ironside, Perry Fucking Mason on wheels?

'Tis it better to have walked and lost than never to have walked at all?

Was it better that Patrick once walked—that he once sprinted up and down Ireland's rolling hills like a thoroughbred and flew across sheets of ice with unbridled power and reckless abandon? Was it categorically better?

It was all you knew, it was your entire young life, and then one sparkling October day it was viciously wrenched away leaving only tortured, fading memories. Until one day, even those vanished too. Wouldn't it be better to have never even glimpsed how good it all could be? Which was more tolerable?

Famous American author John Steinbeck answered the query in this succinct way: *It's so much darker when a light goes out than it would have been if it had never shone.*

Most humans are risk-averse, preferring to keep what they have rather than risk losing it in pursuit of gaining even more. It applied to stock market investing, Patrick well knew, because he'd seen it a million times. But did it apply to losing one's physical abilities or a new, one-of-a-kind love? Too much to consider, he decided. At this moment, he probably couldn't analyze his way to the powder room. If he even had a powder room, which he wasn't certain.

Tilting back his head, he poured the crystal tumbler's remaining contents down the gullet. "Oops." He smirked while capturing a drip with his tongue. "Be careful not to spill any—I'd hate to lose what I already have."

He let the thought go, deciding it would be okay to lose it.

Patrick has a heightened awareness of how loss works. In the early months after his injury, he would dream nightly of walking and running and skating and fucking with abandon. Not that he'd ever fucked with abandon, "thighs good for fucking" aside.

One night his dreams shifted, becoming oddly warped by reality, now bursting with stories in which the protagonist could no longer move from his bed, his school locker, the railroad tracks, or any other scenario, just like in real life. He wasn't riding around in a wheelchair; it was different, not as stark and punishing. He was instead constrained, somehow unable to be with the others, no matter the script. He was the camera watching the action from a distance, the only person sitting in the audience watching the play unfold onstage, never able to spontaneously jump in. Always the observer, never the player. There were other characters in the scene, some familiar, some not, but he was never precisely with them. He was in some other story within the story. And once his dreams made that shift—he never walked or ran or skated or fucked ever again. With abandon or otherwise.

How cruel. Weren't dreams supposed to be a release where your mind and spirit were able to run free? Run away from one's reality?

Speaking of running away from reality, an early Woody Allen movie, *Sleeper*, introduced a device called the "orgasmatron." Exactly why, it was impossible to fathom. The silly futuristic story features the Woodman as Miles Monroe, a jazz musician and health food nut who'd been frozen before waking up two hundred years later. The population in his future world was apparently frigid or otherwise impotent, except for Italians. That part made sense. The non-Italians invented a white cylinder-like sex machine that looked suspiciously like a hot water heater. The door slid open, a person entered it with or without a partner, and a virtual experience of orgasmic proportions ensued, leaving their eyeglasses all askew. Or at least Woody's.

Patrick always wanted to own an orgasmatron—if only in his dreams. Of course, it probably wouldn't work for cripples or blue guys or even the "otherly-abled." In Woody's future world, it appeared they hadn't bothered building an accessible sex machine. The one group which probably needed it the most. Maybe they'd thrown all the cripples off the Cliffs of Moher by then?

It was no different with commercial airliners today. Zero accessible seating or access to bathrooms. Zero. Blue folks had never been a large or powerful enough voting block—either now or two hundred years from now. Plenty of money for waging war in Iraq and Afghanistan, never-to-be-built bullet trains, CEO's yachts and mansions, and politicians' world-class healthcare, pensions, and expense accounts, but never enough to help poor cripples travel comfortably. Mandating more sensitive labeling was a lot less expensive.

On a positive note, blue folks were still getting fucked, and they would still be getting fucked two hundred years from now, so maybe Patrick should stop his complaining? Wasn't that what he wanted?

Happy recollections continued rolling in. There was the time he realized being blind in one eye took away his ability to see in 3-D. He was in a Disney theater sitting in the accessible row, the last row, with his young family. The film began, and within a minute, everyone started screaming and jumping and dodging objects hurtling at them from the screen. Everyone except Patrick. He just sat there befuddled, frozen-smiled, having another one of his half-assed experiences. He could only see in 2-D or 1-D or 0-D—meaning "fucked-again-D." It was immensely better than not seeing at all, he still wanted to tell the UM pool toy, preferably while she was straddling him.

At the same Disney parks, his toddlers would ride around on his lap the entire day. He was their stroller. They would step on his sneaker tops, grab his extended hand, and climb aboard with big smiles on their faces. His broad shoulders would propel them for miles around the park from one exhibit or ride to the next. To the kids, this was normal. In fact, they were special. One of a kind. A Disney prince and princess riding in their own parade. That was called healing. The yin and yang. Joy and woe. He wore the same broad smile now at the memory.

But that was all it was—a distant memory back for a short visit. It faded away as fast as it arrived, and when it did, the loss was twice as painful. How long would it be until he couldn't conjure Finnie's face, couldn't feel her touch on his fingers, feel her feathery weight on his lap, or her soft, fine hair on his chest? Months? Weeks? Days? Hours? He lumbered into the bedroom and opened her wardrobe drawers to spy once again the void—the utter desolation. Lowering his head, he breathed in slowly, deeply, consciously, for any intimation of her resplendent scent. Only the bland oaky aroma of emptiness was evident.

Let the great fade begin.

Dusk was setting in, and shadows painted the walls reminding him of an echoing church or an antique furniture warehouse. "Jesus friggin' Christ," he lamented. "What the hell do I do now?"

Committing one venial sin after another, he poured another splash of pinot and reached onto his treasure shelf once again, this time for Joyce's *Dubliners* tales. Flipping to the last story, considered by some the greatest short story ever written, he looked squarely at the title and murmured, "'The Dead.'" Recognizing that Joyce was hard enough to read when sober, he closed the cover and tossed it back on the shelf. Besides, the subject matter seemed a little morbid, even for today. Latching on to Yeats, his comrade in grieving, he turned to something short and sweet:

> *Down by the salley gardens*
> *my love and I did meet;*
> *She passed the salley gardens*
> *with little snow-white feet.*
> *She bid me take love easy*
> *as the leaves grow on the tree;*
> *But I, being young and foolish,*
> *with her would not agree.*
>
> *In a field by the river*
> *my love and I did stand,*
> *and on my leaning shoulder*
> *she laid a snow-white hand.*
> *She bid me take life easy*
> *as the grass grows on the weirs;*
> *But I am young and foolish*
> *and now am full of tears.*

"Christ alive," he growled. "Here we go again—another foolish man left at the weirs." *What in hell is a "weir" anyway*, he thought, *never mind a "salley garden"?*

Yeats was a much younger man when he wrote "Salley Gardens." *Never too young or old to be foolish in love*, Patrick mused. *Did the guy ever bother to write a poem when he was happy in a relationship?* Or was he too busy straightjacketing his current squeeze and forcing her to read his latest weep-fest? Had he heard any recent off-color jokes he could pass along, for Christ's sake? Had he thought about taking her out to the local pub for a reckless night of drinking and dancing? Probably not. It was more, "Hey honey, come over here and read through my latest poem—it's about when you'll ditch me in a field by the river, or a garden, or both." Talk about greasing the skids of her imminent departure.

And with that impressive academic analysis completed, he tossed the iPad aside in favor of his crystal stemware.

Late into the second night of his "poor me pity party marathon," desperately needing sleep, Patrick's bleary eyes batted up and down in defiance. But he was done—desiccated—and it was past time to bid the ghosts a restful night. Reticent to travel down the dark hallway to his chamber, knowing his loneliness would only grow more vicious, he decided to tuck in right there surrounded by the things he most loved. Inanimates that couldn't pick up and leave at their earliest whim.

Before settling in with his old friend, his weathered leather chair, he clicked on the fireplace. Its flame wavered throughout the room, illumining the barren harp and timeless record player, where he engaged with another old friend, placing him gently on the turntable. Sidling back alongside the comfy chair, he braced his worn shoulders and forearms, shifted left, and lowered his exhausted cargo into the supple leather's welcoming embrace.

Eyes moving one more time around the room, point to point to point, he recognized its shimmering intimacy and loveliness. It wasn't the desolate space left behind after Becky had cleared out; it was instead home, a reflection of everything that made the man. A life well-earned and well-lived. Maybe Finnie had left her mark in a way that wouldn't soon fade away, he considered, as a deeper breath tugged down his eyelids.

Ethereal sounds filled the space and he meekly opposed the drifting away. *How sweet,* he thought, not remembering this Van piece included strings. The melody rose to something harmonious, then angelic, sounding familiar but freshly alive at the same time. The strings intensified to outweigh the recording, forcing open his eyes. The glow cast by the fireplace gave the harp's strings the appearance of vibration. Prying open his left eyelid to clear his vision, it was then that he saw her. From the child's stool, a diminutive, lustrous figure with misty hands gently stroked the strings.

"Finnie, is that you?" His blood began to pulse wildly as he pressed up and shifted back into his wheelchair, rigid legs and feet jumping in spasm. Stomach jumbled, heart aflame, mind now acute, he said, "Finnie, baby doll? have you come home to me?" Straightening in his chair, he sat still in his incredulous stare. Her translucent white face turned directly toward him. Without saying a word, she seemed to be answering him with her eyes and her music.

He moved in on the harp, whispering, "Finnie?" But with every inch closer he crept, her image faded—her face and hands losing their form, becoming wispy, cloudy, like the work of a master impressionist. The sweet sound became muddled with static. Halting his forward motion, slowly backing away, the mist reformed into her image, and the harp's sound clarified. Not removing his eyes for a moment, he transferred again into the leather chair where her figure was most apparent and her music vivid. From this vantage point, Finnie's appearance before him was unambiguous. She had promised she would be here if he needed her. And he needed her. And she was here.

"Thank you, sweet Finnie, thank you." His husky voice was gripped with emotion.

Floating for as long as he was able, he finally sailed into the mystic where his dreams took over. And she kept them graceful. [58]

50

SKATING AWAY

"You okay, Pat?"

"Sure, Marie. I'm doing just peachy."

"Peaches have color. You look a little pasty—like you've seen a ghost."

"Interesting. Maybe I have."

"I'm just worried about you, that's all."

"Really, I'm fine. Remember, it's better to have loved and lost."

"That's a pile of crap, Pat, and you know it. Losing sucks, plain and simple."

"I can't argue with you, Marie."

Belying his ashen look, Patrick was feeling a little better with each passing day, especially once his whiskey soak began to dissipate. The pinot provided a good easing off. He calculated that in a few short weeks, he was already decades ahead of his old friend Yeats in his emotional healing.

The little secret he kept in his den made it all the easier. Ghosts couldn't fill physical needs, naturally, but they sure could provide good company, along with angelic music. Finnie's late-night concert also reminded him that magic continued to exist. As she and Larry had often said, he just needed to keep his heart open and drop the mind swirl of analysis and worry; stay peaceful, humble, and wide awake to the possibilities, and the magic would find him. With that as his "hopeful strategy," he planned to keep alive the memories of his enchanted winter and spring seasons and welcome many more in the months and years ahead.

Memories recede, taking up space in the archives—*probably to keep us sane,* he thought. The process cleared the way for new experiences, each time from a slightly wiser perspective, helping people stay resilient and moving forward. Experiences were stored in the attic, like a tattered sweatshirt we're not quite ready to discard. Locked away in a tissue, a muscle, or a nerve, the most meaningful were certain to make their presence felt from time to time. Something would occur to you: a longing, a sense of disconnection, like something's missing, and off you go on an unconscious search through your attic. You come across that old sweatshirt and think, *Oh yeah, remember when.* You linger in the smile, or the chill, or the ache. A tear forms; on occasion, an inundation.

The appearance of the ghost could be triggered by any of the senses: Maybe a scent shows up in a throb or a twitch, like when an eyelid's spasm won't cease until it's sure it has your attention. Or maybe a piece of music elicits a tiny electric shock in your spinal cord, or a shoulder-shaking shiver somewhere in the vicinity of your ears, spreading a coat of blush across your face and a tingling into your skull. Like a shooting star leaving an incandescent trail along its dark way before finally fizzling away. Each of these may be sensory gateways into our attic. Or they may be an indication of a serious medical condition. *Let's dwell on the former and hope for the best. I meant "strategize" for the best, of course.*

As events of the recent past began to take up residence in Patrick's attic—the bad, the good, the superlative—his spine became more erect, his breathing deepened, his head lifted higher, and his wise-guy chortle could again be heard on occasion.

It had been a time—hadn't it?

Things around the office were returning to some sense of normalcy. He handed the management role over to a newly assigned conscript with her heartfelt promise that he'd be left alone: no meetings, no teaming, no velocity postings, no "eating what we kill," no deep dives or deeper penetrations without the client's enthused consent. He would be left to do his stockbroker thing, at his pace and in his style, taking care of the clients who appreciated his value. In doing so, he'd make an ample enough living to cover his expenses and pay Marie well, put a little away for the kids, and give something back where he could. He wished for enough left over to stay well-stocked in shepherd's pie and Smithwick's, and enough to keep him snug in his SoSo den steeped in the things he loved the most: his music and books, his writing desk, his sports, his taste of the brown (and the red and the amber), and his harp.

They postponed plans for jumping firms or going independent, not deep-sixing it, just putting it on the shelf for the time being. It would be right there to dust off when one too many promises were broken, and the heat turned back up to intolerable. Soon enough, he knew, every pledge made would be tempered. They couldn't help themselves —they were in the money business.

"Hey, Connelly, your numbers are down this month," and "Hey, Connelly, only thirty-one percent of your clients have three or more of our banking services—we've got to get that up," and "Hey, Connelly, have you noticed how Josh or Gillian or Jason is totally crushing it with the new mortgage platform?" and "Why don't we set up a lunch with Josh or Gillian or Jason, just to talk," and "Tsk, tsk, Connelly, such language—it's just a lunch."

The firm had a calculation for everything, including how much his desk was worth and how much he needed to produce per day to justify sitting at it. Especially the desk in the corner office with the eastern view overlooking the Isle of Castles.

It's nothing personal, he thought, *just capitalism made manifest.*

To the best and most resilient workers, the performers, go the spoils. The fittest vessels stay afloat, sailing on to new shores, while the others rust away in the scrap yards, if they hadn't first lodged in the ocean's depths.

It was just over the horizon, he knew, and the office thermometer would begin its ascension as surely as the prevailing winds would shift one late April day from brisk and invigorating to dank and oppressive. Steeped once again in the clammy, day-to-day grind with all its perspiring demands and strivings and expectations. The 8-to-6 focus on money and preserving the wealth of the wealthy.

Where was the magic in that?

He still read his horoscope assiduously, always looking for the message. And whenever he saw a folded-over newspaper lying around on a table, he'd nudge himself over like a vagabond in search of a freebie. Flipping open the paper, he'd quickly scour the headlines and date only to find the mundane news of the day. Like Yukon Cornelius searching for silver and gold with his pickaxe: "Sniff, sniff, lick, lick—nothing."

Driving west on Southern to Kerry's warehouse one last time, he wondered where in the world his charming little friend had gone. His heart dropped when through crisscrossing security gates locked tight, he saw the red letters announcing the antique business and its proprietor had been scraped away. A sign hanging on the door instead said, "For Lease." Peering in through murky glass to the shadowed, concrete gray room beyond, it appeared to be barren warehouse space. Kerry O'Connor's miraculous Irish cottage and antique business had vanished. Just more evidence of life's impermanence. *Here one day and . . .*

He called the number on the realtor's sign. "They just listed it," she said. "The owner, a foreign entity, hasn't given permission to discuss any further aspect, but it could be a wonderful space for any number of businesses, from storage to auto-parts to furniture." She added, "One of the wealthiest enclaves in the world sits just across the bridge to the east." He declined her invitation to see the space.

On his way home, he again crossed the Old Dixie tracks and arrived at the traffic lights. There was an effort underway to remove the panhandlers and homeless from the streets around West Palm, and it was working. The argument had been successfully made that they were drug-addicted, mentally ill, and in some cases swindlers—homeless by choice. Their intrusions were besmirching neighborhoods, increasing crime, and bringing down property values.

So, just move them on their way, get them out of sight, and poof— like magic—problem solved.

While the consensus opinion regarding the tragic condition on the streets might be correct, he didn't really care. It was a lousy life was all he knew, and he felt an agitating blend of sadness, guilt, hopelessness, and obligation. There must be a better way to relieve these poor souls' sufferings. *Get them off the streets and into the proper facilities to help them, for Christ's sakes,* he thought, *including incarceration in the rare case they are dangerous to society.*

The nation's founders would be ashamed to observe modern-day America, he considered. The miracle they began was on life-support. Politics had become a sewer of selfishness and corruption, not much better than a banana republic. The whole thing needed to be reimagined, starting with more competent, courageous leaders across all of government: national, state, and local. Men and women from all backgrounds working together for a common purpose bigger than their own ideologies, public relations, and pocketbooks. Return power where it was meant to be—as far away from DC and as close to the people as possible. A good start would be term limits—twelve years, max—in "public service," then "thank you very much and Godspeed."

Because none of this was possible in the current system, it was time for a complete do-over.

Patrick believed fervently that for his entire five decades on earth, the ruling class, particularly elected officials collecting taxes and managing the country's wealth and social mores, had mostly been abject failures. And the hapless beings suffering on the streets were among the primary victims of their collective dereliction of duty. The political and corporate bosses got fat and ugly with wealth and power, while so many others were emaciated and shriveling away to nothingness.

Since the turn of the new century, these so-called leaders kept short-term interest rates close to zero percent. The result? For one, the national debt continued to skyrocket. The debt payments seemed manageable, nearly nonexistent, so why not borrow more and more? Meanwhile, rich investors and speculators leveraged the value of their assets into skyrocketing wealth, while the middle and lower classes, many of them asset-less, earned nothing on their savings. Insidiously, bankers and retailers encouraged credit cards for consumption while continuing to charge ancient rates of 14 to 24 percent on unpaid balances, depending on the dupe. This travesty, sanctioned by regulators, ensured the financially illiterate lower class would remain buried in debt and incessantly under the heels of the elites. This was abhorrent behavior, pure and simple, and when the ruthless game finally ended, the ensuing wreckage would likely be horrific.

Worse still, if that was even possible, these blowhard, incompetent politicians coldly pour our soldiers' precious blood and trillions of dollars into "solving" the world's troubles. *Solving? Ha!* They've left everything they touched worse off while relentlessly, heartlessly presiding over the ever-collapsing middle and lower classes in America. They hadn't a clue how to help their own suffering citizens effectively, never mind the world.

Modern-day Neros—every one of them.

The well-meaning politicians—and there had been many—found themselves hopelessly trapped in this ruinous system, no different than the fly caught in a spider's viscous web. They talked a good game but accomplished relatively little other than securing their own world-class healthcare, pensions, book deals, and streaming celebrity for the expanses of their privileged lives.

The solution wasn't simple—nothing of value was—but it should be the nation's urgent priority. Hell, Patrick even had a few ideas. Nothing new for the preeminent "idea guy." For today though, all he could do was pray for the miracle that was so desperately needed.

Anybody here seen my old friends, JFK, MLK, and RFK, who once upon a time were our best hopes for a brighter tomorrow? Anybody here seen my old friend, Ronnie, our Great Communicator, who once upon a time restored a decrepit America's rightful place in the world? Can you tell me where they've gone? We miss you, old friends, and need you more desperately now than ever before.

He arrived home that day feeling sullen and uncertain. With the Kerry O'Connor chapter now formally closed, the entirety of the past winter's mythical Palm Beach cycle seemed fully ordered and sealed in the archives. He made his way to the den and dropped his Tumi on the floor by his ancient nesting place. Unable to quell a stirring in the attic, he tapped up the Sonos app on his iPad.

In the same year of his injury, 1974, in the very same month, October, his favorite Celtic rock band released an album called *War Child* that would resonate for all the days ahead. From across the sea, one prophetic song titled "Skating Away" was written only for Patrick, he was certain, and no one could tell him otherwise.

Nearly four decades later, with all that entailed, he grabbed his latest mystery read, popped open a bottle of Smithwick's, and sank into his battered leather friend. Together they went skating away one more time. [59]

51

WAR CHILD

A persistent pounding on the front door startled him from his slumber. He lifted groggily into his wheelchair, dropping Tana French's latest from his chest in the undertaking. The den was ensconced in a foreboding darkness indicating night had descended in the meantime.

Skating away down the shaded corridor, intent on curtailing the impatient beating, he called out: "I'm coming." He flicked on the wrought iron lamp sitting on the vestibule's long, narrow, double-leafed table before igniting a series of exterior lights. "Coming!" he called out again, this time in a more irritated tone. Turning the two deadbolts, he gripped the ornate brass handle and backed away, pulling the heavy mahogany door with him. Only the lighted porch and front steps beyond were apparent. "Hello?"

he appealed, scanning the brick-paved entryway for a package or note or any sign of life. Pausing a moment to listen, a southeastern breeze rustled the clicking palm fronds interrupting the starlit silence, but nothing more. Thinking it was still a month premature for such a Halloween trick, he swung closed the door until it slammed harshly against the night.

About to secure the deadbolts and shut the lamp, he discerned a bumping, dragging noise over his right shoulder. Ratcheting his head in its direction, he saw nothing in the shadowy hallway beyond. *Just more evil spirits,* he thought, turning back to attend to the front door.

"How goes the battle, sitting man?" came the sudden, startling words from the gloomy passage. Spinning sharply, the evil spirit he'd perceived took the form of a bedraggled Jeff Saunders, standing to the rear of the foyer pointing a gun at his head.

Pulling up a chair to "take a load off," his ex-boss appeared to be talking aloud to himself, or maybe to the draped and bound body lying in a heap to his left. His plan was "simple in design," he said, "and even simpler to execute."

Stunned pale, Patrick scanned the mound on the floor as a fluttering sickness pervaded his belly, and the balls of his feet jumped in panicky spasms against his foot pedals. Leaning forward and pressing down hard on his knees to stop the tremors, his chair tipped forward, nearly propelling him to the ground. His feet were in no mood to cease their war dance. [60]

"What plan, Jeff'?" he managed to stammer. "Why are you here?"

Waving the gun at Patrick, then down at the pile, he said, "I told you no one was gonna take away my golden shovel and get away with it, especially useless pieces of shit like you two."

Jumping up suddenly, Saunders wrapped his black boot around the foyer lamp's electrical cord and wrenched it from the socket, dampening the light even further. Then he swept the lamp off the table to a shattering crash on the stone floor, swiftly raised the two leaves until they locked, and hoisted the shrouded body onto a tabletop now wide enough for a wedding reception—or a casket.

"You should be more careful about locking your doors, Connelly," he said in a tone drenched with loathing. "Why not join me for a drink in the den?"

Led by his predator down the hallway and into his refuge, Patrick's quivering voice asked, "What in Christ's name are you doing?"

"Doing? Umm, not too much," he replied snidely. "I've had quite a bit of free time on my hands if you hadn't noticed." One black-gloved hand placed the gun on the bar top while the other poured a tall glass of whiskey. "Can I buy you one?"

"I'm good."

"Really, Connelly? I wouldn't be so sure about that," he said with an infernal laugh. "Cause you don't look so good right now."

"Who's in my foyer?"

"In due time," came the agitated reply.

He'd been stopping by SoSo for the last few weeks, he said, even staying in the guest house for hours at a time—watching and planning. He knew who was going to pay for his fall from grace, but the scheme had only recently come together.

"You sure spend a lot of time alone," he said derisively. "Makes sense—I guess you have a hard time making friends, huh?"

Sitting erect in his wheelchair, wide awake, just a few strides away from his leather chair, he asked, "What do you want, Jeff? How can I help you?"

"Help me?" His voice was raised now. "That's a fucking laugh, a real fucking laugh. You've done more than enough for one lifetime, believe me."

"I never did anything to hurt you," he said. "You did the damage to yourself; if you had any help, it wasn't from me."

"That's a nice story, Connelly." His words knocked around the lofted walls. "But I'll be writing the final chapter here—the resolution let's say—and you're just gonna have to sit there and take it, like you do everything else."

Patrick eyed his Tumi leaning black against the brown leather chair, his cell phone resting in the outer, unzipped pocket. Trying to suppress another surge of panic, he asked, "Who's in the bag, Jeff? Is he dead?"

"You're an impatient fucker, aren't you?" came his answer after a long draw of the whiskey. "He's just knocked out, but he'll be dead within the hour; and guess who's gonna do the deed?"

"This is crazy, Jeff. What the hell are you talking about?"

"I'm talking about an unfortunate incident of home invasion by a crazed former adversary of yours leading to a violent encounter, that's all."

"I'm not shooting anyone if that's what you mean."

"Oh, no worries, Connelly; you won't have to. I'll take care of all that."

Stepping away from the bar, Saunders pulled from its wall mount a decorative medieval sword, saying, "Whoa, this is much heavier than I imagined." Pulling the weapon from its leather sheath and running his fingers along the gleaming blade's edges to its pointed tip, he said, "This will do the job just fine."

"What job? What are you talking about?"

"I figure you discovered the intruder and grabbed this for protection. It's perfect, the sitting man from the Middle Ages riding into battle with his sword. And in self-defense, you stabbed King right through the heart."

"King? Come on, Jeff, you can't be serious. Ian's just a kid—and you know I'll tell them everything."

"Oh yeah, that's the other unfortunate part of the incident. It seems King had this pistol here and simultaneously blew your brains across the room in the struggle. Two heroes fighting to the death. A regular clash of fucking titans. Whaddya think, Connelly? Not a bad plan, huh?"

"Christ," he nearly coughed out. "This is insane; you'll be caught within hours."

"Hours? Ha!" His look was growing more crazed. "Your bodies will be rotting here for days before anybody even thinks to look. It'll probably be some neighbor walking her dog who can't stand the stench anymore, so she'll call the police. By that time, I'll be long gone."

"Your door will be the first the police knock on," Patrick said with a trembling voice, trying to use reason.

"I've got a cabin deep in the Georgia mountains where I've been ever since you two fuckers got me banned for life," replied Saunders. "I've got an airtight alibi and witnesses too, and I'll be as devastated to read about this terrible tragedy as everyone else."

"This is madness."

"No, Connelly—not madness," came his considered response. "It's actually quite rational. I've measured twice, and I'll be cutting once, to borrow a term from an old back-stabbing prick employee."

"It was only a job, Jeff, just a fucking sales job in the useless money business. For that, you're willing to give away everything, including your freedom? That's not a good trade."

"That job was my ticket across that bridge!" he raged. "And you two losers stole it from me. I'll give you a good trade, gimpy: In one stroke of brilliance, I'm wiping out the lying little prick *and* the useless sitting man. There's no downside. It's a home run, really."

Patrick's head was a swirling pool of fear and memories, with images and voices flitting in and out. His attic was emptying out. His father and mother were there, "Don't worry, Paddy, everything's going to be okay." His Bronx friend, "Let's get out of here, Cuz; it's a beautiful, sunny day out." When they'd spun away, his children's faces came rushing in, their individual voices saying, "Are you okay, Dad? we miss you." He lingered here the longest— the most important goodbyes needed to be said to them.

Other faces spilled in when he was done: relatives, friends, love relationships, quickly flashing in and out. Becky made an appearance. She'd dropped the animus, replaced with a worried look. Then came Marie and Larry and Kay and Justus and Kerry, all looking as concerned as Auntie Em. Finally came Finnie. He was so glad she wasn't here to bear the risk or witness his shame.

There would be no hero tonight—no rushing the gunman and wrestling away his pistol just in the nick of time. These were actions ascribed only to the brave and physical—men and women of great strength and dexterity and courage. The Queen Maeves of the world. Instead, he would die a passive death in the decrepit place where he sits, ever the feckless observer.

Putting down his emptied glass, Saunders picked up the pistol and walked out from behind the bar. "It's time to get this show on the road," he said. "King's first. Spin around there, Connelly. I'm following you to the foyer."

Feeling the gun's menace, Patrick made a left turn from the den and moved unsteadily through the corridor toward the entrance hall with Saunders tailgating him. The bound, lifeless body was still prone on the sturdy table.

"I'm getting tired of dragging that big son-of-a-bitch around," Saunders said while tucking the gun into his belt. "Why don't you give him a ride back to the den?" He grabbed the rope tightly wound around the upper torso and dragged it onto Patrick's lap. "Now we have two sitting men," he sneered. "At ease, Ironside, I'll give you a push. No one can say I don't take care of my advisors, even if they suck at what they do."

The heavy cargo and dank smell of confinement weighed on him. The rush of forward motion, his chair's straining groan, the hard right turn, the sudden termination, the body wrenched from his arms falling hard to the floor.

"I've pictured this a hundred times." Saunders was breathing heavily from the exertion. "The confrontation is right here in the middle of the room," he explained while positioning the cloaked body. "He's so drugged up with pain pills, it explains both his delusional, murderous behavior and how someone as useless as you could actually take him down."

He loosened the ropes around the body and pulled away the canvas shroud. It was, in fact, the deathly white face of Ian King—his thick blond hair matted on a forehead oily from perspiration. Silently inspecting his unmoving eyelids, his bruised face and gagged mouth, Patrick had never seen King so meek and reposed. He probably hadn't slept this well in years. Still pointing the gun directly between Patrick's eyes, Saunders picked the sword off the bar top and removed it from its sheath. Running his hand along its length once again, he directed it down and pressed in against the left side of King's chest as if he were measuring twice before the cut.

"Don't do this, Jeff. Please—Christ; you'll regret it."

"Back off, Connelly," he ordered with a threatening wave of the gun. "I want your brains sprayed all over the bar here." Patrick backed up a few paces. He knew he had to do something, anything, or he never would again.

> One by one they were all becoming shades.
> Better pass boldly into that other world,
> in the full glory of some passion,
> than fade and wither dismally with age.

Saunders glanced to the left and saw the antique record player. "I've noticed you're quite fond of music," he said with a tittering snarl. "Play a little something on that old jukebox, and we'll call it your swan song."

Moving to the pedestal table where the gramophone sat, hands shaking, he put the nearest vinyl on the spindle, fiddled with buttons and knobs, and watched the turntable come to life. Pistol still trained on his prey, sword at the ready, Saunders plopped down into the cozy leather chair. Patrick moved a stride closer as the music began its ascent. [61]

Sé mo laoch. mo ghile mear
Sé mo chaesar ghile mear
Suan ná séan ní bhfuaireas fhéin
Ó chuaigh i gcéin mo ghile mear

The strings of the harp stationed at the far end of the den started to vibrate and glow with a faint light as it joined in The Chieftains' ghostly melody. "Hey, that's really cool, Connelly," Saunders said, stifling a yawn. "You've got some computer hookup thing working the harp; maybe I'll just take that with me when I head back to Georgia." His voice was taunting. "You won't mind, will you?"

The sound from the harp grew dreamy in its surrounding mist, and he watched Saunders's head starting to droop. Once, and then again, his head bounced down and back up while furiously batting his eyelids. The gun tilted down a notch, and the sword rested on the nearest arm of the chair.

A proud and gallant cavalier
A high man's scion of gentle mean
A fiery blade engaged to reap
He'd break the bravest in the field

Hearing a light snore now, watching his face intently, Patrick carefully leaned forward and ever so quietly picked his Tumi off the floor. Saunders's eyelids wavered as he murmured, "This is nice, Connelly, real nice." He froze in place with his Tumi flat on his lap, watching Saunders's eyes sag and close again.

Come sing his praise as sweet harps play
And proudly toast his noble frame
With spirit and with mind aflame
So wish him strength and length of day

Studying his active eyelids, Patrick inched in again. Bracing himself on his chair's frame with one arm, he reached out tenuously for the sword until lightly brushing its blade. He wasn't sure whether to thrust it away or plunge it into his despicable chest. He never got to find out. At that moment, Saunders's reddened eyes snapped open and stared menacingly into Patrick's. A wicked smile crossed his lips as he raised up the wilting gun barrel and growled, "Time for your deep dive, Connelly."

Just then, the Mediterranean home in SoSo, so laden with evil spirits, suffered an outage. Lights both inside and out shut down, dispatching the room into blinding darkness. Patrick abruptly shifted back in his chair, grabbing one wheel and spinning away.

A yellow flare accompanied the thunderous burst that propelled him back into a haze of ear-piercing commotion. The last thing he recalled was feeling a crushing pain in his ribcage as he took flight.

When the lights flashed on again, law enforcement was streaming into the room to a soundtrack of blaring sirens. Patrick's chair was flipped over on its back with its front wheels still spinning. His ejected body was prone on the beveled wood planks, his head angled awkwardly where the floor met up with the bar's brass footrest. A stream of blood trickled from his ear and pooled below.

Ian King, still partially bound, was slumped on his knees in front of the brown leather chair now sullied with a viscid, steaming black liquid. Jeff Saunders, partly sitting and partly airborne, arms thrashing, screeching in mortal anguish, was pinned to the chair's back by the full brunt of the medieval sword. Only its blood-soaked hilt was visible in his left side where his abdomen and ribcage converged.

Standing guard over the scene, with a pistol in one hand and a 911 operator in the other, was Larry Devlin.

52

OLD HAUNTS, MYSTERY, AND BLISS

For likely the final time in their lives, Ian King and Patrick Connelly shared the same quarters, this time the intensive care unit in St. Mary's Hospital. King spent ten days there suffering from a nearly fatal drug overdose, internal organ damage, and the emotional torment inflicted on him by his ex-boss. Patrick spent a week there suffering from three fractured ribs, internal bleeding, a concussion, and the emotional torment inflicted on him by his ex-boss. Their tormented ex-boss, barely hanging on to life, was raced from St. Mary's to Jackson Memorial in Miami by Trauma Hawk.

Even more sensational than the recent money laundering news, the events in SoSo qualified for a week of national media attention. They camped out in Clematis's triangular park near the firm's Intracoastal-view office building and on the formerly quiet street outside of Patrick's home, endlessly regurgitating the whole sordid money and vengeance story. Becky and the kids never left his side during his extended recovery, acting as both his nurses and security guards. Becky did everything she could to help, short of wiping his ass, that was. It harkened back to earlier, happier years when they were one cohesive family.

The flood of calls, emails, and text messages requesting interviews hadn't abated. The most interesting was for a photoshoot of Patrick posing with Larry Devlin and the medieval sword, which along with his sullied leather chair was in the hands of the authorities. The firm asked that he reject this and any other publicity request, and he was happy to comply. Their public relations nightmare didn't need any added fuel.

His new partner in the business, Marie, stopped by often while she kept things organized at the office. She suggested they call the business "MC²."

"Is that the name of our new rock band?" he asked.

"I was thinking 'McCarthy & Connelly-squared,' representing our combustible energy. Clever, huh?"

"Yes, clever, but I'm not so sure," he responded. "It sounds like I might have to work a lot harder to live up to the name."

"Would that be so terrible?"

"By the way, Marie," Patrick said, leaving her sinister question unanswered, "just because your name is first, it doesn't automatically mean you'd get the higher payout."

"Hush now, Pat," she responded, "and get your rest. This isn't the time to talk about money."

Well-wishes poured in from scores of clients, old friends, neighbors, and former colleagues. Even Kay gave him a call, "pro bono," she said. He decided that calls with Kay hadn't nearly the value of in-person sessions and promised to schedule one soon. Even his siblings sent along their heartfelt wishes, probably in case he died and left them in his will, which he didn't, and he hadn't.

When he was strong enough physically and emotionally to discuss that evening, he detailed whatever he could remember to the detectives. With their ongoing investigation, they were able to fill in most of the gaps.

Larry Devlin had returned to West Palm Beach from Ireland a few days earlier to take care of some business. He felt an overwhelming intuition that evening to visit Patrick's house, he'd said, including seeing images of Kerry O'Connor and hearing his voice. He didn't mention that part to the police. After his knocks went unanswered, he entered the unlocked front door.

Following the noises, he watched the last minutes of the spectacle unfold from the hallway just outside the den. When he realized the gravity, he quickly backtracked to the garage and shut off the electricity. Then, guided by a light emitting from his burgundy leather pouch, he raced back to the den and directly at the leather chair. The sword's blade was visible by the glow of the harp. Just as Saunders was pulling the trigger, Larry was acting swiftly and surely. Cleared by the authorities, he was spending time at his home in the Gardens recovering from superficial cuts on his hand and the emotional torment inflicted by his friend's ex-boss. Watching his bird friends flitting here and there in the marsh was helping, and he was planning his imminent return to the magical Dingle Peninsula.

The bullet fired by Saunders's pistol, destined to pierce his adversary's midsection, instead ripped a hole in his Tumi, which he'd held up at the last moment. When the police examined the bag, they found the bullet lodged inside a shredded burgundy leather pouch.

Things slowly returned to normal, or some new type of normal. Things could never be old normal again. Patrick was back to a more reasonable office grind with Marie taking hold of her new role with authority, if not nobility.

"Are you gonna do any work today, Pat?"

"Since when did thinking become not working?"

"When they stopped paying for it a few thousand years ago."

"How about if I lower my percentage of the partnership a touch to compensate you for your extraordinary work ethic, stoicism, and undying loyalty."

"That'll work."

"Good, then we have a deal."

"Pat?"

"Yes?"

"Could you define 'a touch'?"

"Oh, for Christ's sake, Marie," he said with a broad smile. "How about if I just write you a check?"

"That'll work, and we'll talk about 'touching' the percentage later?"

"Yes, my dear Marie, that'll work."

Once the money business, always the money business.

South Florida's broiling summer heat was blessedly giving way to a lighter crispness in the air. A few old sweatshirts were extracted from storage in celebration. All dressed up with nowhere to go. His horoscopes of late had been mostly throwaways as if the magic had also been locked away in some inaccessible attic bin. One caught his interest, though, in saying: *Visit old haunts, reengage in old routines. Get out into nature and be governed by the cycles rather than the clock. That's where the true mystery and bliss are hiding.* He clipped it out and left it sitting on his kitchen table to ruminate over.

One old haunt and routine he'd abandoned was visiting Murphy's for an afternoon of cheer. Ghosts remained in residence there that he had no interest in stirring up.

Maybe that should end today, he thought. *Why not?*

He wasn't afraid of ghosts; in fact, he'd learned to rather enjoy their presence. And he could stand a pint or two along with some human interaction. Hopping into his silver bullet, he took the scenic route north along Flagler.

It was a cloudy Sunday afternoon only a few days shy of the overcrowded, plastic-cupped Halloween celebration. Clematis was quiet—just the way he preferred it. Parking along the waterway, he made his way up the hill past the theater, the patisserie, and west toward Murphy's. Pushing through the heavy entrance door, he was surprised at the buoyancy of the Sunday afternoon crowd. A familiar voice rang out, "Patrick Connelly, is that you? It's been a faerie's age."

"It's a blessing to see you again, lovely Molly-O, and to hear that sweet Irish lilt. I've missed you so."

"You as well, Patrick," she said while administering her warmest welcome. "Follow me. We just cleared a table. Will you be joined by anyone?"

"No, just me. The good old days."

"You've come to the right place," she said, placing a knowing hand on his shoulder. "Set you up with the usual—Smithwick's and Bushmills?"

"Perfect," he answered cheerfully. "By the way, any abandoned newspapers in the house?"

"I'll check around."

"Thanks, dear," he replied. No harm in trying.

Unzippering his new black Tumi and slipping out the iPad and writing tablet, he was feeling a little more at home with every resurrected ritual. A different server moving about the active room looked familiar. He did a double-take, thinking, *So familiar, where have I seen her before?* Molly brought his drinks and a basket of soda bread, and he dismissed the thought. Minutes later, head down in his reading, he heard a voice say, "I haven't seen you here before. Is this your first time?"

"First time in a while," he replied to the familiar server. "It used to be my favorite haunt in a former life."

"Favorite haunt—that's funny," she said, glancing at the Halloween decorations all about the room.

"Sorry," he said. "Unintended."

"That's okay," she said. "It was still clever."

"Thank you," he said while extending his hand in introduction. "Patrick Seamus Connelly."

"I know very well who you are," she said. "We were colleagues in *my* former life. Well, maybe more like venomous enemies. I'm so glad to see you here—looking healthy and cheerful." Reaching out and shaking his hand up and down, she said, "Mia Wolfe."

"Oh my God, Mia Wolfe."

"Patrick," she repeated. "I like that. I was instructed to call you 'Connelly' by my former bosses."

"Why was that?"

"It was a form of disrespect, I think. They wanted to get your goat, as Ian put it."

"Nice. That sounds just like Ian."

"Come to think of it," she said with a laugh. "He used to call me Wolfe."

"What a guy," he replied, still a little flummoxed. "I thought you were his partner?"

"I was called that briefly," she said. "But it sure didn't feel that way. The only thing we partnered in were orders. He gave, and I followed."

"Sounds about right. What is Ian doing now?"

"I really haven't kept up. He's recovered and healthy, so that's good. Last I heard, he was still suspended from the securities business, maybe banned for life." Then with a note of distress, she said,

"But not as banned as Jeff Saunders. I couldn't believe what he did—or tried to do. I was horrified when I saw the news."

"You should have been there," he said without thinking. "Sorry, just an expression. I'm glad you weren't, and it all worked out okay."

"Not for Saunders," she said, attempting a smile. "I heard he's still at the rehab center in Miami."

"True," he responded. "But he's going to be okay, I think. First, he needs to get through the next few months, see how much recovery he gets, if any. They have miraculous therapies today compared to my day, so there's reason for optimism."

"I hope you're right, but I'm not so sure," Mia responded. "He might be wishing he had died that night instead."

"You mean it might be better to be dead than paraplegic—living his life in a wheelchair?"

"No—I'm sorry—that's not what I meant at all," she said with a disconcerted look. "Forgive me."

"Of course. Please go on, I was rude and interrupted you."

"Thank you." Wolfe gathered her composure and continued. "It's just that Jeff did this to himself, and he still has the trial ahead, and it doesn't look good; it's a lot to deal with, losing your ability to walk and maybe your freedom too. It seems overwhelming, especially for a macho, kind of crazy guy like Saunders."

"I agree with that," Patrick nodded. "There's no doubt his life is awful, brutal, right now; and it's all his fault, as you said. But who knows, his condition might benefit him in the criminal proceedings. In an odd way, he's in a kind of jail now—he's already lost his freedom. The judge might decide he's suffered enough and go easy on him."

"Maybe," she contemplated. "I'm sorry, Patrick, this must be a very uncomfortable conversation for you."

"Not at all, Mia, but thank you. I was over my grieving process so long ago—I can barely even remember it. It's all tucked away neatly in my attic." Then with a smile, he said, "I have no complaints. I'm enjoying my life and feel nothing but gratitude. I'm a lucky guy."

"That's very impressive, Patrick, and I'm not surprised."

"It's nothing special, believe me," he replied. "Millions of people live with a disability and do very well, especially now in the 21st century. It's the best time in history to give it a whirl."

"I think I'll pass, if you don't mind."

"That's a good choice—you're smarter than I thought," he said, meeting her smile. "It sounds like Jeff may have no choice. He's in shock right now, denial, I'm certain, but he's still young and fit, and he'll eventually get on with his life. He may even beat the odds and walk again. But, either way, he'll probably have a little more humility, and a lot more patience than the guy I remember. Living with a disability will require both.

"How would you know?" she said with a glint.

"Just a guess," he replied, returning her glint. "Before you know it, he'll be back pursuing his golden shovel."

Before hustling away to the waving arms of a patron, she said, "Funny—I never got that whole golden shovel thing anyway."

"Join the club."

When Mia returned, she placed her tray on the table, saying, "I have a few minutes now, I think."

"How about you?" he asked. "How are you doing?"

"Okay," she answered. "I was fully exonerated, and then I banned myself from the business. I was never happy there anyway. I'm working here part-time, trying to get a new business off the ground."

"What kind of business, if I may ask?"

"Certainly, you may," she responded. "It's a non-profit. I want to take all the education I'm still paying for and use it for something meaningful. There are thousands of people, millions really, who are living month-to-month, overwhelmed with debt, working two jobs, barely putting enough clothes on their kids' backs, or food on the table."

"So true," he said. "And they could be the next destitute, even homeless."

"Yes, if they give up," she said. "I want to help them not give up."

"That's admirable, but how?"

"Financial planning, starting with getting rid of debt, especially credit cards; prioritizing their decisions, managing whatever resources they *do* have. I'll provide advocacy, helping them with schooling and finding better jobs. They want better lives, and they're willing to work for it; they just need opportunities and someone to help guide them."

"Like the concierge wealth management services that we provide to the rich?"

"Sort of, but more rudimentary," she answered. "Financial literacy for people who desperately need the services."

"Again, I applaud you. But who pays for it all? And how do you make a living yourself?"

"Hey, you're raining all over my parade."

"Sorry," he said with a smirk. "But that's not possible."

"Why is that?"

"Because it never—"

"—rains in an Irish pub," she finished.

"You've heard it."

"Once or twice," she said with a smile. "I know it sounds crazy. It'll take a boatload of fundraising—public and private—appealing to government agencies and corporations and people with wealth who want to help."

"That's not easy," he warned. "There's lots of competition for philanthropy." Glancing to the sky, she put her hand out to feel for raindrops prompting him to say, "Jeez, Mia, sorry again. I don't mean to be a doom and gloomster."

"That's okay," she responded. "You're correct—but nothing important is ever easy. And some of the richest communities on earth are right here in Palm Beach County. There'll be plenty who want to help, I think, once they see what I'm doing."

"I'm sure you're right," he agreed. "And it's way past time to improve this terrible problem."

"You are so right."

"Well, I'm very proud of you, Mia," he said. "I'll absolutely be there to help you if you'd like."

"Of course, I'd love your help," she responded quickly. "In fact, my heart would be broken otherwise."

Batting his eyes a few times, he said, "Then you'll have it. So, in the meantime, why Murphy's, of all places?"

"Why? My Scotch-Irish heritage, of course," she answered with a sparkle. "I feel right at home here."

When she hastened off once again to take care of her thirsty patrons, Patrick tried to refocus on his iPad. Not a chance in Purgatory. Instead, his eyes trailed her backside around the pub room. The thick black hair he remembered, once held in place by trendy, oversized frames, had been transformed to an auburn mane flowing to her mid-back, reddish with a sprinkling of ginger. It was a profitable trade. There was a natural beauty about her, even more alluring than her days on the pinstriped battlefield. The accountant unleashed. That tends to happen when a person exits the money business. The stress lines fade. A natural glow reemerges. They let their hair down if they are lucky enough to still have some.

After a time, Mia stopped back to his table and said, "I have a confession to make."

"Should I get my frock and light a candle?"

"Thanks, but that won't be necessary," she laughed. "This confession doesn't include my sins."

"Too bad," he said. "Please, the confessional is yours."

"Okay," she started. "I used to pray you'd join our team, or we'd join your team, or however that's supposed to work."

"When someone has 80 percent of the assets, and like 60 percent of the production," he explained, "you're supposed to join his team if you're fortunate enough to be invited."

"Got it—that makes sense," she said before continuing. "Well, even while under constant stress, threats even, I admired your demeanor, your eloquence, your quiet strength, and the way you treated Marie, always with respect and dignity. I was hoping you could do that for me, for our team. You're a kind and courageous man, Patrick Connelly."

"Well, now you've done it," he said. "I'm blushing." After a noticeable pause, he continued, "Honestly, Mia, thank you. That is very generous of you. I could never live up to such accolades."

"You don't have to live up to anything," she chimed in. "I had plenty of time to take the measure of the man."

"Like measuring twice and cutting once?"

"Ugh," she said with a grimace. "Please, don't remind me."

"Sorry again," he said. "You forgot to take measure of my wise-guy-ness."

"You're an Irishman," she responded. "I expect nothing less."

"I kissed the Blarney Stone, after all."

"I did too."

"You did?" came his surprised voice. "When?"

"A long time ago—nearly two decades," she said. "I studied in Dublin for a year during college and traveled the country. I even wrote my thesis about the Troubles—the Irish Nationalist, British Loyalist conflict. I was there just ahead of the Good Friday Agreement."

"I'm very familiar," he said, "and very impressed."

She scurried away once again to take care of her tables, saying over her shoulder, "Please don't leave yet. I'll be back as soon as I can."

"I'm a fixture," he said, smiling and glancing about the convivial pub in search of his Molly-O.

Speaking of the Troubles, Patrick tuned in to the background as the extraordinary Luke Kelly lamented the near ruin of his beloved town of Derry. [62] *What's done is done*, he silently concurred, *and what's lost is lost and gone forever. Nothing was won*, he corrected. *All we can do now is continue praying for a brighter tomorrow.*

When Mia returned, she said, "I'm getting off in a few minutes; would you like to take a stroll down to the waterway with me? It's quiet and so beautiful watching the moon rising on the Intracoastal."

"That sounds like a wonderful idea, Mia," he said, a little flabbergasted. "Are you sure? This isn't a setup, is it?"

"I left the firm," she said with a laugh. "Remember, silly?"

"I recall you mentioning something like that," he replied, working through a moment of reminiscence. "Oh, why not—my horoscope said I need to get back to nature."

"I read horoscopes too," she said. "But I never told King or any of our clients. Probably not a good look for a financial advisor."

"No, probably not," he said.

Settling the tab and giving Molly a warm hug, he pushed open the not-so-heavy front door and joined Mia Wolfe's stroll east on Clematis.

The air had a cooling mist, and the sidewalk was slick from the remnants of a late afternoon sun shower that had pushed east over the Atlantic. When they reached the front of the office building they once shared, she paused. "I probably shouldn't say this."

"Then you must," he encouraged.

Warily, she continued, "I have this crazy feeling we knew each other once, maybe in an earlier lifetime. We may have even been lovers."

"That would really be something," he said, with halting breath and an emerging tremor. "But it's impossible to believe, don't you think?"

Looking directly in his eyes, she said, "Someone much smarter than me once said, 'Believe it all unless you can prove otherwise.'"

"That sounds like something WB Yeats would say."

"Yes, Patrick, it does," she said. "Yeats believed in unseen worlds and magical creatures, keeping our hearts open and seeking joy in the mysteries of the natural world. He believed everything exists, whatever our minds can conjure. What could be more fun than that?"

"I can't think of a thing."

And with that, they cut across Clematis and through the oak-shrouded triangular park leading to the waterfront. As they crossed over Flagler, off in the distant clouds, Patrick noticed a still vibrant rainbow ascending over Palm Beach in the general direction of the Emerald Isle. [63]

POETRY AND QUOTES

Title Page:
Quote from W. B. Yeats—From a letter to Olivia Shakespear, December 6, 1926.

Chapter 7:
Quote from *Chariots of Fire*—1981—written by Colin Welland— produced by David Puttnam—distributed by Warner Bros. (domestic) & 20th Century Fox (international).

Chapter 15:
Several quotes from Irish playwright Samuel Beckett—1906-1989; One quote from Robin Williams—1951-2014

Chapter 18:
From "The Song of Wandering Aengus"—Published by W. B. Yeats in 1899 in *The Wind in the Reeds* collection—Public domain.

Chapter 23:

Quote from Mark Twain—1835-1910

Chapter 26:

Kerry O'Connor's description of St. Patrick was inspired (not plagiarized, but probably similar enough) by *How the Irish Saved Civilization* by Thomas Cahill.

Chapter 36:

"The Lake Isle of Innisfree"—Published by W. B. Yeats in *The Countess Cathleen and Various Legends and Lyrics* in 1892—Public domain.

Chapter 40:

W. B. Yeats verses from:

Fairy and Folk Tales of the Irish Peasantry, published in 1888.

"The Stolen Child"—*The Wanderings of Oisin and Other Poems*, published in 1889.

The Land of Heart's Desire, a play written in 1889, first performed in 1894, in the Avenue Theatre in London.

The Countess Cathleen and Various Legends and Lyrics, published in 1892.

The Celtic Twilight: Faerie and Folklore, published in 1893.

"A Drinking Song"—published in 1916.

"Among School Children"—*The Tower*, published in 1928.

"In Remorse for Intemperate Speech"—*The Winding Stair and Other Poems*, published in 1933.

"Mad as the Mist and Snow"—*The Winding Stair and Other Poems*, published in 1933.

All the verses were written by W.B. Yeats and are in the public domain.

Chapter 40:

The dialogue briefly references language found in the following poems from Seamus Heaney: "The Cure at Troy," published in 1990; "Beowulf: A New Verse Translation," published in 1999 by Farrar, Straus and Giroux, and "Robert Lowell: A Memorial Address and an Elegy," published in 1978 by Faber and Faber.

Chapter 41:

Verse from "Auguries of Innocence," from the *Pickering Manuscript*—William Blake—written in 1803, first published in 1863. Public domain.

Chapter 42:

Quote from Tommy DeVito (played by Joe Pesci) in *Goodfellas*—1990—Written by Nicholas Pileggi and Martin Scorsese—produced by Irwin Winkler—distributed by Warner Bros.

Quote from *Chariots of Fire*—1981—written by Colin Welland—produced by David Puttnam—distributed by Warner Bros. (domestic) & 20th Century Fox (international).

Chapter 48:
W. B. Yeats verse from: "September 1913"—from *Responsibilities*, published in 1914—Public domain.

Quotes from Mark Twain—1835-1910.

Chapter 49:
"When You Are Old"—from *The Rose collection*, W. B. Yeats, published in 1893. Public domain.

"In Memoriam A.H.H."—Alfred Tennyson—1850—Public domain.

Quote from *The Winter of Our Discontent*—American author John Steinbeck—1961.

"Down by the Salley Gardens"—*The Wanderings of Oisin and Other Poems*, W. B. Yeats, published in 1889. Public domain.

Chapter 51:
Quote from "The Dead"—*Dubliner Tales*—James Joyce—1914.

Mac Domhnaill, Sean Clárach (1691 - 1754). "*Mo Ghile Mear*" with reference to the poem "My Heart is Sore with Sorrow Deep" (c. 1746).

Author's Disclaimer

I've described *Sitting on a Rainbow* as part memoir, part fiction, and part fantasy. There are three integrating parts to protagonist Patrick Connelly's story: Living with a disability, working in financial services, and exploring Irish history and folklore's present-day relevance.

The memoir portion of the story involves the author's experiences of living with a spinal cord injury (since age nineteen) and his memories of working as a stockbroker/financial advisor (for three decades). This is where the story leaves the memoir genre and spins off into fiction and fantasy. Along with genuine memories of the author's time "on the desk," the main plot (Patrick Connelly's dilemma and how he goes about trying to solve it) is a purely fictional account. Thus, it is not intended to, and does not, depict any real-life person or specific experience the author had in his thirty years in retail financial advisory. Rather, it is an imaginative tapestry woven from snippets of people he encountered and moments he recalled, with a generous supply of blarney sewn into the fabric.

In addition, any public agencies, companies, institutions, or historical figures mentioned in the story serve as a backdrop to the characters and their actions, which are wholly imaginary.

While the story was meant to deliver morality-based messages along the way, and the author hopes that has been achieved, its primary purpose was to be interesting and entertaining, all meant in a lighthearted spirit.

Thank you for your interest, God bless, and I hope you've enjoyed sitting on the rainbow with Patrick Connelly.

Best Regards,
James P. Rooney
Author

CPSIA information can be obtained
at www.ICGtesting.com
Printed in the USA
LVHW080757080323
741035LV00037B/423